For Such a Time as This

By T. L. Kelley

I1005602

Illustrations, cover design and photography by T. L. Kelley.

Unless otherwise indicated, all Scripture quotations are taken from the HOLY BIBLE, NEW REVISED STANDARD VERSION®. Oxford University Press: Oxford, New York (2001).

Available from Amazon.com, CreateSpace.com, and other retail outlets.

ISBN-13: 978-1530444762
ISBN-10: 1530444764

FIRST EDITION: April 2016

✝ ✝ ✝

J L Kelley
7/2/16

In loving memory of
my sister, Pamela

Preface

Dear Readers,

This story arose from a desire to know Priscilla (Prisca) and Aquila, Judeans who lived in the heart of a burgeoning and oppressive Roman Empire. Who were they? How did they come to follow Christ? We find only hints of them in Scripture, diminutive traces written into Acts, Romans, I Corinthians and II Timothy.

When a seed was planted in my heart to write about them, there was an overwhelming sense that early followers of The Way must be cast within an honest historical setting in order to reveal what challenges they had to face, what fears they must have met, and what burdens they may have carried. Knowing these truths would expand our understanding of how they came to faith in Jesus. Such began years of researching history and examining Scripture, ever seeped in prayer, believing in the Lord's gentle whisper and earnestly seeking truth concerning life in ancient Rome. I am forever grateful to a loving, wise, and patient Father who took me on this remarkable journey.

Paul writes, *"Greet Prisca and Aquila, who work with me in Christ Jesus and who risked their necks for my life, to whom not only I give thanks, but also all the churches of the Gentiles"* (Romans 16:3-4).

As Paul suggests, please greet Prisca and Aquila through this writing, which illuminates a period of history that precedes their service with Paul. May you join them as they travel into darkened places where *Jesus*, the *"light of the world,"* shines forth. And, like Prisca and Aquila, may you be changed.

Sincerely,
T. L. Kelley

Note to Reader: The setting for this story is First Century AD, the Roman Empire, a time and place known for intense violence. In an effort to present a story that is both Biblically and historically accurate, some scenes of violence are depicted.

Table of Contents

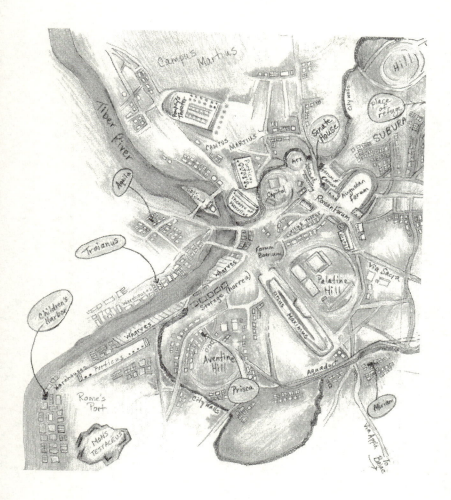

Rome – 37 AD

<u>Note</u>: This map is to assist the reader as to orientation. Locations are approximate.

~ *I* ~

"Be still and know that I am God."

~Psalm 46:10

Rome – 37 A.D.

Hannah and I sank into shadow, silent and watchful. From our balcony perch, air was damp and unmoving, though just below us mobs of angry men churned as in a boiling pot, waving branches of fire that pressed smoke into our hideaway, watering my eyes.

Fueled by wine and bitter memory, they shouted in brash, uneven chorus: "To the Tiber! To the Tiber with Tiberius!" Their barks and bellows landed loud and hard against buildings that grew tall from both sides of our narrow road.

"Prisca?" Hannah called out to me. Her voice was a tiny tapped bell, almost lost in the escalating din from below.

"To the Tiber!" the crowd blared. "Let his body be defiled!"

Tiberius, the emperor of Rome, was dead. Hannah had come to me hours earlier with the news, and then chaos erupted, hurrying us to our place of frightened surveillance. My shoulders shook with chill, and I considered Hannah's appearance as we huddled together, realizing her wan figure mirrored a pervading anxiety that was all too familiar in Rome. How could I answer her, knowing the dread seeping into my own soul … fear of the unknown.

We overlooked the Vicus Albus. It was the street I lived on, a name meaning "White Way." When Rome was yet a village, there was a small quarry of dazzling white stones on our side of the hill. My road must have been only a footpath then. I longed to see those few pale stones still dotting its course, but they were hidden beneath hobnailed sandals, flaring robes, and shifting flames.

A fresh barrage of voices struck the air: "To the Tiber! To the Tiber with Tiberius!" My head pounded. Their grief, even their rage, garnered sympathy. The emperor had used the Tiber River to carry executed bodies away, and many had been put to death for treason in the years ending his reign. Most, like Hannah's parents, were innocent victims.

My stinging eyes closed, recalling a day when Mama was yet alive and a much younger Prisca beheld tumbling green waves and gentle shaded coves. The Tiber had been a beautiful waterway then, a life-giving force for the people of Rome. But in recent years we looked upon a darkened funeral procession with rust-tinged currents bearing bodies of the condemned.

Leaning near balcony's edge, heat pricked my skin. "Yes," I said. "To the Tiber, you horrid man."

Hannah touched my arm, and I turned. Her widened eyes reflected sparks of fire and beckoned my return to shadowed obscurity.

"And now what will our lives be?" she asked. Her words, filtered through a raw and parched throat, directed the question we'd been avoiding all afternoon. We had

10

talked of everything except that which we most wanted to know and could not answer.

I had not been disappointed to hear Hannah's news. "So, old Tiberius is dead!" I'd responded. "The world is finally rid of his meanness." My friend had only nodded, eyes downcast, but I begged to know more. "When did you hear? How did it happen? Who will be the new emperor?"

Hannah chose to answer my last. "Miriam says it's to be Gaius."

"Gaius?" I asked.

"His full name is Gaius Julius Caesar Germanicus," Hannah replied. "Miriam says the soldiers call him *Caligula*."

Wise Miriam, gentle woman of God, who loved and taught me like her own child. Of course, Miriam would know.

I asked, "But what does that mean for us? What is he like?" I didn't wait for her answer. "Gaius. Wasn't he the one who gave the funeral speech for Livia, the old empress?"

Hannah's shoulders rose. "Yes. Because her own son, Tiberius, refused to return to Rome, refused to honor the memory of his mother," she replied.

Livia, Rome's first empress. She was quiet, dignified. All of Rome, rich or poor, grieved her death. There were some disparaging rumors, of course—the gossip trail was the swiftest of Roman roads—but Tiberius' efforts to tarnish his mother's image resulted only in disgrace to himself.

I asked Hannah, "So Gaius is the dead emperor's nephew?"

11

She nodded. "But remember, Tiberius adopted him." Hannah kept account of such things. Like Miriam, she contemplated government affairs, ever aware of our political scene, while I was more interested in picking flowers and baking cakes.

"Adopted as Tiberius' son," I'd replied. "Quite convenient for Gaius now, I think!" Adoptions were common among the Romans and were as binding as if the same blood existed between men. Our people, from the land of Judea, the children of Israel, were very unlike them in that way. The blood of our father Abraham coursed within us. And, like Abraham, we were blessed. The Lord's everlasting covenant belonged to us.

"The soldiers call him *Caligula*?" I asked. "What kind of name—it means 'little boots'?"

Hannah smiled. "Miriam says, when he was a boy, he lived in the soldier camps. You know, his true father was the famous general, Germanicus—"

"Germanicus! Is Gaius handsome like his father?"

"Be serious, Prisca," Hannah said.

"But that's important, don't you think? He'll be much more tolerable if he's good-looking." I fluttered my eyelashes.

Hannah laughed and shook her head. "In truth, I've never seen him. Anyway, living in the camps, he wore little soldier clothes and boots, and Miriam says the soldiers started calling him *Caligula*. Can you imagine? Someone named 'Bootikins' in control of an empire?"

I couldn't imagine it at all.

Smoke surged, causing me to cough and returning me to the moment. Wisps of charred air merged with amber rays of setting sun, and Hannah's face appeared to move in the strange light. Her question still hung suspended between us: *What will our lives be?*

"I don't know," I replied. "But could anyone be worse than Tiberius?"

Hannah said, "I suppose we'll have to trust in a man named Gaius."

"You mean 'Bootikins'?"

"You'd better not be heard calling him that," she said.

My mind conceived a vision of young Gaius, our prospective emperor, dressed all in armor and leather, wearing a child's version of soldier boots. Wouldn't that be better than the towering, intimidating presence of Tiberius?

All my life, Tiberius had been Rome's emperor, a descendant of Julius Caesar like the Emperor Augustus before him. My father described his policies as noble and reasoned at first, but then Tiberius had changed. According to Father, that transformation came about because emperors possessed unnatural power. The Romans called it *imperium*. It meant that one person could decide every issue, including life and death. And I agreed, that kind of power could change someone.

Peering into the blistering scene below, I realized that change again had come ... and it was not subtle, like the washing away of fine pebbles along the riverbank. It was change like a turbulent wind, upon which we were as helpless as brittle autumn leaves.

Hannah moved toward the steps. "I've stayed too long," she said.

My stomach squeezed. "Don't go. Not now."

"But you know Miriam will be worried," Hannah said.

I bit my lip. No longer were Miriam's feet young and swift, and she had sent Hannah to alert me. Our eager conversation had then stolen the hours. Just as angry sounds began to trail away from the Vicus Albus, so our sun was fading from spring day. It was unsafe for Hannah to go alone.

"But Miriam sent you," I said. "She would expect Father to bring you home." I gathered an edge of her cloak into cold fingers. "Stay."

Hannah nodded, and we crept down the stairs, a reeking remnant of fire following us. At the hearth, I stirred a bronze pot filled with steaming legumes. Hannah crushed herbs, mixing them with oil. The soothing aroma of herbs and stew soon filled the kitchen.

Our home—a Roman *domus*—had at its center an atrium, which was a large square room with shallow pool and opening above. From its wide opening could be seen sky and sun or stars. It was the place light entered our home, reflected in the pool, and then was imparted throughout, as all rooms bordered our atrium's airy space. My eyes strayed often toward that central room, eager for Father's steps on its tiled floor. When at last he came, I ran, allowing him to fold me into a warm embrace.

Eben Lucullus Priscus, my father, was a freedman and a scribe, keeper of the senate's official proceedings. His position brought us financial security and civic freedom, but often I feared the discovery that we led a false life: Roman by appearance, Judean by blood. It was an unstable edge to stand on.

"Hannah came with the news," I said. "Are you all right, Abba?"

My father tensed. "I will not have my daughter worrying." He sighed and embraced my chin. "Ah, well … I am breathing yet," he said.

Since last spring, Father's hair had paled, his face thinned, making me uneasy. "And among the senators," I said, "was there trouble?"

"Speculation, a few outbursts and lengthy rants," he replied. "But some quota of insecurity is expected in times like these." Father's position carried grim responsibilities, but he never spoke of them. In his view, mine was to be a carefree existence.

Hannah inclined her head, responding to a hearty greeting from my father. "Prisca thought I should wait for you," she said.

"She is right—this time," he replied. "A young woman should never walk Rome's darkened streets without aid. And today, this is a city unsure of its future; that increases the danger." Father took her small hand and patted it. "Come. We go to Miriam."

I jumped to his side. "Abba, may I—"

"You will remain here. Betna is on the way—with a surprise." He turned away, but I observed his cheeks swell with pleasure, increasing my curiosity. What could Betna be bringing?

My friend raised her hand to mine in a silent good-bye, and they were gone.

Leaning against our solid door and sealed away from Rome's unsettled atmosphere, I thought of my father. When fear crowded my heart, his clear voice would say, "It is the Lord's purpose we must be looking for." The next hour was then consumed with learning what possible purpose Adonai might have. Only a few days earlier, Father had spoken in just that way.

"God Almighty has allowed us to be here," he said. "And like Abraham, we sojourn in a distant land. Be patient, my daughter. Blessing will come." Patience! It was a grueling assignment.

And then I remembered my grandfather, who, though a child, had been taken in slavery from Judea to Rome. With him began our family's history in the bustling heart of an ever-expanding empire. In bondage to the prestigious Licinius Lucullus, known for extravagance, my grandfather turned misfortune into good.

Over cups of tea and with yellowed scrolls unfurled, Father explained how a young boy's cleverness delivered him out of slavery.

"First, you must understand," Father told me, "that most Romans believed our people were uncivilized. They thought our faith was nothing more than superstition. And so Lucullus speculated, 'How could there be intelligence in this slave boy whose people believe in only one God?' But then he read this." Father opened the scroll.

Seeing the ten-year-old slave's witty notations in the timeworn scroll, it became obvious how Grandfather's fresh intellect had intrigued old Lucullus. My grandfather had been teaching himself from texts in the household library! So the nobleman began to school him, training him to read and write in many languages. One day, the boy having grown to manhood, Lucullus granted his freedom and influenced Grandfather's appointment as official scribe to the Roman Senate. Years later, my father was granted a similar position, each day enhancing the family legacy with relentless study and ardent prayer.

≈ ≈

Betna stooped through a small door that opened from the garden, his brown-wool tunic smelling of outside air. "Good evening, child," he said. To Betna, I would always be a child.

"Good evening, sir." Exaggerating the "sir" and bending a knee, a tittering sound escaped my mouth.

"Ha!" Betna laughed in a loud, short blast. He held out a package wrapped in soft linen. "For the naughty child, your father sends me with this gift." Betna's eyes shone bright, eyebrows raised in a dark, moist face. His clothing was not unlike the masses filling Roman streets, but shining hoops adorned his ears—a hint of exotic past.

Betna was born in Nubia, a country many days' south of Rome, across yawning sea and searing desert. *Nubia.* Its name derived from the word for gold. Betna's vivid stories would take me to red-sanded ledges and meandering rivers so wide that you could not see the opposite shore. He had so filled my head with scenes that his bare feet could be seen running swift through hot sands, passing under trees of twisting shapes and thick leaves, and then halting … to release an arrow at a spotted cat.

Pondering the package in my hands, shame pierced like a dagger. Just last week, I had ignored Father's orders and gone to Pompey's Theater, rationalizing my behavior with pathetic excuses.

"But it was educational," I had said, "an opportunity to see true Greek tragedy!" My father's eye had twitched with irritation, but my words continued in a swarm. "I dressed like a Roman girl—no one would have known otherwise—and slipped away without notice." Father was so annoyed that he spoke only to say my freedom was limited to collecting water at our neighborhood fountain.

My head sank lower at the memory. "But I don't deserve this," I said to Betna.

His cheeks lifted with amusement. "It is certain, child." He laid a large hand on my head, withdrew it, and exhaled another "Ha!"

Inside the wrapping was a beautiful scarf, its fine weave shimmering with colors like a rippling ocean.

"It must be like the Tyrrhenian Sea!" I held it to my cheek. "Does the Tyrrhenian look so blue, yet vibrant green?"

Betna stared at the fabric in my hands. "It is so," he replied. He looked past me in a way that reminded of the first night Father brought him home. It was a night of anxious voices, and I'd peeked from my room as Betna was carried in. Father found his friend under an outcropping alongside Aventine Hill where he had crawled for shelter, expecting to die. His legs had been shattered beneath a load of fallen bricks, and hardhearted fellow workers then cast him onto a scrap pile. I was small and whisked away by a doting mother, but Betna's face held the same pained look those many years before.

"Betna?" I touched his arm.

His eyes blinked, and then he bowed as if I were an empress and left the room.

18

Our lamp-lit pool became my silent audience. First, I was a dancer perched on pointed toes, and then one of Adonai's heavenly messengers singing hymns with the *malachim*; and, at last, my own self, wrapped in a blue-green sea.

ℬ ℭ

In two days' time, word came that Gaius was bringing the body of Tiberius to Rome. Young boys in clean white tunics and excited faces ran door-to-door heralding the news. Tender sprigs of budding flowers were woven into wreaths that hung at every crossroads within the city.

On the appointed day, Father, Betna, and I united with swarms of people pouring into the forum to get a glimpse of Gaius, a son of Caesar.

Golden sun drifted in and out from behind puffed, white clouds ranging in blue sky. Gaius' entrance was not signaled by horn blast or shout. Instead, every voice was hushed, when in the solemn presence of a billowing shadow, he rose from the lower road, grand and heroic atop a very large white horse. He was draped in black, an extravagant cloak extending over the back of his steed. Paying close attention to his feet, I wanted to cry out "Bootikins!" as he proceeded down the Romans' Sacred Road but pressed my lips. Father would have been horrified.

Gaius neared the Temple of Vesta, ancient goddess of the hearth, who had been worshiped since Rome first came to be. All eighteen Vestal Virgins stood in front of the cylindrical temple in arched rows.

Six young girls made up the lowest row. Inducted as children into the priesthood, they were being trained for future obligations that included a promise not to know a man until their thirty-year vow was complete. Six elder priestesses, nearing the age of forty, stood on the highest step; it was their responsibility to mentor the young and inexperienced. The six remaining Vestal Virgins were positioned in the center, married to their commitment and diligent in daily reverent tasks. Contemplating their long days cloistered within the silent hallways and rose-filled gardens of the Vestal home, it was difficult not to admire such devotion.

Gaius trotted by, and Rome's Vestal priestesses lifted dainty bouquets in his honor. Long white gowns of sheer Egyptian linen were puffed by a breeze into filmy wings, and white verbena blossoms quivered in shining, curled hair. The temple's flame glowed in orange, yellow, and golden bursts at their backs, and it appeared their delicate bodies were somehow united to its fiery brazier.

From every corner of the forum, solemn hush gave way to shouts of cheer. Many were waving. Some were singing songs. Others called out words of endearment: "Welcome, pet!" or "Our star has come!" Men in formal *togae* and women in elegant cloaks leaned over laurel-draped balconies. What a different scene from the one Hannah and I witnessed just a few nights before! Rome's citizens were so eager for a new leader—son of the popular Germanicus—that anger had flown like swift starlings eyeing a patch of water.

It was an extraordinary day. Businesses were closed, tented awnings rolled away, giving the forum a trim quality—at least until hordes of city residents filled the fresh-swept space. A mixture of scents encircled Rome's fluted pillars, lingered in its doorways, and wafted up shining marble staircases: Incense and exotic spices, animal flesh seared in sacrifice, fresh-cut laurel boughs, sacrificial bread baking. My lungs burned with sensation. Side streets emptied thousands of pedestrians onto marble-paved floor, and we were caught up in the whirr of pressing bodies, desperate for a glimpse of the black figure on a white horse.

The *rostrum*, a large platform designed for political or theatrical presentations, was one of two that graced the forum. Bronzed ships' prows had been inserted across the front—like bird beaks—each prow symbolizing a defeated enemy ship. Gaius climbed *rostrum* stairs, and hundreds of soldiers clad in red tunics and bronze breastplates gathered around him like a wall. Exhilaration coursed through me. To be in Rome at such a momentous time seemed important. I felt very grown-up.

There was no eulogy; that formality was reserved for the week to come. Gaius did, however, deliver an emotion-filled oratory in honor of the deceased emperor's service to Rome, emphasizing his own profound sorrow. We listened until he made a plea to Jupiter that Tiberius would arrive safe into "the heavenly realm." Thousands stood, faces upturned, rapt with admiration.

It crossed my mind in that moment what God Almighty was thinking. Did our Most High God understand the forces that shaped our lives? Were we wrong in submitting to Rome's government? In doing so, had we, as the prophet Hosea warned, forgotten our Maker? And if the east wind came in a blast from God, unleashing destruction on Rome and its people, would we Judeans be rescued from such devastation? Such questions made me realize that I was not so grown-up after all.

People began to disperse, voices increasing in volume. Father followed bristling soldier plumes toward the senate house, and I returned home with Betna, enthused by a zealous and hopeful crowd. My eyes probed every litter leaving the forum for glimpses of sparkling jewels and painted faces behind sheer drapes. Exclamations poured from my lips. Betna attempted to calm my enthusiasm with little success. His sweetest blessing was that our walk was not a long one.

As home came into view, I warmed to its welcoming façade. A builder from years long past had shaped our doorway with those white stones the Vicus Albus was named for, and its shining arc greeted us day or night. Ours was not the largest dwelling in the neighborhood, but it was luxurious compared to other Judean families. Once the *domus* of a Roman tribune, during the later conflicted years of Rome's Republic, it had been remodeled. Floors were added to a wing of the initial residence to accommodate a growing population of commoners, transforming the structure into four levels of multiple dwellings, termed an *"insula"* in Roman tongue. Our family dwelt in the original and lowest portion of the building.

Adjacent to our home and accessed by a diminutive door from the kitchen was our petite walled-in garden—a space I loved best. Within its peaceful, vine-covered walls were three bricked steps leading to an upper terrace and a narrow alleyway, a passage that was abounding—according to my active imagination—in clandestine pursuits.

Walking with eager steps at Betna's side, my head spun toward every sound. A note of festivity still resounded in our neighborhood, the first time merriment had emanated from doorways in many long months. All of Rome supposed that young Gaius would bring goodness and healing. Wilting floral wreaths at the crossroads were our only hint of dimness to such splendid hopes.

⁞  

Father returned later from the senate house, brightening upon my entry from the garden. He poured out cool, refreshing water to bathe our hands before the evening meal. As I'd been taught, our tradition of washing was an invitation to ponder the work of my hands, and I considered each tender seedling that had sprouted in recent days and the threatening weeds now plucked away. A contented breath sailed through my lips.

Father was quiet and reflective. The sound of pouring water filled our little kitchen. It was odd that Betna had not joined us, and I glanced into the atrium.

"Shall we wait for Betna?" I asked.

"He had errands at the forum and will return after sunset," Father said.

Our meals were always taken together except when my father was kept late at his work, and Father's businesslike demeanor increased my bemusement. He took his place at table and nodded for me to take mine, but I was still carrying food.

"We all have responsibilities to live up to," Father said.

"Responsibilities?" I asked. His eyes followed my busy hands, loading a platter with olives and sliced cheese. "What are you trying to tell me, Father?"

He cleared his throat, avoiding my question. "There's something I wish to discuss with you," he said. I paused in anticipation, expecting a lesson, a lecture or both. He had the same tone when he was about to say something that was good for me, correcting my manners or critiquing my recitation of a Greek epic.

"With recent events, my studies have fallen behind," I said. "Is that what you're talking about? Have you a new book for me, something you want me to learn?"

His eyes were on our table, platters of varying sizes holding food for our meal, but he appeared detached and far-off in thought. "I believe it's time that you learn the ways of a good wife."

I huffed and planted a round bread loaf before him, taking my seat. "But I already know those ways. At least all that I want to know."

We bowed heads, and Father's tone was solemn. "Blessed are you, Lord our God, Ruler of the world, who brings forth bread from the earth." We sat quiet for a moment, and he added, "Lord of all that has been, that is, and is to come, we offer our thanks for these bountiful gifts. And may my daughter learn the value of respect for her father and the willingness to abide by his wisdom."

My jaw tightened. The man Father chose would be, first, respectable and devoted to God. He would be a good provider. He would be strong but kind. He would be—oh, he would be ugly, fat, and very old! I didn't want to marry at all.

Father raised a hand over my head and gave the daughter's blessing: "May God make you like Sarah, Rebecca, Rachel, and Leah." He knotted his fingers under a clean-shaven chin, leaned forward and grinned. "I've met a man who traveled here from Pontus—"

"Then he must smell like fish!" I frowned. Pontus! It was worse than expected—a leathery old fisherman from the Black Sea, cackling with bulging eyes over his mound of wriggling fish.

Father's brow furrowed. "Prisca. You interrupt me." Lowering my head, lips compressed, he then continued. "You knew this time would come. The Lord's plan is for you to marry." His fingers tapped the table, eyes brooding. "And proceedings each day in the senate house remind me to consider your future, your safety."

"But I am safe, Father … with you." I wanted to relieve his worry.

"Your eyes deceive you then. I am no longer a young man." He flexed misshapen fingers and swollen joints, blackened from ink, and searched my face. There was an odd sense of separation between us, that he was releasing me, even pushing me away. Life without him was my gravest fear.

I said, "It's just—I understand you're only concerned for me, but I know how to take care of myself." That was a lie. In Rome, a woman was not protected by anything … except perhaps a strong man.

Father was considerate and didn't acknowledge my foolishness. "You are now fifteen," he said, "even beyond marriageable age. This man, his name is Aquila. He's a good man, from the line of Benjamin. In three days' time, he will escort you to market and to Miriam for a visit. I have arranged it."

My breath held, aware of my father's commanding presence, wondering if it were possible to change his mind.

"I trust that you will be respectful—and obedient," he said. Tearing off a piece of bread, he waved it at me. "And what did you think of the festivities today, Daughter?"

My brain had conjured up a vision of Aquila as a thickset and mindless fisherman, lifting a veil of fishing nets from my submissive brow. I swallowed hard.

"The festivities?" Inhaling a large breath, I worked to forget the man from Pontus and to recall the splendor and beauty of Rome's forum. "Hmm, the best-dressed of Rome sauntering through the forum, the Vestal Virgins resplendent and holy looking, Gaius Caesar entering on a grand white stallion ... I wanted to stay longer, Father."

"There was a lot of glory filling the forum"—he raised his brows—"though perhaps a bit displaced." The sound of his cup scraping across the table made me uneasy, and he ingested a mouthful of wine.

Banishing all thought of the man from Pontus, my enthusiasm began to mount. "Really, it was—well, it was entertaining."

Father grimaced.

"The new emperor—Gaius—he spoke zealously about old Tiberius. It was like an actor in a Greek tragedy without even a painted mask! His dreary lamentations persisted like a sluggish drain … groaning and groaning, tears and moaning." The memory made me giggle.

"This man has not been proclaimed 'emperor' yet, Prisca," Father said.

I shrugged. "But that's what everyone expects."

"Nevertheless," Father said, "we shall hope for better things from this man in days to come."

೮০ ೮෪

The next three days passed as if one day. Father would tell me very little about Aquila, so my imagination created the most incorrigible, unkempt man in Rome. It was disclosed that he was a tent-maker and that his family had done leatherwork for many generations, also that he lived across the Tiber River. That last concerned me, because artisans and laborers with the dirtiest, smelliest businesses were kept on the other side of the Tiber, away from the "noble" and "glorious" of Rome. My fears were confirmed.

Hannah visited the day before Aquila's arrival and advised how to dress for the occasion. She pointed to a light brown tunic. "Wear that one, the one with the cross-weave. It will remind him of fishing nets!"

A groan left my lips. Hannah's comment breathed the old, dimwitted fisherman into reality.

"He'll think he's caught the prize fish," Hannah continued, "a mullet!" My friend's humor, so unlike her, shook me with laughter. It was an effort to reply.

"A mullet, am I?" I pouted. "Then he will not want me. A mullet sours fast, and I intend to make him wait a very long time." Acting the part of an old woman, I spoke with rattling voice. "A very long time." We both fell back onto bed cushions, giggling so that tears came.

Hannah turned toward me, propping her head on one arm. "There's something I need to tell you," she said. Her finger traced a floral design stitched into the cushion between us. "But you must promise me something."

"And now you expect promises, after you've called me a mullet!" Waving a hand, I stood and positioned myself like a Roman goddess, eyes lowered and unfeeling. "Hmm ... you expect too much," I said.

Hannah looked offended.

"Don't start taking me seriously!" I tossed the brown tunic at her. "Go on."

"Prisca, you have to promise, or I won't tell you." She looked at me as if scolding a small child.

"All right. But what am I promising?"

"You can't make fun of me," she said.

Sitting again by her among the cushions, I regarded the person long known as my dearest friend. Shafts of light made her hair shimmer like rich, dark fabric. Her smile was always honest, and she found goodness in every person. Hannah had telling hands, much like leaves gently swaying on an oleander tree. I was the clumsy one; she was composed and steady. There was a thriving bond between us, more than sisterhood. We fed one another. Much like a seedling needs both soil and sun, what sprang up between us was green and living.

I shook my head. "I won't make fun of you."

Hannah filled her lungs and then exhaled a string of words. "Do you remember the young man who lives on our street? The man with dark eyes and—and big feet?" She covered a smile with her cupped hand, appearing shy at the memory. "You were there when he brought fresh eggs to Miriam and me," she said.

My mouth flew open. "The one who splashed mud all over you!" It had rained all morning. She and Miriam were about to cross the road when a man came by in a hurry and stomped into a giant puddle. All three were left dripping with brown, mucky water.

Hannah said, "And the eggs were a gift and an apology."

"I do remember him," I said. "His father was with him, and they had a basket filled with eggs. His name is— oh, trying to remember. It's Aaron or—"

"Alon," Hannah said. Her face was flushed.

"And now he offers more to you than eggs, I think."

Hannah laid delicate fingers across my arm and leaned close, eager to see my reaction. "I cannot believe how blessed I am. His father came to see Miriam. He has asked to arrange a marriage."

My arms were around her in an instant. "How wonderful!"

"Do you really think so?" she asked.

"Of course." Hannah was sixteen and soon to be a bride. Days of picking flowers and singing through the house were long past. Our friendship would be very different.

Hannah chewed her lip, searching my face. "You remember that he and his father do woodworking and build moving carts." She tilted her head, a hand pressed to her lips, eyes dreamy. "Alon showed me the first one they ever made, a four-wheeled wagon. He is quite skilled, and their little workshop is busy. They are now making carts and wagons with painted designs. Some even have canopies. When last he came to visit, he rode in a carriage pulled by a horse!" Her face was filled with color and looking to me for response. "You don't disapprove?" she asked.

I hugged her. "He seems a good man. I'm happy for you."

"So we really are growing up, Prisca. I have my Alon, and you will have Aquila," she said.

Scenes passed through my mind of us sharing market days or baking cakes together for special feasts, children scurrying underfoot, playing as we once did. But fear then tickled its way into my middle.

"Not sure I'm ready," I said. "Father needs me. I could never leave him, Hannah."

Hannah's fingers tightened around mine. "But I think he wants to see you married." She brought her beaming face closer. "He will be a good grandfather."

"Now you really are rushing me!" My smile faded. "Be patient with me, friend."

Hannah stood to leave. "I am patient, Prisca. But you may find that Aquila is too good to keep waiting. You may be surprised."

I replied, "Tomorrow. Maybe then we'll know."

Following her into the atrium, our figures were reflected in its center pool. We were no longer children. But must that mean marriage? Marriage meant leaving home, perhaps to live in faraway Pontus. The thought was terrifying.

৩০ ৫৩

On the morning of Aquila's scheduled arrival, I looked into a shallow basin of water, its tremor emulating the state of my soul. What would he see, this man from Pontus, when first I stood before him? My eyes were too round, and there was a greenness to them that seemed out of place. "So like your mother's," Father had said.

Like mother's. I could see her gazing at me from the basin. Her eyes, her hair—and there were her hands, smelling of olives, packing her willow basket. It brimmed with healing balm, rich broth, and herbal remedies for someone in need. With Mama, there was always a need to be filled, a purpose to be satisfied.

I remembered standing before her, a whimpering child holding tight to a wooden doll. "But I don't want to go, Mama," I was saying.

Lowering to her knees, gentle fingers hugging my shoulders, she breathed her pet name for me as if she cooled a hot bit of food. "Kisbah," she said, "my little lamb. Our friend, Elah, cannot walk. She cannot cook for her children."

My face had puckered, not willing to go, thinking of new clothes laid out for Dassah, my doll. "But I just want to play with my baby," I said.

"Hmm, I see," Mama replied. She stood and sighed. "I was sure you would want to see the puppies."

She began to move away, and I tugged at her tunic. "Puppies?"

Mama smiled. "They have five!" And so Dassah was tucked away for a nap, and off we went.

Memories flowed clear and fresh, as from a fountain. An image appeared in my mind of a low-slung farmhouse built of rutted stones. It was our destination that day. Lush vertical trees guarded it roundabout like sturdy soldiers, and bright yellow flowers danced near its door. There were puppies, also chickens and burly young goats. I ran through a hedged yard for them to chase me and later watched—a safe distance—when Elah's oldest son milked a cow.

Elah's husband had been killed while working on an aqueduct, and in her hurry to be near him, she had fallen. Elah rested on a blue pillow embroidered with Hebrew letters, most of its decoration hidden beneath black, frizzy waves of hair. Her face was rosy and plump. I crept closer and saw dark eyes fringed with thick lashes, lingering with care over each of seven children. Mama held broth to Elah's rounded lips and applied balm to swollen knees. Elah never cried.

"How old are you, Prisca?" Elah asked me. I held up six fingers. "What a good girl you are," she said, "to come all this way with your Mama."

But I remembered my doll and—well, I had not been a good girl at all. Elah lifted my chin and peered into my eyes. Looking back at her, I knew she was someone that Father would have called *bona fide*, good and faithful.

As we left the house, I remember hugging Mama's legs. "What is it, Kisbah?" she asked.

"I'm glad you take care of people, Mama," I said.

She combed my hair with slender fingers. "You have learned today. It is good."

Halting the flow of memory, I leaned away from the basin and breathed, exhaling words into the silence of my room. "Oh, Mama, if only you were here, I would be a good girl always."

Memories rushed upon me. Somehow, the spillway had opened, and like rapid waters, events tumbled on. I saw our journey home that day. We were skipping. We were happy. Mama's feet strayed from the road, and I followed her into tickling green grasses. She picked mint and thyme for her basket and sang a song about children on a hillside. I gathered orange, papery poppies into short-stemmed bouquets, squealing as flowers slipped through my fingers and blew across the grass.

By late afternoon, we could see Rome's gates ahead, and then, like a mounting storm, hundreds of Roman soldiers marched fast on our path. Their armor glinted in brilliant sunset, and tight rows of helmeted heads filled the roadway. Horses were whipped to an urgent pace, black hides twitching—so near, I could smell streams of sweat. They pulled a stout cart, its thick planks restraining a load of metal weapons.

Swathed in a shroud of dust, I heard a thump and a cracking sound. The cart had hit something. Its wooden wheel shattered into splinters. Horses cried out and bolted. The cart shot upward; turning, falling, and coming at us. Mama's eyes were large and scared, and I ran to her.

"No! Prisca!" She tossed me away, and like my lost flowers, I sailed into a grassy sea, Mama's face growing smaller, until the world went silent.

Withdrawing from those thoughts, I leaned so close to the basin that my nose breathed in wetness. My eyes closed. That last day with Mother I both wanted to recall and wanted to forget. Can one erase all the bad memories that are mixed in with the good? And I reasoned, perhaps the contrast between good and bad makes each one more potent.

My eyes opened with recollection. Holly leaves were all around, sharp-edged and scratching. Where is Mama? My heart beat faster. Calling to her, there was no answer. I blinked and looked again. There she was, just across from me, where little sparkles of dust floated in amber shafts of light. Flowers and herbs lay in a wreath around her, trembling on a breeze that raised the shawl from her shoulders and fanned dark ringlets into webs over her face. I thought Mama could see me; her eyes were open.

"Come get me, Mama." She didn't move. Words screeched through a tight throat. "I just want to go home."

Grasses waved to and fro before my eyes. I watched as men gathered their artillery and moved away but remained still, fingers in my mouth, while day hardened into long shadows.

And then Father came, his figure like a black ghost. He trembled as he held her, moaning her name, "Nessa. Nessa." I kept telling my mouth to open, cry out to him. "Call to Abba. Call to Abba." But my mouth would not obey. No sound would come.

Father searched for me. "Prisca," he said. "Kisbah!" he called. But my limbs would not pick me up and carry me to him. When, at last, he found me, pulling me close, only a queer sound came from my throat. Abba cried new tears and said my name, and we walked away from Mama forever.

The images ceased. My basin's water was tranquil, unmoving, and I touched it, tracing a moistened finger across dark, arching brows. That my eyes were like Mama's made me glad. Remembering her face and her ways filled me somehow. It was as if the voice of my God had reminded how good and blessed my life had been having her as my mother, even for a brief time. "If I could be more like Mama ..."

Fastening my hair into a bundle with linen ribbon, I sailed the new scarf overhead, securing it behind my ears. The reflection made me pause. How did Father know? His sensitive gift revealed rich color in my eyes and silky tone to my skin. Who was the young woman in the water before me, cheeks aglow with scented oil?

My hand went quick to the odd lump at my ankle, another remnant of the day Mama died. I slapped the water, diffusing its image. "Who wants a girl with a twisted foot?" Shrugging my shoulders, I exhaled a long breath. "I'm not interested in an old fisherman anyway."

Betna appeared in the doorway. "The man, Aquila, is arrived." I dropped my head and groaned.

ဆ ℭ

Standing silent in the atrium was a man so unlike what was anticipated, it was startling. He was tall, at least six feet. He had dark, wavy hair that framed a tanned face and lessened the severity of a firm jaw line. Aquila's presence and demeanor spoke to me of forthrightness and truth. His eyes were of the darkest brown and moved about the room as if memorizing every detail. When I entered, he searched me as well, looking into my eyes until I tipped my head away, afraid of revealing secret thoughts.

"Greetings," he said. "My name is Aquila, and I come from Pontus, many days north from here."

My own voice was timid. "And I am Prisca. Of Rome."

"Yes." He smiled. Aquila's entire face filled with it, eyes narrowing into golden glints of light.

"I suppose you know that," I said. Why was I so nervous? My foot seemed twice its usual size, and I pulled at my tunic to conceal it.

He looked nervous as well. His hands found it hard to be still, and he clasped them behind his back. In contrast, his voice was calm, lighthearted. "Do you need a basket for the market?" he asked.

"It's just in the kitchen," I replied. Imagine, thinking I wasn't capable of remembering my own basket! I slipped from the room, emptied a basket of herbs, and pushed my arm through. Betna saw everything, his hand restraining an explosion of laughter. He was spying on me, it was certain.

Faces set toward the marketplace, our journey began. Betna followed behind, shoulders back, head high, revealing a once-impressive physique. It was both a reassurance and a distraction to know he was there, but I remember thinking how tender was his heart. In all my years of knowing him, Betna had never smiled as on that day.

Father had instructed that we purchase items for Miriam, and I tallied those, one by one, as we walked the Vicus Albus.

"Would you like to take my arm?" Aquila asked. He raised an elbow.

His comment caused my fingers to tighten on the basket's handle. In Judea, men would not even speak to women in public. To touch was forbidden. Even in a metropolis like Rome, it was not common practice for our elders to converse with women. I sighed. Aquila was from Pontus. Perhaps contact between men and women was more relaxed there.

I replied, "No. I really—I don't really know you."

Aquila straightened his posture, brows raised. "What would you like to know?" He had a face that became animated when he talked, open and revealing, unafraid to share. He also had a very short growth of beard around the base of his chin.

What would I like to know? What learning has he had? What does he believe about God? Would he expect to live in Pontus again one day?

"How do you know my father?" I asked.

His response was quick. "Your father, I met him in the forum on my first arriving in Rome." He ticked off the time on long, sturdy fingers. "It has been eight months."

"He seems to think highly of you for such a recent acquaintance," I said.

"Your father has been kind," Aquila said.

"How is that?" I began to relax, enjoying the warm sunshine and—what was it? Sincerity? Gentleness?—that seemed to radiate from this tall, handsome man.

Aquila said, "When I came here, the city seemed—it was large, but mostly it was confusing. In the land I come from, there are many languages spoken. But in Rome it is increased several times! People are from unfamiliar countries, and there is urgency in all they do. They were scurrying in every direction, speaking languages I had never heard. They—they buzz, you know. Like insects. All buzzing at the same time."

I recalled one summer afternoon under a tall, arching pine when insects had chorused in a loud and steady trill that was almost disturbing. Rome was like that, a never-ending blur of numberless sounds all competing for attention.

Aquila continued. "On that day, I visited a shop and asked about homes to rent. The man waved me away, saying, '*Go home*,' and turned his back." Aquila held a finger to his lips and paused.

I said, "There are those here who reject us. '*Strangers*,' they call us. '*Foreigners*.'"

"Some more coldly than others," Aquila said. He waited before speaking again, and the clatter around us seemed to cry out: Woolen canopies flapping, our footsteps grinding into pavement, children playing a game with small bones that snapped the ground when tossed.

Aquila looked around and above to the tall buildings touching a clear sky and then turned to me. "Your father overheard the man's remarks and led me to another *taberna*, a small shop on a nearby street. It had a painted awning over its entrance, all flowers and swirls." He gestured with his hands, drawing a diagram of the shop's location and outlining its entry, then continued. "There, a woman—a rather boisterous woman—gave me directions and arranged for my dwelling."

I looked into his eyes, the rich color of moist garden soil. "My father is knowledgeable about many things," I said.

"And he came to visit me," Aquila said. His stride was so long, I found myself taking two steps to his one.

"Oh?"

"To see if I liked my new home. He brought me a fresh loaf of bread."

My eyes opened wide at the realization. Father had me baking bread "for a needy family." I turned away so Aquila would not see sudden awareness spreading across my face, but it was too late. He was laughing at my side.

"He told me about you. He said you were an excellent cook." Aquila stopped and looked into my face. "It was very good bread."

I smiled plainly. "My father is not very discreet."

"But he is a good friend." Aquila said. "I think you are like him."

It was an awkward moment, appraised by a man yet unknown to me. Increasing my pace, I edged around growing numbers of persons filling the street, and then an unexpected hand closed around my arm.

"Your father would never forgive me if I lost you in this crowd," Aquila said.

"That would never happen. I probably know these streets better than you."

"Even so, please allow me to be cautious, for your father's sake," he replied.

There was no sense in refusing. The protective grip on my arm felt supportive ... and delightful. I nodded agreement and addressed my efforts to the path ahead, but I began to question: Could this be the one Adonai has chosen for me?

The road began to curve. Scents of cinnamon and pepper from a spice merchant tickled my nose, and a bright-colored market opened before us. Tradesmen boasted their quality goods, chants rising and falling like swells of lashing rain. It was an interesting mixture of dialects from all over the empire, mingled with animals howling and birds clucking, though every voice spoke the fundamental language of Rome, the language of "money." In the eyes of these purveyors, Rome was the prime location in which to fill their purses.

Idols were everywhere, recalling the firm command of Almighty God: "I am the Lord your God, who brought you out of the land of Egypt, out of the house of slavery; you shall have no other gods before me." Glancing above to a cloudless sky, I shuddered. Most Romans embraced the worship of any new deity, not wanting to miss whatever blessings the latest golden statue might bestow. Pouches were tied about their waists containing miniature clay figures to ensure protection from hunger and lack of gain. "Oh, that *bona fortuna* would smile," they would say. But small helpings of bread that came free from the hand of the emperor did little to satisfy empty hearts.

A familiar voice rang out above the din. "Priscilla, my sweet! Here is a lovely silk to caress your skin." Few people called me by my full name, and hearing it from this man made me cringe. A smooth, lemon-colored scarf was lifted high, its translucence undulating on wafts of air. Only a man's chubby fingers could be seen holding the trim edges, but I knew his voice and sensed his burning gaze. Eliam.

He peeked from behind bright fabric, arching wiry brows. "You see? It is the color of sunlight!"

I wanted to rest my fingers on the soft, sheer silk, but the presence of Eliam commanded caution. In his bearing, one could recognize the features of a serpent, though perhaps the character of the man influenced my vision; he was low and cunning. The pockmarked skin beneath his bald head; rounded, protruding eyes; and snubbed nose prompted the children to call him "toad face." Eliam was a man of many trades and even more vices. He was influential among certain Judeans because of hidden dealings with Roman officials, and his excess of power lay in an ability to betray the weak. Many feared falling out of favor with Eliam, for he was known to bring offense against his own people. Though he was a son of Abraham, a man of Israel, the god he served was himself.

"No. But thank you." Aquila moved closer, and I sensed Betna's approaching presence as well.

"And who is your gargantuan friend?" Eliam asked. He leaned back, puffy hand curled against his chin, assessing the stature of my companion.

Aquila edged between the exuberant vendor and me. "I am Aquila, come from Pontus. And your name?"

Eliam extended a grandiose bow, waving his short arm in an arc overhead, ending at his rounded middle. He wore a tunic of golden fabric that only emphasized a repulsive figure.

"And I am Eliam, master of many trades." He winked at me as if we shared a secret, tapping a finger against lips so thin they were almost hidden by a pointed, wiry beard. "But my prime skill is negotiation. Come see me, and I will get you connected in this community, my friend."

Aquila looked at Eliam with an intensity that appeared to be memorizing every feature and word. "I will remember your offer," he said. He then took my arm and led me beyond Eliam's booming voice.

"Aquila!" Eliam shouted. "I will remember you!"

Once the crowd had hidden all view of Eliam, Aquila stopped. "Who is that man?"

"Not one to be trusted."

Aquila dropped his face near mine. "That much I knew," he said.

Peering in the direction from which we'd come, Betna had blocked any view Eliam might have of us. Eyes alert, face glistening, Betna appeared much younger than his almost sixty years.

Turning to face Aquila, I sighed. "Father once told me, 'Eliam has little regard for the living. He will do whatever it takes to advance himself.'" I paused. "He told me, 'Be polite, but never tell him anything.'"

Aquila appeared desirous of more information, but I moved away, stopping to dip my nose into fragrant yellow blooms.

"Your father gives wise advice," Aquila said.

"Maybe that's why he's come to like you, Aquila. You respect him."

It was uncomfortable again, and I turned for sun to warm my skin. Miriam always told me, "When the day is fair, lift your face to the light and rejoice. For God is the author of life, and a bright day reminds of His brilliance above the heavens."

We were distracted then by the antics of a spindly monkey, screeching and jumping up and down on a severed tree bough wedged into the next booth. We strolled close, laughing as he ran the branch's width and flipped head over tail. Then, in one swift tug, his nimble fingers pulled my scarf, causing my hair to tumble in lengthy waves.

The scruffy animal's owner was from far in the East, a small man with thin brown eyes, wearing a bright pink coat. He appeared frantic, raising and lowering his hands, chattering so fast in a foreign tongue that he sounded much like the monkey at his side. After returning the scarf, he bowed with clasped hands and presented a silver ring from a wooden tray. Though I begged him to keep it, he kept pressing it into my hand and nodding his head. The ring was an endless circle of delicate silver leaves entwined.

Our journey beyond the market took us by a road that hugged the Circus Maximus. Evenings saw rough behavior in this neighborhood so close to the site of Roman games. On this day, no chariots could be heard. Soon we passed outside the city wall where there were sounds, to be sure, but they were not the impatient yells and tempting sneers of buyers and sellers in Rome's shopping districts. In Miriam's neighborhood, you could hear tradesmen working with hammers and carts being pushed or pulled over steep paths. Stopping for a moment, I could hear a bird singing. Betna also paused to listen.

We approached a row of gray *insulae* that Miriam called home, and there was a small gathering of children tucked into the shelter of a pomegranate tree. The tree's horizontal branches were bursting with green buds, enclosing the little flock in scattered shade and fat drops of sunlight. A bearded man, perhaps twenty years of age, sat on a rock facing the children and appeared to be telling them a story. Traditional Judean robes—at one time apparently rich in color—hung from his slender frame. Thick and unruly dark hair framed a playful and engaging expression, and little children leaned forward, captivated by his words.

A melodic voice drifted out to us—or was it even audible? No one else in our little party seemed to hear.

The man was saying, "And then they allowed all of the children to sit near him. Because, you see, he had told his followers, '*Let the little children come to me, and do not hinder them, for the kingdom of heaven belongs to such as these.*'"

A thin reed of a boy stood among the group, his clothes threadbare. Gold-tinged curls crowned a little body. When he spoke, a delicate voice matched his appearance. "You mean, even little children like me?"

Surprising, I seemed to sense emotion stirring in the storyteller. He reached out and rested a palm on the boy's head.

"That's right," the man said, "just like you."

৪০ ৫৪

Miriam's days had been privileged ones until an ill-warned siege near Jerusalem had ended her husband's life and left her defenseless. Everything she possessed was then seized by the Roman army. Even Miriam herself was bound and carried to Rome. Enslaved by a Roman consul as caretaker for his children, she learned the ways of Roman nobility. When the consul died, Miriam was freed but left without home or livelihood, landing in *Subura,* the slum region of Rome. It was then that a chance meeting between Miriam and Father's mother made them friends. Father was only a boy then.

Years later, Tiberius exiled all Judeans, and Miriam was herded outside southern walls into a rough tumble of *insulae*—and she was among the blessed. Many foreigners were separated from family and cast to far limits of the Empire. Because of Father's official position and Roman name, our household was spared exile, and Father did what he could—and what Miriam would allow—to provide support for her.

It was a joy to be Miriam's pupil for most of my life and a terrible disappointment when, due to growing instability in Rome and walking distance to Miriam's *insula,* Father prevented my regular journeys to see her, even with Betna at my side. I missed her. It was hard to give up our daily conversations, steeped in wisdom and nurture.

Miriam lived on the third floor, accessed by a narrow wooden staircase. Her little balcony brimmed with colorful flowers and herbs, distinguishing her home to any who knew her, because Miriam taught that all plants of the earth were to be appreciated as precious gifts from God.

Hannah answered our tap, opening the door wide. She pinched her lips into a grin as I entered, impressed by my companion. Miriam sat reserved in a shadowed corner, soft wrap caressing her shoulders. She appeared smaller and weaker than our last meeting, but her eyes glowed with fierce spirit. Ever a child in her presence, I dropped to my knees before her, and we sang together a favorite psalm:

> *I am like an olive tree, an olive tree, an olive tree,*
> *Flourishing for all to see,*
> *An olive tree in the house of God.*
> *I trust in God's unfailing love, unfailing love,*
> *   unfailing love,*
> *I trust in God's unfailing love, for ever and ever.*

With our fingers, we played imaginary cymbals, and Miriam tapped her toes to an invisible drum. All of a sudden, I remembered Aquila was standing by, and a hand flew to my lips. He was smiling and stepped back a pace.

"Betna, there is a particular tradesman I've been wanting to meet," Aquila said. "His shop is nearby. Will you come?"

Betna nodded, and Aquila pulled the door behind them.

Hannah slid fast beside me. "He is quite handsome!"

Miriam closed wrinkled hands around mine. "Your father believes you need a husband, I think," she said. "This young man reminds me of him—of your father." She drew me closer. "Tell me. He is a son of Abraham?"

"Father says he's from Benjamin's line."

"That will do," Miriam said. "Yes, that will do." She leaned back in her chair, examining me.

"We've been apart too long," I said.

Hannah stood, touching my shoulder. "I have vegetables to prepare." She moved to a table across the room.

Miriam smiled and embraced my face with a gentle hand. "It is time I show you something, child. Come," she said.

Across the room was a shallow recess in the wall. Inserting her hands, she withdrew a narrow wooden chest carved with Hebraic symbols and embellished with metal edging. There was a leather hasp and a smooth wooden dowel that held the lid closed. Miriam swept a sprinkling of dust from its surface and carried it back to her cushions. My soul sensed an importance about the box in her hands, and I waited while her blue shawl rose and fell, rose and fell, in perpetual rhythm.

At last, Miriam spoke. "You know, child, my family has strong and enduring ties to the past—holy and righteous bonds—to the faithfulness of our people."

I nodded. Miriam had told me this long ago.

Her voice softened. "When I was a child, my mother told me of a brave boy, a simple stable boy, who did a kind service for a priest named Matthias. My mother was given this story by her father, Benaiah. It is one you have heard, in part. It was the time when wicked Antiochus, the Syrian King, set his murderers loose upon Jerusalem."

Jerusalem. The very name meant it was a place of peace. I thought of our Temple on Jerusalem's hill: The Meeting House of God. To the people of Judea, children of Israel, it was simply *HaMakom*, "the place." Righteous and learned priests walked its holy passageways. A cold chill tickled my spine. Antiochus had invaded that sanctuary, the dwelling place of God. Yes, I knew the time.

Miriam rocked forward a little, her breath brushing hairs of my head. "It was a troubling generation," she said. "Our people must bear some of the blame, you see. They had turned from God, and they relied on their own prideful ways instead of the goodness of *Yahweh*. Many had become corrupt with greed and earthly pleasures. It divided us, brother against brother"—she tapped my chin—"sister against sister. Some had begun to worship other gods and looked to Greek wisdom instead of seeking the Lord. We no longer acted like a blessed nation."

It was hard to imagine our people in the heart of Jerusalem turning to idols instead of Almighty God, yet just days before, I'd been drawn to an event-filled forum and sparkling jewels within draped litters. What must Adonai think of me? How could one remain true to God in such a place as Rome?

Miriam, unaware of my thoughts, continued. "There was a certain man among our people, Menelaus was his name, who used gold to gain favor with evil Antiochus. The Syrian King made this corrupt man to be our high priest. Imagine, such a thief performing the most holy duties unto Adonai!" Miriam sighed. "But our people rejected Menelaus. We forced his removal from the Temple!"

"That must have angered Antiochus," I said.

"Our people had proven themselves steadfast in the might of the Lord. Yes, Antiochus was outraged." She paused. "You must understand. It was not just a battle of men." Her voice grew. "This was a battle against God."

Images of fire and of angels with golden swords filled my mind.

Miriam inhaled a long, slow breath and then spoke with intensity. "Antiochus sent his cruelest armies to attack Jerusalem, led by the heartless general, Apollonius." With her finger, Miriam traced engravings on the box in her lap. Her eyes misted. "Once they tore down our defenses," she said, "the Syrian soldiers were merciless. Men were slaughtered, women and children taken as slaves." Settling a hand on the wooden box, she inclined her head. "It was a savage fight."

"What about the stable boy?" I asked.

She brightened. "The stable boy, he was named Shema, because, at his birth, a horn was sounded and his cries silenced, and he turned toward the sound." Miriam cupped fingers around her ear and smiled. "He was a good boy," she said.

I moved closer, hugging her knees, and Miriam resumed her story. "Matthias, the priest, was wounded by a Syrian dagger and left to die. He was one of the *Hasidim*, the pious ones of our people, and targeted by Antiochus' men. Though Shema was still very young at the time of the battle, he dragged Matthias into a cattle stall, hiding him in the hay.

"While the city slept, little Shema would seek food for them, risking his life by cover of darkness. Always he prayed. He prayed to the Lord to heal Matthias. He prayed to the Lord for provision and safety. And God Almighty heard his prayers. Matthias became healed. And when he was well enough, they fled into the hills."

"But what does that have to do with this box?" I asked.

Miriam held a finger to her lips. "In time, child. In time." She closed her eyes, returning to the past. "Dark days became like night. You see, dear Priscilla, it was Antiochus' desire not only to kill." She paused, her face tight with pain. "He wanted to steal our faith. Antiochus took the golden candlestick and other of our holy treasures and, by his command, the Temple was soiled with unclean sacrifice. Our sacred books were burned. Our most holy acts of faith were punishable by death. We were even made to worship *Baal Shamem*, whose very image was set upon the altar." Miriam closed her eyes and emitted a mournful sigh.

I covered her hand with mine. "We can talk of this another day," I said.

"No." Her voice was firm. "A light comes forth now. This you must know."

With a light squeeze on her hand, I nodded.

"You see," Miriam said, "Matthias loved Shema and taught him God's truth. The little stable boy became a mighty warrior, not by wielding a sword, but by proclaiming the powerful Word of our Lord. He gave our people hope at a time when all hope was lost."

She paused there. My mind had filled with questions, but I restrained them and waited for her to proceed.

"And little Shema, a mere boy, also taught the priest." Miriam leaned forward, radiant, cradling the box. "Because of Shema's selfless act, the priest learned the importance of risking one's life for love of another. Matthias was transformed by this humble lesson, and he became known for compassion and selflessness."

"What a marvelous story," I said.

"It is a living story." Miriam smiled. "And now I tell you what is in this box." Her frail hand patted its wooden surface. "You see, when Matthias became very old and had no son but Shema, he gave to him this scroll."

"A scroll?"

"It survived the evil destruction of Antiochus because Matthias had hidden it in a secret place." Miriam opened the chest to reveal a thin stretch of animal skin, rolled and bound with thick cord. It was ragged around the edges and dark from age.

She raised my chin, guiding my eyes into hers. "First, you must know that my own grandfather, Benaiah, was descended from Shema. Benaiah told my mother about Shema, when he transferred this chest into her care. The scroll still exists because I, too, believed and understood that important duty and hid it away in my homeland. It has since been delivered to me by a trusted friend."

"Few would have been so careful," I said.

Miriam replied, "The scroll must go to a faithful one of God. It is a weighty responsibility."

Her tone, once again, became light and eager. "I keep the scroll in this chest always. It was fashioned by those who feared the Lord; among them, the prophet Malachi."

Almost afraid to breathe, I stared at the fragile document, thinking it might shatter into pieces. Miriam was reverent, inclining her head toward mine.

"And now, my child, it will come to you," she said.

Something so delicate, so precious, and she was giving it to me? The burden of caring for something so important was terrifying.

Miriam continued, overlooking my panicked expression. "It is said to be written by the very hand of Malachi." Unrolling it, she read the inscribed words:

> *'They shall be mine,' says the Lord of hosts, 'my special possession on the day when I act. I will spare them, just as in compassion a man spares his son who serves him. Then once more you shall see the difference between the righteous and the wicked, between one who serves God and one who does not serve Him. For you who revere my name, the sun of righteousness shall rise with healing in its wings.'*

I closed my eyes. "Praised be the name of God Most High," I whispered.

"Yes. Praise Almighty God." Miriam returned the scroll and closed the box. "And this I have never told anyone," she said, "but it has been on my heart to share it with you, dear Priscilla. I believe Messiah will be more than a Savior, more even than a king. He will be a holy bridge between us and the Almighty, allowing us to speak to God much as children come to us with a scraped knee. That is how merciful our Most High God is." Miriam's words were spoken with heat and breath. "Priscilla, child, I do think he will bring life into our dying souls!" She pressed a hand over her heart.

"It frightens me when you speak this way," I said. "It's like you're going away, like you're leaving me."

Miriam kissed the crown of my head. "But one day I will be gone, child. And you must go on, carrying your faith like a shield."

"Without you?" There was no hiding the worry in my voice.

Her hands took hold of my shoulders, and emotion filled her face. Wide gray eyes probed mine. "And who should this treasure be given to?" she asked. "Who might be so faithful before the Lord? These words I have prayed every day." Her voice intensified. "God has made clear to me. It is you."

My body shivered in her grasp. "But why?"

Her look softened. "I do not know the task before you. The scroll itself is not to be honored above our Lord; you must remember that. But it is a special blessing, a reminder of our Lord's prophetic utterance and of the importance of belonging to God."

"Belonging to God." My head bowed, repeating words from the scroll. "*The sun of righteousness shall rise with healing in its wings.*"

Miriam sighed. "I have always felt that, when Messiah comes, I will know it somehow. I wonder if, even now, he is coming."

"But how can we know?" I asked. "Oh, Miriam, what if we've missed it?" My stomach tightened. "We're so far from the holy places."

Miriam smiled, tilting her head, and I envisioned her as a young woman, beautiful and lively. "We are children of Abraham, of Isaac, of Jacob," she said, "blessed with a promise from God Almighty. I think we will know ... as long as we keep watching."

"Please say you will not leave me." I rested my head in the soft cradle of her knees, clinging to her.

Miriam lifted my chin. She kissed my forehead, my eyes, my cheeks, as if I were six again and mourning my mother. "Do not cry for me, dear Priscilla. For, somehow, I know it is Messiah who will carry me in death. Even beyond death." She smoothed strands of hair from my face. "You must understand. I believe that I will go to a greater place. Greater even than this." Waving her hand to encompass the small square room that served as her living quarters, she started to laugh—at first quiet, then full and strong. Leaning into her arms, she rocked me, murmuring a psalm.

"I shall always remember this moment," I said, "and you."

"And now who is talking as if I go away?" She chuckled.

A knock at the door interrupted us. Hannah went, inviting Aquila and Betna to enter, and we assembled for our humble meal. We dined similar to Roman fashion, though our cushions rested on the floor rather than on narrow, gilt couches. A low table bore cheese and bread; in the center was a plate of vegetables seasoned with herbs and oil. We had brought a gift of spring berries, and those were placed in front of Miriam, sparkling with droplets of fresh water. Betna and Aquila sat together on one long side,

Hannah and I the other, with Miriam nestled at table's short end. Her calm was a marked contrast to my exuberance, and I worked hard at maintaining a respectful demeanor.

Once blessings were offered to our Lord, it was Betna—the quiet one—who was first to be heard. He inclined toward Miriam. "You bring good to this table," he said.

"Dear man," Miriam said, "it is a blessed table, surrounded by good friends." She grinned at Hannah. "And there is delicious food!"

"A feast!" Betna agreed.

"And what news comes from the market?" Miriam asked. Her eyes were wide and interested.

"Ah, the market," Betna said. He linked his arms, leaning back. His one-word description of the market was "Noise."

More excited tones and colorful descriptions passed my lips in describing the market. The people were intriguing, and if one looked beyond their masks, what might they be? What did they do when no one could see?

Aquila cleared his throat and broke into the conversation. "We were approached by a man named Eliam."

"Eliam!" Hannah said. "What did he want?"

"He was trying to sell me some silk. It was a yellow silk scarf. Very pretty," I said.

"Eliam was once a good man," Miriam said. She was so serene, her words might have been missed, but their meaning caused all faces to turn her way. "He was not always so selfish, you know, so scheming."

"But he's been so all my life." I drew a quick breath and changed the subject. "Anyway, something funny happened. A skinny little monkey attacked me. He yanked the veil right off my head!"

Aquila chuckled. "It has been an interesting day," he said. His eyes searched mine, and warmth crept up my neck, filling my cheeks.

Hannah turned toward me, brightening. "What did you do?"

"What could I do? I placed it back on my head, and—here. The man at the booth gave me this ring to make up for it." I lifted my smallest finger to Hannah.

Sliding the ring onto her palm, she turned it over and over. "It reminds me of the vines in your garden."

Aquila was solemn. "Excuse me," he said, "but because I'm fairly new to Rome, I'm unaware of the people here, their history."

Betna was watching Aquila, appearing to like him, eager to listen. Stranger yet among us, Aquila appeared calm but inquisitive, interested in Miriam and her opinions.

Miriam asked, "What is it you want to know?"

"What caused this Eliam to change, and could he— do you consider him a dangerous man?" He gave Miriam his full, patient attention.

She stared at the basket of berries in front of her for a moment then returned Aquila's gaze. "There was a fire," she said, "a terrible fire. Eliam was not there when it started and arrived too late. He lost everything, his wife and his small son. From that time, he has been a tormented and evil man."

"Roman *insulae*, they are not safe." Betna groaned. "People who live more than three floors, they do not get out."

I thought of the narrow staircase to Miriam's dwelling, made of splintering wood. The first couple of floors were built of stone, but dwellings above were like the stairs, a neatly constructed funeral pyre.

Miriam restated Aquila's question. "And is he dangerous? That answer is not yet clear." She and Betna exchanged glances.

"Why have you never told me of this?" I asked. "I just assumed—"

"You were quite young, Priscilla," Miriam said. "Children are not generally told of such things."

"And it is many years," Betna said. "Some stories lay under a stone, and sand blows above it, and the stone we do not see. One day, we cannot remember there is a stone."

Our good cheer had vanished as fast as our delicious vegetables and berries, and I found myself irritated at Aquila for pressing the subject of Eliam. Monkeys in the marketplace were much more exciting.

Hannah moved us on to happier things. "Spring is my favorite time of year," she said. "The sun was bright and warm today; flowers are beginning to bloom."

I said, "And the birds! Betna, I saw you stop and listen."

He nodded. "The birds are liking branches on a tall pine."

"Were the birds in your homeland much different?" I asked.

Betna replied, "In my Nubia, birds are many colors, and they are large. To speak truth, in Rome, many are the same." Betna's eyes widened, as if about to share a mysterious secret. "But understand, my friends, they are always in Nubia first!" We laughed.

Aquila said, "It would appear that many Roman things were once something else."

Glancing around our table, grateful for honest smiles on trusted friends, thoughts turned to the man from Pontus. Did he fit us?

Miriam spoke as if she knew my thoughts. "And, Aquila, will you tell us what brought you to Rome?"

"Two years ago," he said, "my parents died. Father first, a man who had always been robust, filled with purpose." Aquila looked at me. "It was a disease, they said. My father worked with leather, making tents, and he thought to expand a profitable business, so he traveled east, investigating new and different materials. But the journey weakened him. In the end, he could not survive the sickness."

"But your mother too," Hannah said.

Aquila nodded. "They had known each other all their lives. When my father died, she could not bear living without him." His brow creased. "It was hardest to watch her fade, the life disappear from her slowly. She was a woman blessed with joy and could find something fine in everyone and everything." He smiled at Miriam. Did Aquila see some of his mother's spirit in her?

Betna lowered his head, and Hannah looked toward the balcony and flowers bending in delicate wind. Death was all too familiar; it had scarred each of us. And there, on

58

the surface of my thoughts, was Father. How hard it must have been for him to go on when Mother died, but he always told me, "It's my job to see you grow up properly!"

Aquila shook off his reverie and half smiled. "Our home was so different with them gone. Too many reminders of what life had been. The thought came to me, 'Should I move away, seek a new place?' That very day, a rabbi took me aside, said he heard there was a need for making tents in Rome, for the soldiers. I thought it must be a direction from the Lord to come here."

"It is many miles," Betna said, "even for a young man."

"I didn't come alone," Aquila said.

His statement was unexpected, and my head veered toward him.

"Tamar, my young sister, has come as well," he said.

Miriam said, "You must bring Tamar next time."

"Yes," I said. "If I had known ... she could have come with us today."

"She has missed much," Aquila replied.

Laying my hand on Miriam's, I said to her, "My father believes that Adonai brought our family to Rome, even though they came as slaves. Do you believe our Lord directs us in that way? After all, Abraham was brought to a new land too."

Her face, lined with long years of smiles as well as sadness, leaned close to mine. "There are many mysteries with our holy Lord," she said. "For those who walk blameless before Him, their paths are sure."

Could she see the fear in me? Blameless! Was it possible for one to be blameless before the Lord? How many sacrifices might it take?

Miriam rose, appearing tired, signaling the end of our time together. Aquila grasped a hand to steady her. Far too soon, the time had come for us to leave.

"It is good meeting you, young Aquila," Miriam said. "I think you would do well to look after our Priscilla."

My face burned. How could everyone be so confident about this man? Even Miriam! Yes, he was interesting, and if Father liked him, that was important. He was handsome, but would he be faithful? He was strong, but could he also be gentle? He had traveled many miles to Rome, but would he stay?

It was hard to leave Miriam, and our hands clasped as she whispered into my ear. "When the time is right, I will send the treasure box to you." Tiny glints of light shone in her eyes.

"As the Lord wills," I said.

Hannah followed me to the door. I said, "I want to meet Alon. On Sabbath perhaps?"

She lowered her gaze to our feet. It was a vain hope. Living as they did, outside the gates, the walk to our holy assembly was too far, beyond the limit Judean law allowed.

"Perhaps we can find a way," Hannah replied. She raised a hand to mine and smiled.

ꙮ

Night had come, and there were many thoughts to fill waiting dreams. Taking a small twig, I lit an oil lamp from glowing embers at our hearth. Its flame wavered on subtle swells of air. That a light so small could drive away night's dark shadows amazed me. In like manner, Mama's fragrance still pervaded our household; it was her healing smell of chamomile, myrrh and olives. Closing eyes to a remembrance of her wiping away childish tears—tears shed for a lost toy now forgotten—Mama's tender voice filled my ears. "Kisbah," she said, "believe that it will be found. Always live a life of hope, child." Such thoughts lulled me to sleep.

ଽଡ ଔ

In dreams, I saw a newborn baby, its cry sounding hollow and far off. Cool air, perfumed with a scent of spring blossoms, roused me. Breaths quickened, and I realized that the child was real and crying outside.

For the Romans, any child born with a deformity was an ill omen. Imperfect or fatherless children were cast out—"exposed" they called it—helpless to survive. Such children were traditionally left upon the *mons testaceus*, the mound of refuse near Rome's port, and I could only speculate why a child might be left within city walls. Could it be that a compassionate slave gave the babe a meek chance of survival? Or a midwife could not bear the newborn to be discarded in a trash heap? Either scenario would require the compassionate act of another. Another … like me?

The feeble cry tore at my soul, but fear stalled me. Fear, as real as those condemned bodies washed down the Tiber. To rescue this child would break Roman tradition, Roman law, placing me at the emperor's mercy. Pressing hands over my ears, I tried to think of it as someone else's problem, an imperfection, but then I sat upright, swept by a wave of nausea. What if a slave trader found the child? "Adonai, please hear me. Please help." Slaves were prodded, probed with rods, bodies displayed and examined as if meat in a butcher's shop, girls and boys sold into prostitution to make money. Always the desire for money!

But the child would require a wet nurse. Where could someone be found who would keep such a secret? One clear truth blazed before me: Miriam would never let a child die alone in the cold. On that very afternoon, she had spoken of the importance of risking your life for love of another.

Passing through the atrium, I reached the small garden door with ease. My hands felt hard wood, cold metal hinges, and I tugged at the bolt, trying not to make a sound.

Outside, my feet sank into loose soil. In the distance was a glimmering flame atop Rome's city wall where soldiers maintained the night watch. The alley, however, had only the changeable moon for light. Hearing a sound, I jumped next to the wall, peering just above its line of flat stones, afraid even to breathe.

Defined by moon's light, a figure approached—a woman—coming toward my hiding place. She came so close that I could see a scar on her left hand, one that caused her first finger to be misshapen. Her hair was long and trailed her swift movement. In passing, she muttered to a small bundle in Greek—and in Hebrew, saying, "Quiet, little one. It will be all right, Kisbah."

My lungs stretched wide, filling with night air. Kisbah! Little lamb!

Pressing my back against garden wall, I slid to the ground and sat, still quivering. The strange woman must be kind. After all, didn't she speak soft to the child? And couldn't those arms have been mine? And I would be a stranger too.

But the woman cast in silver moonlight had been fearless; and I, with shame sagging my shoulders, drifted back into the warm quiet of our *domus*, resentful that someone else had such courage.

⟋ ⟍

~ *II* ~

Do you know the balancings of the clouds,
The wondrous works of the One
whose knowledge is perfect,
You, whose garments are hot when the earth is still
because of the south wind?
Can you, like Him, spread out the skies,
hard as a molten mirror?
Teach us what we shall say to Him;
We cannot draw up our case because of darkness.
Should He be told that I want to speak?

~Job 37:1-20

Our dreams of peace and security were not fulfilled. Fast as a vicious weed will sprout, Rome's new emperor brought his own barbed thistles to bear. It began with *ludi publici,* the public games. Romans loved games of all kinds, but first among Roman delights were those mortal combats taking place in the busy forum or the teeming circus. There were contests between men, between animals and men, and between women, often a fight to the death. Gaius Caesar wanted his people to love him, so he offered games and celebrations, banquets and festivals. Just months after he came to power, more than 160,000 persons were slain in his dreadful games. And the people adored him. They craved his opulent presence, crowding him, touching him, plying him with gifts.

When Rome's young emperor collapsed from illness eight months into his reign, some offered their very lives as gladiators, believing that, by their sacrifice, Gaius Caesar's health would be restored. Even the mighty Parthian king paid homage to Gaius and offered sacrifices for his health. The man who was nicknamed "Bootikins" had become famous beyond the bounds of his own empire.

To foreigners in Rome, the emperor cultivated a charitable image of himself. He recalled exiles and dismissed charges that old Tiberius had fomented against them. One of those released from prison was Herod Agrippa, who had been a boyhood friend of Gaius. Not only was he released, the young emperor also granted Herod a position of governance over imperial territories, and by that, many Judeans expressed hope for our future. Miriam, however, refused to reside within Rome's fortified walls. She declared, "A man who decorates himself with jewels and silks and wears woman's slippers in public is not to be trusted."

Was he a leader we could trust? I sought Father's answer to that question when Gaius Caesar returned from Pandataria bearing the ashes of his mother and brother. It was an honorable act on his part, returning their remains from exile, thereby absolving any shame that had been ascribed to them by Tiberius.

"Caligula appears to be kind, even thoughtful," I said. "At least he's considerate of his family, don't you think?"

Father was silent, his brow furrowed. He was composing a letter, making rapid black strokes across parchment.

"I mean, bringing his mother and brother back to Rome. Don't you agree, Father?"

He laid *stylus* aside, lifting eyes to mine and speaking in an authoritative tone. "His proper name is Gaius Julius Caesar Germanicus. And we must dutifully call him 'Gaius Caesar.'"

"Yes, Father," I said.

"And if he had such concern for his mother and brother," Father continued, "why did he not intercede when Tiberius first sentenced them to exile?" The muscles of his face were taut.

"Perhaps he felt powerless to do anything."

He grunted and returned to his letter-writing. "Perhaps," he said.

Kneeling at his desk, arms folded and resting on its cool surface, I inquired further. "What is he like—I mean, in person?"

Father stopped writing but did not look at me. "He is a man, merely a man."

"But a good man," I said, "at least a good Roman?" I sought his eyes, needing assurance.

Father stared into vacant space. "We can only hope," he said. "We have no other choice."

I swallowed the tension in my throat. Father was right. What could anyone do? The population had so loved Germanicus and so hated old Tiberius that the young, enthusiastic Gaius gained immediate favor. Tiberius' own blood grandson had been named co-heir in his will, but those particulars were ignored. Gaius Caesar raced into power, senators at the reins, his true character nothing but a figment. He was, at once, granted the title *"Augustus,"* meaning "venerable one," and never failed to remind his subjects that divine blood flowed within him; he was a Caesar from birth.

Early on, coins were circulated among the masses, engraved with Gaius' likeness on one side and Augustus Caesar—Rome's first and favorite emperor—on the other, linking them explicitly. The new emperor's shining image was soon in every hand across a vast empire, and the dangerous truth was realized too late: Gaius Julius Caesar Germanicus had absolute and unrestrained power over us all.

As it happened, Miriam was accurate in her mistrust. When Gaius Caesar edged into his second imperial year, it seemed that true evil was now living among the painted frescoes and marbled halls atop Palatine Hill. First, Tiberius Gemellus, the emperor's co-heir, killed himself. As he was still a boy, those soldiers sent to perpetrate the suicide had to instruct him in positioning his sword.

I asked my father, "Why kill Gemellus? What did he do wrong?"

Father's grim expression told me it was beyond explanation. My question, though, was answered more patently by others: In the murmur of common people on the streets, in frightened glances from aged faces, and in silent precautions taken by members of the senate. The boy had been far too gleeful during Gaius Caesar's illness.

The next fatality was Gaius' former father-in-law, a senator named Marcus Silanus, whose daughter died in childbirth four years prior. He was a man that others called *facile princeps*, a natural leader, and one who had earned my father's respect. When Silanus declined to board Gaius' ship in a pending storm, the emperor alleged that he was intending to seize the empire if the boat sank—officially, a charge of treason. Upon hearing these allegations, Father slammed a fist on his desk and shouted. "But the man was only afraid of rough seas! Silanus was never a sailor," he said. Before any accusations could be litigated, the good senator was forced to cut his own throat. Father's health was concerning in those days—at the very least, he could become bald, so fierce was the pulling of hairs on his head.

Last was the death of Naevius Sutorius Macro, the emperor's Prefect of the Praetorian Guard, his trusted mentor and advisor. Macro had acted much like a father to young Gaius, even nudging him when he fell asleep at banquets. But the emperor charged Macro with adultery, and again, before any trial could be held, both he and his wife were obliged to kill themselves.

Though these deaths were labeled "suicides," everyone knew the frightening truth. Gaius Caesar, one I would forever remember only as "Caligula," was using his figurative boots to stamp out any competition. Rome's nobles began to live a most precarious existence, regretting any wealth or prestige that might entice the emperor's attention. The richest families sought refuge in resort cities like Puteoli and Capreae or found refreshment in the hot springs of Baiae and Tibur. Whether noble or lowly, pleasing the emperor became an arduous but necessary task.

Father continued at his work, and I knew his first priority was to provide for Betna and me. Often he came home, hair matted with perspiration, disappearing into his room. His woolen curtain remained closed, buffeted by steady, whispered prayers. I thought of inviting Father to share his burdens but, instead, willingly participated in the thick wall growing between us. Father's side of that wall was meant to protect; mine was rooted in fear.

ೞ ೞ

Trees leafed and flowers bloomed, warm days of rain brought freshness to the land, and I was determined to remain optimistic. Father encouraged my friendship with Aquila but did not rush us into marriage, and I was thankful, still clinging to childhood memories and life with Father and Betna. On those days, however, when Aquila escorted me to market or to assembly, or when he crossed my path at the neighborhood fountain, I believed myself to be the most blessed young woman in Rome.

In the Hebrew month of Adar and the time of our festival of Purim, I stood over the kitchen table, wrapping fruit-filled cookies in embroidered scraps of linen. One of the most important activities of Purim was giving gifts to the poor, and I'd been bustling about all day, packing baskets with food. Purim began with a reading of the scroll of Esther. It was my favorite feast, not just because of the delicious banqueting; Purim was special to me because of the courage and faith of Queen Esther. Each year, as the scroll was unrolled, the story read aloud, and menorah candles flickered golden, I sensed my faith warming anew. Only God Almighty could have arranged for a Hebrew girl to become Queen of Persia! Might the Holy One call upon me one day as he called upon Esther? My heart quickened.

Esther's story told of Haman, a wicked man who convinced the king to order death for every Judean. But faithful Mordecai sent word to the queen, beseeching her to plead with her husband to save their people from death. It was my favorite part of the story, because it allowed Esther to demonstrate her courage and devotion. What a difficult place she was in! She was facing sure death, because no one could approach the king without invitation—not even his own wife! When she voiced fear at seeking the king's presence, Mordecai prompted her by asking, "Who knows whether you have come to the kingdom for such a time as this?" Mordecai's words moved Esther's heart. Believing that God called her to a holy purpose at that precise time, she committed herself to obey, telling him, "If I perish, I perish."

I sighed. "Might there be a time and purpose for me, Adonai," I asked, "perhaps for such a time as this?" My eyes wandered through kitchen's narrow doorway into the atrium, searching clouds and sky reflected in its serene pool. "I'm not beautiful or faithful like Esther," I said. "Could you ever call on someone like me?"

A subtle tapping echoed in the vestibule and, at my answer, Matron Helah pressed into the room. Matron Mara and her daughter, Keziah, poured in behind her.

"Good day, young Priscilla," Helah said. Her voice grated, as if filtered by grains of sand. Nearing seventy years of age, Helah's tall, slender form was forceful and alert. She was an esteemed woman, and her aging husband was still an authority among men.

Words of greeting came quick from my lips, inspired by numerous lessons in hospitality. "You have blessed our household by coming," I replied.

"I suppose you question the purpose of our visit," said Mara. She was a woman of about fifty, active in many charity functions that supported our flock of worshipers, often humming unknown melodies or chattering as she toiled. Her stout shape hurried about most days, gathering various stores for the needy, sharing tidbits of news. Pitiable Keziah, looking much like her mother and always in attendance upon her, was never allowed to speak. She made up for a lack of voice by contorting her face into grieved and distressed expressions.

"No—no, not at all," I responded. "My first thought is that you've come to wish me well and tell me about Purim festivities." The two older women stood emotionless. Keziah stared around the room as if searching for something.

Mara said, "We have come because it is our duty."

"Duty?"

"Absolutely, dear," Helah said. "Since you have no mother, it falls upon us to see that you are instructed correctly."

"Instructed?"

"Instructed properly," Mara declared, "regarding the behavior of a young, marriageable woman." Mara wobbled as she spoke, making one think that her words were conjured up and out by the movement. Her relentless scrutiny was unsettling, and my comfortable kitchen with its cheery baskets beckoned.

"Oh. Well, I—my—my behavior?" Why did I always stammer when these women spoke to me?

"Of course," said Helah.

I said, "But it's just that—that I've been honored with instruction from Miriam. She's taught me—"

Helah shook her head, and each word she spoke sounded like a hammer's tap. "Oh, no, no, no," she said. "Miriam has not been sanctioned by the Rabbi to teach."

"Positively not," Mara echoed. She made a clicking sound with her tongue.

Helah cleared her throat. "Had we been called upon before now, your marriage might already be in hand."

The two women exchanged knowing glances. Keziah sniffed and pinched her lips.

"We are your guides." Mara raised open palms, presenting herself as sacrifice. Her smile was lavish. "Our little committee has been sanctioned—duly sanctioned—by the rabbi to assure proper upbringing and training for young wives."

I replied, "You—you are kind, but between Father and Miriam ..."

"Oh, it is quite sad," Helah said. "Your clothing is too—it is far too colorful." She pinched her mouth into a wrinkled beak.

My mouth opened but no words came, staring at the draping of gray and black standing before me.

Mara paced a small circle, gripping small tucks of my tunic as she went. "And your tunic is entirely too snug," she said. "You must loosen your garments." She shook her head, and the skin around her mouth began to joggle. "You must not appear impious, child."

"You—you think I appear impious?" My eyes opened wide. These women were beginning to irritate me.

"Appearance is the outward design of inner purity," Helah said. Her eyelids wilted, and she lifted her face to incoming light.

Mara smoothed her woolen *palla*, twisting its decorative fringes with swollen fingers. "We are not to present ourselves in disgrace before the Lord, dear."

Disgrace? Be polite, for Father's sake, I admonished myself.

"May I offer you some refreshment?" I asked. "There is fresh-drawn water and also sweet wine. And I've made cookies for our festival, so ..."

Mara leaned back as if struck. "Food gifts are for the needy!" she said. "Are you inferring that we—"

"No. Please," I said, "it's just that I—I've made so many and—"

Helah breathed an immense sigh, and white strands crept from beneath her dark veil. "There are two more young women who need our services," she said. "We must see them before Purim begins." Her posture straightened in dismissal.

Mara filled her chest with air, rising to maximum height. "Yes. Let us go, Keziah."

They never spoke a farewell, and I embarrassed myself by stuttering and waving at their swaying backsides. The little trio sailed from the house, Keziah's heaviness like the ballast in their wake. As the door closed, my lungs heaved. Having those women assigned to instruct me would be miserable.

I looked down at the fabric of my tunic, dyed its soft green color by using pouches of lichen Betna had collected from the forest. Threads of white and blue were sewn into a floral design along the neckline. Impious?

༄ ༺

Market days were a welcome diversion from daily chores and carried me beyond our familiar walls. Betna, ever tolerant, trudged along at my side, waiting as I debated choices of fresh vegetables and fruit. Sometimes he would step away—though never further than road's width—and could be seen gazing at bone-handle knives or dipping his nose into small pots of frankincense. These were the things of Nubia.

In the month the Romans named for the Goddess Juno, it was a fair day for an outing. Betna first endured a brief—and dutiful—call on Mara and Keziah, from which he offered to carry a bundle of tunics Keziah had outgrown, all in dreary and colorless hues. A walk to the burgeoning marketplace followed our visit. The sun was intense, and Betna appeared sluggish, overheated. Nearby was a fountain with a flat sill.

"Please sit," I said. Betna started to protest. "I know Father's orders, and we're abiding by them. But we need fish for a special meal, and I'm only going to the *piscatoris*. You see? It's just there." And I was gone before he could pull me back.

Being in the market made me think of my first acquaintance with Aquila, and my body became more fluid in its motion, lifted and free. Every vibrant awning, every vendor's shout, the racks of exotic silks ... all reminded me of him.

Across and to my left, Eliam just arriving. He was late—illegally late. Magistrates issued fines for anyone pulling a cart on city streets after sunrise, and it amazed me that he dared attempt such a feat mid-morning. It was hard to suppress my mirth, though, observing what he had done to his wagon. It was always adorned with trinkets and bright fabrics, but this day the centers of his wheels were covered with circles of animal hide. They twisted as the wheels turned, reminding me of a cow chewing mouthfuls of hay.

The *piscatoris*—fish vendor—had several varieties of fish, alive and swimming in narrow troughs. An awning, crafted from golden reeds and white seashells, shaded the stall. The strong smell of fish wrinkled my nose, but the man was cheerful. He held a large eel for inspection.

"Caught while you were sleeping," he said. "We take care to deliver these fresh, to bring the best to you." His voice softened. "Especially to you."

The man's eyes were bright but not bulging, like Aquila's were imagined to be, when first suspecting he was a fisherman; it made me grin. I shook my head, not very interested in fresh eel, though it was a delicacy to Romans.

"Would you recommend that fish?" I pointed.

"Fresh trout," he said, "from a cold-water lake in Etruria. Some olive oil, a splash of lemon, a sprinkling of herbs and," he closed his eyes and shook his head as if savoring the aroma, "it is a banquet to please even the emperor."

His friendliness lifted my spirits. "Thank you. I'll have five."

"That will be four *sestertii*," he said.

"Four? That's more than I expected."

Rubbing the stubbles on his chin, he began to nod and then tapped a drumbeat on the side of his cart. Finally, exhaling a loud sigh for emphasis, he responded. "Allow me to be generous, young woman. On this bright day and for your kind smile, I can offer them for three."

"That is a better price." I dropped the brass coins into his basket.

The *piscatoris* turned away and busied himself with wrapping and bundling the fish for me to take home. In that moment, there was a slight shaking of my basket from behind and another man's voice whispering. It was a familiar voice and words that were gentle yet brisk.

He said, "I know someone who fed five thousand men with just two fish and five loaves of bread."

Pausing, trying to make sense of his words, I then turned in the direction of the whisper, but no one was there. Narrowing my eyes and searching the hundreds of faces bobbing among decorated carts and wagons, no face was recognizable.

"Excuse, please," the fish vendor called.

Oh! The *piscatoris*! Spinning around to face him, I accepted my purchase and then ran to Betna while the neglected vendor was still speaking.

"Please come again!" he shouted. All thought of him vanished, however, in contemplation of the extraordinary encounter.

Betna was already moving toward me, a look of annoyance on his face. "That man," he said. "What did he want?"

"Well, I—I'm just confused. What he said was not frightening. It seemed rather mysterious, like a question to answer or a riddle to solve. He talked about someone who fed five thousand people with two fish and—hmm, what an odd thing to say." A woman, arms filled with cabbages, appeared to lean closer, her interest lured by our enlivened tones. "Maybe we should talk about it at home," I said.

Betna patted my hand. "And home we are going."

"But we need more foods for our dinner, and I think that Aquila would enjoy—"

"Aha, and I see. A special meal—for him!" His brows lifted.

"We need to purchase a few lemons—oh, and some honey for a cake," I said.

He took the basket from me. "And when do I get honey cakes?"

"What? I've made many cakes for you!"

⟐ ⟐

Later, as we rounded the corner toward home, hanging from our door latch was a woven leather satchel hugging a wide-mouth clay pot that brimmed with yellow roses and sprigs of mint and thyme. Betna bent toward me, humming a melody I'd heard from him on occasion.

"What is that song, Betna? Does it have a name?" I asked.

"An old song," he said. "The words come from wise Solomon, a man who knows love." He ambled into the house, closing his eyes to the cool air greeting us.

As usual, I wanted to know everything I didn't know. "But what are the words? Sing it with words. Did you learn it when you were a boy?"

"Today it is for humming," Betna replied. "One day, I will give you words." He set the packed market basket on a table and went his way.

The sweet-smelling flowers were arranged in a vase, the fresh herbs tied for drying. Oily fragrance clung to my fingers, and I hugged my nose time and again, inhaling lush scent. When my basket was almost empty, I paused, holding my breath. There, nestled among the lemons, sat a single polished pomegranate.

"But I did not purchase a—" I started. But my basket had moved when that whispered voice spoke riddles in my ear. It was the same gentle voice that told stories to children under a budding pomegranate tree.

ༀ ༃

The next day I woke excited. We were having guests for evening meal. Miriam and Hannah were coming, and Aquila was bringing them.

We had the luxury of a working kitchen in our home. *Insula* residents surrounding us were forced to share a community stove, and even they were fortunate. Most of the commoners living in Rome had no cooking facilities at all and took meals at city cook-shops, where pots of vegetable and bean soups were always steaming and tables were filled with hungry customers. I loved cooking, and so my little stove was kept busy.

I'd decided to please my father with a cake that Mother used to bake, a honey cake with oranges and dates. Already, the room was pungent with orange peel, and I reminisced about the man under a pomegranate tree. Many months had passed, but his tender words remained clear in memory: "He had told his followers, '*Let the little children come to me. The kingdom of heaven belongs to such as these.*'" Who was this man he spoke of, the one who had followers? Who could have said such marvelous things? And how could a lone storyteller in stippled shade have ever noticed me that day, a passing observer on the path, when he had a passel of captivated children at his feet?

Maybe the storyteller didn't remember me at all and approached me at random in the marketplace. But then why drop a pomegranate in my basket? And what about the two fish and five loaves? On that first glimpse of him, he wore Judean clothing, so perhaps it was a legendary tale, a story from long-forgotten days of our ancestors. What a mysterious incident! It was a topic to discuss with Miriam.

Hours passed, and to my enormous grief, Miriam did not arrive. Fish was steaming, vegetables were washed and seasoned, and the cake—my pride—was ready to be sliced. But our guests did not come.

By the time Father arrived from the senate house, panic had risen higher than Rome's Capitoline Hill. "Abba! They should be here! What has happened?"

He remained calm. "They must have been held up. Or perhaps Miriam was not up to the walk today," he said.

"We should go to them," I said. "We would have heard something by now." Father stood shaking his head. "What if Miriam has taken ill?"

"Now, Prisca—"

I whined, holding a hand to my mouth. "Could they have forgotten it was today?"

He assured me they would never forget, that Aquila would get a message to us if there were troubles, and then drifted into a square-shaped room behind our atrium called the *tablinum*. It was Father's place of refuge, and I knew that he was also concerned when he picked up a manuscript borrowed from the library; it was one he'd been trying to become interested in for weeks.

Feathery pink wisps appeared in a dusky sky, and fear expanded in my stomach, leaving little room for food. What had been prepared could not be wasted and was shared in silence between Father, Betna and me, the remains of which were stored away. Father and Betna were gracious, plying me with all warm and generous compliments, but I became sulky and depressed. When stars peeked out of a black sky and oil lamps were glowing, there came a light knock at our door, and Aquila slid into the room without being greeted. His clothing was torn and soiled, his brow feverish.

"Forgive my—my trespass." His breath came in short bursts. Aquila nodded my way. "I'm sorry to miss your fine meal."

It was hard to shake the burning beneath my skin, anger that had been nurtured all evening, but it was clear that something was very wrong. Aquila must have rehearsed his apologies all the way to our house, and those regrets having been said, was unable to speak more.

Father urged him to a chair and gestured me out of the room. "Prisca, bring us something to drink," he said.

Scampering away, Hannah's name could be heard, but everything else was beyond understanding. Dread filled my mind so completely that I forgot how much wine was added to water and stiffened, trying to make sense of it.

At last, rushing back to their discussion, Aquila was saying, "She's in my home. Miriam has come to look after her."

The conversation was interrupted when cups were passed to them.

"Is Hannah ill?" I asked.

"You need to sit down," Father said.

"What is it?" I asked.

Aquila's eyes were intense, disturbing me even more. "Please sit down," he said.

I dropped onto the couch beside Father. "What has happened? Is Hannah all right?"

Father laid a hand on my shoulder. "Hannah—she's been the victim of a terrible harm."

"A terrible harm. What do you mean?" Twitches of panic were multiplying. "She's alive, isn't she? Tell me what's happened."

"She is alive," Father said.

Looking to one and then the other, it appeared that Father was attempting to shield me; Aquila was slack with fatigue. Shifting on the cushions, muscles tensing, I leaned forward. "Tell me what's going on."

Aquila made an attempt at calm. "You must trust that Hannah is safe. I've done what I could to protect—to help her."

"She's safe? But what's happened? Why does she need protecting?" It was all so vague, noncommittal and terrifying. My friend was hurting and hidden in a maze of unknown streets.

Aquila began to explain, his words tentative. "I went to Miriam's home as planned. It was just past midday, the sun still high. When I came near the crossroads, there were sounds—muffled screams—coming from inside a shaded archway. Two youths were there. They each wore a *toga virilis*. They were violating a young woman." He hesitated. "It was Hannah."

I jumped to my feet. "Take me to her."

Father stood and held my hands. "You can't go to her now. Not now."

"But she needs me. You can't keep me from her," I said.

Aquila touched my arm. "Your father is right. It's not safe." He was concealing his right hand. It was bleeding. He stepped away.

"Your hand," I said.

With unwavering concentration, Aquila looked at me. His voice was firm. "I came here with care, knowing others may be watching." Letting out a huge breath, he turned to leave. "I endanger you by being here."

"But you're wounded." I reached for him. "Let me help."

He walked fast toward our garden door and then swiveled, his body cast in flickering lamplight. "Trust me," he said. Then he pushed his way through the low doorsill.

I ran to the door in a childish attempt to call him back, but Father held me. "Sit down, Priscilla," he said.

Instead, I pressed my forehead into his broad chest and moaned. He guided me to a low couch where he wrapped arms around me.

"How could anyone do such a thing to Hannah?" I ground my teeth, wanting to do something, but bound by the laws of our people and the fear of Rome, there was nothing within my power.

Father swept strands of hair from my face. "I assure you, when it's safe, I'll take you to her."

"But I don't understand. Why is it so dangerous? Why did Aquila say it was dangerous to even come here?"

Father's jaw tightened. "Aquila confronted the two men. He fought with them. Others will be looking for him, searching everywhere. He was a witness to their crime."

The scene was becoming more distinct. Aquila had come to Hannah's rescue, fighting to free her. They must have seen his face.

"You said 'others' will be looking for him. Who do you mean?" I asked.

His tone was intense. "Whoever can be bought," Father said. "Only sons of senators wear the *toga virilis*. Their resources will be vast." He stared into our quiet room where frescoed walls danced in subtle lamplight.

The significance of what happened that afternoon began to weigh on my soul. "What can be done?" I asked. My heart was beating loud and fast.

"Pray. Aquila needs the intervention of our all-seeing and merciful God."

Leaning against him, lifted by his inward-outward flows of air, I recognized how Hannah deserved a father who could hold her when pain was too much to bear. Alon would be a comfort—I sucked in a breath and my eyes filled with tears. Everything was changed now, in the tiny space of an afternoon. Would Alon still have her?

That night, sleep came in fractions. Every sound—the wind, the hoot of an owl, the chirping of insects in the trees—terrified me. Yet there was a constant circle of light outside my bedroom door and a shadowed image in the gathering folds of my curtain ... Father keeping watch.

ರಾ ೧೪

The next days, turning into weeks, were misery. Hannah's attack was revisited in sketched scenes. Unexpected sounds brought on terrified spasms. Nighttime found me layered in blankets, even as summer heat soared, body curled into a rounded lump under the covers. Father would not allow me to leave the *domus*, but in truth, I would not have left anyway unless to see Hannah. Even the company of Betna was not enough to overcome worry.

Would there have been less pain if the victim had been me? Hannah was the one who wanted marriage. To stay with Father would be sufficient. In the year after Mother's death, my father had said, "You cannot change what happened, only be thankful for blessings we've had. We learn and grow in times of pain." How could such pain make me grow?

"Do you hear me?" I asked of my God. Prayers became mingled with ancient words of the psalmist, *"Hear my prayer, O Lord; let my cry come to thee! Do not hide thy face from me in the day of my distress! Incline thy ear to me; answer me speedily in the day when I call."* But what is "speedily" in the infinite realm of God?

෨ ෬

~ *III* ~

But as for you, return to your God,
hold fast to love and justice,
and wait continually for your God.

~Hosea 12:6

Still confined to our *insula*, I ascended the stairs one day to call on Valeria, two floors above us, perhaps to seek understanding? Comfort? Simply to hear a woman's voice?

Valeria and her artisan husband, Crispus, had been our neighbors for four years. Seeking work, Crispus had brought his pregnant wife from Campania, a region south of Rome, longing to carve beautiful friezes and decorative panels for the wealthy patricians of Rome. But his connections did not lead into circles of nobility, and to feed his family, he'd been forced into the drudgery of construction labor, re-facing or renovating aging structures from Rome's celebrated past.

Valeria was five years my senior but looked younger. She was so petite, so slender, I had doubted whether she could deliver her child. Yet, when Tertius came, the birth was pronounced as an easy one and very quick. In traditional Roman way, Crispus described birds in flight as their son was born, proclaiming: "The gods have favored us!"

Having finished my chores by mid-morning, I gathered a trio of round honey cakes and carried them to the young family. Climbing stairs to their *insula*, thoughts of Tertius made me smile. He was nearing four years old, and I loved him. An audacious child, his hair was always rumpled; most days, his pink, excited face was painted with dirt. Little boats, carved from pieces of wood by a doting father, were lined up by steady plump fingers readying them to do battle with sea monsters made from small rocks and sticks. Surely Tertius would jump into my arms when he saw the sweet cakes!

But it was Valeria's pale face that met me, eyes reddened and anxious, brown hair limp and uncombed.

I scanned the *insula* for signs of a small boy's activity. "Where is Tertius?"

Valeria was silent, and I took her hand, eyes adjusting to dim light. Her gaze came to a pallet below their small, iron-gated window—the only window. Tertius was waiflike among the cushions. White slants of light revealed damp, blotched skin. All around him were wooden boats waiting for a young adventurer to rise and play, but the glazed face on the pillow was unmoving.

Rushing to him, Valeria hovered over me like a shadow. "How long has he been like this?" I asked.

"Since the sun left us yesterday." Her voice was so faint it was hard to hear. "I—I bathed his face through the night."

A bowl sat beside him with only a puddle of water left and a tattered cloth drying in summer heat. The room was stifling. How Rome's impoverished survived in these wooden boxes ... all I could do was shake my head at the gloom and stagnant air.

"And Crispus?" I asked.

She sniffed, fighting back tears.

I pressed her to answer. "Where is your husband?"

"He's gone to find a physician," she replied.

"Oh, I see." It was an effort to mask my anxiety. Rome's physicians were seldom available for those with lean purses. "He is certain to return soon."

Valeria searched her young son's face and held a hand to her mouth. A slow stream of tears rolled down her cheeks.

I handed her a water pot. "You go outside, get some air. Gather fresh water from the fountain. I'll stay with Tertius and tend him." When she hesitated, I promised not to leave him.

Once her steps sounded on the stairs, I set about freshening things. Thoughts carried me to a happier day when Tertius was an infant. Valeria was sitting on a wooden bench inside my garden, suckling her small child as I planted seeds in early spring. Fresh young blossoms peeked from green shrubs, scenting the sun-filled air, and birds chirped in happy tune. We had spoken then about Almighty God, and I had shared in eager tones about my belief that a perfect God had formed the boy in her arms.

"And if that is so," she said, "if your God is truly perfect, then so must be my son."

"If only he lived in a perfect world," I had replied.

The memory lingered as I ran fingers through Tertius' dark, wavy hair. "Oh, sweet boy—that we could live in a perfect world," I whispered.

He felt hot. While washing his face and rubbing oil into his skin, a strange, thick moan came from his chest, and I leaned close to understand. He was crying, calling to his mother, but lungs clogged with sickness could not release clear words.

Crispus then burst into the room, eyes wide and searching.

"My son," he said. His voice dripped like dense liquid from a tortured heart. Seeing me on the floor near Tertius, he hardened. "Why are you here?"

"I came bringing cakes." It sounded senseless to my own ears.

Crispus replied, "We have no need of cakes. Go home."

The door opened again. It was Valeria, a black shape outlined by sun's light. Crispus stood over their rickety table, fists upon it, every muscle tensed. Seeing that no physician had come, Valeria slumped against the doorframe, water spilling from her pot.

"He called for you," I said. She ran to her son.

A heavy heart drove me down the long stairs, eyes fixed on feet that expanded into the leather of my sandals at every step.

When sun burned hot in a vivid blue sky next morning and Valeria's wail rose above us, we knew that Tertius had died. He deserved better. He deserved more. His bright mind had such potential. Why did he have to die?

I knelt at my bed, begging the Almighty to hear me. "It's not fair. Even in the wilderness, you remained with our people. Are you yet here in this horrid wasteland?"

Burrowing my head into the crook of my arm, body aching with sorrow, tears would not come. "Oh, Adonai, why? Why must the helpless suffer and die? You are great, but are you not also merciful?"

It was a small procession. Neighborhood children came, scrubbed and oiled, carrying gifts to lay beside Tertius for his journey to a place the Romans called *Elysium*. Valeria staggered along, downcast. She leaned on Crispus, their unsteady pace lagging behind a blue-painted cart bearing their son's body. Crispus wore no expression, his eyes shadowed and distant.

My own sorrow was borne in quiet, in spades of garden soil turned over, in violent harrowing and weeding. My father, concerned, came and wrapped arms around me.

"Do not let grief steal your faith," he said. "Remember, King David was pursued by many, assaulted on every side. He saw friends die in battle and fled for his own life. But he remained true to the Lord."

"I am not so strong as King David," I said.

"You are stronger than you know." He lifted one corner of his mouth in a half smile. "And who are we to question the Almighty?"

My eyes began to tear, not with sorrow but with anger. "I thought our God was merciful."

"And so he is." Father nodded, still calm, always patient. "Remember the wonderful works he has done. God will bring good from this sad time."

"I cannot see it," I said.

"Exactly. How are we to understand his grand and mysterious ways? Even David could not always see. But he continued to trust," Father said.

During the weeks that followed, many succumbed to a vile fever plaguing Rome. Money and choice physicians did not protect even the wealthy. Sitting high above the city in his grand *domus* on Palatine Hill, the emperor himself was stricken when his favorite sister, Julia Drusilla, died of fever. She was twenty-two years old. All of Rome was summoned for an elaborate funerary procession, a *pompa funebris*.

On our way, we saw Aquila standing near the Circus Maximus entry, watching and waiting for us to pass. He had brought a friend, Tychon, who worked with him in tent-making. Tychon was a block of a man, square and muscular—not tall, but the breadth of his shoulders was wide. As Tychon drew near to make my acquaintance, vivid blue eyes opened to mine. His bearing and demeanor spoke of intense loyalty with and for Aquila, a friendship like that between Father and Betna.

Hannah and Miriam were woefully absent, and we turned together down a street named Vicus Tuscus along with half of Rome. Heat was unbearable in the crowded street, but the smell was worse. I was thankful for my veil and covered my nose. Throngs of Rome's occupants pushed through wearing traditional mourning clothes: Men in black, women in white. As we neared the forum, horns were blaring, a signal that the procession was about to begin. Wide steps of the Basilica Julia were packed—no room for us—and we were funneled in the direction of the Temple of Concord. It would be more difficult to see the procession from there, but I could think of nothing but Hannah anyway. Pressed into the line of mourners, we stood in searing sun and watched.

The cornu players came first, their spiral horns heralding the coming of divine presence. I never quite understood that "divine" aspect of Roman tradition. These were people, flesh and blood, who had been born, lived and died just like everybody else. Gaius Caesar had elevated Drusilla to divine status, chronicling her death among those who had "ascended into a godly realm," on a level with Julius and Augustus Caesar. With a jolt, the blare of horns right beside us woke me from melancholy, and I became focused on approaching figures.

Behind the snail-like cornus came bearers of incense, ten of them, all men. They each carried a round bronze platter suspended on chains from a hooked rod and wore black robes. Their faces shimmered with golden powder. Perfumed smoke rose from their platters and mingled with the odor of the crowd, upsetting my stomach.

Women followed, each one blowing high and airy notes through an *aulos*. Men came close behind, adding the soft strumming of *citharas* for fresh and pleasing harmony. Young children joined the song, tapping miniature cymbals. Next in the procession were ladies in tunics of gauzy white linen who stepped on tiptoe, tossing rose petals into the air. I only recall seeing Drusilla once but somehow knew she would have enjoyed the musical and visual display. I exhaled through parted lips, mesmerized by the delicacy of movement made ethereal with wispy white and pink petals floating all around us.

Drusilla's family members came then. They wore the *imagines*—wax masks—of honorable ancestors. Caesar Augustus, as if raised from the dead, appeared in black robes. "Oh" and "Ah" rose from the crowd while proud, clipped steps carried him toward the *rostrum*. Germanicus then appeared in military garb, an adoring Agrippina at his side. The procession of ancestors was strange and frightening to me. Individuals were chosen to fit physical attributes of the originals and fitted with the deceased persons' masks. There was an eerie sense that those long dead had sprung back to life.

Julia Drusilla was carried after them, seated upright on a curving couch made of ivory. Her gown was white silk, trimmed with golden threads, her hair sculpted into shining coils around a powdered face. She appeared as though in dreamy sleep.

I have heard it said that the emperor was not there that day, that it was Drusilla's husband, Lepidus, who gave the eulogy. But with my own eyes I saw the emperor walking beside Drusilla's body, a jeweled hand caressing the couch she reclined on. A mask of Julius Caesar hid his face. Passing close to our party, he stole a tender, longing glance at a much-loved sister. His eyes were reddened and moist. I knew in that moment it was Gaius himself.

Brother and sisters ascended the *rostrum*, and the molded face of Julius Caesar came forward.

"Citizens of Rome, today I stand before you aggrieved," he paused, "but honored to delight you with the extraordinary life of Julia Drusilla, a daughter of Caesar." There was a slight tremor in his voice. He hesitated, filled his lungs, and turned toward the lifeless form reclining among pillows.

Resuming then with more vigor, he spoke to her as though she yet lived in a voice the audience could hear:

"My Drusilla, by your lovely and refined character, you have remained devoted to your parents, to your brothers and sisters, to your husband. I honor you. When your parents were wrongly accused and fatally attacked, you exhibited honor and commitment. Though robbed of your dear family, you always expressed loyalty to your father's *genius*, honoring him in life and in death. You have never failed to be a faithful friend ..."

Nothing could be heard but the musical voice of a heartbroken man and the fluttering leaves of an olive tree. Could it be that Gaius Caesar was not the monster many believed? Might he be a man of some benevolence?

"... I seek to honor you by striving to bring greater glory to all of Rome. And now— now, my Drusilla, I must attempt to bring these statements to a close, for I would not seek to dwell at length on your deeds that they might appear unworthy of you. You are to be praised, my dear Drusilla! May the gods grant you rest and protection until you arrive at your own glorious destiny."

He concluded the eulogy, bowing before Drusilla's body, and she was lifted in silence. The emperor, along with his remaining two sisters, followed. Another figure walked, head shrouded and hanging low, behind them. Her husband, Lepidus? My heart was torn for that man, denied the ability to honor his own wife.

Pure-toned voices of small boys and girls echoed in perfect harmony against marble-clad monuments, a mournful chant to send Drusilla on her journey. We were not required to attend the lighting of her funeral pyre, and there was then a parting of ways for those who returned home and those who followed grief-stricken wails and beckoning tendrils of incense. Father chose an alternate route for us, and it was a relief. After weeks of confinement, our walls were growing closer.

Tychon left us then, and we walked north and west along a narrow road that took us by Pompey's Theatre with its elegant colonnade and well-ordered plantings of conical trees. Father and Betna led our little party. Aquila walked beside me. Masses of Rome's residents still crowded, but in the shaded, tranquil vista imparted by the theatre's lengthy portico, I saw an opportunity to question Aquila about my injured friend.

"What news of Hannah?" I asked.

"She's comfortable." Aquila was working at looking cheerful. "My sister is grateful for the opportunity to be hospitable."

"But is she improving? Is she well?" I searched his face.

Aquila would not look my way but faced toward our direction of travel. "Miriam is with her. Hannah is receiving the best care," he said.

His detached answers were annoying. "Don't shield me from the truth," I said. "Tell me what you don't want to say."

He slowed his pace and lowered his voice. "I believe her gravest wound is not a physical one."

My jaw tightened. The anxieties I'd carried grew heavier. "I need to go to her," I said. "It's been too long." What I knew but couldn't explain to Aquila is that Hannah couldn't carry this pain alone. That was one of the beautiful measures of friendship; we were to help one another. And the very person who had taught that noble lesson was Hannah.

Aquila stopped in the road. "I don't know if the men still pursue me," he said. "They haven't been seen since that night. But we cannot risk disclosing where Hannah is, and it would not be safe to connect Hannah with you."

Trying to make myself taller, my voice gained volume. "But why today? Why today is it all right to connect me with you?"

He shifted his weight and looked at his feet. "We agreed that today, all men robed in black, attention focused on the procession, I would go unnoticed. And then the different route home—"

"*We* agreed?" My body pulsed in anger. "I don't care if someone finds me! Take me to her. You must. Take me in the dark if you have to. But I'm going. I just need to know where she is."

Father raised his hand to quiet me.

Aquila said, "You can see her when it's safe. Not before." He resumed his pace.

"That is all you can say?" I asked.

He walked on. I ground my teeth. Why must men control every action? Why were women not allowed some freedom or voice of opinion? I hated the world at that moment. My body inflated with hate—for the world of men. And I did not know what to do about anything.

Aquila, Father, and Betna were stalled ahead, waiting for me, and I didn't care. Let them wait. In time, practical concern, however, overcame defiance. The route Father had chosen was new, the way home was uncertain. Straightening my shoulders, I refused them any attention and just walked.

We had gone some distance, our path following an old bridge across the Tiber, when tension eased. Different scenery was diverting. On either side were rows of small storefronts and cheap cookhouses that bordered the pier. Their upper balconies and wooden staircases were narrow, revealing shoddy *insulae* above each shop.

A few paces ahead, a woman was sweeping an entry to a cook-shop called *Troianus*—the Trojan. Businesses had closed in official mourning, but food was not the attraction; it was the scar on her hand that had me entranced. Here was the mystical woman of a moonlit alley, whose slender arms had enfolded an abandoned baby, and we had stumbled upon her workplace. From that point, every landmark and was locked in memory. This path I was determined to take again.

๛ ๛

On Sabbath, Father and I attended assembly to worship and pray. It felt quiet in the women's section, and I kept to myself, face set toward Jerusalem, lifting silent prayers for those I loved.

The Eternal Lamp shone bright, symbol of God's never-ending presence, but for me its brilliance revealed the stark contrast between God and humankind, and I despaired that life was so dark. We returned home, silence hanging between us like a wet drape. It was one of those occasions when I valued the assurance of *mitzvot*, the commands of the Lord, for nothing else seemed right; nothing else seemed certain.

As we crossed our threshold and passed fingers over the *mezuzah* on our doorpost, the inscribed blessing that it housed filled my mind: "Blessed are you, Lord our God, Ruler of the world, who sanctified us with his *mitzvot* and commanded us to affix a *mezuzah*." I was a baby when we came to our white-paved roadway but imagined my father's hands carving the niche and placing the crafted metal container, my mother praying a blessing over his labors and over our new home.

Betna recited the Sabbath Prayer for Father, and we all joined hands and lifted them up to the Lord, trusting that our sad hearts could be seen by Almighty God—*El Ro'I*, God of Seeing.

That night, rains came, and it rained several days without stopping. Why, all of a sudden, it would be safe to go to Hannah in the rain was hard to understand—perhaps because the Romans lived their lives according to the *auguri*, those mysterious men who interpret signs of nature. Storm clouds, dense rain, and lightning did not breed good fortune. Rome's men and women were fancied cowering beneath their couches as thunder rumbled their world. Father came to my room on the second stormy day, large cloak over his shoulders, and insisted that we should go with all swiftness.

Streets were slick with mud. More than once, my flimsy sandals slid from the stones, requiring a steady hand from Father or Betna. Our splashing steps made me think of Alon. Did he know what happened to Hannah? He and Hannah had already begun dreaming of married life together. Were their plans of marriage now impossible?

Though it made a longer walk, the best place for us to cross the Tiber was Pons Fabricius, a bridge dating to the old Republic, taking us through Tiberina Island and then across a second bridge to reach the other side. Near the first crossing, Father strolled ahead, watching for any signs of danger. Betna and I waited by Octavia's Porch, a magnificent double-columned building housing a library and school. Even through curtains of rain and graying light, it was a pleasing edifice.

Father signaled for us to come and walk slow, as if we were taking Betna for healing on the island. The Romans had erected a large temple there in honor of Aesculapius, Greek god of medicine, and many persons made pilgrimage there. It was a good cover for us. Our only difficulty lay in retreat from the island on the other side. A vigilant observer might ask why someone might go for healing and not stay? Some visitors stayed overnight in the temple, sacrificing, imbibing strange concoctions, and waiting for a miraculous sign of healing.

When we reached the second section of bridge past the temple, a familiar face emerged from a trio of dripping pines. It was Aquila. He wore the clothing of a foreign merchant and accosted us as if to sell some merchandise.

We proceeded from there with caution, but few persons were out in the rain, so our journey seemed secure.

It was not far to arrive at the residence situated above Aquila's tent-making shop, where our knock was greeted by a young woman. Her happy countenance I would not forget. She was welcoming and open to our wet figures tramping into their small, immaculate apartment where a loom with intricate weaving filled a corner space. Resemblance to Aquila lived in the shape of her mouth and texture of her hair, and I knew at once who she was.

"You are Tamar," I said.

She took my hands and pulled me into the room. "Prisca," she said. "If only we were meeting for happier reasons." She had such expression in her eyes. At once, I could see her gladness at meeting me but sorrow she felt for Hannah's pain.

After entering, all focus turned to my injured friend. She was resting on a low couch softened with cushions, her expressionless eyes framed in shadow.

I knelt and held her hand. It was cold.

"Hannah," I said.

She turned away. "I'm not—oh, please, I just want to die."

"No," I said. "You are special. You are loved. And you are going to live." I rubbed her fingers.

Miriam was seated opposite. She spoke not a word but nodded, trying to force an uplifting smile. Weariness lived in her, and I recognized the effort it must have taken each day to nurse someone in such despair. It was good that Tamar was young and supportive.

I set about fluffing pillows, straightening the coverlet, tucking it around her. It was summertime, but Hannah was cold. Aquila brought wine, and she also drank some broth that was carried from home. All of these ministrations Hannah accepted with little response, and I asked the men to leave us for a time.

Once the room was quiet, I knelt on the floor, bringing my face closer to Hannah's. "My friend, don't let this evil steal your hope. My mother—I've not spoken of her in many months—told me to live '*a life of hope.*'"

"But what hope do I have?" Her tone was vacant, like it lacked air to fill it. "A woman's finest treasure is her purity; it is a treasure I no longer possess."

"I think—oh, I'm learning too—but I think we have to search for hope; it hides from us in sad times." As I held her familiar but delicate face in my hands, it was like I was holding so much more … her very life.

Dark eyes looked into mine. The spark that had always glittered in them was missing, and its loss was a stab to my heart.

"I feel empty," Hannah said. "It's as if everything right and worthy has been taken from me. There is nothing left, Prisca."

"That is not true," I said. "Do you know how much I've longed to see you?" Hannah didn't respond. "And it's a selfish thing. My main desire has been to be at your side, to tend and heal you. But I've also been desperate to see you—desperate for myself."

Hannah's dull eyes explored my face.

"When I'm with you, I know that something good still exists in this life. It encourages me." Pausing, there was an ache growing in my middle. What possible words could help her? "Hannah, it seems that there is a purity beyond our bodies. That purity is still in you."

She closed her eyes, wincing as if in pain, and then opened them. "But where does one find hope?" Hannah asked. "You know that Alon will never care to see me again."

"If you can trust me, together we'll seek the hope of God."

Hannah didn't answer, but her fingers clutched mine. Tears flickered on her cheeks, and I pressed a soft cloth to them.

Raindrops were pelting tree leaves and rooftops outside. "When I think about the rain," I said, "it reminds me that flowers will grow again. That gives me hope." I grinned. "And if that doesn't work, maybe a funny little man in a pink coat can bring his monkey to cheer you."

Hannah offered a tenuous smile. "You always make me laugh, Prisca. Like no other, you make me laugh."

"And you make me better. I mean, like I can do important things. You make me want to try," I said. "Live, Hannah. Let us laugh together again, and we can both be better."

"Maybe—maybe I can," she said.

"Oh, please."

Hannah lay still for some time, and I started to repack my things. She stopped me with her voice. "Wait."

"Here I am, my friend."

"There's something I believe is meant for you to know," she whispered.

"What is it?"

"First, would you to speak to Alon?" Hannah asked. "I'm trusting you to explain." She swallowed and continued. "Miriam can show you where he lives. Either Miriam or Aquila should go with you."

That she wanted Alon to hear was a positive change—a wink of hope.

"And there is something else," Hannah said.

A bandage had slipped from her brow, and I reached for it. "Oh, Hannah, I must fix this for—"

"Prisca," she said. Her hand fumbled about on the coverlet, and I clasped it. "Listen. I believe it—it is from our Lord." Her voice sounded warmer, stronger.

I stopped, heeding the urgency of her voice.

"There is a man who talks to children. He sits—he sits under a tree." Hannah stared, eyes averted from me. "He is someone you need to know."

She was talking about that man of riddles and storytelling who left a pomegranate in my basket. "I've seen this man," I said, "telling stories to children. And he was sitting under a pomegranate tree." His secreted words at the market came to mind. And he wants me to know something about fishes and bread.

Miriam dressed Hannah's wound, and she drifted into sleep. We became aware that the men had rejoined us, and it was time to say our sad farewells. Father, Betna, and I then set off to brave the wet journey home.

80 03

~ *IV* ~

Are you not from of old,
O Lord my God, my Holy One?
You shall not die.
O Lord, you have marked them for judgment;
And you, O Rock, have established them for punishment.
Your eyes are too pure to behold evil,
And you cannot look on wrongdoing;
Why do you look on the treacherous,
And are silent when the wicked
Swallow those more righteous than they?

~Habakkuk 1:12-13

It was very peculiar that the next siege upon Rome's populace was because Gaius Caesar needed money. And how was that possible? He had inherited a fortune that amounted to twenty-seven million gold pieces! Unbelievable to our minds, every tiny *dupondius* had been wasted on outrageous and frivolous pursuits.

The siege began with an edict that demanded a five-percent tax on all food purchased within the city and a three-percent increase on legal transactions. No public decree was announced, and most people discovered these new tax rates when soldiers, rather than the customary tax collectors, came to their doors to collect. Any who lacked the requisite funds were fined or beaten; some were jailed until a patron came to their aid. Rome, a city that had witnessed so much violence in its history, became a battleground once again—over taxes!

Desperate for revenue, Caligula's debauchery grew. He compelled wealthy citizens to bequeath entire estates to him, and if they had the impudence to continue living after doing so, he presented them tasty gifts seasoned with poison. He also opened a brothel within rooms of his own palace, forcing married women and freeborn boys to perform immoral acts. Payments for such services were then added to the imperial treasury.

Rome became a community of closed doors and darkened shutters. Daughters and wives of those with means were taken in secret to the country. The rich pretended to be poor. Everyone wanted to hide. But with the populace already awake with panic, Caligula's macabre behavior evoked even more terror. He was seen wearing godlike clothing, carrying on animated conversations with statues, and often demanding that people address him as "Jupiter."

It was during this disturbing time that I pondered how to meet Alon, as promised to Hannah. Weeks had passed with no news, and she was constant in my thoughts. Father described Rome as a "warren of sin," and that only increased my resolve. Everything would be different once Alon understood. He would come to Hannah's side and profess his unwavering love, and she would be healed and whole once again. It became my mission, my daily aim. "Are you brave enough to risk?" I asked myself.

One thundering morning, when Father and Betna were out, our open ceiling revealed black clouds amassing. It reminded of the day we'd visited Hannah using storms as our guise and prompted thoughts of Roman *auguri*, the belief that storms not only bred misfortune, but that the flight of birds and other occurrences were signs of either bad or good. A nameless woman then wafted into my melancholy. Lean and scarred, she was insignificant to Rome's world, yet navigated its abysmal alleys while others slept, to give babies a chance at survival.

Stirred by her daring ways, I stood and spoke with a loud voice. "Adonai, use me like Esther," I said. "If I perish, I perish."

Hidden beneath a veil the color of storm clouds, basket of bread tucked under an arm, I left through the garden door. Without knowledge of Alon's location, I would first have to go to Hannah. She could tell me the way. Perhaps Aquila would accompany me from there and return me home before Father arrived.

Upon reaching Octavia's Portico, I recognized a trickle of roadway between its dignified columns and the enormous Theater of Marcellus. We had traveled that very passage after Drusilla's funeral into the neighborhood of the unknown scarred woman. Dare I take it? Inhaling a long breath and rearing my shoulders, I set a course for the Trojan cookhouse. Purple sky shouted driving rain and few people were on the streets. It was exhilarating. I was free— and I was soaked.

Colonnades sprang up near the harbor, and pots of dripping flowers leaned out of every opening. My confidence grew as buildings, fountains, and colorful shop signs looked familiar, having been committed to memory for this particular quest. Soon, drenched and freezing, a wooden sign painted in bright red scrawling letters hung just above my head. It read *"Troianus."*

The Trojan cookhouse was not decorated in finery or graced with elegant dishes like restaurants that catered to senators; however, a hearty aroma of vegetables flavored with fishy essence of *garum* greeted me, and I stepped near a marble-topped counter where giant, steaming pots were inset and heated by flames from below.

Behind the counter stood a man with the largest face I had ever seen, his head capped with thick, black curls. Coarse hairs poked from wide, rounded nostrils, and a grease-smeared apron—insufficient to cover his massive frame—hung from a fat neck. When he opened his mouth, he had but three teeth, one on top and two on bottom.

"You—girl—what do you want?" He barked the words in Greek and bent his face into a scowl.

"I came—I'm here for—I ..." At my loss of words, the man staggered away. He shoved a couple of logs into glowing flames beneath bubbling soup pots, wiped thick hands with his apron, and then dropped his forearms on the counter, staring down at me.

"Out with it," he said. "Why are you here? This is no public toilet."

I inhaled a fortifying breath. "Can I eat?"

He slapped a flat palm on the counter, causing my feet to leave the ground for a moment, and his mouth opened in a large howl. "Ha! That's what we're here for!"

"I'd like to come in, please," I said. More than food, I craved cover from rain and warmth from his fire.

"If you buy my food, you can stay all night." The man's eyes thinned to slits, dark brows arching.

His behavior made me queasy, but I made no reply and moved into the dining area. Three tables were squeezed into a shallow concrete room; a fourth was broken and laying in a corner. The floor looked clean, though. Walls were painted white with garlands of red and yellow flowers, and a steady tapping of raindrops overhead lent coziness to the space. The mysterious woman, reason for my search, was cleaning pots in a rear alcove. I ordered a small bowl of vegetables and then chose a table nearest her.

The food was not bad, and it warmed me. Taking small sips, I hoped that the woman would move my way. In time, she did, carrying a broom. The fabric of her tunic was worn and patched. She had no shawl or cloak for warmth and wore no jewelry, no adornment of any kind. Her face was lined beyond her age—she couldn't have been more than twenty years old—and her left hand bore the unmistakable scar.

Lifting my own hand in greeting, I asked her name. When she didn't respond, I repeated the question in Greek.

She looked around before answering, her voice an anxious whisper. "My name is Lo-Ruhamah. I am called Lormah. It is easier." Her eyelids lowered. "It is better."

"Lormah," I said. "You look familiar. Do you know me?"

"No." She pinched her brows together, and the alarm in her face forced my quick return to the steaming dish of vegetables. Lingering over my food, attempting to look disinterested, questions wanted to leap from my mouth, but it was clear that *Troianus* was not the place for them. In time, turning away from the little cook-shop with its bubbling stew to be battered again by raindrops, I mused that the woman of moonlight now had a name. Surprising, it was a Hebrew name: Lo-Ruhamah. Though tattered and uneducated, Lormah seemed alert to everything around her, a condition that a hard life would teach.

Black clouds had multiplied while sitting in Lormah's cookhouse, and twinges of fear assaulted me when passing from its doorway. Rome's flooded streets were still mostly empty, but the occasional sneering traveler pinched my stomach in alarm. And what did I have to defend myself? A soggy loaf of bread.

When green swells of the Tiber River had softened at my back, the shop-front belonging to Aquila was not hard to find. Having no sight of him inside the busy workroom, I mounted the stairs.

At the door, I made a light tap. No one answered. Knocking again, I stated, "Aquila? Is anyone there?"

Halting footsteps sounded from inside, and I waited, standing back from the door. Tamar's brown eyes enlarged when she opened the door.

"Hello, Tamar." I shivered in a breeze that crept up the stairs.

"How did you come here?" She gulped. "You came alone?" Tamar leaned out the doorway, looking past me. The expression on her face made me self-conscious. Strands of sodden hair plastered my face, every fabric on my body sagged and dripped, and my self-assurance was sinking as well. I had disobeyed Father.

Tamar stepped aside. "Come in. Please."

The room was changed. The low-lying couch was gone and, to my alarm, so was my friend. "Where is Hannah?" My heart pounded.

"She wanted to go home. They left this morning."

"They left?" I asked.

Tamar motioned to a chair. "Forgive me. Please sit down. Aquila and your two friends, Hannah and Miriam—"

I interrupted. "Then Hannah must be better." My body relaxed into the chair.

She pulled a stool near, sitting down and inclining her head. "In truth," Tamar said, "I don't think she is. At least, not much better. I'm sorry."

"But then why—"

Tamar tapped my hand to calm me. "Matron Miriam said she would heal better in her own home. If you had seen their sad faces, you would understand."

At my feet, a circle of water was growing on Tamar's clean floor. My voice was hoarse. "You—you must think me ridiculous, to have come here like this."

Tamar shook her head. "I could never have done it." She leaned forward in her chair. "You are so brave."

I groaned. "Not brave. It did seem thrilling, at first, doing something like this on my own. Now—oh, Tamar, Father will be so angry. It's just that I was overcome with worry and wanted to risk myself for someone I loved."

"Risk yourself?" Tamar asked.

"It's something that Miriam told me. You know, the kind of courage Esther had, risking her life for our people." I bit my lip. "A nonsensical idea, isn't it, trying to be like someone legendary? And even more embarrassing now, knowing that Hannah isn't here. All of my 'excellent' plans have ended in failure."

"I've never had a friend who would risk so much for me," Tamar said. "Hannah was improving after your visit. And then one day—I'm not sure why—it was like she gave up."

Glancing out her high window, Tamar wrinkled her brow at murky sky.

"It's past time for me to leave." I pressed a wrapped loaf into her hand. "Please keep the bread. Sorry ... it got moist. The rain ..."

Tamar held me. "But it's dark."

"And I should have been home long ago."

She tightened her grip. "Please," she said. "Remember your friend, what happened to her. Wait for Aquila."

Cramps had started in my legs, leading me to question whether I could make the walk home alone. It was helpful that Aquila came through the door at that moment. He lifted a drenched cloak to a peg near the door and started speaking. "Greetings, Sister. Tomorrow we'll need to fix that—"

He saw me and then glanced around the room. "How did you get here? Tell me you did not come by yourself." His disapproving look reminded me of Betna, and I felt like a misbehaved child.

"I—I know it was foolish," I said, "but needed to see Hannah."

His lips tightened. "I was thinking of a stronger word than 'foolish.'"

Tamar stepped forward. "My brother," she began, "it has been good of Prisca to visit us, and I'm thankful for this time, but she must go right away. Her father doesn't know she's here."

He yanked the door open and turned to me, tension apparent in his voice. "There is scant light," he said. My fingers touched the air in a fleeting farewell to Tamar, and we left without another word.

There was no conversation between us, but during our steady pace over puddled roads, I began to understand better the man at my side. There was a sense of complete safety—and even more. It was an awareness that I belonged with him, like a piece of fruit on the right tree, like honey that goes into my mother's cake. There was a tangible, growing knowledge that we required one another.

Nearer to home, dark clouds lifted, and a pale orange glow appeared at that division between day and night. It was strange to see light at the close of such a black day. We attempted to avoid prying eyes by entering from the outer stairs and climbing down and inside via the balcony steps.

Betna was pacing the floor, and he took my hands in his. "Soon my hair will be gone, child."

Shame colored my face. "I'm sorry."

Betna shook a finger at me, and then his eyes took in my pathetic figure, and he hastened from the room, shouting as he went, "But we will have food!"

Without Betna in the room, Aquila's presence grew. I gestured to a couch. "Would you stay awhile, allow your cloak to dry?" I asked. "I'll get you something to drink."

His hand stopped me. "Nothing to drink," Aquila said. "But will you sit ... please."

Shedding the wet shawl, I draped a coverlet over my shoulders and sat on the couch.

"It's important"—he hesitated, walking a few steps away and then coming back. "Prisca, I will be speaking to your father, but I have to know." His tone was serious.

"I understand. You're right. My father will be angry, and you—you think it's important that he should know." Lowering my head, I was too exhausted to argue. "It was wrong to go today without—"

He shook his head, smiling. "But what I mean is: Shall we be married?"

My mouth opened. "I—I didn't expect—things have been so difficult, life is uncertain, Hannah ..."

He said, "It has been difficult." Turning slowly away, his chest inflated with air. "It's made me think, Prisca. I don't want to face more days of uncertainty. I want to know something real, something sure." He moved closer. "My life will be more certain if it includes you."

Our traditions were old and firm; Aquila did not have to ask me. Father could compel me to marry whomever he wished.

Aquila's eyebrows lifted, petitioning an answer.

"I will not say 'no,'" I replied. "But—but I cannot say 'yes.' You see, I—suddenly, I feel very young and a little afraid."

He sat near me on the couch, our knees almost touching. My own body betrayed me with a tide of warmth, craving his protective arms around me. Unprepared for such feelings, I forced myself to turn away.

"Give me time," I said.

Aquila stood. "It is late."

"Please wait. It is unfair to ask you ..." Needing separation to raise confidence, I stood and walked among plants in the atrium, but then the distance seemed dishonest, as if unspoken thoughts had perched high on a wall between us. "You owe me nothing," I said. "In fact, you've given so much to my family and to me."

Aquila said, "Ask whatever you will. I like your questions."

"It's about a promise made to Hannah. There's a man named Alon who is a friend to her," I said.

Aquila nodded. "I know this man."

"She asked me to speak to him and said that you or Miriam must take me. Hannah wants me to explain about her—her injuries." Aquila was watching me, listening. Since first meeting this intense and capable man, he had become my version of a champion, brave but also compassionate. It struck me as rare indeed that he was sincere about wanting to know what I valued. "Is there still danger for you?" I asked.

Aquila said, "I'll take you to Alon. And, yes, there is danger. But I'm careful. The men who attacked her have not hunted me ... for now." His solemn expression was reflected in the pool. This was a man who worked hard at keeping others safe.

He continued, "It's an insecure time for all of us. This empire and those who dwell in it are menaced from without and within." He paused. "All the more reason for my question of you tonight."

I rushed to answer. "And I haven't said 'no.' It's just that I need time."

"Again, it's late," Aquila said. "I'll send word about a meeting with Alon." He departed by the small kitchen door to pass through my garden.

ಲ ೞ

"You directly disobeyed me!" Father's face was puffed in anger. "I'm trying to protect you." He huffed. "Not to mention the disgrace to me and to our people by your defiant behavior."

My hands were busy kneading dough. "But I'm not a child—"

"And that is a big part of your problem! Did you not learn anything from Hannah's experience?"

Setting my mound of dough aside and covering it with a damp cloth, I washed my hands. Unshed tears spilled down the sides of my face, and my back remained turned, hiding them from him.

"The world has changed, Father. Our world has changed." There was a tremor in my voice. "I don't want to dishonor you—ever. But when someone I love needs help, then …"

"Do you even listen to me anymore?" He sat down hard.

I studied his sad expression. "Hannah is in my thoughts every day, and I've tried to be strong, positive—hopeful." Hovering again over my blanketed bread dough, I patted its powdery surface, moving it into several positions, folding and unfolding the cloth around it. "What is really happening in the senate, Father?"

He shifted on the wood bench. "There is always strife among the senators. You know that. It has been that way since before you were born."

It was an effort to steady my voice. "You preach to me of danger but withhold any facts that might explain it. It would help to know the truth."

He grunted. "You are not ignorant. Much of it you surely see. Hannah's experience is ample evidence."

I replied, "But there is much you conceal."

He looked tired. "Perhaps I only long to forget."

"You want to protect me from it," I said. Sliding next to him, I lifted one of his wide hands and hugged it with my own. "Share it with me. Let me help you forget."

"You are so like your mother," he said. He took my hands. "Kisbah, some things were meant for a father to bear, if it allows his daughter to sleep and to dream. Maybe tomorrow." He cupped my face in his hands. "Promise me you'll use better discretion," he said.

ᛞ ᚳ

Restless about my earlier conversation with Aquila, I asked Adonai, "Is this the man you've created for me, a man who builds things from animal hides?" Would my days be spent stretching leather and sewing while children ran circles around us? Pulling blankets over my head, I drifted into sleep.

Sometime later, the hem of my door's curtain flapped, and bursts of light played against it. There was low rumbling of thunder and pounding of raindrops, as if launched from a boundless height. And there, in the midst of the deluge, was the sound of a baby's cry.

"Again," I said. The thought of an abandoned baby in the storm stirred me from bed. "Oh, God, please lead me."

The floor was damp and cold, sending chills and aching up my legs, but I kept going. Please little one, don't give up. Don't give up.

116

My feet plunged into mud outside the door. Rain came hard and fast so that only my ears could find the wriggling boy, just hours old. Taking him into an embrace, he continued to cry, hands flailing, and I rubbed his little limbs trying to warm them, holding him close. "Oh, little one, please live."

In a sudden sting of light, there was an outline of someone coming. Alarmed, I slipped and fell back with a splat, still cradling the child. Though my backside was bruised, an odd little chuckle rose from me. What might Aquila think of his prospective wife, legs straddling a flooded alleyway, screaming infant in her arms? And then I remembered the dark figure still approaching and tucked the boy close to my heart.

Hoping to appear bold, I rose to my knees and spoke to the stranger standing over me. "You will not take him," I said.

Another bright flash revealed it was Lormah, her arms outstretched and pleading.

"Lormah," I said. She stopped, shrinking back and narrowing her eyes.

"I do not know you," she said. "But I have seen you—yes?"

"Yes. In the cookhouse, *Tro-* ..."

She pressed a swift finger to her lips and knelt down, leaning close.

"Is not safe to speak here," she said. She looked up and down the alley. "Give me the child." She reached for him.

"No." I held tight.

Lormah frowned and plopped into a puddle across from me as if we played some silly childhood game. But a frail infant squirmed between us, and Lormah looked nothing like a child. In fact, she looked awful. The hair that before was long and flowing had been cut into uneven lengths, and she had a bruise across the bridge of her nose. Raindrops beating against her scalp seemed to explain everything else about her.

"Why do you take children from here?" I asked. "What is it you do to them?"

"I take them so they will live. If I want to hurt them, I will leave them here." She raised both hands and arched thin brows to mock me.

"But where do you take them?" The babe was beginning to feel warmer and had calmed.

Lormah wrinkled her brow. "I will not tell you, stupid girl. Not here." Her face relaxed. "But it is a good place."

I opened my arm a trace, peering at the pale, helpless form. He had begun to suck on his fist.

"He needs care," I said.

"He needs food," Lormah said. "And you do not have what he needs."

"Well, I would see that he gets it," I huffed. "You don't take these children to slave traders, do you?"

Lormah looked stunned. "I will die first," she said. She swiped moisture from her face. "And what will you do?"

I had no answer. There was little chance of sneaking him into my home unnoticed, and his presence there would put us all in peril. One of the crucial lessons my father impressed upon me was not to interfere in the Romans' way of life; the consequences were grave. I shrugged my shoulders and pressed my cheek against his downy head. He deserved a chance.

"I know to hide the child where he is safe," Lormah said. "And you? Can your neighbors not see you have a baby?"

"I just couldn't leave him to die."

Her face softened, and she reached out and touched my arm. "There are others," she said.

"Others? Like him?" I asked.

She didn't reply. Her features sank into sadness. Lormah. What mystery lived in this woman? She looked forsaken and alone, like the child in my arms.

Running my finger across the babe's brow, I hugged him once more and, opening my arms, lifted him to her. She wrapped him quickly and secured him in a makeshift sling, leaving her own hands free.

Lormah began to leave but then leaned to my ear, her voice low. "I come to this gate in two days, when it is dark. Then I tell you of the others." As she vanished into waves of rain, I sat motionless, listening until all sound of her was consumed by storm's flow.

An unexpected sound of splashing steps first made me think that Lormah was returning—but no, her steps were lighter, more cautious. Chafing my legs on brick steps, I slid into the garden and pressed against its wall, becoming one with black shadows.

Someone was breathing hard, looming. And then a guttural voice contended with roaring skies. "Where is it?" he asked.

I heard—and felt—rocks thrown against the very wall I crouched behind.

"By the gods! Where'd it go?" A man belched. "He won't like this." Feet slapped the wet pavement, marching back and forth, only a few inches of stone between us. He was looking for the child.

Holding tight to the slick stones, legs knotted under me, the man's vile breath made me want to retch. Rivulets of rainwater rushed by, loosening the soil, and every lightning blast brought terror that I might be seen, but fear held me there. In time, the only sounds were those of the storm and earth's response to it, and I came away in silence, opening our door just enough to slip through.

Shedding my wet clothing, I fell into bed and lay there until fingers of light crept beneath my curtained doorway. Sleep eluded me. Lormah and her mission of rescue whirled in a busy mind. What kind of woman wandered the alleys looking for exposed children? It was frightening what could happen to her. And where did she take them? She said it was a good place—and safe. I believed her.

ᛒ ᚳ

Next morning while I was preparing food, Father drew me aside. "Are you ill?" he asked. "I've never seen you so pale."

He answered for me. "Recent events have been too much. Go. Rest." He almost pushed me out of the kitchen.

It was a dreary day. For a brief moment, the storms abated, but then thick clouds tumbled about in our sky and water flowed everywhere. Betna was busy hauling filled jars from our flooding atrium pool. Thunder and lightning kept senators at home, so Father worked on private business in his *tablinum*.

I dozed a little, but it was muddled sleep. The voice of Miriam called to me in dreams. "Remember your Hebrew, child," she would say. She tapped me on the head with her finger. "Remember your Hebrew." Our people's language was not used in everyday life, at least not in Rome. There was Hebrew on Sabbath and in readings that came from the *Torah*, from Psalms of David or the prophet Isaiah.

"Remember your Hebrew," I whispered to myself. What could that mean?

I also dreamt of Aquila. Did he like the way I smiled or the things I said? Did he appreciate my fine needlework? Perhaps not. Did he admire me for a quick mind? Not likely. In my dreams, we walked together, and always our hands were joined. They were warming dreams. What was it he said to me? "My life will be more certain if it includes you." I enjoyed thinking of myself as a stable force for him.

At midday, Betna came to my curtained door. "Your father asks for you," he said.

The *tablinum* was where a typical Roman patriarch would occupy himself with financial matters, perhaps receive guests, and apply himself to letter-writing and personal affairs. In our home, it was a comfortable room, furnished with things of my father. The rear wall had a ledge built of smoothed stone, and all along its surface were special writings and keepsakes, many of which were given to my grandfather while he was growing up in the

Lucullus household. The oldest books were engravings on stone. My father had also collected items during his years of service to the senate, including his very first writing instrument, a stylus carved from bone.

From a senate auction, Father had obtained writings by Vergilius, a Roman poet, and they spoke of shepherds and goats and singing—*ta bukolika* in Greek, because they were about life in the country, the fields and the hills. The poet's words were delicate, full of sensory meaning. Hearing Father read them transported me beyond dusty city walls and into fields of growing, living things: "*But soon as thou hast skill to read of heroes' fame and of thy father's deeds and learn what virtue is, the plain by slow degrees with waving corn-crops shall to golden grow. From the wild briar shall hang the blushing grape, and stubborn oaks sweat honey-dew.*"

By far, my favorite among Father's possessions was a thin-sided silver cup. It was the cup he had crushed when he married my mother. The cup had an important function, to unite a couple by the sharing of wine and to bring honor to their celebration. But it was purposely damaged so that no crafted thing would become an idol for worship. No object would ever be cherished above our Most High God, and no object would ever be cherished above the person who was given by God. Its crumpled condition served to remind us of our human brokenness and sin, urging us to live by God's law.

At those times when I had felt my mother's loss the most, when I began to think that life with her was only imagined, I would run to the *tablinum* and wrap my hands around the small bent cup, stained dark with wedding wine.

Touching it, knowing she drank from it, helped me to remember that she had once really lived.

Father was sitting at a narrow writing desk, and I watched him at his work, pressing his stylus into a wax tablet. More important notations were made on papyrus, which was too expensive for everyday matters. I preferred writing on wax, because my secret notations—and mistakes—could be smoothed from the surface and never seen.

He spoke to me without looking up. "Prisca, please sit down."

I settled into a small chair at the corner of his writing table. "Hmm. You have that serious look, Father." There was no response, and I thought for a moment he did not hear me, but he set the stylus aside and looked up.

"While you were resting, a message came from Aquila. He's offered to be your escort, to meet Alon tomorrow."

"Will that be all right, Father?" My mid-section began to flutter.

"It would have been all right," he said, "but another matter may make it awkward, even impossible."

"What do you mean?"

"Some news has come." He shifted his chair, moving it closer, and took both my hands in his. "It may be difficult to bear."

"Difficult?" Already, my stomach was tightening.

"Miriam and Hannah have been taken into custody by Roman authorities," he said.

"Into custody?" My head was throbbing, trying to understand.

123

He nodded.

"You mean they are jailed?" Warmth drained from my face.

"At the *carcer* near the forum." He scowled. "The charge against them is avoidance of taxes."

"Taxes? But why would they be prosecuted for taxes?"

Father looked grave. He ran a hand through his hair. "Do you remember what Aquila told us about Hannah's attackers?"

"They were sons of senators," I said.

"And you realize that these men will want to avert others' eyes from their own wrongdoing."

I nodded.

He stood and faced the atrium, fingers locked behind his back. "My understanding is that these men have accused Hannah of prostitution, and they have involved Miriam."

"What?" I sprang from my chair. "But it's a lie! They're criminals! And how can such accusation have anything to do with neglecting tax payments?"

He stared at the floor. "Even prostitution is a business that is taxed in Rome," he said.

"But Hannah has been abused. She cannot survive imprisonment. And Miriam"—I closed my eyes—"she is too frail." Sinking back into the chair, I moaned. "Oh, Father."

"A young man brought the information. It was this Alon whom Hannah asked you to meet."

My voice trembled. "Did you know that he and Hannah were going to be married?"

124

"His face told me as much. He said that Hannah and Miriam sent him. He must have been there when—he delivered this." Father held the engraved wooden box Miriam had shown me. Taking it onto my lap, I laid my head against its beveled surface.

"We must do something," I said. "But what? What can be done?"

Father took my shoulders into both hands. "Now, Daughter, this is not something for you to deal with. I will look into the situation—with caution. Making impassioned accusations will only provoke the emperor's anger."

"But the emperor needs to hear the truth. I will go." Shaking his hands free, I placed Miriam's box on the desk. "It doesn't matter what he does to me."

"What you do not realize is that you would most likely endanger our friends by doing so! Trust me in this."

I ran from the room. It was hopeless. How could we persuade authorities to release them? Hannah, the beautiful and eager young bride, planning her marriage to Alon, accused by the very men who assaulted her! And Miriam. I could see soldiers forcing her from the *insula*, down the steep stairs, and—rushing to my garden and dropping onto swampy ground, I yanked at weeds. Each deep-rooted thistle was an enemy, an attacker of defenseless women, and I ripped at them until arms lifted me and gentle hands washed mud away. There was Father's face and then Betna's, each of them careworn, and they wrapped me into blankets in the quiet of my room.

Whispered into the folds of my coverlet were the words Miriam had once taught: "When I am afraid, I will trust in you. In God, whose word I praise. In God I trust; I will not be afraid." Over and over, through pleading lips: "I will not be afraid. I will not be afraid." At some point, exhausted, I began to sleep.

⊱ ⊰

Father was true to his promise, looking into circumstances of our friends' arrest the next day. He went to Miriam's neighborhood and asked questions of those who were willing to speak. He spoke to the few senators he could without attracting undue attention. He met with individuals within our assembly who had contacts in key positions. Information began to surface.

When he arrived home, torches were already burning atop city walls, and Betna had lit oil lamps in the atrium and kitchen. Father looked worn. Rome's senate house was an unpredictable place; senators were touted with high esteem one day and then forced to run several miles beside Gaius Caesar's golden chariot on the next. These were sorrowful and confusing times.

"Abba. Welcome home." I met him at the door.

He took my hand, and together we walked into the atrium where we sat under a spectacle of stars. It was enchanting and beautiful and did not fit at all with the circumstances of our lives.

Projecting his voice toward the kitchen, Father called Betna to join us. He then took his time, weighing hard words. "Miriam and Hannah were not arrested by the Praetorian Guard," he said. "And that is good news. If the Praetorian Guard had taken them, I would have assumed it was Gaius Caesar behind the accusations somehow."

"You mean he isn't?" I asked.

"The persons responsible for the arrest are Lucius Cornelius Sulla and Gaius Nonius Asprenas, powerful and noble men—senators," he said. "There is relative certainty they are the fathers of the attackers."

I cleared my throat, a little afraid of our discussion. Actions of senators and emperors were often impulsive and never beneficial to foreigners, especially Judeans.

"Do you mean, Father, that it would be worse for Miriam and Hannah if the emperor were behind it?"

"Yes," he said. "I fear, if Gaius Caesar were the apparent enemy, they would have little hope."

"But you do believe they have hope," I said.

He patted my hand. "A tenuous one." He paced the dim room. "Gaius Caesar does not like it when senators apply the law for personal reasons. He may be suspicious of their actions." Father answered my puzzled look. "I believe it has something to do with vanity, with pride. The emperor would rather be the one to make such decisions."

I shuddered. Everything in my being told me it was not wise to make Gaius Caesar suspicious.

"That unexpected detail may give our friends a way of release," he said.

"Is it possible to see them?" I asked.

He shook his head. "It would be very unsafe at this point, Prisca. The *carcer* is a dismal group of cells beneath the Stairs of Mourning. Its entrance is near a busy section of the forum. What we must pursue—and quickly—is some form of absolution for their crime. We must convince the authorities that it's a mistake or generate whatever restitution may be in order."

"But they've done nothing wrong. Wouldn't it make them appear guilty by paying restitution?"

"It may," Father said. "If it saves their lives"—he paused and drew me close. "We will always know the truth."

Covering my mouth with a tight hand, I nodded. And what of Alon? Would he even acknowledge Hannah after this?

"There is another unpleasant aspect to this situation you should know," Father said. "In my conversations with persons from assembly, a comment was made that Eliam was somehow involved."

"Eliam!" I said. Anger pulled me like an armed bow. "What did they pay him?"

"We must be cautious about such information, Prisca. There is a possibility of endangering those who have placed trust in us. There is also a possibility that Eliam is innocent of any deceit."

"I don't trust him, Father." Rising from my seat, I stared into our starlit pool. "Something tells me he was mixed up in this. But why?"

"There could be any number of reasons. I'll look into it. But wait until we know more facts before you judge him."

Betna said, "One day, it was Eliam who did a good thing." Both Father and I stared at him with stunned expressions, and Betna continued. "It was a day with worry. Later, it is something forgotten, and already Eliam is a hard man, one you cannot trust."

Father asked, "What was this good deed?"

"It is Eliam who brings news of Nessa, of her dying," Betna said. "Eliam comes to me, and I go to find you."

I never recalled seeing Eliam those many years ago. If he had not told Betna, where would I be? In debt to a man like Eliam?

Father's expression softened. "We can all be fooled by how things appear. As with all men, I will believe him guiltless in this circumstance until we learn something different." Betna nodded agreement.

"But how are they?" I asked. "Hannah and Miriam, what is their condition?"

He lowered his head. "I only know they are imprisoned here in Rome; they've not been transported out of the city."

"You haven't seen them?" I asked.

His jaw tensed. "This morning I started in that direction, hoping to make some inquiry of the prison guard. But Gaius Caesar and several others came out of the senate house just then. For our sakes, I must maintain a discreet profile. I'm sorry." He sighed and patted my shoulder. "Prison conditions are not good. We can't expect that they are well."

"But can I do something?" I asked. "I could take food to them."

He shook his head.

I said, "The waiting is hard. I imagine countless horrors."

"Yet that is what we must do, Daughter. We wait together. We pray."

The hour was late, and the three of us went our separate ways, extinguishing lights, washing dirt from our faces, seeking sleep that would not come.

ဆ ભ

~ *V* ~

"I remember my affliction and my wandering,
The bitterness and the gall.
I well remember them,
And my soul is downcast within me.
Yet this I call to mind
And therefore I have hope:
Because of the Lord's great love
We are not consumed,
For his compassions never fail.
They are new every morning;
Great is your faithfulness."

~Lamentations 3:19-23

Morning met me with worry like a ball of yarn crammed in my throat, but golden rays tread on soft feet into my room, breathing color into faded frescoes on familiar walls and calming my soul. In the corner, there was a wide chest where fresh tunics were folded and stored and a slim painted shelf holding a pot of flowers and linen ties for my hair. This was my room, my peaceful sanctuary.

Into the stillness, I whispered. "Where are you, God?" My heart burned with an urge to pray. "Blessed be the name of Almighty God." The blessing came swift to my lips, but to express more? What were my commonplace words compared to the dazzling majesty of *Yahweh*, the powerful *I Am*?

My brain tallied the many times I had disobeyed Father and brought indignity to our household. Matrons

Helah and Mara I imagined standing over me, fingers wagging. How could my prayers do any good?

Perching on feeble knees, I bowed my head and tried. "Please, Adonai. Hannah and Miriam—they are good, they are faithful. Help them. Please set them free." Waiting, listening, I remembered the heart of King David, words of his psalm: *"Before a word is on my tongue, you know it completely, O Lord."*

A gust of air kicked up the amber-colored curtain at my door and blew fresh scent into my face. I was encouraged.

It was a pretty morning. Clouds the color of fresh goat milk were stirred into azure sky, a concoction of perfection, and I wanted to be angry. How could evil men be allowed to receive such a day when Miriam and Hannah could not? Even more, my own guilt regarding the expedition that was soon to take place brought torment. Lormah was coming, meeting me after dark, and I fretted about seeking adventure when my friends were in such horrible circumstances. Why was it so hard to know what God was calling me to do? Was life always to be filled with indecision and trouble? Sweeping floors and freshening bedding, I thought of Lormah. What kind of life did she have? Did she ever struggle with such questions?

Day wore on. A pink sun dipped low. When I begged to seek refuge in my room, Father and Betna did not question. Each kissed my face and bid me good night, and my throat tightened again with shame, but soon all was quiet.

Outside, a single twinkling star overhead gave me courage, and I listened for Lormah's remembered steps and her characteristic sniff in the cool, moist air. She found me, and we crouched out of sight.

"So ... you are able to escape." Lormah spoke in a husky tone. "Are you ready?" she asked.

"Y—yes. At least I think so."

"Are you afraid?" She tossed a veil over uncombed hair, pulling it close over her forehead.

I hesitated. "Yes."

"Good. We need to be careful." She stood and pulled me from the ground. "This way."

Hiding beneath my veil as Lormah had, I followed her down the alley to our right, heading west. We had traveled a short way when she motioned for me to be quiet, shoved me into a slim crevice between two *insulae*, and then wedged in beside me. Her movement was so unexpected—what could it be? A smell of vegetable soup filled my nostrils, and it reminded of the shop where Lormah worked; the fishy essence of *garum* was all about her.

Footsteps were heard, and they were near. They sounded unstable on the cobbled stones. A sandal slipped, and then came a man's thick voice.

"Aw, by Jupiter!" The man hiccupped. "'Bout lost my way there." He snorted and then made a shrill laugh.

I wanted to giggle, stifling the urge by pressing fingers against my lips until they hurt. Lormah made no move. It occurred to me that her body was a shield. Thin, battered little Lormah was my personal guard.

After what seemed hours, Lormah stepped from our cramped hiding place and tugged me out. She held a finger to her lips. "Those we cannot trust," she whispered. "Not ever." Her caution brought to mind the terror of Hannah's attack, and from that moment, my senses were attuned to every sound and sight.

We took a turn, going southwest, until Lormah flattened herself against a wall, eyes skyward. Roman guards were on watch. They overlooked a city gate named for the goddess *Laverna*, so-called "protector of thieves." A few feet from us stood a grove of trees where bandits were known to seek shelter. By this point, my jaw was beginning to ache from holding it so tight. Lormah took my hand, and together we flitted through the gate like a couple of small night birds. Once through, slumping to the ground, we crawled until our path turned down a slope, and then we walked again.

Air smelling of fish and a sound of rolling waves meant we had come near the Tiber, and our journey ended with an abrupt stop at the back of a tall building. At first, I thought we stood behind an *insula*, but it was more like a large storehouse. Lormah pushed through a door, and we stepped into a vast, dark space. Flickering on a dilapidated bench beyond the door was a rustic oil lamp, enabling me to see that it was a place where products were prepared for shipping. There were *amphorae*—tall jars used to store olive oil and wine—some coiled round with ropes and set into crates, ready to be loaded. A scattering of fishing nets and a couple of small riverboats could also be seen, but the majority of the room remained in darkness.

To our right was a stairway, and we climbed it, wooden planks creaking beneath our weight. There were children's voices, speaking low, and my feet increased speed, ushering Lormah up the stairs.

The second floor was a sizeable room, and its few random lamps only extended the shadows. Lormah left my side to approach a man sitting near an opposite wall, and my eyes explored the area. For such a large room, it was crowded. Children, from newborn to perhaps fourteen, were shrouded in ragged blankets. Every infant appeared to have an older caretaker, a child of ten years or older. Babies were cradled in wooden crates, some padded with fishing nets, others with tattered clothing or blankets. Though screened by a thin curtain, two women could be seen at the far end of the room. It appeared they were each breastfeeding an infant. Conversation was going on, but like the filmy light surrounding them, all was soft.

Lormah returned to escort me, and as we neared the individual who appeared to be her mentor or guide, my heart beat faster.

"I remember you," I said. "You are the man who speaks to children under a pomegranate tree." He was also the man that Hannah urged me to meet, giving me a sense of certainty about being there, that it was right. Thinking back to a single pomegranate found in my market basket, it made me smile.

He gave a brief nod. "I am that man," he said. Dark whiskers shone in flickering lamplight. "And my name is Ethan."

"You must tell me, Ethan, the answer to the riddle."
Lormah wrinkled her brow. "Riddle?"
"About feeding thousands with only two fish," I said.
"And five loaves," Ethan said.
I nodded. "Oh, yes. And loaves."

"Barley loaves," Lormah said. She stood at my left elbow, grinning.

"What did you mean by that," I asked, "and why—why would you talk to me about fish and bread?"

Ethan replied, "For the answer, I ask your patience. The Lord's timing is perfect in all things, and I am prompted to wait."

"You can't tell me now?" I asked.

What kind of people dwelt in this obscure place? A part of me was annoyed, but there was also amazement at the ability to wait for things. Ethan's response made me realize how seldom I waited for anything.

He said, "I believe you're here tonight for another reason. Lormah tells me you wish to save the helpless."

I swallowed hard and scanned the room. "Yes, though there are—there are just so many."

"As you say, there are many in need," Ethan replied. "But even in this dismal place we believe miracles can happen." He smiled and motioned me to follow. "Let me show you."

In a city where people rushed at all hours, Ethan's slowness was astounding. He would not be hurried. Dipping his lamp beside a crate filled with fishing nets, its glow revealed a babe nesting in a frayed woolen blanket that was cushioned with fishnet.

"This is the boy you found in the storm," Ethan said. "Perhaps he was rejected because of the mark on his face."

I bent over the makeshift cradle. There was a reddish birthmark above his left brow, no larger than a wee pebble or coin of small denomination. A meaningless little mark and unnoticed on that stormy night. He was sleeping, and I stroked the short, fine hair covering his head.

Ethan knelt at my side. "We have named him Ira, because when he's awake, his eyes are bright and curious, watching everything. I think maybe he watches for you." He winked at me.

"Ira, '*watchful one*,'" I said. "A good name." I lingered there, not wanting to take my hand away.

He led on, introducing me to Rome's forsaken, now rescued, concluding at a small table where tattered scraps of parchment and papyrus were arranged in neat order and stacked next to a *stylus* and pot of ink. The notations were graceful and precise. It was clear that we had arrived at Ethan's private work area, a place where he kept careful record and spent time in prayer.

"Ethan," I said, "How could the Romans abandon these defenseless children? It is beyond my ability to understand."

"In truth, these come to us for myriad reasons. Not all are abandoned at birth," Ethan replied.

Round faces bobbed in amber light, like gold-tinged bubbles on a shaded sea. "But how do they find you?" I asked.

Ethan raised his chin and smiled. "That is part of the miracle," he said. "The Lord places them in our paths."

My attention was drawn to a brittle twig of a girl with straight lengths of yellow hair. Sapphire eyes were ringed in unhealthy shadow, and her wretched little form was worrying. I asked Ethan her name.

"That one," he said, "she is new to us. From Gaul, perhaps." He lowered sorrowful eyes. "When she came, her body was bruised and ... the women took great care. We have offered many prayers. She has not yet spoken."

The girl appeared slightly older than young Tertius. I wanted to assure her everything would be all right. But would it?

The count came to thirty-three children of varying ages, most of them girls. How was one to care for such a number?

"All are awake," I said, "except the babies, though it's nighttime."

Lormah laid a hand on my shoulder. "These learn to sleep by day," she said.

A sigh left my lips. "But how is it possible to feed and clothe them all?"

"Nothing is too great for God," Ethan said. "There is a need, he fills it. We have much to be thankful for." He offered me a chair. "Do you trust me enough to speak your name?"

"My—yes. My name is Prisca."

"Prisca," he repeated.

"My mother called me Priscilla." My eyelids lowered. She also called me her little lamb ... and here was a room filled with unwanted lambs.

Ethan said, "We're thankful for your willingness. There are needs in our humble calling that require immense faith."

"Somehow I believe—I don't know how to say it— I'm supposed to be here. A dear friend has spoken to me of the importance of risking your life for love of another." My eyes began to tear, and I blinked them away.

"Your friend is wise, for that is a dear sacrifice." Ethan paused in silence, staring into the room, and then his eyes sought mine. "Do not be surprised that you were led to us."

"Led to you?" I asked.

"God's remarkable plan is being carried out," Ethan said. "He alone directs every move."

God was directing. What a thought. Lormah turned to me with an expression of complete peace, and the hardness of her life seemed to float away, softening the lines of her face. My breaths were shallow, and I thought of Esther in that moment when circumstances had compelled her to act. There was such mystery to God's plan. Was I really a part of it? Could I be part of it?

"What we ask first," Ethan said, "is to send food. There is always a hungry child among us."

"I'll bring what I can."

He shook his head. "Lormah will carry it. Traveling the streets by night is perhaps the most perilous task, but she has chosen that willingly."

And now I'd made a commitment. Would Father approve? And what about Aquila? Would he think me a fool? Worse yet, would he think me inappropriate? Disrespectful? Compared with tradition, my behavior was disobedient at best. But in a world where innocent children were left to die, it would deny my faith in a loving God to ignore them. What had Ethan said that day, many months ago, just a short walk from Miriam's door? "Let the little children come to me," he had said. Somehow it was fitting to be among such people.

"I do want to help, Ethan." I cleared my throat. "And, in fact, to risk myself. Though I'm not as strong as Lormah, nor as daring."

Ethan stood. "We will meet again, and we will talk of fish and bread." He smiled. "And, Prisca, what the Lord seeks is children of faith. He does not need our strength."

Lormah led me to the stairs from whence we came. It was painful to leave, and I gathered one last glance for my memory's pocket: Darkened planks of wood burnished with lamplight, windows dressed with blankets or boards, an odor of urine-stained swaddling cloths and burning olive oil. And over all, a veil of peace, as tangible as the fishnets fitted for a new and worthy purpose. It was a haven for the helpless, a safe port midst turbulent seas ... a children's harbor.

Lormah led on. We traveled downward, hesitating at ground level. Tapping her arm, she turned to face me.

"Do you know anything about the prison of Rome?" I asked.

Lormah squinted and tilted her head. "Is your friend there, the one you needed to cry for?"

She was as watchful as baby Ira. "Yes, but she is not alone. They have taken a young woman with her—also my friend." I paused. "They were falsely accused by two senators."

Her eyes, small and dark, appeared to glisten in dim lamplight. "I know," she said.

"You know?"

"I know it as well as I am knowing you. Our people always are suffering from untruths," Lormah said.

"But what can be done?" A knot grew in my throat.

"You know what camp they are in?" she asked.

"Camp? Only that my father says it's in the city." I chewed my lip. Emotion was rising in me again.

"The *carcer*, at the forum," Lormah replied.

"You're right. He did say 'the *carcer*.' But how can you know?"

Lormah's worn look had resurfaced, and she turned aside. "I have been there. By God's mercy, I was released."

"When were you"—

She laid a finger against her lips. "Shush. I will take you. But you will follow my instructions."

The thought of seeing Miriam and Hannah was encouraging. "What must I do?"

"Bake round loaves, only this size." She arched her hands around an invisible ball, fingers just touching. "Bake at least five. Ten is better."

My mind was already planning how and when to do the baking.

"You have a large basket?" she asked. "Fill the basket with loaves. Cover them with an old cloth. An old one," she repeated. "It will be torn, thin. You understand?" She looked at me with intensity, as if to emphasize the importance.

"I see what you're saying, but ..."

"We will look like those with no money for fine wool. And your clothes"—she shook her head—"not like this." She pointed to my tunic, embroidered with delicate thread.

"But what should I'"—

She waved a hand across her dress. "You will look like me."

Lormah's tunic must have been worn every day for months. Neat rows of mending looked almost decorative, so many holes had been repaired.

"For now, you do these things. I come for you after tomorrow, before sun rises." She turned and descended the stairs, motioning me to follow.

When we reached street level, Lormah brought her face close and spoke low. "Quick," she said. "We are too long here. No more talking."

It was a swift passage. I had a sense now of our direction, and the children's harbor was not so far from home. We met no other travelers along our way, arriving at my gate before dawn. Creeping inside, curling at last into the comfort of my bed, my brain whirled from excitement. How could I possibly sleep? That was my last thought.

″ ′

Midmorning, Aquila came to our garden door. After customary greetings, we both were quiet. His eyes trailed my movements as plants were tended in the atrium, and my hands became clumsy blocks, strewing dirt over my clothing as well as the floor. It was an embarrassing mess. To prevent Aquila from chuckling, I decided to talk.

"We—we're becoming friends," I said, "and I am glad. It is good. But there is something I must share with you."

Aquila looked apprehensive. "You know, Prisca, you speak out more than most girls your age," he said.

"Does that irritate you?" Both Miriam and my father had taught me the duties of a proper Judean girl—respectful, devoted, courteous—though my nature often

142

nudged against those boundaries. There was an uncommon desire to challenge Aquila, perhaps tease him, but I didn't know why. Maybe it was because he seemed so serious and somewhat authoritative, making me seem even more the child.

"It may appear that I'm proud," Aquila said, "but it's more to do with determination, striving to learn my father's trade and care for those he left behind. There have been hardships because of coming here, although now blessings are near." He became more animated. "Often, I think of our people's past, which has been marked with grave extremes. By the decree of our sovereign God, we have experienced moments of miraculous victory and periods of harrowing defeat and exile. Those who have gone before us have borne scars that marked steadfastness in the face of difficulty—even in the face of death."

He lowered his head like those who served at assembly, respectful and solemn.

"My father was a good man, Prisca. He taught me to work with my hands, to provide well for myself ... and for my family." Aquila paused, and his eyes searched mine. He then continued, "He also taught me the importance of walking in the way that God commands. I believe we must be constant in our devotion to the One God, that we should be resilient and committed in carrying on, living rightly before Him." He softened, moving closer. "The devotion I see in you is what I've prayed for. You have compassion. And your friends attest to your goodness." He stopped and pinched the base of his chin; enjoyment sparked in the darkest centers of his eyes. "As for your wisdom, it will surely increase."

"And as for speaking my mind?"

He said, "The answer is 'no,' it does not irritate me."

"Well—"

He silenced me with a hand, but it was clear he was holding back laughter.

"As long as you speak wisely." His face broadened into smile. This was something I liked in Aquila, that flash of mischief that surfaced in surprise. "And you had something to discuss?" he asked.

I crossed the room. "Where to begin." Staring into Father's *tablinum*, ordering my thoughts, my desire was to do right by this man of principle, this man whose presence produced security and delight.

"You know there are abandoned children in this city," I said.

"I am well aware," he replied.

"Well, I—I want to help them ... so they can have a chance to live." Passion punctuated my words.

"As do I, but this is dangerous business you speak of," he said.

He walked toward me, standing so near I could smell the oils he used for working goatskin into tent leather. A light breeze from overhead caught the ends of my long scarf and blew them against his chest. His tone grew more intense. "It is especially dangerous for a young woman."

"But it would be against all that I am to do nothing," I said.

"You can pray. Allow God to intervene."

"I have prayed," I replied. "Is it so hard to believe that God could use me to intervene?" Was it really true? Was our wise and powerful God responsible for the compelling force within me?

"And what are you intending to do? What are your plans?" he asked. "This is not something you should attempt alone."

"I have met someone."

He pulled away. "I see. And how can he help you with your calling?"

"It's not like you think." I walked toward him. "My friend—"

"Your friend is not likely to be trusted." His face was becoming red.

"And how could you know that?" I asked. "You don't even know her."

"Because—her?" He closed the distance between our faces.

"I met her—you see, we—I met her when—on an unexpected occasion. She's already begun helping orphans in this city. It is a risk, which is why I wanted to talk to you."

Aquila sighed. "You wanted to increase my concern?"

"I wanted you to know, because I'd hoped you would stand by my decision to help—"

"Stand by? But it sounds like a hasty decision, and you don't know—"

"—and because my answer to your question is 'yes.'"

"Your answer—" He stopped, and his features relaxed. Taking my hands in his, he pulled me with him to the couch. "You say 'yes'?"

My face was flushing, and I raised a hand to my cheek in an attempt to cool it.

"Today I am a happy man," Aquila said, "for I shall be joined to the woman with dancing eyes."

"Dancing eyes?"

"From the moment I met you," he said, "they have danced." He lifted my chin. "I love you, Priscilla, daughter of Eben Lucullus Priscus."

"And you, Aquila. I love you."

He touched my face as a soft breeze might caress the skin. Unfamiliar warmth filled me and a longing for him to press his lips against mine. Years of training restrained me, however, from yielding to temptation. The laws of our God forbid any touching before marriage. My mouth curved into a smile, thinking of Betna and his constant presence; he was probably listening from the kitchen. What if he barged into the atrium and began chastising us? It would be too shameful to bear.

"Will you then be speaking to my father?"

"Today," he said. "It will be announced at assembly on Sabbath."

"Remember what I told you, Aquila. About helping the children."

He said, "Let me be the one to help. Or your friend can do it. You can give her supplies, if necessary."

"Why has God excited me with such compassion?" I asked. "I feel directed, urged, led by his beseeching hand." My demeanor softened towards his uneasiness.

146

"Please trust me. I give you my solemn promise to be discreet, to be cautious and protect my reputation. All of this I do for you. But it is a calling I can't ignore. There is such need, Aquila."

His eyes were steady. "Allow me to assist you then, to look after you."

"Do you trust me?" I asked. "Can you trust me?"

Hesitating for a moment, he studied me. "I will trust." He tightened the grip on my fingers. "But, Prisca, if there is trouble, you must send for me."

"I promise." Was the floor moving beneath my feet? This man had such effect on me. My voice thinned to a whisper. "I will not be careless with our love."

From the direction of the kitchen came the sound of Betna humming. We both turned together, and Aquila laughed.

"I will leave you now, in Betna's capable hands," he said.

My insides were tickling as if filled with flying insects.

Aquila moved his face close to mine. "I will come again ... soon."

I grinned. "Perhaps I'll bake you some bread."

"Ah. I've heard there's a needy family and will take them a loaf." His smile faded, and he took my hand in his. "Remember your promise. Be careful. Call for me."

I squeezed his hand in reply, and he left this time by the upper stairway, following it through the *insula* and exiting behind.

After he left, I sauntered toward the kitchen, a stern look on my face. "Betna," I said, "how much listening were you doing?"

He stood near the stove, crushing dried herbs and placing them into little leather pouches, still humming. Turning, he looked startled. "Oh! There you are," he said.

"Come now, old friend, your hearing isn't that bad."

He continued to hum the familiar tune, smiling and rocking his head as if remembering a long-ago dance.

"And what is that song?" I asked. "You said you would tell me."

"It is poetry of wise old Solomon," he said, "a simple song about a garden."

ഊ ൠ

Our *domus* felt hollow after Aquila had gone, and Betna agreed, upon my urging, to take me on an errand. We walked to the meat and banqueting shop of Aedias and Hesperia; together, they owned *Epulatus*, which meant "To Feast Upon." Like Father's family, the ancestors of Aedias and Hesperia were brought from Judea as slaves. At some point, their families had earned freedom, and Aedias' father became a successful meat merchant.

Epulatus was situated in the center of a well-traveled road just beyond the *forum boarium*, at one time a busy cattle market. The area still retained an atmosphere of trade and marketing, and we passed along the rim of its wide expanse, meandering through colonnades and porticoes to avoid the jumble of animals and people. The butcher shop was soon within sight, its broad doors open to a group of customers extending into the street. It was not uncommon to see slaves collecting packages for a wealthy master's feast, and several were in line, wearing shallow sandals and coarse-weave tunics.

In physical and emotional terms, *Epulatus* was owned by Aedias alone. He simply belonged. Short and stout, body coated with black, bristly hair, he appeared to have been plumped for his own clientele. Every inch of his skin was taut, his miniscule black eyes anxious and alert. As we neared, I could see him scurrying about like a fat rodent—absent only a leathery tail. Aedias was a talented and zealous cook, once disclosing that he had received instruction from a famous culinary expert named Apicius. Making the most of his learning, Aedias catered to Roman clientele with delicacies such as chicken drowned in wine and spiced flamingo tongue—such dishes a devoted Judean would never imbibe.

Just outside the shop's door was a giant hook with counterbalances for weighing large cuts of meat. Red-and-gold-painted interior walls were hung with peacocks and gray-feathered geese. Wild hares dangled from hooks, and a boar's empty eyes gawked at me from a shaded corner. Just upwind from *Epulatus* was a baker's stand, and I leaned away from the smell of wild game and into the aroma of fresh bread.

Betna entered the shop, intent on purchasing a modest portion of lamb, while I strayed from the entry to greet Hesperia. A tall woman and robust, Hesperia was always attired in latest Roman fashion by capitalizing on her prime talent, weaving and adorning cloth. Such intricate stitching! Her clothing was among the finest in Rome. I supposed that her children had little care for style of dress, and her husband Aedias—a more bombastic and carefree man was never known—would not desire decoration. His tunics were always covered with thick aprons stained with animal residue. In contrast, Hesperia was meticulous as a carved statue, her flowing hair braided into extensive ropes, looped and pinned high above a square face.

Aedias and Hesperia had three sons: Cassius, eleven, built like his father; Aulus, age eight and a masculine version of Hesperia; and Livius, nearing the age of five, plump and wide-eyed, an intelligent and inquisitive boy. In addition, there were two girls within the household: Balbina, a lanky, rather anxious girl of twelve; and round-faced Hortensia, a very subdued six-year-old. The girls had been taken in by Hesperia and, after having visited the children's harbor, I found myself curious about their beginnings.

"Good day, Hesperia," I called.

She grunted a reply, her eyes focused on Aulus' hair, running a comb through thick waves. Aulus had been pulled from a game the boys were playing, their small stones resting in wells of a game board that had been carved into a step near the shop entrance.

"Aulus will soon be taller than me," I said.

"Mmm." Hesperia nodded.

"Where are the girls?" I asked.

"They have chores," Hesperia said. She tapped Aulus on the back, returning him to the game with his brothers. "Don't make a mess of yourselves," she said.

"I wonder—well, where was it you found your girls?"

She furrowed her high brow, and searched me with thin eyes.

"If you don't mind my asking," I said.

"I heard them," Hesperia replied. She brushed at her gown, straightening the folds. "They were whispering beneath the road."

"Beneath the road?"

She sighed with a slight jiggle of her braids. "You know, under one of those iron grates covering the sewer."

"From the sewer?" I wrinkled my nose. Rome's sewer was a nasty and dismal place. "What were they doing there?"

"Hiding there from—from whoever. Their previous owners, I suppose."

"So they were slaves." They must have had hard lives indeed.

"Foolish girls thought they could make it on their own. No one can survive in such filth," she said.

"And you took them in," I responded.

"They get along all right," Hesperia said. "Thought I would never get them clean, though."

"I'd be happy for them to spend a day with me. We could bake together. Perhaps I could braid their hair," I said.

Hesperia raised trimmed eyebrows. "They are not behaved enough for that."

"Just for an afternoon?" I asked.

"We'll see," Hesperia said.

Betna came into view with a wrapped package, and I said farewells to all. Overhead, a large curved balcony extended the home Aedias and Hesperia shared above their busy storefront. Searching its dark cavity for any glimpse of Balbina and Hortensia, neither appeared, and we returned home.

ဆ ၄

Day disappeared. Night birds could be heard from outside, but indoors all was silent. I sank into the cushions of my bed, enjoying a vision of Aquila, when an ache began growing in the very center of me, tension that could not be waved away. Somehow, the prospect of being Aquila's wife made me more apprehensive, more fearful of the challenges already set in motion. That he might be hurt by my actions was a powerful deterrent, and I considered waving Lormah on, telling her I couldn't go to the *carcer*. But loved ones filled my mind, beckoning. "Please come."

Finally, unable to sleep, it was time to go, and there seemed no other choice. Pulling one of Keziah's cast-off gray tunics overhead and gathering an old robe about me, I slipped through my bedroom door, sandals in hand. The sun would not be up for a while. My basket of rounded loaves had been secreted away beneath the stairs, and I folded a ragged cloth against its woven sides.

At the back gate, huddling in shadow, it occurred to me that nighttime adventures had become a profession. Though there was a sense of fright about them, I also felt alive and involved, part of the kindling that ignites a fire. Shuddering in pre-dawn chill, I prayed that it would be a contained fire.

It was not long before recognizing the slim silhouette of Lormah. My fingers extended just above the wall, in hopes that she alone could see me. Her familiar footfalls brought comfort, and she fell swift to my side.

"How are you?" I asked.

"Tired." Pulling her knees snug, she rested her chin between them. "A hard day tending soup, a long night tending children." She sighed. "But my life belongs to God. He carries me."

"What do you mean?"

"He makes a way. When my feet can walk no more, he makes them strong. I do not know how, but he helps me. Only my God." She leaned her head back, staring into starlit sky. Lormah was not a beauty, but she seemed to have—oh, to explain it—a brightness, a gleam, some confident assurance that was calming and safe, when all around there was worry and trouble.

"I love the Lord," I said, "but I'd like to sense his direction, to know he guided me."

"It shall be, friend. The Holy Spirit tells it to my soul."

"The Holy Spirit tells you?" I asked.

She tapped my arm. "Now, we go. I have left the house of children. Soon I am dishing soup."

I said, "I've made it hard on you. This is more work, and you are tired. Maybe we should not—"

"No." Lormah pulled my face toward hers. Her fingers were rough, but her touch was gentle. "We go where there is need. It is for the purpose of God. I know it."

"God's purpose? How can one know such things?"

Rising, she surveyed the alley and then gestured to close my lips. "We move with no noise," she whispered. "Follow me."

153

We started off, Lormah leading, our destination the *carcer* of Rome. Slipping behind walls and ducking into slim doorways, we soon arrived at the sprawling mass of buildings that enclosed the forum's paved floor. Once there, we had no place to hide. It was a location where people were present at all hours, and we were forced into a mode of deception, entering the broad plaza of the forum as two impoverished women who earned a pittance baking bread for prisoners.

"Silent," Lormah reminded. She pressed a hand down for emphasis. "Pretend you cannot speak."

I nodded in reply.

Together, we walked toward the northeast end of the forum. Shopkeepers were beginning to open *tabernae* around the perimeter, raising awnings and arranging merchandise for display. We passed the painted cart of a *pomarius*—a fruit vendor—and my stomach began to grumble at the fragrance of bananas, fresh berries and coconuts. Continuing our steady pace, a couple of men shouted obscenities, coming close enough to impart a stench of strong wine and urine. There was then a sudden, unsettling sense that someone was following us and watching our movements. Did Lormah sense it too? We plodded on, however, toward those ominous Stairs of Mourning.

As we walked by the senate house—the Roman *curia*—there was an alcove ahead. Though many journeys had been made to the forum with Father or Betna, here was an opening never noticed before, and it was one through which we must pass to gain access to the *carcer*. On our left, the Stairs of Mourning climbed high to the *Arx*—

Rome's fortress—above. I shivered, thinking of bodies that had been cast upon those stairs. Hannah's own parents were among them, and she now resided beneath. A sorrowful sigh left my lips, and Lormah squeezed my arm in warning.

Two guards were posted at the *carcer's* entry, their armor glossed by a single torch. Lormah walked toward a guard on the right and spoke to him in the only Latin words I ever heard her utter.

"We got bread for prisoners," she said. "Let us pass."

The guard was a towering man with a rounded paunch. He snarled. "Let me see 'em."

Lormah stood, staring. It appeared she did not understand, so I lifted my basket to his chest and pulled back the cloth to reveal stacked brown loaves, nine of them.

"Get on then," the guard said. He shoved the basket at me, causing a loaf to topple out and onto the ground. Before I could recover it, a sharp sword pierced its grainy surface, and he stripped the blade clean. "They don't need all of 'em." He grunted and bit into the bread.

I held my breath while passing into something like a tunnel, though with no solid roof overhead. It was damp, chilling. Set low into the hillside was a dingy row of cells, like black holes in a bricked wall, their fronts enclosed with a crisscross of metal rods. Fading moonlight allowed me to see dim outlines within, and I strained for a glimpse of Hannah or Miriam. Most prisoners were silent. A few forced arms out between the rails, opening and closing hands in wordless appeal. It was frightening, and I thought Lormah heroic, handing out bread in silence, enduring lewd sneers and groping.

At the fourth cell, something about the shapes of its inhabitants stalled me, and I pulled back the cover on my basket and edged closer. By this time, moonlight was dissolving into approaching dawn, making the cave-like cells appear dark violet in color. Being outside, my own face must have been more visible.

A whispered voice claimed my ears. "Prisca!" It was Hannah.

"Oh, Hannah." I leaned against cold metal.

"You risk too much, child," said Miriam. Her approach was slow and sounded difficult. "Leave here. It's not safe." A frail hand emerged, waving me away, but the unevenness in her voice told me she was near tears. "Go, child."

"But I had to come, to tell you … your being here is wrong." My voice broke. "I love you."

Hannah came near. "Miriam is right. You must go before they see."

I pushed my hand through a narrow opening, wanting assurance that they were alive. Hannah's cold fingers wrapped around mine. A moldy odor brushed my face, causing me to wobble. Oh, Adonai, how can they be in such a place?

Lormah grabbed my arm, her voice low but insistent. "Too close, too close. Guards will see."

I turned a tearful face toward her and saw the largest guard coming our way, leather flaps slapping his muscled thighs. Panic stabbed my chest. Lormah pulled me into the tunnel, distributing bread—only a few more cells to go. We reached the end and started back, and a citizen was talking to the approaching guard, saying something about "information regarding cell number two."

Lormah and I looked at one another, baffled by what was taking place. We revisited previous steps, moving at a careful pace. Taking advantage of the guard's distraction, we lingered again near Hannah and Miriam. I pressed a hand to my lips, motioning a kiss their way.

Hannah whispered as we passed. "We are all right. Don't worry," she said. "We may be excused soon."

"It is my prayer," I said.

Hannah said, "I am with child, Prisca. And—" Her voice became choked with weeping.

I almost stopped, almost turned back, but Lormah pressed me onward.

Miriam's sweet voice met my ears. "Do not fear. Hannah will be—" I could hear no more.

To leave, we had to walk around the apparent confrontation between the guard and unknown man. They were not talking; there was some kind of written tablet being reviewed. We bowed our heads and passed by. When exiting the prison, the stationed guard tossed a few coins in my basket, and I flinched.

We escaped into open forum, and fresh air filled my lungs. Only then did we see that a soft mist had dampened our clothing, but those mists began to lift, and there came a luster to building façades, a rosy preface to sun's rising. I was struck with an odd sense that, on one singular morning, I would behold the magnificence and splendor of Rome, its gilded marble reflecting bright colors of dawn, and almost in that same moment had experienced its desolation and depravity, the squalidness of its prison.

Lormah herded us over gleaming marble pavements and past an assemblage of priests in vivid attire, preparing a bull for sacrifice. Our steps were swift, and we worked hard to pass without notice.

As we neared *Circus Maximus*, I became more alert and again sensed someone close behind. Jerking Lormah to me, we disappeared behind a broad arch near the circus entrance. Charioteers were preparing for races later in the day, horses whinnying and chariot wheels spinning. A thin powder from the sandy track floated all around us.

Finger to my lips, I pointed toward the intersection we'd just left. A man stood there, the same man we had seen at the prison, hidden beneath a hefty cape. His body turned in every direction and his hands raised in anger. It appeared certain he was searching for us. We remained motionless, bodies pressed against cool travertine, until he was gone and we could gather courage to go on.

As the white arc of my doorway came into sight, relief overwhelmed me. I wanted to run, but my feet felt like bricks. Turning to the faithful companion beside me, a long-held breath escaped my lips.

"You have proven a dear and trusted friend," I said. "How can I thank you?"

Her eyes met mine, and her words were sluggish, like cold honey. "Stay my friend," she said.

I answered by gripping her fingers in mine.

She lowered her head and spoke low. "To many, I am judged—named—as one not worthy of love." With a quick nod of her head, she left, never looking back.

What Lormah had done that day flooded my soul. She had given so much to help me, someone still quite unknown to her. Dizzy with emotion and relieved to be home, I stumbled into the garden gate, landing atop my willow basket. As I sat, wiping wetness from my brow, I realized something of who Lormah was.

"Her name," I whispered. A tingling sensation met my skin. "Her name is Hebrew. Lo-Ruhamah." I shut my eyes. "Lo-Ruhamah." What kind of person would name a child '*not loved*'?

∽ ∾

The iron handle of our garden door felt familiar and reassuring as my fingers held it and shoved the door open. I sighed, my eyes adapting to low light, not seeing Father at first. But then I knew—dark cape across his shoulders, clay tablet resting on the table—he was the one who distracted the guard, allowing us to pass unhindered.

"Have you no thought for the safety of your family?" His voice reverberated with anger.

"Father, I know it was wrong of me, but—"

"Wrong of you?" He wore that incredulous expression I'd seen before, when I took a bite too big for my mouth or when Betna first stopped calling him "sir," only this time his face was nearly violet with rage. "Priscilla, what you have done this morning was not simply wrong; it may be the cause of someone's death."

Shifting my broken basket to the floor, I slid onto a bench. Many sacrifices had been made in order to execute the little plot that morning—bread baked, lack of sleep—but it never crossed my mind that someone could be hurt by it. Yet my own dear father, guardian and guide of my life, would not lie to me.

"When I noticed your absence," he said, "I knew where you were headed. You're quite predictable."

My eyes concentrated on the table's surface, afraid to look at him. "I realize it was selfish," I said, "but I had to see them. A part of me really believed I could help. At least give them hope."

"It's difficult to have sympathy for you." He shook his head, standing and walking away. "You risk too much."

"I risk myself, Abba. For the ones I love."

He spun toward me. "And you do not think how losing you would affect me." He leaned over the table, facial muscles constricting. "Or how it could affect Aquila?"

"It's hard to see your own value through another's eyes." I thought of Lormah.

He shook his head at me. "Foolish girl! Your desperate need to fix others' problems is unbearable! If your disguise today failed ..." He combed hands through his hair.

My stomach squeezed in pain. "I don't understand. Have I harmed Miriam and Hannah somehow?"

"We will know soon. If someone heard you speak to them ..." He stood, picking up his cloak and hanging it on a hook near the door. "Do not go near the prison again." His voice toughened. "Let me make it clear. I forbid you."

I pressed my lips until they hurt.

"When I realized that guard was headed for you," he hesitated, "it was like losing your mother all over again." He looked away.

My throat ached, holding back emotion.

Father continued, "Today's behavior has made me realize your ignorance in these matters."

I started to object.

"Yes, I see your response, Daughter. You struggle with believing you have any ignorance. Proud and strong." He leaned back, appraising me. "You are also a woman."

"This speech is sounding like many I've heard, Father. But you don't understand. Women can do many things."

He sat next to me. "You mistake my words. What I mean is that women are a more likely target in this empire." He tapped the table as if to call me to attention. "Come now. You know the legend of the Sabine women."

I frowned. "Ancient history. The original patriarchs of Rome needed wives. So they stole them from neighboring Sabine men."

"Simply stated, but essentially correct. Take it in. Work it into your mind. That tradition is established here. Men fully believe in domination over women, and they will apply whatever power or influence they hold." He leaned closer. "You must be alert, cautious, and never alone."

"I do understand."

He smacked the table and then stood in silence, turning his back. When he spoke again, it was quiet, controlled. "Miriam and Hannah are scheduled to stand before the court in two days' time."

"Day after tomorrow?"

"I have withheld that information from you. Perhaps I shouldn't have done so." He turned again to look at me. "I thought you might do something impulsive, if you knew, attempt something unsafe." He shook his head.

"What does it mean, Abba, to stand before the court?"

"In the old days, there was always a jury. Now, there is no assurance of that." He exhaled. "Two impressive senators, men who have maintained the favor of Gaius—not an easy feat—have accused Miriam and Hannah. Worse yet, there is a personal impetus to the accusation, although many would not know that. And, quite honestly, Hannah's apparent condition is potent evidence against her."

"You knew," I said. Father's declaration had made her condition real. It seemed Hannah's words that morning were spoken in a dream.

"The outcome is not certain," he said. "Nothing is."

"But she was attacked!" I said. "How can they prove prostitution?"

"Unfortunately, Hannah cannot prove otherwise." He hung his head, face written with sorrow. "She is yet unmarried."

"Aquila can testify that she was attacked. He was there."

My father leaned close, speaking with clarity and slowness. "Consider what you are saying. This man whom you are to marry, do you want more threat to his life?"

"But is it really a threat to one's life to tell the truth?"

His shoulders fell. Turning toward the atrium, he braced his body within its doorway. "Truth does not carry the importance it once had. I tell you, family of the attackers could swiftly take his life. They are members of respected nobility. If they called upon their extensive list of clients, some simply glorified assassins," he sighed, "it would be over—and quick."

Chills ran through my body.

He turned to face me. "I will tell you what kind of man seeks your hand. Aquila went to the senate three days ago. He insisted he had information that would liberate Hannah and Miriam. It was a bold move. But when Hannah and Miriam were brought before a tribunal for questioning, they insisted they did not know him."

"But why? Why would they deny him?"

"My perception is that they preferred to protect him." His face reddened, his speech became unsteady. "They may end up protecting him with their very lives."

"They protect him for me," I said.

"Yes," he said. "They do."

"And I thought I was being brave."

"Brave?" His shoulders slumped. "What we need is to act with wisdom. Most of all, we need miracles."

Ethan had proclaimed his reliance on miracles in a room filled with abandoned children who never saw daylight. "What miracles?" I asked. "Only in bedtime tales, Father. Children are weaned on the legendary heroes of our people."

I stood, walking the length of the table, fingers tracing the grain of wood in its surface. "And if we prayed for another Joshua or David, would God actually send such a leader to Rome?" A weight of hopelessness seeped into my heart, and I shook my head in anger. "No. Not here."

My father's face slackened. "I've not always taught you as I should, about our people, our ways."

"But you have, Abba. And what you have not taught, Miriam supplied."

He came to me, took my hands and squeezed them, attempting a smile. "No. I mean about miracles. My own father believed, really believed, that slavery came to him as a miracle."

"But how could slavery ever be a miracle?"

Father replied, "It led him to become educated. He learned languages. He learned to read, to write. He received valuable skills that were passed on."

"To his brilliant son." I patted Father's hand.

"To us." His eyes were intense. "Think, Prisca. So few are given that gift of learning. Most are wealthy. What if your grandfather had never been taught such things?"

I couldn't imagine what life might have been without the knowledge that originated with Lucullus.

"In days such as these, we must be attentive," he said. "Dwell on those gifts that have come to you. Savor them. Realize how they can be used in the service of God."

His words reminded me of Lormah's statement from earlier that morning, that her work was "for the purpose of God." I sat down hard on the bench.

"When those you love are in jeopardy, it's hard to focus on anything good," I said.

Father nodded. "But when difficulties have come to me, I have perceived my own father's face in memory and how, in all earnestness, he spoke to me of miracles. He literally glowed with faith, Prisca. Because a worthy man like him believed, so can I. It helps me to know that the Lord still leads us."

We sat together in the melodious welcome of morning birdsong, sunlight coloring our atrium. In that moment, it was easy to believe God was shining goodness upon us.

"I promise to look for miracles, but it's just that I have heard the legends of our people over and over, and God did not do it alone. He used people, men and women like us. How do we know—I mean, could the Lord be asking us to do something? And if so, don't you think we should try?"

He laid a hand on mine. "I have paid the indebted amount required under Table III of Roman law. We can now only wait, see if Gaius Caesar will be just."

"There is more troubling you."

Father sighed. "It is the current state of things, the emperor's recent behavior. His actions are—there is no predicting what he will do."

"What do you mean?"

Father explained. "This week, an officer of public games came to Gaius Caesar with a requisition to purchase food for circus beasts. The cost of meat, you know, has escalated."

"But the emperor has money. Ours," I said.

"Money flies from his hands like winnowed chaff upon wind." Father lowered his gaze. "Rather than pay a high price, the emperor responded with an order for a number of prisoners to be brought in. He then selected every third person to be hauled into the circus as food for animals."

I moaned a reply, and Father held my hands so tight they ached. It occurred to me what burdens he had been carrying.

"Gaius Caesar has changed," he said. "He is not the same man. His mind has been twisted somehow."

"But would he—please tell me he would not do that to Miriam and Hannah," I said.

"I can tell you this: He is determined to punish those who will not sacrifice to him, who will not call him a god. To the emperor, such disobedience amounts to treason. And treason is a capital crime."

"What if Miriam and Hannah are put to such a test? Would they give in? Would they sacrifice to the emperor?"

His eyes were piercing. "Never."

I lowered my aching head, closing my eyes.

Father stood and paced to the end of the room. "The sad truth is Gaius will manipulate the laws when he can. He chooses, in particular, to torment those who are not Roman citizens. They are used to set examples for others."

"How can God leave his people at the mercy of men like Gaius Caesar?"

Father came to me, laying a hand against my cheek. "We live in an evil world. Blood and smoke from Rome's sacrifices assault us every day, sacrifices dedicated to bronzed or golden images. Our own emperor has been seen whispering into the mouth of his god, Jupiter, as if they are conspirators. As long as good and evil coexist, Prisca, we will see suffering."

I walked into the atrium, troubled in spirit. Could we survive here? Could we make it? Our traditions—with every new day, it became more difficult to live by them;

they were not the Roman way. I turned to my father, the man who worked hard to protect my life, my future. "Forgive me, Father. I dishonored you today."

His voice wavered. "You were wrong to go."

"I will be better," I said.

He came near, taking my face within his hands. "Please. For all of us."

Shame flooded my soul. How—oh, God, tell me how—to follow the calling of my heart and still comply with the expectations of a dutiful daughter?

ಬ ಚ

Our discourse had taken us into dawn, and Father hurried off to rolls of parchment, cups of black ink, and aged men in crisp white togas. Betna soon followed with errands at the market. I longed to go with him but was left with my worry. What could happen to Miriam and Hannah? Was Aquila safe from pursuit? The cloak I was weaving became knotted and uneven, and several rows of yarn were tossed to the floor.

When Helah, Mara and Keziah appeared, it was a relief to see them. We shared greetings, and Mara was first to speak.

"We are alarmed that you are not in the garden," she said. "It needs tending, dear."

"Perhaps later today I will make time for—"

Mara interrupted. "It is not good that a young woman becomes derelict in her chores."

I struggled to contain a sigh. "Matron Mara, I assure you it is important to me." I paused. "Today I've been preoccupied, but ..."

"We must express our best efforts in all things," Helah said. "There are expectations you must recognize— standards—for young women who intend to marry."

"And the community will be watching closely now," Mara said.

Keziah narrowed silent eyes, and I dreaded what this visit meant. It appeared they came to me with some specific intent.

"I don't understand," I said. "Watching closely?"

Helah's eyelids were fluttering. "Well! That young girl you have associated yourself with. You know that will cause others to consider your suitability."

"My suit- —are you speaking of Hannah?"

Mara raised a hand to her mouth, eyes wide. "You would do best not to mention her by name. We will not speak it again, will we?" She cast glances at Helah and Keziah while patting my shoulder. "If we were in our homeland, hmm, things would be quite different."

"But she is my friend." It was an effort to keep my voice steady.

Helah tensed. "Shush now. That is the image you must correct."

"The law of Moses is clear," Mara said. "A woman like that is to be cast out. In Judea, she would be stoned."

"I could never"—if not for Father, I would take a broom to these hags, I thought. "Forgive me, Matrons. You do not know everything that happened."

Helah pinched her lips together and pressed an arthritic finger to her forehead. "Words we have heard many times before." She sighed.

"Ah, yes," Mara agreed. She arched her brows. "But we are not blind."

Emotion fueled my voice. "Hannah was wounded. She was a victim. She has done nothing wrong," I said.

Helah shook her head.

Mara came near and patted my shoulder once again. "Come now. It is not our wish to upset you." She and Helah looked at one another and nodded. "But you must understand. This girl is merely bearing the consequences of sin."

My eyes began to water. The law. Sin was the dark, swollen cloud that kept us from sunlight.

"We saw the same thing with Lavan's daughter, didn't we, Helah?" Mara asked.

"Yes," Helah replied. "And she had such boldness!"

Mara shook her head. "Sneaking around, attempting to speak to my Keziah about such matters, trying to vindicate herself!"

Keziah frowned, twisting an end of veil around her pointing finger.

Helah huffed. "That girl was carried on swift wheels into the country. Matter resolved. Lavan did his best."

"It is a pity," Mara said. "Your—well, this girl has no father to handle such matters." She turned to Helah. "We may need to present this issue for the rabbi."

"Excuse me," I said. "If you knew the entire circumstances—"

Helah ignored me. "Hmm, that is a pity," she said. "It will only be more difficult."

"But back to you, dear." Mara radiated friendliness. "We will do what we can to break off the connection. No one need know that you have been—well, that you have been acquainted."

Helah raised a finger to my face. "But you must follow our instructions."

"Thank you for your concern," I said. "But I feel it is only fair to tell you I believe Hannah. I believe she was wronged. I want to remain her friend."

Three wide-eyed owls puffed their chests at my words, their shawls expanding like wings.

"I will stand by her." I lifted my chin. "As far as my own moral standing, I have been obedient to the law, have remained chaste, and will continue to be so."

Mara's lips went white. "Well! I am quite troubled by your statements." Her voice sounded coarse. "We may have to ask Rabbi. We may even be required to decline your case."

I did not respond.

Helah turned toward the door, head held aloft, and her summoning call reminded me of a rooster at morning. "Shall we go?" Without waiting for the others to respond, she exited. Mara and Keziah followed. I heard the door thump, and they were gone.

"Bearing the consequences of sin! Oh!" I paced around and around the pool, my hands rolled into tight fists till they ached. Like the garden, my weaving was left unattended.

ଚ୍ଚ ଓ୪

As the next day came and again I attempted normal household tasks, nothing about life seemed normal. What was to become of my friends? Mara's words tormented me and left me grumbling. "There is not a sinful thought in Hannah's head!" I shouted.

Anxiety became a burdensome stone that I carried, and each moment it drew more weight. Betna had journeyed to a farm some miles away to help a friend in need, and I missed his uplifting presence, his low-pitched hum that made me smile. Our *domus* was a cavern of gloom, and it was late when Father came from the *curia*. In a manner unlike him, he went straight to the *tablinum*. He collapsed into a chair behind his writing desk, head hung low. At my approach, he waved me away.

"I dare not speak to you, Daughter."

The dismissal stung. What had caused him to rebuild a wall between us? Hannah and Miriam would not be taken to the magistrate for another day, and I reassured myself their situation had not changed.

Forcing myself into the garden, which did indeed need attention, if the matrons were evaluating my chores— no, it was better to remember that the garden was a healing and valued place. Weeding and pruning with vigor until the sun was gone and then collecting a few autumn vegetables, the exertion refreshed me. I was on my knees, humming a childhood tune when Father seized my arms and pulled me to my feet, almost carrying me into the *domus*.

I protested, but the look on his face arrested me. Father's skin was blotched with red, eyes pinched. His hands were feverish, holding my arms in a firm grip. For the first time ever, there was fear in his presence.

"When the sun sets, you stay inside," he said. "And you will never—never be alone!"

My eyes were wide and staring, trying to make sense of what was happening.

In the slight time it takes to turn a spade in loose soil, his manner altered, and then the benevolent father I knew released me. "Adonai, Adonai," he sighed. Shuddering, he pressed his forehead against the wall.

"What—Abba, what has happened?" I asked.

There was no movement, only labored breathing, and then a pained moan rose from his chest. "The emperor is insane." He slapped the wall. "He is insane!"

Stroking his arms and speaking soft, I managed to pull him into a seat. "It will be all right, it will be all right. Talk to me. Tell me, Abba." We sat for some time listening to familiar house sounds, gentle winds outside, and then he began to speak.

"Today, three persons were brought before the senate and the emperor," he said. "They were all believers in a new religion. They said they followed someone—a man—claiming to be Messiah." He passed shaky fingers over parched lips.

"You mean our Messiah? The Messiah promised to Israel?" I asked.

"That's what they said. And, like us, they were—two of them—were from Judea. But they believe that this Jesus, this man from Nazareth, came to earth as the Son of God. They said he died '*To atone for the sins of mankind.*'" Father shook his head. "I don't know, I don't know. It doesn't make sense."

"A man from Nazareth," I said. Excitement coursed through me. Hadn't Miriam sensed that Messiah was coming? "Even now," she had said. Turning attention full upon Father, I mellowed at his haggard look. "Why did these people upset you? I don't understand."

"It was not these people." He stared into distance.

"Was it"—I hesitated, already knowing the answer. "It was the emperor."

He nodded, filling his lungs. Words were slow, despairing. "Gaius Caesar told them—I'm trying to recall exact—first, he said, '*I will allow you to worship this man, this Jesus.*' Then he slapped his hands together." Father ran a finger across tense lips. "I will never forget the shrill pitch to his voice and the look on his face when he said, '*I might add him to my list of gods too!*'"

"How strange," I said.

He continued. "Gaius—Caligula—he looked dim, shadowy. His body became rigid, and he had an odd grin. Then he told them, '*But you must get on your knees and pay me homage, for I am your god here in Rome.*'"

"He said he was a god?"

Father nodded.

"And did they do it?"

He shook his head at me. "They told Caesar they respected his authority, but their faith forbids them to worship any but the One God and His Son, Jesus. The woman called him '*Emmanuel.*'"

"Emmanuel," I breathed.

"It means '*God is with us.*'" Father sat very still.

I laid my hand on his stiffened fist, and he opened it, embracing my fingers.

"Could it be? Has the Messiah truly come?"

He bowed his head. "I don't know."

I asked, "What did the emperor do then?"

"He—you should not hear such things."

"I am no longer a child."

Holding his head, perspiration obvious in rumpled locks of hair, Father's words came slow. "The first, a man. He said his name was Uriel. He was not a large man but stood very erect. His eyes were clear and focused. There was next a woman, a young woman. Her name was Chaya. I still can see her face, so pale it seemed. But it was not pale like one who is sick." He paused. "There was a pure quality that—words fail me."

"And a third person?"

"Last was a Greek by the name of Kyriakos. He was a very large, muscular man. But none of them needed to be restrained. They were calm ... as I have never seen."

Father stared at the hands in his lap, and I waited for him, listening to his intakes of breath. He said, "Caligula called for the executioner. He was certain the men would give in, if the woman were tortured first." His voice softened. "She was stretched across a stone bench, and a metal saw was carried to the center of her body."

"Oh, Father," I gasped.

"The emperor said, '*Woman, worshiper of this Jesus, a dead man, will you now swear by my* genius *before this audience? After all, I am alive, though you may not be for very long.*' Then he laughed, Prisca. He laughed."

I huddled tight against my father.

"She said it would deny her faith to do so. And the men—the sorrow for her pain was evident, but they did not cry out. They seemed to be looking at something in the distance, something beyond … oh, I don't know."

Father wrenched his face, his heartache manifest. His mouth had become so dry that speaking was difficult.

"She was—she was sawn in two," he said. "Gaius had the executioner stop at one point, crying out, '*Make her feel that she is dying!*'"

We leaned into one another, and it seemed we each craved whatever stability could be found by sharing the agony.

"The worst"—he covered his face with his hands— "the worst is that I did nothing to stop it."

"You cannot blame yourself."

"But I watched—I watched it all. And did nothing. My pen kept moving across parchment, listening, writing. I kept doing my job, faithful—faithful to that tyrant!" My father reached out, brushing my hair with his fingers. "I kept seeing your face. All I could think of was my daughter's face."

We sat there holding one another, mourning a young woman neither of us knew, a young woman named Chaya.

After a time, my voice broke the silence. "Father, what happened to the men?"

His body was used up; it seemed he had no breath to speak, and the words eked out. "Their faces remained set. Their only words were, '*Jesus. Lord Jesus.*' They displayed a mysterious peace." He shook his head, staring. "Perhaps I was the only one in the room who noticed."

"Did the emperor hurt them too?"

"The large Greek is to fight the beasts tomorrow morning. His legs were broken to bring him down to their level. The other man, Uriel, was flogged and imprisoned in a narrow cage like an animal. He will be executed in some brutal way after Caligula feels he has suffered enough."

The oil lamp was beginning to flicker, almost out of oil, and Father walked me to my room. He drew a blanket and tucked it round like days long past, and I wanted him to stay and tell me stories of Daniel surviving in a lion's den or Joshua bringing down the walls of Jericho with a blaring horn, to feel safe in his arms and wrapped in the legends of our people. But the young woman I was becoming knew his spirit was too brittle to entertain me.

"Do you think they are right? Has Messiah come to us?" I asked.

"I can tell you that these followers of Jesus truly believed. They said he was '*the Way.*'"

"The Way," I repeated.

His face was aglow in lamplight. "That is all I know." He stood then, disappearing into shadow, carrying himself off to bed.

When all was dark and murmurs of nighttime became large, I thought of Miriam and Hannah and the expectation of court next day.

"Adonai, please protect my friends." Turning into my pillow, giving myself up to tears, I begged, "Please ... keep them from going before the emperor."

Father's grief and the suffering of three strangers tore at me. But, oh, what models of faith!

"Jesus," a name that means "God saves." Did I truly believe that our Lord—*El Gibbor*, God of Strength—would

176

restore his people? Did I believe in the promise? I must remember to ask Miriam ... I choked back a hard knot in my throat. "Adonai, bring her back to me."

Closing my eyes and turning on my side, one clear thought pursued me, and I stared into the darkened recesses of my room. Jesus. From Nazareth. Has Messiah finally come? Recalling the innocent face of a little baby named Ira, I said to myself, "Be watchful."

ဆ �%

~*VI*~

The Lord is my shepherd, I shall not want.
He makes me lie down in green pastures;
He leads me beside still waters;
He restores my soul.
He leads me in right paths for His name's sake.
Even though I walk through the valley
Of the shadow of death,
I fear no evil; for You are with me;
Your rod and Your staff—they comfort me.

~Psalm 23:1-4

All day, I occupied myself: Cleaned, gardened, paced the floor. There were baskets and garments that needed mending, herbs to bundle, fruits to cut and dry. The sun was constant. I thought it would forever sail overhead. Would we never know? Would Father never come? Betna had returned, yet even his familiar presence was flustering. He was brooding and restless, just like me.

When at last footsteps drummed through the entry, I tossed my washcloth and ran. Betna was there before me. Father stood tall, looking at each of us in turn with tenderness.

"Abba?"

The sound that emanated from his chest astonished me. He was laughing, and his whole body moved with the sound. "They are to be freed!" he cried.

I stood staring. "Can it be?"

Father planted his hand on Betna's shoulder, gesturing with the other. "A tribune named Papinius reviewed the case. He glanced at our friends and then applied his seal to the documents. *'Because the debt is paid,'* he said, *'the prisoners shall be released.'* We receive them from the prison just after dawn."

"It seems too simple," I said. "Are you certain? Will they be all right?"

"There is no reason to doubt," he said. "The mood in the Senate today is unstable, at best. After yesterday"—he stopped, eyes downcast. "Those in judicial positions are maintaining a low profile today. Perhaps the lives of three innocents were given for a larger purpose than we know." He lifted his eyes to mine and reached for my hand. Betna's solemn expression told me he and Father had talked.

We drew ourselves into a tight circle, embracing, and my tensed muscles began to ease. But then there was something else in our presence, something good and right and true. Squeezing Father's hand, I leaned into him. "Today," I said, "I believe in miracles."

ℬ ℭ

Morning was yet to arrive when I woke to the sudden presence of my father, his face enlarged by lamplight, standing at my door.

"Would you like to come?" he asked.

In seconds, I was fumbling through my clothing chest for a tunic, stopping only because Father's chuckle resonated from across the room.

"I thought you might," he said. His tone became serious. "Do not come near the *carcer*. Stay with Betna in the forum. I'll show you where." At my nod, he continued, "Once Miriam and Hannah are freed, we'll walk toward Aedias' shop. You'll meet us there."

I fingered the fresh clothing in my hands. "Shall I bring them something to wear?"

He nodded. "A light cloak for each."

&) C&

Soon we stood in the forum, sun warming our shoulders. Gold-trimmed columns shimmered. It was early, but people were crowding. Considering our mission, the festivity was unfitting. We did have cause to rejoice, but my last encounter with Miriam and Hannah prescribed months of healing and care. My lungs felt bound. It was hard to let go of worry.

Near the center of the forum, a gladiatorial combat was being staged. Slaves, glistening with sweat, emptied teeming buckets of *harena*, the fawn-colored sand that kept blood from soiling a white marble floor. Seating had been erected around a temporary wooden perimeter. The deepest platform would soon accommodate the emperor's illustrious chair with ivory chairs flanking it for senior members of the senate.

There were two featured gladiators, and the city prefect summoned them to swear oaths before battle.

"Uri, vinciri, verberari, ferroque necari," they declared, meaning, "I will endure to be burned, to be bound, to be beaten, and to be killed by the sword." As each condemning word was pledged, I pondered what these men hoped from the contest. To be free? With one swift victory, a gladiator could gain the *rudis,* an inscribed

wooden sword, declaring freedom. To be rich? The most hardened gladiators chose to remain in slavery, attached to their fondness for gold coins. Money often came to the gladiator as well as his master.

Rome's spectators had a single goal, and that was to be entertained. It was life triumphant versus glorious death, Rome's paradigm for courage and honor. My thoughts turned to innocent Chaya, helpless victim of Gaius Caesar's perverse mind, and I shivered to think of cold metal pressed against her bare skin. Hers was true courage. But to die with peace as Father described? That was unrestrained faith, wasn't it?

One gladiator wore powerful armor and carried a sword; a dull bronze helmet capped his stout figure. His right leg was exposed except for a red silken scarf tied into a knot above the knee. I searched the audience for a woman who appeared to favor him with this token of good fortune, and a beaming face drew my interest. Though her skin was powdered, her wide-set eyes darkened with kohl, such artificial adornment could not conceal flawless complexion and luxurious lashes. She held the elbow of a well-built senator and so had no apparent favorite in the games. Who was this enchanting couple?

I pressed Father's arm, directing my regard toward them as they approached. He looked disgruntled.

"A senator," Father said.

"Yes, but who?"

"One called Poppaedius." Father's voice was low. His glance was averted toward the gladiators, who were being sponged with seawater prior to combat.

"And she?" His look made me embarrassed for asking. I knew his thoughts were elsewhere.

"She's an actress," Father said. "Her name, Quintilia."

"Such perfect skin," I said.

He grunted and quickened his pace.

The gladiator's opponent wore meager attire and had no scarf tied around his thigh. He wielded a woven net; a trident; and, tucked into a wide leather belt, a small dagger. His hair was long and gold-colored, his head unprotected. Only his heart had been shielded: A curved plate of metal embraced his left shoulder and, within its concave center, a gold medallion bore the likeness of Hercules.

I understood this competitor to be a *retiarius* or net-fighter, whose essential skill was to confine his adversary with the net and then attack with his small blade. I compared him to a spider capturing its prey. A net-fighter's foremost advantage was in swift movement and occasional sprints, forcing his armored challenger to tire. Today's match provided him the perfect opportunity, because the first gladiator was a pursuer, or *secutor*, whose bulky accoutrement weighed against him with every step.

A procession had formed at the lower end of the forum to launch a full week of Caligula's "spectacular" games. The emperor, in streaming colors of silk, stood in a painted chariot behind four pale horses. Even the breeze seemed to be his conspirator, elevating his cloak for dramatic effect.

Voices multiplied around us. A *nuntius* shouted into the swarm of onlookers, igniting their fervor. "Today's fight is just a taste of what's to come! Tomorrow's games shall be our luscious banquet! Gladiator combats! Chariot races! And something new to excite your palates!" He leaned into the crowd, hissing. "The emperor has brought panthers to Rome! His savage black cats will challenge our most talented *bestiarii!*"

The masses responded with shouts, clapping hands, and stomping feet.

My heart was thumping. Mesmerized by the colorful displays and rollicking mood, I was drawn into its wild contagion. It helped that Father had a plan. Just past the central forum, Betna and I parted from him, stepping away to the south, while Father continued on toward the *carcer*.

Extending my joy, Aquila appeared with Tamar, and I remembered that, according to Father, Hannah's attackers had been deployed abroad, assigned to military duties. Could it be that we were released from fear at last, Hannah and Miriam returning home, Aquila no longer to hide? Hopeful air plunged far into my lungs.

We strayed near the cart of a fruit vendor, purchasing slices of red apple and sipping cool water from a nearby fountain. Tamar was excited and lively. She mentioned more than twice, "What a special day this is!" Aquila, cautious elder brother, would then take her hand and hold it, after which Tamar would exhibit a period of calm. Betna remained reticent, sometimes looking toward the north end of the forum, but always watching the crowds around us.

We talked of the approaching cool season, noting already brisk mornings and a hollow clattering of ripe leaves. Our conversation was lighthearted. Undermining it, however, was a current of tension creating wetness at the back of my neck. Betna lifted his eyes to mine, and I turned to see Father trudging past the senate building with two women. Hannah was in the center, supported by the others.

"They are coming." A long-held breath released. "Shall we go?"

Aquila said, "We'll go to your home by another way. It will attract less attention." Perhaps he sensed my apprehension at his words. "We're just being careful," he said. He offered a hand, and I laid mine upon his.

At that moment, musicians began to play, and the imperial procession marched toward Rome's Capitol up the Sacred Road. At least a dozen men, each blowing into the double pipes of a *tibia*, produced a cheerful and airy sound, proclaiming the passage of Rome's supreme ruler. All heads turned toward a glittering vision of majesty that was heading our way.

Aquila looked pleased. "The parade will allow us to depart unnoticed." Tamar took his arm, and I watched them blend into throngs of jubilant citizens. Aquila stood tall, trim, and muscular, Tamar a more petite version of the same form, her earnest face tipped in admiration upon a beloved brother.

Betna raised an elbow for me, and we turned down the road. Our friends were approaching *Epulatus*. I wanted to run into Miriam's arms like a child, but the goal was to be discreet, and I patted my own thighs to keep them steady.

Today Hesperia was minding the shop, piling meat onto a scale for a waiting slave, a boy of perhaps sixteen years, his features and complexion suggestive of Carthage. A line of customers stood behind him. Hesperia's adopted girls were busy nearby, Balbina with a broom, Hortensia catching swept dirt in a metal scuttle. Hesperia wrapped the weight of meat with three layers of cloth, sprinkling each with salt and placing it into the boy's basket. Braids twice circled her head and draped her brow. I had seen this style somewhere—on a new coin minted by Gaius Caesar, and it was a coin bearing the image of his mother, Agrippina.

All thought of Hesperia faded as our loved ones neared. Miriam's face was so haggard that prominent bones were evident. Hannah's skin was colorless, her once-shining hair thin and broken. She was the one I reached first, pressing my face beside hers.

"How I've missed you," I said.

"And I you," she replied.

My arms went next around Miriam, and it seemed her fragile body might fold under the pressure. "You have come back to me," I said.

Miriam appraised me with tired eyes. "I begin to believe you are no longer a child." We hugged again. As I pulled away, concern filled her face, and her hands moved to my shoulders. "Did you receive the box, Priscilla?"

"Let's get you home," I said. "We can talk about your treasure later." I kissed her cheek.

"But you did receive it?" Miriam's brow creased with alarm.

I patted her hand, leading her toward home. "Yes, yes. Do not fear." My arm went around her waist for support. "Come now. There is water to cleanse, food to nourish."

185

Father and Betna almost carried frail Hannah, who strained for every breath at my side. Tears shone on her cheeks. Once home, our actions gained speed. Into my room Father and Betna had carried another couch. Both women would be resting there, and I would sleep outside their door, on the atrium's fringe. It was my task to gather water and cloths and assemble clean clothing. Betna warmed a nourishing soup that had been made.

Next, I gauged our friends' health and set about tending to their needs. Miriam was bathed in water infused with myrrh and fennel and then her papery skin rubbed with oil. She had no apparent injuries, but her body had wasted away.

Likewise, Hannah was bathed and oiled. She had countless bruises, and there was an inflammation on her right leg that was concerning.

"My friend," I said, "I'm not sure what to do. I am no physician."

"To be here is healing enough," Hannah said. "To be warm and clean"—her voice caught.

My eyes pinched with worry. "There was a man lecturing one day near the forum—a sophist, I think. He taught lessons from the Greek physician, Hippocrates. '*It is not possible,*' he said, '*for anyone to know medicine who does not know what man is and how he is made.*'" I leaned close. "Hannah, I do not know how a body is made."

"But you know the One who made me," Hannah said.

"But—"

"My life is in God's hands," Hannah said. "You are merely his servant."

186

Closing my eyes, I willed myself to remember Mother's ministrations. Brief glimpses of long-ago scenes passed through my mind. Chewing my lip and setting my jaw, I began with wine, cleaning the wound and then dressing it with a salve made from myrrh and pounded grapes. After boiling a handful of mullein leaves, fig leaves, and pomegranate leaves, I laid them across the salve, careful not to prevent air from reaching the wound. Once finished, Hannah lay very still. It was encouraging to see her in fresh, clean clothing and breathing evenly. My hands could not resist caressing the small mound of her belly, whispering to the child growing there.

"It will be all right," I said.

Betna brought soup to our door, and they ate well. Very little conversation took place; they were too weak. Preparing to leave, Miriam called to me, and I took her hand. Cool fingers closed around mine, her eyes fluttering with fatigue.

"The box," she said. "You have it?"

"Yes," I replied. "Don't worry. It is safe."

Miriam's brow clouded. "I've had many thoughts about it."

Kneeling beside her, my words came in clear, warm tones. "All is well. When you feel better, we'll preserve it in any way you wish."

Miriam tensed. "No. You—you must hide it. Now."

"But soon it will be restored to you, in your own home," I said. "It should be with you, now that you are safe."

"You misinterpret our release," Miriam said. "We shall never be freed from pursuit."

Panic crowded my lungs. "We'll keep you safe, even if it means we must leave Rome," I said. "Father won't let harm come to you."

Tears pooled in Miriam's eyes, and her words poured from a raspy throat. "There is evil that pursues us. Only by God's hand will we be secure."

Her body was weak and traumatized. After such an ordeal, it would be hard for her to see that things were improving. I patted her hand and turned away, but she stopped me.

"Hide it now. Please." Her eyes implored me. "You must hide it where it can be retrieved if"—she drew her face as if in pain. "It must be hidden outside of your home."

Looking at her in confusion, my heart quickened. Miriam was the wisest woman I knew. What was this rising fear?

"Trust me, child," she said. "Do not question."

Long years of knowledge had been nurtured in Miriam's devoted soul. It was an insight that physical infirmity could not suppress.

Taking her face into my hands, I kissed her forehead. "I promise," I said. "Tonight, once it is dark, I will hide it in a safe place. Please rest."

Miriam nodded, sinking into her pillow. The lines of her face relaxed. When I heard her breathing become steady, I left the room.

The contrast from one room to the next caused me to sway. Aquila, Father, and Betna had straight shoulders, heads held high. A table, abundant with food, had been carried into the atrium. There were gifts of seasoned cabbage and palm-sized cakes from Tamar, who was dressed in a yellow tunic, small jewels dangling from her ears.

It was a celebration, a formal announcement of my betrothal to Aquila. And though those attending were few and intimate, Father presided over us with ceremony and spirit, his demeanor one of complete reverence unto Adonai. Gone was his Roman-style tunic; he had donned traditional Hebrew attire. Though we knew well our traditions and what would be said, everyone was eager to hear what he had entitled a "pleasurable pronouncement."

Before the ceremony began, I whispered a brisk "please excuse me" and ran from the room. Sponging fresh water over my face and neck, brushing my hair, I then fitted myself into a tunic of pale blue. From low in my clothing chest came a simple, white, loose-woven scarf. It was Mother's. Smoothing it, I held its softness against my face, breathing its scent and closing my eyes ... remembering her.

With Mother's scarf crowning my head, I rejoined the celebration, Aquila's worried look transforming into one of approval. In the sunny atrium, our canopy was alive—brilliant white clouds floated across cerulean sky, birds spread wings in flight, God's crystalline heavens were shining; all this beauty was doubled, reflected by our shallow pool in the center of the room. Father positioned himself in the midst of this grand scene, his arms extended.

"To all of you," he said, "I am pleased to declare the intended marriage of my beloved daughter." This statement was met with a fierce clapping of hands.

Father continued. "Aquila, descendant of Benjamin, has formed a covenant with myself. The price—our traditional *mohar*—has been negotiated and paid by the groom on this very date."

Attention shifted toward Aquila, who straightened his posture, acknowledging Father's remarks with a firm nod. It was a beautiful tradition, I thought. As Isaac had sent valuables to attest the worth of Rebecca, I felt pride in my own person, content to be a woman of worth to Aquila.

Father said, "To my new son, I say this: Priscilla, child of Judah, my beloved daughter, is now set apart for you. And before God Almighty, I declare, with all faith and truth, she is a virgin bride, consecrated and pure before God and before these witnesses."

It was as if my body contained jiggling bells, all ringing at once. I bowed my head, filled with a sense of both humility and pride. The memory of Hannah's loss brushed my thoughts, but my father then uncovered a shining chalice of parchment-thin silver, and other memories, glad memories, yielded support.

"Beloved daughter," he said, "this chalice has been crafted for your special day, reminding us that the Lord crafted man from dust. May you be so refined by the wisdom and provision of your husband, and may he be refined by your encouragement and compassion."

Into the chalice, Father poured fermented wine, reciting these words: "As our God has deemed it necessary for man to have a helpmate and for woman to receive happiness through her husband, may God Himself unite you, that you may become no longer two separate beings, but one flesh, set apart and sanctified by God alone." He offered the chalice to Aquila.

Every small sound in the room was amplified: Aquila's full breaths, the muffled giggle of Tamar, Betna's "tsk-tsk," Father's long intake of air, and even a whispery rustling of plants in response to gentle breeze. Aquila stood strong yet serene; none of Rome's epic statues could compare. He stepped near and took my right hand, slipping a gold ring onto my raised forefinger.

"Behold," Aquila said, "You are consecrated unto me with this ring in accordance with the Law of Moses and Israel."

Father placed one hand beneath and one hand above ours, holding them secure. "May God prepare you for a marriage free from discord," he said. Old fears threatened, the thought of life without Father, and my body tensed, but the warm bond of our hands reminded that our connection would never be broken, only added to. Cheers and clapping erupted.

Our banquet was delicious, and we offered blessing unto Adonai for his generous provision. My only regret was that Miriam and Hannah were not well enough to join the festivities.

"The elation they sense within these walls will speed healing," Father said. He pulled me into the comfort of his arms. "Today, Daughter, we have reason for cheer."

It was the last occasion that Aquila and I would spend in each other's presence for many months, in accord with our people's tradition. My father asserted that it was a good custom. He tapped my nose and said it would give me "time to dream, time to gain patience."

Toward the close of our gathering, my betrothed called me aside, away from others' hearing, to share future plans and speak farewells. In hushed tones, we spoke of our love.

"You once told me I had eyes that danced," I said. And I know they must reflect a song that you gave to my heart."

Aquila examined me as if to memorize every mark and curve of my face. "And just as singing and dancing belong together, so do we."

"I feel it too," I said.

"It's like being part of God's incredible mystery," Aquila said. "Could it be that our Lord has led us to this place, to this solitary moment?" His words made me pause, because they echoed the comments of Ethan, when he said not to be surprised that God led me.

A warm smile was my answer. "My father believes God brought our family to Rome—even that our being here is a miracle. It is often hard to understand, though."

Aquila gazed into heavens now dark and glittering. "When there is a sky like this," he said, "I think of our ancestors who asked, '*What is man that God is mindful of him?*' Our Creator God is so powerful, Prisca. Do you think our little lives matter to him?" He lifted my hand and held it. "On days like this one, it is easier to think so."

Raising my eyes to the same view overhead, I imagined Aquila in open pasture, looking to the stars like a shepherd or a roving nomad. "This sense, that God has united us—"

"Yes, my love."

"—it makes me question what is going to happen, as if a road has been laid into deep-cut furrows. Could it be that something dreadful is coming?"

Aquila smoothed the crease in my brow. "The city is unsettled," he said, "and you have experienced hardship and sorrow. Maybe it's not something dreadful; rather, maybe it is just different."

"Miriam said curious things to me earlier, as if she were given a prophecy." Her small wooden chest came to mind. "It was so unexpected. Her fears made me wary."

"Miriam is a woman who walks with God," Aquila said.

"His faithful servant," I agreed.

"You are right to heed her." Aquila lowered his eyes. When he spoke again, his tone was grave. "It will be difficult for me to entrust your safety to anyone else," he said. "But your father is strong, and Miriam is wise."

I squared my shoulders. "You forget. I am also strong."

"Hmm." His eyes widened. "Much stronger than you are wise, I think."

"Proving my wisdom, to both you and my father, will be a prime ambition."

"Better simply to gain wisdom, and then you will not have to prove it." He chuckled.

"If you will love me more, I will become wisest of women."

His eyes traveled over my face. "Is it possible?" he asked. "Could you be more precious to me?"

"Aquila." My voice was unsteady.

He straightened with effort. "I will honor you and your father by holding to our tradition. It will be twelve long months of waiting." He breathed air far into his lungs. "But if our situation should change, become strained ..."

"We will look for God's direction in all things," I said. "I trust that more than ancient rules and traditions."

"Be careful, my bride," he said. "Those rules were first set in place by God."

"But God can change his rules, don't you think? Or—well, maybe not. But perhaps the rules will no longer be necessary?" My words were confusing, even to me.

He remained silent, considering my question.

In an effort to clarify for both of us, I broke the silence. "I've heard—some say Messiah has come."

"I have heard of a Jesus from Nazareth," Aquila said.

"Yes." My response was quick. "Do you think it is true?"

"The prophecies must be satisfied for it to be true," he said. "Messiah will fulfill the promises of God."

"I have wanted it to be true, for God to rescue his people. We have been waiting and trusting."

Aquila took my hands into both of his. "God is patient, and we must be like him. Messiah has been promised for long years, and I ask: Why would God choose this time? Our time?"

"It is a question we cannot answer," I replied. "And we may not even know until much later."

Aquila smiled. "And we need not rush to consider it, darling Priscilla."

"We have many months," I said.

Aquila pressed warm lips to the ring on my finger.

"I don't want this evening to end," I said.

"Nor I, but one purpose sustains me," he said. "I go to prepare a place for you, my wife; that where I am, there you may be also."

I closed my eyes, drinking in the scent of him—cloves and mint—soaking it into memory, noting how autumn's chill air covered my skin with little bumps. With difficulty we separated, and the celebration came to an end.

༄ ༅

After Aquila and Tamar had gone, Betna came to me in the kitchen where I was brewing fennel and grape seed into a healing tea.

"Hello, child," he said. Those words had been Betna's greeting since the day we first met. Here was a man who had helped me capture a butterfly, marveling at its loveliness, whose same capable hands had lifted loads of brick and could coax delicate images out of cold marble. Betna had become a second father to me.

I raised my head high in jest. "Well, I am not such a child now!" As soon as they were spoken, I wanted to yank the arrogant words back. Being a child to dear Betna meant joy and shelter.

His chest lifted with a robust "Ha!" He then leaned close and spoke soft. "You ask an old man about a song."

"Will you tell me?"

Betna cleared his throat. "These are words of Solomon, powerful king and wise man of God—his words, but in music."

I pretended to chastise him. "And I've been waiting and waiting to hear them."

"Each thing has a right time," he replied. "These are words for ones who marry." Waving a hand with flourish, he began a pleasant melody:

> *"Where has your lover gone, most beautiful of women? Which way did your lover turn, that we may look for him with you? 'My lover has gone down to his garden, to the beds of spices, to browse in the gardens and to gather lilies. I am my lover's and my lover is mine.'"*

Pressing my hands together, I lifted them to my face in warm appreciation. "I will always try to remember."

"The cup!" he said. His eyes sparked.

"What cup?"

From behind his back, he withdrew my silver betrothal cup. I took it from him and read the words, "*I am my lover's and my lover is mine*," etched into its shining surface.

"It is here," he pointed to the cup, "and always here." Betna pressed a fist against his chest.

He must have made the fine etchings himself. It was exquisite.

When Betna turned to leave, I touched his arm. "Father told me you came to Rome looking for someone, when I'd always thought you came here for work. Tell me, why did you leave Nubia?"

Betna smiled and took my hands in his. He patted them as he began to speak. "When I came to Rome ..." He lowered his head and sighed. "It will soon be forty years."

"A long time," I said.

"But I even remember the flowers in my Ketek's hair. They are big flowers." Betna held out a palm, fingers spread. "My mother calls them *karkadè*. These are yellow, but the center is red and is for cooking."

"Ketek?" I liked the clear, crisp sound of her name. "Tell me about her. Please."

We moved to the table with cups of tea, a scent of fennel steaming the air. Betna sat opposite, his fingers drawing circles on our tabletop. "It is long that I speak of Ketek. I was young ... and beautiful." He pressed a finger to full lips, his body vibrating with silent laughter.

I began to giggle, and he shifted his head into a striking pose.

"Where was Ketek when you last saw her?" I asked.

Delight narrowed his eyes. "Ha! She is scrubbing clothes on rocks at the river. Ketek looks up when I call. The flowers ... she wears them for me." Slowly, the smile left his face. "And next, warriors come, soldiers of Rome. I run for my bow, but there are many men wearing chest plates of metal. And my pouch has seven arrows."

His disappointment was tangible. I pictured him staring at his handful of arrows, knowing it could never be enough.

His words came faster. "My people run to sand, to trees, to water." He moaned. "But my Ketek, they take her. A slave."

"No," I said.

"They tie Ketek's hands. She is crying. I try to help, but I am hit"—Betna laid a hand on the crown of his head—"and it is two days until I wake. And then I go, following big footsteps." He paused, his voice expanding. "My people walk with the smallest marks upon sand."

I clutched his fingers, holding them tight. "Where did they take her?"

"I follow them to a city that has the name of Alexander, he who was king of Macedon."

"Alexandria."

"The River Nile flows near this city." He sipped tea, breathing in its warm scent, and then continued. "There is a tower of fire guiding ships from sea to the land." He looked at me with a face of surprise. "Under this tall light, I see the ships and learn that they will go to Rome. One boat seeks workers, and here is a man who will work!" He slapped his broad chest and grinned. "Even now, I see God marks a path."

"And so you went on that ship as a worker?"

"Ah, yes. I follow Roman tracks over the sand, over the sea. I go to find my Ketek." His eyes became moist. "And then I am given more. On this boat, I learn who is the great *I Am*."

"How could that be?" I asked. "On a ship?"

"A man is on this ship, a teacher of Greek words. He was in Alexandria making holy writings into Greek and now goes to Rome. He does not know my speaking, but my hands talk to him, and then the words come." Betna appeared reflective, and then he laughed. "He is a man with big patience. Ha!"

"He taught you about Almighty God? And he couldn't speak your language?"

Betna sighed. "This is a man who likes words, but even more, he loves the One God. It is many days to cross the huge Roman lake. Adonai gives us time."

I refilled our cups of tea, letting Betna's story fill my mind. What if we could help him find Ketek? After all these years, was she alive?

"What about your family?" I asked. "Did they know what happened to you?"

Betna stared into his stout cup of tea, wrapping long, brown fingers around it. "My mother, my small brother—I did not say good-bye. I was so certain—I knew that Ketek would be found, and we would go home." He closed his eyes.

How many years had I known this honorable, sensitive man? Never to have asked him of his loved ones? I was ashamed.

"But Betna, you never found Ketek? She was not in Rome?"

He looked overhead, into empty space. "I looked. Every day I looked. But Ketek is never there."

"But did she know you followed, that you came looking for her?"

"Ah, yes," he replied. "Ketek knows. She knows I will follow." He paused, drank some tea, and appeared to savor it.

"But you stayed here, in Rome," I said.

Betna looked straight into my eyes. "One day," he said, "Ketek can be found ... always I believe this. And then I find a friend. To this friend I owe my life." There was no need to ask. The "friend" was my father.

Betna's sigh filled the room. "Ah, when I come to Rome, they are good days. Augustus Caesar is building a golden city, a shining city. He wants men to work. My body is strong. I work. And I watch for Ketek ..."

"Did you meet Father then?"

"Priscus? Ha!" Betna leaned toward me, raising an eyebrow. "He is young and pretty. Girls always look at him."

"They did?"

"So I ask him, does he see a girl like Ketek. Your father, he shakes his head and I am going—but he stops me. He asks why. No one before asks why. No one cares but only my friend."

"Betna, I remember when Father carried you in, your legs broken," I said, "but I was too young to understand. What had happened that day?"

He replied, "Because I am a free man, not slave, I am hated in Rome. These men wanted the bricks to fall. They want for me to die."

"It's hard to believe someone could do that ... and to you, Betna," I said.

"There are others who like to hurt people. Your father protects you from this."

"He's beginning to teach me," I said. "I suppose growing up means realizing hard truths."

Betna brightened. "But there is also good," he said. "Adonai wants me to know him. And then also he wants me to know you."

I thought back to my earliest days, all the years of knowing Betna, and realized how rich he had made every one of them. Yes, Nubia had sent a bit of its gold to us … in the form of Betna.

He, as well, was pondering old thoughts. "At night, I dream," he said. "Some dreams are Nubia. Some dreams are my mother." He offered a sad smile. "And always there is Ketek."

"Maybe one day you'll find her."

He began to hum his sweet song and strolled from the room. Though Betna had gone, my body swayed to his tune. *Where has your lover gone?* And I answered: "He has gone to prepare a place for me." My breath held. "For me."

ꟸ ꟹ

The day had been a long one, and we all began to extinguish flickering lamps, craving soft cushions and long-elusive rest. As promised to Miriam, though, I first paid a visit to Father's *tablinum,* locating the wooden box she had entrusted. It was there, positioned among favorite books and sentimental possessions. I had imagined a way to hide it while in the kitchen boiling tea: My garden. It was outside and somewhat obscure. Most important, the box would be simple to retrieve. Every measure of tilled soil had, at one time, touched my hands.

Scooping up my little parcel, I carried it into the kitchen and bound it with cloth, sliding it into a leather pouch. Outside, assuring that no one was in sight, I made a hole in black earth, digging so that Miriam's treasure box would reside beneath any level of sown seed and—a last-minute thought—transplanted a mound of rosemary atop it as disguise. Rosemary signified memory, and I would never forget.

Once the box was hidden, I stopped to look skyward. *"What is man that God is mindful of him?"* Aquila's words sang out to me. It had been a day of miracles. For all the grief of past weeks, we had survived.

I picked up my shovel to go in, but a man leapt over the wall, grabbing my throat in one hand and twisting my left arm with his other. I squealed in pain. He tightened the grip on my neck and brought his face close, spitting his words. "You the one who took that baby?"

I shook my head, fighting to breathe. "What?"

"Behind that wall." He motioned with his head toward the alley, where a discarded newborn, thundering steps, and putrid breath had come together in the midst of a powerful storm.

Lies forced their way from a pinched throat. "I—I don't know what you mean."

He yanked my arm. "Sure you do," he said. "You'll be taken before a noble man, and he'll get truth from you." He rubbed his bristled face against mine, and rotting filth poured from his lips. "Maybe I'll get to help him."

He began to drag me toward the blackened alley, and I realized the shovel was still in my hand. Slamming it against his knee, his hands loosed, and my body collapsed. When his injured knee gave way, he fell hard against my legs.

"Please let me go." My throat ached with each word. "I only enjoyed the stars tonight."

He clamped my arms with firm hands. "You'll be enjoying more than that before I'm through," he said.

"No!" I pushed at him, kicking to get free, and then heard a striking sound. The man fell across me, unconscious.

"Prisca." It was Father's voice, insistent but low. "Priscilla," he said, emotion cracking his voice. "Are you all right?"

"Yes." My voice was hoarse.

"Quick. Go inside." He pulled me to my feet, and I burst through the garden door into the house. Betna was there, face bent with concern. My bruised legs weakened, and he bore me to a chair.

The ministrations applied earlier to Miriam and Hannah were now used for myself, bathing my face in a mixture of myrrh and fennel, inhaling its scent through damp cloth, washing away every odor, every memory of the stranger in my garden. Areas around my neck were reddened, and I pressed cool cloth to the swelling. After Father returned, nervousness began to fade.

"Where have you been?" I asked.

"That is something you will never know," he said.

I made no reply, and he lingered over me, staring and rubbing his jaw. He paced the room a few times before pulling a chair to sit across from me, hands on my shoulders.

"What were you doing outside?" he asked. "You could have been killed." He gripped my shoulders, pressing me away just enough to examine my face. "Prisca, we just talked about this. What were you thinking?"

"I—I was burying the box," I said.

"Burying the—what?"

"The box that—the special box that Miriam gave me." I lifted tremulous hands to cover my face. "She asked me to hide it. I was cautious, looked all around and saw no one. It was dark ..."

"No amount of caution can protect you. Not anymore." He held a lamp to my face. "Let me look at you." He checked for broken bones.

Behind us, Betna was heating wine, his quiet presence adding comfort.

"I came when I heard you cry out," Father said. "What did he do to you?" He looked at me in desperation.

"His hand was around my throat. And my—my legs. When I hit him with the shovel, he fell across them. Those are my only injuries."

"In truth, Daughter?"

"Yes." I shivered.

Father held the lamp to my neck and ran his fingers over bruises that were starting there. "Keep your cloth on this. Let no one see until it is healed."

"Yes, Abba."

"Do you understand me?" His voice quaked with tension, and he held me apart from him, forcing his words to be well-defined and effective. "Someone may come looking, may be expecting to see a woman with injuries."

Tears flooded my eyes.

He lifted my legs at the knees, his touch tender, careful. "Can you walk?"

Nodding in response, I bowed my head. Father pulled me close. "Do not be afraid, Kisbah. I will be frightened for all of us." He looked at Betna.

"Our world is different," I said. "What must we do?"

"What I have seen these past weeks tells me we must look to God. Our only help will come from him," Father replied.

"But today was good. It was better," I said. Only now did I see thin specks of blood on his garment, and my stomach began to twist. "And then this happens and— sometimes I want to give up."

"We cannot give up. God prods us onward, to impart blessing unto others, just as he has blessed us." Father's words were tinged with bitterness. "Wickedness pervades the city and even beyond, to the ends of Rome's world."

Betna's voice joined ours. "But there is good, Priscus. God is larger than this evil." He patted Father's back. "Maybe evil wants to make us blind."

"Do you mean blind to God's goodness?" I asked.

Betna set cups of warm wine before us. "It is a mystery, child," he said. "But never is God blind. He sees. He always can see. And so there is hope." Embracing Father's shoulder with his hand, he left us.

Wine trickled down my throat, stinging at first, and then flooding my limbs with warmth. "Today Betna told me about Ketek," I said.

The tense lines of father's face slackened. "Betna is a better man than you know."

"Oh, I know Betna is good. And so is my father."

He shook his head. "You were small; you don't remember those days. I left you, for a time, you know. When your mother died, part of me went away with her."

"But you were always here."

"In body, yes. It was Betna who reminded me I had a daughter."

I rested my head on his shoulder. "Maybe Betna is right, that evil only rises to keep us from seeing our God. But you told me, Father, about those blessings we have, that we need to remember them and be faithful to our Lord. I'm trying to remember."

He replied, "I believe a time is coming when we shall learn how faithful our people can be."

For a time, we were still and snug, with only the sound of our simmering hearth. And then Father pulled away, looking at me with brows raised. "So you hit him with your shovel, did you?"

I nodded, and tears streamed down my face.

Father patted my back. "That's my brave girl," he said.

He carried me into the atrium where my bed was blanketed, kissed my forehead, and plodded to his room. Sleep soon overtook me, and I awakened only occasionally to a lamp's glow beyond Father's door.

ℛ ℭ

~ *VII* ~

This is what the Lord says—
He who made a way through the sea,
A path through the mighty waters,
Who drew out the chariots and horses,
The army and reinforcements together,
And they lay there, never to rise again,
Extinguished, snuffed out like a wick:

'Forget the former things;
Do not dwell on the past.
See, I am doing a new thing!
Now it springs up; do you not perceive it?
I am making a way in the desert
And streams in the wasteland.'

~Isaiah 43:16-19

Weeks passed. We were the happy recipients of various tiny triumphs: Standing from bed without aid, fingers grasping a cup without shaking, a sudden remembrance of cheery birdsong, and the warm repose of sun on oiled skin. Miriam and I looked with tenderness on Hannah and her coming child. Though Hannah's leg did not show signs of complete healing, it did improve. Betna carved a beautiful cane for her from olive wood, and she was returned to mobility. Father directed us not to leave the house, but we never bemoaned confinement; the three of us toddled around the atrium pool again and again, singing and laughing as we went. Even sore hearts began to mend.

Dedicated to increasing wisdom as promised to Aquila, I flung never-ending questions at Miriam: Who made the best wife? Was it beautiful Sarah, who waited patiently for a child, bearing Isaac as an old woman? Or could it be Leah, the unloved bride and mother of many, finally earning Jacob's love and respect through faith and devotion?

"Both are fitting examples," Miriam said. "Patience. Endurance. Noble blessings unto God."

"How does one become patient?"

"You must be made to wait," she said, "and not be consumed with the waiting." She laid a pale, cool hand over my own. "Endurance is the more difficult; it is learned through suffering."

Suffering! Recent afflictions had defeated us all, and tending to my friends' recovery occupied both mind and body.

Every evening, one of Father's many books came to my blanketed couch, where an oil lamp was poised to illuminate the aged writings. The poet, Horace, wrote of *"pale death, which knocks with equal hand at poor men's hovels and the towers of kings."* Such words were torture! Instead, I turned to Vergilius and found my burdened heart lifted by poems of countryside and harvest. At times I would wake, book pressed tight to my chest, lamp's flame nearly gone, with no memory of what words had been read at all.

One morning Betna came to us, arms extended around a bundle of scrolls that he said the Greek teacher had given him, apologetic that not all had survived from those years past. Our fingers traced precise, inscribed words, realizing we were reading Holy Scriptures that had been translated into Greek. What an inspiring find! Miriam, Hannah, and I pored over them at all hours of the day, reciting and memorizing passages within. In one scroll, we found the book of Ruth, and I lingered over the words, *"The Lord make your wife who goes into your house as Rachel and as Leah, who both together built the house of Israel."* I wanted many children, just like Leah.

Miriam became haunted and unmoving as we began reading from Isaiah. *"He shall be led as a lamb to the slaughter."* She looked overhead, following a slow pace of clouds in bright sky. "Is this a prophecy about Messiah?" she asked.

Miriam's question narrowed my attention to the verse. "As a lamb to the slaughter? A sacrifice?" I asked.

"Moses foretold that he shall be without blemish," Miriam said. "In truth, I've not read these words so closely … until now."

"Without blemish," I repeated.

Hannah asked, "Like our lambs and goats that are brought into the Temple?"

Miriam said, "As with Abraham, I believe that *Yahweh* shall provide a lamb … a lamb that will rescue our souls."

A lamb to rescue human souls? So many men walked the earth. How could we know who was Messiah? I trusted Miriam's faithful leading, but without blemish? *"El Shaddai,* increase my faith," I begged.

During these weeks, my promise to Ethan and Lormah was kept, and food made its way into a basket near our garden wall. Thick shrubs kept those humble gatherings from view, and following mornings would find my basket in the same place, though empty. It was reassuring to imagine the children's delight, giddy over tasty fruits or honeyed cakes. Added contentment lived in the invisible bond shared with Lormah, both of us united in our desperate compassion for children. At times, something in the basket was intended for her: Woolen thread, a carved wooden comb, olive oil infused with herbs; I never knew if she kept them.

Time was kind. Cooler days arrived, sprinkled with peeks at sunshine and temporary warmth. On one afternoon of dappled light, Miriam climbed to the upper balcony, Hannah in tow. While they sat above, Alon tapped on our door just below them. A man of broad shoulders and skillful hands, Alon was not as tall as Aquila. His hair was dark and thick with waves; a short beard rounded out an oval-shaped face. He had high cheekbones; thick, arching brows; and a broad mouth that frequently flared white; features that rendered him a man of almost perpetual mirth. I liked him.

We exchanged greetings, and I waved him into the room. Betna brought Alon a cup of light wine.

"I have been told your friend—that Hannah is here." Alon inspected the room.

To my positive response, his expression softened. "Your husband came to me, he explained what happened. I trust him. I believe him."

Hearing Aquila called my "husband" made me feel light-headed. It was still hard to think of him as such. Many days had passed since our betrothal, and I only saw him in private thoughts.

Alon continued, voice growing. "Aquila neglected nothing. I know all." He paused and quieted. "The reason I came is to tell—to tell Hannah I want us to be married."

My breath caught.

"Is she well enough to see me?" he asked.

"Alon, she has been through harsh treatment and— well, if you will be patient, please. Wait just a moment, and I'll talk to her. We will see."

He brightened. "I will wait."

Nodding to him, I went to Hannah and Miriam, finding them huddled together on the wooden stairs. Their eyes told me they heard what Alon had said.

Hannah spoke in a whisper. "Prisca, don't let him see me like this." Her hands went quick to the roundness of her womb.

"But he said Aquila told him everything. He knows. He wants you still!"

She looked at Miriam. "But I'm not well enough to face him. Not now."

"Can I tell him to come another day? At least that?"

She shook her head and turned toward Miriam as if attempting to read the older woman's thoughts. "I don't know."

Miriam asked, "What if Prisca were to tell Alon you needed more time to recover? Let him know that you will send word in one week's time."

Hannah was silent. She was chewing her bottom lip and looking at me.

I squeezed her hand. "You agree?"

"Yes. All right," she said.

I wanted to run, skip, and squeal with delight but, instead, censured myself all the way back to Alon. "Be calm. Be calm."

He was perched on the edge of his chair, toe tapping. When I asked if we could send for him in a week, his eyes increased in size.

"Yes," he said. "One week." He was so excited he spilled little drops of wine all over himself.

How perfect for Hannah was this trustworthy man. He adored her. He was a man of skill and would provide well for them. He was honest and caring.

"One week," he said. "I will be here." And then he was gone.

৪৩ ০৪

On Sabbath, we attended our holy assembly, and Miriam was well enough to make the short journey.

A man came to speak on that day. Through the veil that divides the women from the men, his face was gauzy and unclear, but when his voice was raised, my face flushed and a hand went fast to my lips.

Miriam whispered in my ear. "Are you all right?"

I nodded assurance, but my heart was hammering. It was Ethan from the children's harbor. How could I explain this man, knowing him?

Ethan began, "'*Sing to the Lord; praise the Lord! For he has delivered the life of the needy from the hands of evildoers.*' These words come to us by the prophet Jeremiah."

He paused, bowed his head, and then continued. "Greetings, friends. My name is Ethan, and I was born a son of Abraham and raised near the northern shore of Galilee's freshwater sea. Today I introduce you to a man who met me there, on a hill by the sea."

His tone was warm and welcoming; it transported me, as if we stood together on Galilee's shore.

Ethan said, "It was some years ago. I was a boy who dreamed of men's adventures, nearly fourteen. The sun was golden, the land was green, and a gentle wind rippled the water that day. My mother had sent me for bread from the mill, and I recall thinking it was a child's errand and wanting to do much bigger things.

"Walking home with five barley loaves wrapped and secure in my basket, the smell of fish and seawater was enticing. It seemed a good thing to bring fish for our supper. And, of course, I listened to myself."

Amusement sprang from among Ethan's listeners.

He said, "There was a spot where springs tumbled into a warm pool and fish were quick to catch. It is one you may know and is called *Ein Sheva*, 'a place of seven springs.'"

"Place of seven springs." Did Miriam know of it?

Ethan said, "*Ein Sheva*, to me, was paradise; it was a rich, well-nourished pool. Abundant warm springs attracted many fish. Two nice ones were soon caught and added to my basket, and I hurried home, certain of pleasing Mother with the prize.

"It was then, while clambering over a spill of rocks that led across River Jordan, that a calm voice was heard and people were seen amassed on the hillside. I was drawn to join them, to heed this man clothed in rough wool, his arms extended in gesture and welcome.

213

"People sat, some in clusters, some separate, but all were intent, hearkening to his words. Among them were those with bodies broken or diseased, and I watched as he healed them. A man whose legs were gnarled and useless stood at once and walked. A woman brought her small boy who was limp with fever, and at the man's touch, this child woke refreshed and well.

"Settling myself against a rock, I considered what was happening—too astounded to understand—and then jumped from rock to rock, always watching, always moving closer to this stranger who makes men new."

Ethan paused and smiled. "And now let me tell you of my part in this story," he said. "One of the man's disciples walked among us, asking if we had food for those who were gathered." Ethan laughed. "On that hill were more persons than I could number! And remember what I had, a couple of fish and five circles of bread. When I told the man, he shook his head and walked away.

"But, my friends, this same disciple came again to me. His face was flushed, enlivened, as if he had just received good news, and he said, 'My name is Andrew. Come. Follow me to Jesus!'"

Whispers surged. I tried in vain to see Father, to note his reaction, knowing we had heard this name and the claim that he was our Messiah. Ethan raised a calming hand, and our assembly quieted.

He continued. "And so I followed Andrew," Ethan said. "He was not a tall man, but his arms and shoulders were sturdy, and he told me he was a fisherman. His robe was soiled and ragged at the hem, and his feet were red and calloused in sandals nearly worn through. I remember

214

being surprised that this man, eager as his steps were, would be careful to avoid trampling wildflowers as he climbed the hill.

"Sitting among the people, there were some I knew. We walked by Joel, the son of a stonemason, two years my senior; we had fished together. And there was the woman with the crimson birthmark—it covered half her face. Every dawn and every sundown, she could be seen nested against the walls of our city gate, a knotted empty bag near her feet.

"Their stares burned into me. The bread in my pack was bought with Mother's money, and my stomach churned with guilt. But I went to Jesus with what I had. And to my amazement, with every step closer to Jesus, the heavier my basket became, until it seemed too much to hold. At last, standing before him, Jesus laid a hand on my head, saying my name—a name shared with no one—and I could see that he had known me all my life."

Ethan's hearers were voiceless. He lifted an imaginary basket to the assembly and told us, "I handed him my fish and bread. He blessed the food, thanking God the Father, provider of every need, and asking that we would be filled. And then Jesus said, '*It will be enough.*'"

Ethan again paused, emotion coloring his face. "Beloved," he said, "I bear witness that, yes, it was enough. More than five thousand men were fed that day, and the women and children weren't even counted. There were so many crumbs left from our meal that baskets had to be passed to collect them."

So this was Ethan's riddle ... a miracle. He paused until murmurings stifled and then straightened, turning clear, wide eyes upon a waiting crowd.

He said, "I'm here today to share my encounter with Jesus of Nazareth and invite you, like me, to follow him, to seek the truth. I know him to be our promised Messiah."

Rumblings escalated, and Ethan raised a hand, a silent request for patience. He said, "I know that Messiah may not have come in the manner you expected, but if you search the prophecies, you will find they are fulfilled, accomplished in the manner of Almighty God. Who but God alone has filled the needy with bread? Our fathers ate manna in the desert; as it is written, '*He gave them bread from heaven to eat.*' My friends, Jesus has said, '*I am the bread of life. He who comes to me shall never hunger, and he who believes in me shall never thirst.*'"

A man shouted, "This Jesus died on a Roman cross! Like a slave! He is dead." The man groaned. "*Yahweh* does not die."

Ethan was undaunted. "True, he faced death on a cross. You see, my friends, he died for us."

The man growled. "For us? You don't know what you say!"

Ethan's tone magnified like resounding thunder. "I do know that, at his death, the veil of the Temple was torn in two; the ground quaked; rocks were split; graves were opened, and many bodies of saints who had fallen asleep raised and appeared. I was in Jerusalem. I was there. I saw these things and bear witness to them."

Ethan declared: "Jesus is the Son of God. I testify to you that Jesus has risen. He died, yet he lives and is now seated at the right hand of God."

Some of those attending our assembly were disturbed. More than one person shouted.

"Blasphemer!"

"You are not telling the truth!"

Ethan was a weight of granite that could not be budged. He said, "I believe that Jesus died on a cross and rose again after three days. And I believe, because of Jesus, my sin is forgiven. If you so believe and speak such words of faith unto God, you shall have everlasting life." He stepped away from the platform and departed in silence.

Miriam said nothing. We met Father and Betna and returned home.

ജ ൗ

Sabbath meal was readied, candles lit, Sabbath prayer spoken. There was a curious peace over us. It reminded of when we had snow in the city—a not-so-common event—its crystalline softness rendering hush to our world.

Father spoke first. "Miriam, have you heard of the man named Jesus?"

Her eyes were downcast. "Only in my dreams."

"You have dreamed of him?" I asked. "Do you mean you actually saw his face?"

"No. Not his face. His presence was white, glowing, and his name was repeated over and over. '*Yeshua, Yeshua, Yeshua.*'" She spoke this last in the Hebrew.

217

Hannah had not been with us, and so we took turns relating Ethan's story. It was interesting to watch the changing expressions on her face as each scene was described.

My father said, "I have heard from others that Jesus was born in a cattle stall in a little town called Bethlehem. Messiah was not depicted in such a way. He is to be a king."

Miriam said, "But he is to come from Bethlehem, the City of David."

I said, "If Ethan's words are true, Jesus is now a king and seated at the right hand of God."

"It seems impossible," Hannah said.

Betna, usually so quiet, cleared his throat to speak. "God is wise," he said. "And it is a wise thing to send a Savior to live among us." His voice softened. "This is how God can feel our weakness."

None of us spoke. I stared at our broken loaf of bread and thought of the Jesus we were learning about, his body battered and slain. According to Ethan, Jesus had said, "*I am the bread of life.*" Bread, such a simple thing. Our basest need.

&) C3

Ever since the attack in my garden, I remained inside after sunset. Generally, provisions for the children's harbor were secreted away in daylight, while working the soil. My garden was looking its best, tilled and ready for warm weather to return—even Helah would be impressed. There had been no more journeys under cover of night, but my involvement in the rescue of children presented danger to the family, and I had made up my mind to tell Father about the children's harbor. In fact, something drove me to tell him. He needed to know.

One day, he arrived home from the senate earlier than normal. Apparently a flock of vultures had flown over the curia's roof, not a good omen for senate discussions. I asked him if we might sit in the *tablinum* and talk.

He was seated across from me, smelling of incense and wood that was burned at various Roman altars throughout the city. How could I explain? What would he say?

"I—I don't know quite where to start," I said.

"I am your father," he said. "Just talk."

Inhaling a long breath, I began to speak, omitting no detail from the hearing of that first baby's cry. I described every perilous expedition into gloomy alleyway, my encounters with Lormah and meeting Ethan, about the man who came searching for baby Ira, and my tour of the children's harbor where babies were given a chance at life. My voice rose and fell, as did my enthusiasm, watching his face, hoping for approval or at least understanding.

"And so, Abba, it's understandable that you would be angry," I said, "but just knowing that children suffer, it was a cause that—well, I had to do something."

Buzzing with spent emotion, I waited for his reaction. When he stood and walked away, fear pierced my stomach. Was he so angry? But he was searching for something in a chest against the wall. He returned with a baby blanket in an outstretched hand. It was made using fine woolen yarns, and someone had crafted it with care, weaving a circular pattern at every edge, adjusting the loom and inserting yarns of brightly dyed colors into soft white.

"This," he said, "was your mother's."

Rubbing the warp, I held it to my face, breathing through it. "It's lovely ... and unlike any I've seen."

"Yes." He reached across, his fingers touching the blanket as well as my chin that had rested on its soft surface. "It's a Roman blanket, Prisca."

"I don't understand."

"Your story"—he walked over and embraced me— "your heart for the helpless seems very natural to me." He knelt before me. "You see, your mother was an exposed child, left in a rubbish-filled alley."

"But I—"

He pressed a finger to his lips and continued. "I was just a boy then. And, like you, I could not bear the sound of a child, deserted and crying, knowing no one would come." Father shook his head and expelled an amused breath. "Miriam ... I was always bringing her things, pebbles I'd found, stray dogs, broken toys to fix." He chuckled. "One night, I brought her a baby."

My mother of Roman blood? Awareness flooded my soul, like morning light warming dew-clothed fields. I was tempted to say, "Aha! Life makes more sense."

"Your mother was raised in Miriam's household as her own. She was taught all things that—well, that you were taught at Miriam's knee, and she grew into a kind and gracious woman. And I loved her. From that first day, peeling back the blanket from her angelic face, I loved her."

Laying a hand upon his, I sighed. "And so you do understand, even more than ..."

His throat appeared choked with emotion. "Yes."

I could see he was grieving Mama all over again. "Abba, I—I'd like to think about Mama for a while."

"Every time I see you I think of her." His eyes were wet.

I folded my mother's blanket, hugged it, and pressed it into his hand. Kissing the crown of his head, I left the room.

ℬ ℭ

Alon came again to see Hannah. We made careful preparation before his arrival, arranging her on a couch surrounded by pillows. She was very uneasy that he should see the enormity of her condition. As he was ushered in to Hannah, now healing, now showing the rose-pink anticipation of motherhood, it was difficult to contain my pleasure. Alon was seated. Sincere admiration widened his face.

Hannah was silent. She had requested my presence, but I sat apart to lend privacy, clumsily stabbing my fingers with an unsteady needle in an effort to occupy myself.

Alon said, "I have longed to see you, little mud flower." He laughed, and I remembered how they first met. Picturing Hannah plastered with mud, I began to giggle as well.

Hannah coughed. "Alon, I am sorry—"

He interrupted. "No!" He tightened his lips as if afraid of upsetting Hannah, and then his features relaxed, became tender. "It is I who am sorry. At first, I—I listened to others and not to my heart. But now I know the truth. I should have been watching over, protecting you."

Hannah began to cry, soft at first. Long-unshed tears then began to flow, and the sound shook my soul. I knew that her utmost pain was from shame, and the depth of it ripped my heart as she sobbed in my arms.

Alon was overcome, sliding down to the floor, kneeling before her. "Hannah," he said, "my feet cannot find their way, my mouth has lost all voice. Please consent to be my wife."

"Not this way. I am ruined."

"My life is ruined, if you say 'no,'" he replied.

"But don't you see?" Hannah's voice wavered, betraying emotion. "Because of my—my attack, I am with child."

"Aquila has told me all." He took her hand. "The child shall be raised as my own."

She did not answer. Misting rain floated on shards of gray light into our shallow pool, kissing flowers along its edge. Love was tangible. What grace I felt to be in its presence!

Hannah began to stir. She wiped her eyes and gazed into the expectant face of Alon.

"I will stand by our betrothal," she said, "if you will forgive ..."

"There is nothing to forgive." He clasped her hands between his. "I believe that our love remains in purity between us, by the power of Almighty God."

Slipping from the room, I pressed my back against kitchen wall. They talked of forgiveness. God Almighty had the power to forgive, but how many sacrifices did it take? Ethan had said one sacrifice was made, and we needed nothing more than to believe, but it seemed incredible. The man Ethan spoke of was far away from our troubles ... and now gone.

Alon could be heard saying those beautiful words of tradition and love and marriage. "I go to prepare a place for you, that where I go you may be also." He brought her hand to his lips and left.

My friend was quiet and reflective when I rejoined her. "Oh, Hannah, there has never been such love! He will be good to you," I said.

"It's hard for me to accept." Hannah lowered her eyes. "Prisca, I have often thought we are a reflection of who we think God is. Most of my life, God has been a powerful commander, overseeing and disciplining us as need arises. I have marched carefully and have always followed the law. Even when my soul ached, when my mind told me another way was more righteous—even then, I held firm to the law. Until one horrible day, and my God did not save me from ruin." A tear slid down her cheek.

"Does the Holy One punish us for the sins of others? I will not believe it," I said.

"When Alon came here weeks ago, it made me think. If he still wants me—I no longer care about laws, Prisca. *Yahweh* did not protect me. I must do what is best for my child, although I fear it is unfair to Alon."

"Unfair? Alon is rejoicing!"

"He deserves better," Hannah said.

"There are none who are perfect, Hannah. Only our Lord. There must be a purpose for what happened. We may not understand it, but ..."

"A purpose!" Hannah said. "I am weak. That is what I know."

My voice rose with passion. "What are the lessons Miriam has taught us? Who are the people that Adonai used? Rahab! A prostitute!" I caught Hannah's shoulders and turned her to me. "You have done no wrong. And if our majestic and holy Lord can use people such as Rahab of Jericho—oh, my friend, he will surely use you."

Hannah sighed. "Prisca, I am judged as unworthy."

"I cannot believe that Adonai holds such things against you," I said. "Together we will study, and we will prove ourselves worthy of his love."

ʘ ʘ

Some days, while dipping my toes into our shallow pool, worries intensified. I saw my father laboring over ink and parchment, recording whatever ridiculous new laws had been manufactured by Caligula and condoned by a terrified senate. He would be silent, ears attuned, fingers swift, pressing hypocrisy into some cavity within, never betraying those he loved.

Though Father was quiet about many things, rumor succeeds in its way, and news of the emperor's exploits found willing ears.

Valeria, after the death of Tertius, had remained inside her *insula* most days and seldom spoke in passing. One afternoon, she called to me with a cheerful "*Salve!*" and leaned into my garden's enclosure. Beside her was a very young slave girl named Charis.

"You've been to market?" I asked.

She set a basket to her side. "It was busy there today," she said. "We've purchased a cabbage, olives, some beans."

I greeted young Charis in Greek, giving her a smooth white stone found in the garden. She rubbed it between both hands, marveling at its shine.

Valeria said, "Finally, my husband has found a fixed project. The emperor is building something grand. It will keep Crispus busy!"

"What kind of project?"

Valeria was pleased to tell. "He's enlarging the palace. In time, it will be touching the forum."

I pressed against my side of the wall, tightening the distance between us. "But the palace is already so large." In fact, his residence had become a city unto itself! "Why does the emperor need more space?"

She laughed. "You must know! The shrine of Castor and Pollux will soon become his opulent entryway. Crispus tells me that the emperor talks of Castor and Pollux as if they're his children. The twin sons of Jupiter!"

"As if the emperor were Jupiter himself?" I asked.

"Mmm." She paused and looked over her shoulder. Charis was smelling flowers several feet from us. "I trust you, Prisca, so I can tell you. The country is different—simpler. Being here in Rome, seeing what the emperor does, it seems peculiar to me."

I wanted to reply that this new construction project made perfect sense. The Temple of Castor and Pollux housed Rome's treasury, and Caligula would be closer to his money.

Valeria leaned over the wall, speaking in hushed tones. "Another thing—and maybe you've seen it, Prisca—the golden statue of Gaius Caesar in the forum. Crispus says it wears the same clothing as the emperor each day! In the country, such things never happened ... at least from what I knew. Country people worked the land or raised animals for food; there was little time for dressing our statues."

Valeria moved her fingers over the wall's roughened surface. "Well, I must get home." She appeared thoughtful, even a little melancholy. "And I want you to know. I'm better," she said. "It doesn't hurt as much." She forced a smile.

I understood. The sharpness of her pain had dulled, but Tertius would always be missed.

"I'm glad you stopped to talk," I said.

Valeria rested her hand on the wall between us and nodded. Gathering her basket, she ascended the stairs.

Later, within the sturdy walls of our *domus*, we talked of the emperor's bizarre behavior, and Father commented on the state of things at the senate house.

"I haven't wanted to worry you," he said. Setting his wine cup aside, he leaned against clasped hands and then began to speak. "Short weeks ago, the emperor developed a disliking for one of the senators and decided that the man should be killed. At Caligula's instigation, the man was attacked as he entered the curia, senators using their own pens to stab him. He, a fellow senator, was torn into pieces and piled at the emperor's feet."

"Could there be some cure for this—this strange behavior?" I asked. "What can be done?"

Father replied, "You're talking about someone who forces fathers to watch their own sons be put to death, who takes other men's wives as he pleases and then tosses them into the street as if they were rubbish." He stood and curled his hands into fists. "I know of no answer. The emperor believes himself to be a god. Demands are made; any who will not comply are punished."

"And the senators," Hannah said. "How could they—they murdered one of their own colleagues?"

"They act out of fear," Father said. "Their purpose is to please the emperor, if it takes even the blood of friends or family."

Miriam's face was solemn. "Evil has been set loose. We must all be vigilant." Ever since leaving Rome's jail, Miriam had become pensive, and her statements were often delivered in the nature of prophecy or warning. It distressed me, making me look over my shoulder.

"But what should we watch for?" I asked.

"We must watch ourselves," Father said. "Be careful of your actions; be cautious of your trust."

Hannah looked depleted. Her time was drawing near, and the child lay heavy, summoning all her might. "But it's impossible to hide ourselves from the entire world," she said.

I asked, "If we harm no one, what can he do to us?"

My father groaned. "That is the most difficult thing. The emperor does not choose his victims based upon morality or virtue. People suffer and die based on his own foolish whims. He cleans the *carcer* by sending prisoners at random to the arena!"

Hannah bent over, a muffled cry escaping her lips. I went to her.

"I am sorry," Father said. "Too much time is spent in the company of those who are deceitful, the very ones who demand my respect. It has been my intent to protect you from them, and I have failed so utterly. Forgive me."

"Do not apologize," Miriam said. "You are an excellent man, Priscus, but you cannot do everything."

Hannah lifted her head. "She's right. We've been living a lie, trying to believe we're safe. What future do any of us have?"

"Don't speak that way, Hannah," I said. Aquila was preparing a home for us, and it was a future that kept me striving, believing that better days would come.

"The eyes of the Lord are on the ways of man," Betna said.

"Betna is right," Miriam said. "We must rest our hope on the Holy One, the incomparable *I Am*. I have been thinking that we need to know more about this Jesus."

"His very name is a promise," I said. "'*The Lord saves.*'"

Hannah said, "But *El Shaddai* has commanded that we have no other gods before him!"

"It is true," Miriam said. "But if Jesus is God's Son—I have been recalling the prophecies. We have been promised a Savior, one who would '*take up our infirmities and carry our diseases.*' If the man spoke truth to us at assembly, then a promise has been fulfilled." She embraced Hannah's hand. "Let us consider. The promises of God are meant for our good."

"Prisca knows this man who spoke at assembly," Father said. All eyes turned toward me. "Shall we send for him, ask to hear more about the one called Jesus?" Heads were nodding on all sides.

"Betna," Father said, "I have come to rely on you as a man of wisdom. Have you some word of caution or encouragement?"

Betna replied, "You say I am wise, but I say two things: I learn the words of Solomon, and I learn from many faults."

"But what do you believe we should we do?" I asked.

He straightened in his seat, eyes closed, chin in hand. I would always remember Betna in this way, applying wisdom and experience to every discussion.

He said, "Solomon tells us to look for wisdom like it is silver. Search for wisdom like you search for treasure that is hiding. And this is how to find knowledge of God." He paused. "How do we know, if we will not look?"

&) (3

~ VIII ~

*"But from there you will seek the Lord your God,
and you will find Him if you seek Him with all your heart
and with all your soul. When you are in distress, and all
these things come upon you in the latter days, when you
turn to the Lord your God and obey His voice (for the
Lord your God is a merciful God), He will not forsake
you nor destroy you, nor forget the covenant of your
fathers which He swore to them."*

~Deuteronomy 4:29-31

Betna's words inspired me. "Look for wisdom," he
had said, "like you search for treasure that is hiding," and I
thought of the carved box with its precious scroll buried
under rich, moist soil in my garden. My soul hungered for
knowledge of God as never before.

My morning basket from Lormah held a square of
rough wool. Upon the fabric's woven surface were six even
stitches of gray thread. It had been prearranged between us:
A piece of cloth containing a straight row of three stitches
was a request for meeting. If the recipient added three more
stitches to make a line of six, it meant circumstances were
good to meet. In contrast, if there was a single vertical
stitch sewn below the first row, it was unsafe. I smiled,
thinking of Lormah and her neat handwork. It was a rare
kinship we shared, and her coming was anticipated with
every breath.

Wrapped in nighttime's cloak and curled into a tight corner between garden wall and *domus*, I was not afraid. This time, Father was posted in a hiding place of his own, watching. There was a nervousness, however, that shook my limbs, and it involved the security of old traditions and powerful convictions. Generation after generation, our people had watched for Messiah. Myriad stars pulsed overhead, each one conceived by a loving creator, reminding that our God was one of order, and he had given explicit commands for us to obey. How could we be certain that Jesus had come to fulfill prophecy and not to blaspheme the Holy God that I loved?

At that moment, Lormah slipped beside me like a whisper. We had only a sliver of moon to see by, and I pressed her arm, wanting assurance that she was real and alive. Her quick intake of breath spoke pain.

"Have I hurt you?" I asked.

"It is nothing," she replied. "Today, my master reminds he owns me."

"He struck you?" It was difficult to keep my voice low.

"It is nothing," Lormah repeated.

"You are wrong. You do not value yourself," I said.

She took some time before answering. "Every day I wake up believing Gallus Urbanus will be new. I tell myself, '*No hitting me today.*' Most days, it is true."

There was a tremendous knot in my throat. "Stay with me. I will protect you."

Lormah sighed. "And so I would go from one prison to another. You are my friend, but you do not see."

"Your safety is important to me," I said.

"You cannot protect all people," Lormah said. "You are not God."

What life did Lormah have? Was there even a room or bed for her own?

She said, "The Lord has placed me where I am. He leads me. I have freedom to do his work. He gives me strength to bear what pain comes with it."

I responded through grinding teeth. "I cannot leave you in that place."

"Then I pray God to build you up. He will lead me to a better place ... in his time." Lormah laid a hand on my shoulder. "And why do you ask me to come?"

"We—my family—would like to talk with Ethan. He came to assembly and told us of Jesus and fishes and loaves. Will he come?" I asked. "Will he tell us more?"

"He lives for this task," Lormah replied. "It is certain."

"But when? How?"

"When sun falls is best. I will give a sign on that day."

"But how will I know?" I asked.

"You will know," she replied.

And then Lormah was gone.

ಬ ೞ

In three days, I discovered a tied piece of wool enfolding a single pomegranate seed. Gripping it, I whispered, "Tonight!"

Before dusk, seating was prepared in the atrium, and I had baked a fruit-filled cake. Ethan's arrival was met with solemn greetings. Father began the discussion.

He said to Ethan, "We should make clear, it is our first desire to worship the one God, the God of Abraham."

"My desire agrees with yours, Priscus," Ethan said, "for I believe that Jesus, the Christ, was sent to us from God Himself."

"How can you know that?" Hannah asked.

Ethan looked like someone starting a race. He said, "Jesus fulfills the prophecies."

Miriam cleared her throat. "Young man," she said, "before you speak of prophecy, tell us how this Jesus came to be. We hear he came from Nazareth, but what of his family?"

Ethan nodded. "You are right ... and wise. I should start there." He looked upward, the palms of his hands open. "Oh, merciful Father, by the power of Your Holy Spirit, speak truth through me, I pray."

Bumps appeared on my arms. Lormah had told me of the Holy Spirit—the Holy Spirit revealed something to her? It was as if she and Ethan actually understood or heard direct from—no, it could not be. Yet they were two people who had said such things, people that I trusted.

Ethan began. "It was about forty years ago, and our people had been suffering under the harsh hand of the first Herod, King of Judea, for more than thirty years. At that chosen time, our merciful God sent an angel to a woman named Mary in Nazareth, one who had not yet known a man but was betrothed to Joseph of the house of David. The angel Gabriel came to her declaring a marvelous promise: The Holy Spirit would cause a son to be conceived in her womb, a child who would be Son of the

Most High God and would reign over the house of Jacob forever."

"But why this Mary?" I asked. "Why was she chosen by God?" My eyes strayed to the lovely form of Hannah, full with child, and I was overcome with compassion. How would Mary have explained her pregnancy to family? To Joseph?

"Only Adonai knows why Mary was chosen," Ethan replied, "though I have been told she is humble, a woman with immense faith. Why are any of us chosen by God?" He looked into our faces, his eyes sparked with cheer. "Perhaps a day will come when you may meet the mother of Jesus. She yet lives."

Hannah whispered, "Chosen ... by God."

"You have spoken to this woman?" Miriam asked.

"Sadly, I have not." Ethan's face clouded. "Though I saw her once."

I shook my head at him. "What makes you believe such a story? If she did not tell you herself, then how—"

Father was nodding. "Yes. What witness was there to such an event?"

"What witness." Ethan inhaled and gazed into glittering sky framed by the opening above our heads. "A star shone over Bethlehem," he said. "It was where Mary and Joseph had gone to be counted at the command of Emperor Augustus."

Father looked doubtful. "I have seen many stars."

"But this was such a star!" Ethan replied. "It shone upon a lowly shelter where they had come to rest, where a manger became the bed for newborn Jesus. God's bright star was so resplendent that magi followed it from far in the East."

Hannah said, "Our Messiah? In a manger? But our Savior is meant to rule as King." As her words met the air, a sense of calm swept over me, and I contemplated another humble lodging, one where baby Ira slept in a tumble of fishing nets.

Ethan replied, "These are questions that many times I've pondered, and it has come to my mind that we live in a world filled with men of power. Is it not more wonderful, more astounding, that all people would be saved through one whose life began so lowly?"

Our room fell silent until Ethan spoke again.

"In the hills near Bethlehem there were shepherds tending sheep." He waved a hand overhead. "Across the indigo sky came a chorus of angels declaring in song, *'Glory to God in the Highest!'* One aged shepherd still tells it. He now speaks only in song, but his eyes flash bright when he recounts the angels' message: *'Born this day in the city of David is a Savior who is Christ the Lord.'*"

"So you say he is the Savior? The Christ? The One promised to us?" I asked.

"Mashiach." Ethan said the name in Hebrew and with reverence. "The Anointed One from God. The prophet Isaiah predicted his coming in such a way, saying, *'The virgin shall conceive and bear a Son, and shall call his name Emmanuel.'* Jesus is called by this title. It means *'God is with us.'*"

"How can it be?" Hannah asked.

Ethan's eyes were soft and resting on Hannah. "It was Adonai's merciful plan. Jesus did not come to condemn the world, beloved. He came to save it."

"'*A little child shall lead them,*'" Miriam said.

Betna sat up in his seat. "Ethan of Galilee," he said, "how is it you believe Jesus is Messiah? Tell us this."

He said, "Few persons ask about my coming to faith." Ethan tugged at his beard and leaned back. I remember Jesus with hands always open, always giving. People were freed of demons—a startling sight. No one was beyond his sight and care. All of these moved me, my friends. They move me still. But when he spoke, when he touched me, there was complete peace and bold awareness that he had always known me. How was I convinced he was Messiah? In his presence, I just knew."

"Complete peace," Hannah said. Her eyes were moist.

Father said, "We live in a world devoid of peace."

"And the peace Jesus brings is for each of us," Ethan said. "He came as an outpouring of the endless love and mercy of God. He came for you."

My breath was slow to come. In older days, angels had visited earth, carrying messages from our Lord. They say Moses' face shone with the glory of our Lord's living presence. But how many generations had gone since any one of our people had experienced something miraculous? It was incredible to think that *Yahweh's* own Son had come to earth and that he could know me.

Ethan said, "Moses told us that God would raise up a prophet from among us. I once heard Jesus say, '*If you believed Moses, you would believe me; for he wrote of me.'"*

Hannah was leaning forward, silent but clearly interested.

I asked, "Why would Adonai send his own son to live in this world?"

"It is a marvelous mystery," Ethan said, "but I believe God wanted to provide a better way for us to reach him. Jesus, being fully human and fully God, understands our temptations and, by his life, demonstrates our Father's unlimited mercy."

"Fully human? Fully God? But that is blasphemy!" Father said. "You speak of worshiping Son and Father, and we shall have no other gods before *El Shaddai!*"

Ethan bowed his head and pressed a finger to his lips. He said, "John, an apostle of Jesus, explained it to me this way: '*Jesus is the Word. He was with God from the very beginning, and all things were made through him as the Father spoke them into being.*'" Ethan paused and then said, "And the Father's Word again has come forth—this time, clothed in the helpless form of a human child." Ethan looked into Father's eyes. "And so the Word became flesh and lived here with us. Jesus, the Word, is at once a part and still the very fullness of God."

"I understand the power of words," my father said. He then shook his head. "But there is much to consider, Ethan. Much is at stake."

Miriam was tiring. "Tell us how this man died," she said. Hannah drew a *palla* across Miriam's thin shoulders.

Ethan replied, "Priests became critical of Jesus. When crowds followed and believed, they were overcome with anger. When he performed healing on Sabbath, they were outraged and began arranging his death. They wanted to be rid of one they considered a troublemaker."

Father said, "Priests and rulers do not like opposition, it is true. But what response did Jesus give for healing someone on Sabbath?"

Ethan raised his brows. "Jesus spoke of the healing before it took place, asking them, *'What man is there among you who has one sheep, and if it falls into a pit on Sabbath, will not lay hold of it and lift it out?'* He then said, *'Of how much more value is a man than a sheep?'*"

Betna repeated, "Of how much more value is a man."

Ethan said, "He told them it was lawful to do good on Sabbath."

"And so they sought to kill him," Miriam said.

Ethan nodded. "The chief priest turned Jesus over to Roman authorities, and the governor, Pontius Pilate, had him flogged. I think Pilate merely wished to appease the rabble."

"But flogging wasn't enough?" I asked.

"They wanted more than blood," Ethan said. "They wanted his life. And Pilate sentenced Jesus to crucifixion. *'King of the Jews,'* Rome's soldiers called him. They twisted thorns into a crown and pressed it onto his head."

Hannah sighed. "King of the Jews," she repeated.

Ethan said, "I saw him then. The one who had accepted my petty meal of fish and bread, his body now dripping in blood, having been shredded by Roman whips."

Miriam whispered, *"'By his stripes we are healed.'"* Her eyes were intent upon Ethan.

238

"Did no one help him?" Hannah asked.

"Even his closest followers hid themselves, afraid," Ethan replied. "Jesus' disciples told me he had prophesied his own death, though they had not understood. He had said to them, '*Greater love has no man than this, that he lay down his life for his friends.*'" Ethan paused. "They told me this with tears."

Miriam lifted her head. "Nailed to a tree," she said.

The room fell silent once more.

In a soft voice, Ethan continued. "It was there, on that hill near Jerusalem, that I saw Mary, his mother. I heard Jesus speak to her while hanging from the cross. The apostle named John was at her side, and Jesus said, '*Woman, behold your son!*' To John he said, '*Behold your mother!*' Even in the midst of torture, he was a comfort to others."

"I have never heard of such compassion," Hannah said.

"He told us he came to serve," Ethan said, "and he served us with his life and breath."

Father was grim. "But this man has died, Ethan. How can he be of service to anyone now?"

"That is the glorious gift!" Ethan was revitalized, eyes bright. "Jesus was without sin. Hell could not hold him. He is alive again!"

"He's alive?" I asked.

"If that is true, if he was without sin, why did he even have to die?" Hannah asked.

Ethan smiled at her and inclined his head. "But you see, he died for us," he said. "On his body he carried the sin of the world. Our continual offerings of goats and lambs could never be enough. Almighty God has provided the sacrifice: His own Son, Jesus, the spotless Lamb of God."

Betna held his chin, eyes intense. "How can you know he lives? Did you see this?"

Ethan replied, "I did not, friend. But I believe the testimony that came to me. Mary of Magdala went to the grave. She saw the stone cast aside. Jesus himself appeared and told her, '*Say to the disciples, I am ascending to my Father and your Father and to my God and your God.*'"

"And did others see him?" Betna asked.

"Jesus later appeared to the disciples, and then to many others." Ethan's voice was fervent. "As expressed to the congregation, I witnessed many other acts that confirm his victory. He died, yet he lives."

Days later, those words still rang in my ears: "He died, yet he lives."

Ethan told us that the last command of Jesus was to go forth and make disciples, to teach others what he had taught them. It was why Ethan had come to Rome, guided by the Holy Spirit, ministering to children.

As I lay upon my bed, speaking blessings to God, I prayed, "Adonai, please plant truth in my heart." A vision played over and over in my mind's sight, a picture of Jesus ascending, fading like mist into sun and saying, "Lo, I am with you always, even to the end of the age."

⋈ ⋈

Though these thoughts followed me, the coming days were busy and demanding. Hannah's time was close, and preparations were under way for her and the child. We had woven blankets and made clothes for her baby. My prediction was that she would have a girl! Miriam cautioned me to be practical, and I did not allow my embroidery needle to create unnecessary swirls or floral designs. There were also duties to be done for my wedding and for Hannah's. It was decided that she and Alon would marry early in summer, before what we called "the sweating season." Aquila and I had to wait some months after that for our marriage ceremony—our *nisu'in*.

It was exciting to make the cloth that would adorn our new homes. We needed blankets, new clothing (for married women), and sacred cloths for feast days. Miriam impressed us as we sat day after next at the loom. Her aged fingers were nimble as a young woman's upon the shuttle. My impatience was evident in uneven warp, but Miriam never complained as we opened the yarns and began again and again.

After our feast of Purim and annual reading of Esther, the Romans celebrated *Kalends*. Theirs was a festival of rekindling fires to the Goddess Vesta, and it included a celebration for their god named Mars. Our neighborhood was rowdy with merriment, dancers frolicking down the street and rattling up the stairs, visiting one home after another for elaborate banqueting.

Mars was Rome's god of war, so also during this time soldiers were assigned to military campaigns. Father remarked that men of authority crowded the forum; soldiers wearing dark-red tunics and leather skirts, sons of senators looking important in their manly *togae*, and senators themselves were present and eager to fill the rosters of Rome's legions.

241

Our household was restless. Arrangements had been made for a midwife to attend Hannah—all was readied—but outside noise continued into late hours. She was not resting.

Even before all dancing to Mars had ceased, another celebration began! *Equirria* was yet another festival to honor Mars but with chariot racing. Thankfully, it drew the hordes away from our neighborhood and into *Campus Martius*—the Field of Mars—where two-horse chariots pounded across grass-stubbled parade grounds. Father, in consensus with Rome's senatorial retinue, rose at dawn to perform an ancillary duty, keeping a record of the day's oratory. He remarked that Seneca was speaking. Lucius Annaeus Seneca was a talented orator (even though his look was one of chronic pain), and I was interested to hear Father's comments upon returning. Very soon, however, the poet was banished from all thought, for it was on this occasion that Hannah's pains began.

Betna was sharpening tools near an outer stairway, and I ran to him. "Quick! It's Hannah's time! We need the midwife!"

He laid aside an adze and patted my hand. "Yes, little mother. I will go."

It seemed we were forever waiting, and when Betna returned, it was without the expected midwife. The leathery-skinned, spindly woman before me was a stranger.

"I don't understand. Where is Ora?" I asked.

"I am Michal," she said. "Where's the woman with pains?"

Betna's unhappy eyes searched mine. "Ora is gone," he said.

"But we don't know you," I said.

Michal's hands were grimy, her fingernails long for a midwife. An unkempt child of about ten years old was hiding behind her threadbare cloak. I ached to see Ora's strong arms and cheerful face.

"Be glad I'm here," Michal said. "Word of the woman's uncleanness has reached many ears."

"She is not as you say. And you shall not touch Hannah until you have washed." I ground my teeth, unable to say more.

Michal's response was lost when Miriam called out. Swallowing anger, I ran inside. Racham, the pitiful waif who had come at Michal's side, followed without a word.

Hannah's room glowed with lanterns. As the Holy One had blessed Job in days of long ago, guiding him through bleak and desperate days, so would Hannah's baby pass from darkness into blessed light. Her labors were rhythmic, steady. She was positioned on a firm bed until birth became imminent, when we would move her to a special chair. Miriam had cushioned the birth chair, and we had tied soft rings of cloth for Hannah to cling to.

When her pain faded, Hannah turned to me, flushed and smiling. "Worry is written on your face," she said. "Better wash it off."

"Is it that obvious?"

She answered me with a smile.

"Women have borne children since the beginning," Miriam said.

Hannah labored into the ninth hour of day, and the room became stuffy. We were all showing signs of heat and fatigue. Michal appeared to know the duties of midwife, and she cared for Hannah with precision, if not affection. Miriam sang or recited psalms of praise with unexpected vitality. Dashing back and forth with fresh supplies, I kept Betna apprised. More than once, the day's chariot races came to mind—not wishing to be there, but I felt like a racehorse!

Little Racham soon became attached like a stitch to my tunic. She carried more than her own slight weight, toting pots of water and armloads of cloths. During the long hours, there came a visible change in her. Within our hopeful environment, her frightened countenance had been exchanged for one of helpfulness.

Between pains, Hannah squeezed my fingers. "You must promise me," she said, "if anything does go wrong, that you ..."

"Ah! Do not say this!" I clapped hands to my ears.

Hannah clasped the sides of the bed and pinched her face. The swelling of her body tightened to a peak.

"It will be soon," Michal said.

I ran fingers over Hannah's abdomen, feeling the tension, thrilled about the new life inside. Miriam stroked her hair, speaking psalms. "*Behold, children are a heritage from the Lord, the fruit of the womb is a reward.*"

A cry left Hannah's lips, and Miriam spoke with more intensity. "*I will lift up my eyes to the hills; from whence comes my help? My help comes from the Lord, who made heaven and earth.*"

Michal spat her words. "Breathe, woman."

My stomach tightened in sympathy. "Soon, my friend. Soon."

Rapid as the pain came, it faded. Hannah's body began to release. Her skin was moist with perspiration.

Michal nodded to me. "Move her now."

I helped Hannah to the edge of the bed, and with my friend's roundness hanging between us, Michal and I shifted her into the birthing chair, bringing an immediate pain and another wail from Hannah.

Michal raised a limp rag and wagged it my direction. "I need more," she said.

Laying a hand to Hannah's swollen belly, Michal commanded her, "When the pain comes, you push."

Hannah didn't respond. Her body was already arching again, her abdomen taut.

"Push!" Michal said.

Hannah's head mirrored the pressure she exerted, bowing toward her chest, tight and red.

"Push!" Michal repeated.

A head with streaks of dark hair was emerging. My pulse quickened.

Hannah groaned.

"I see the baby!" I said.

"Push!" Michal said.

"Blessed are you, Lord our God, Ruler of the world," Miriam whispered.

In one swift movement, the child was in Michal's hands. A boy. I was not sorry to be wrong. He was perfect in form and cried with a loud voice.

"Perhaps he will be a singer," I said. A few giggles parted my lips, lifting Hannah's newborn babe and cradling him against my body.

Miriam was praying, and Hannah held an arm outstretched for her child.

I washed him in a mixture of olive oil, salt and warm water and then rinsed his pinked skin with fresh, clear water. It appeared he had Hannah's beautiful eyes, but they were puffed with newness, how could one be sure? After smoothing oil over his flailing body, I wrapped him tight and carried him to his mother.

Hannah kissed her son's face. She examined his hands, his feet, checking his completeness, and then swept his silken hair with her cheek.

"And you, my son, shall be Menahem," Hannah said. "For you brought me comfort even before your birth … and a will to live." She kissed him again and pressed him against her breast. He fed eagerly, and Hannah relaxed against the cushions, closing her eyes.

"Menahem," I repeated. "Comfort" would not have been my word. Regarding Hannah with her son, though, I could see it was right.

Next, Michal made an odd movement, stepping away from the birthing chair.

"What are you doing?" I asked.

"This woman's sins have condemned her," Michal said.

"Don't say that," I replied. Moving closer, I saw red—everything was red—with my friend's blood.

"Miriam!" I cried. My heart throbbed. "Michal, you must help her."

The midwife looked at me with disgust. "I was good to save the fatherless child. I will do no more." She walked away. Racham's eyes were haunting, afraid once again; a small, pale fist pressed against her mouth.

Hannah's low moan signaled me to action. She was shivering.

I shouted at Michal. "At least help me move her to the bed."

Michal nodded her stony face. We eased Hannah onto the bed, and Miriam raised her legs with several cushions.

There was then a gripping fear that came over me, and my body could not move. Miriam spoke louder, directing me in clear tones. "Prisca, listen to me. I will gather blankets. You must pack cloths into her. Do you hear? Put pressure where you can—firm pressure. Try to stop the flow."

Grabbing cloths, one after another, I applied pressure, summoning whatever strength my muscles held. Each cloth came away soaked. Fear was mounting.

Hannah whispered, "Take care of my boy."

"No! Hannah! You will live," I cried. Again and again, I said those words, pushing against the bleeding, begging it to stop. "You will live, Hannah. Live."

Hannah began panting for air, her limbs quivering. Miriam laid her own body across Hannah's for warmth.

My tower of folded cloths had vanished. Tears tumbled down my face. "Hannah, it will not stop. The blood will not stop."

Noticing the hollow sound of my words, I surveyed the room. Lamps had burned low. Michal and Racham were gone. Miriam was cradling Hannah's beloved face. There was only Menahem's cry to be heard. A finger's width of sunlight passed through an opening in the curtained doorway, and it was unwelcome. Light did not belong.

Miriam turned to me. "The baby, Prisca. He needs to be fed."

I hugged Hannah, unwilling to let her go.

Miriam's face was wet with tears. "She is with God."

I moaned.

Miriam rested a hand on my back. "You could not have heard, her voice was so small, but she said to tell you, from the prophet Isaiah, '*He has sent me to heal the brokenhearted.*'" Miriam strained to say more, her throat choking and tears falling anew. "She said, '*Tell Prisca I believe.*'"

The wriggling life beside Hannah cried louder. Miriam, woman of wisdom, the one I always turned to for counsel, begged me with tired eyes. "Priscilla, you must help him."

Food. He needed food. Where might one find a wet nurse, one we could trust? My throat cramped to think we might settle for someone like Michal. Dearest Adonai, please help.

Bundling the boy into my arms, I kissed Hannah and ran. Bursting from the garden door, my legs rushed into the alley. Darkness was descending. Holding Menahem tight, he cried against my pulsing neck, his wails loud and shrill. Every shadowed balcony held probing eyes. Peaked temples seemed to shriek, and billowing smoke from temple altars stung my nose. There were blurred faces; some turned away, some stared at me with pressed lips.

Be brave like Lormah, I urged. My feet carried me toward the Tiber, stopping for no one.

A narrow wooden door set into brick wall soon stood before me. The door was stained from hands grasping its latch. Stairs inside were familiar, lifting me higher, closer to that place of provision—the only one I knew—for Hannah's infant boy.

Several individuals stirred at my sudden arrival, and I remembered—Oh, yes. Lormah said they slept by day.

Ethan's expression confused me. He walked forward, brow furrowed, mouth parted. It occurred to me that my entrance was alarming, clothing stained with blood, holding a screaming infant.

He spoke in a whisper. "Prisca, what have you done?"

"He needs food," I said.

"Friend, have you brought the wolves to our very door?" Ethan asked.

"Hannah has—" I couldn't say the words. "This is her child. There is no one to feed him."

Ethan raised his hand, and a woman emerged from the shadows, face obscured by a veil. She took Menahem, her voice soothing.

A sound emanated from behind. Ethan, startled, looked past me, and I turned to see Betna, sparkling with sweat, feet planted apart, surveying the room.

My own voice sounded slight. "I'll come back for him," I said, and began to leave.

"That is all?" Ethan asked.

"What do you mean?"

"Do you not see? Do you not know?" He raised his hands in the air. "Why must these children sleep in the day? Why must we all be silent? Cautious?" He walked away, pressing his forehead into an open palm. "In one evening, my friend, you've consigned us all to death or arrest—perhaps torture ..."

My shoulders dropped. "Ethan, I don't—don't know what to say. I—I could only think of the child."

His voice was strained. "One child may affect the lives of many."

"I'm sorry," I said.

Ethan looked heavenward, a hand pressed to his lips. "We must move quickly. But where?"

"It is time to load a ship," Betna said. He stepped closer.

"Load a ship?" Ethan asked.

"Ships are full of containers, and containers hold valuable things." Betna gave a slow nod of his head.

Ethan inhaled, his brows rose. "All right. I see what you're saying. But what ship? There are many arrangements to be made for what you suggest."

"I know about ships. And I have a friend."

Their words then became jumbled in my mind, their faces seen as if through shifting clouds. Betna's large hand took hold of mine, Ethan tossed a cloak over my bloodstained clothing, and we left the children's harbor, a place never to be seen again.

Brokenness hampered our journey home, but Betna was a ready crutch. At our door—cold death awaiting—sorrow hit like a fist, folding me at its threshold.

Even glowing oil lamps could not overcome the chill within our walls. Someone had cleaned the room where Hannah died. I touched the bed. Just hours before, we had laughed together in that very place.

In the next room, the *taharah* was already under way; Hannah's body was being purified for burial. Whispered prayers floated from within, the doorway's curtain fluttering as women's deft movements stirred the air around Hannah. Anger stung my throat. Where were these women when we needed help? Why did they wait until Hannah was dead?

Miriam dozed fitfully on a couch in the atrium, and Father met me with a cup of wine. My limbs collapsed as though they were tied with bronze weights. The wine, coupled with a strenuous day, made me drowsy. Still, it was turbulent sleep, filled with aching and tears.

ꝏ ꝏ

Hannah's funeral was remembered in abrupt scenes: The grim-faced few assembled at our door, Alon's hunched frame straggling behind the small procession, our family's listless walk behind Hannah's coffin, tearing at our clothing—tearing my own so harshly that Miriam had to press a hand over mine—budded branches swaying under cold sky. Like my clothing, life was forever torn by Hannah's passing. It would never be the same.

At the end of our procession, Betna recited, "'*A woman of valor who can find? For her price is far above rubies.*'"

Father, his voice weakened and halting, delivered a psalm. "'*The Lord is your keeper; the Lord is your shade at your right hand. The sun shall not strike you by day, nor the moon by night.'* Rest," he said. "Rest, dear Hannah."

There was little that comforted me in that time. In dutiful blessings unto Adonai, I begged for answers. Why take Hannah? Why not me? Burst into flames from your infinite skies and explain why this happened!

Each day was viewed through a continual haze. Chores were completed with forced effort. At night, curled into a tight ball, my chest was bound with tears that could not be freed.

There was no knowledge of the children's harbor, beyond some awareness that Betna had led them out to sea. Hannah's baby—Menahem—I would imagine being rocked by gentle waves. I ached for him as for my departed friend but kept reminding myself we had no way to feed him. Poor Hannah. The crime against her had infected us like a plague. A vicious rumor remained that Hannah was unclean, and that censure would extend to Hannah's son. Finding a wet nurse under such circumstances would be impossible. I resigned myself; Menahem was better with Ethan.

Days were struck, one by one, from the perpetual calendar. Food had no taste. Tunics flagged upon my frame; my countenance equaled them. In time, desolation won my embrace. I forgot what happiness was.

ЕᎧ ᏣᎧ

~ *IX* ~

"Indeed, you are my lamp, O Lord,
The Lord lightens my darkness."

~II Samuel 22:29

When summer's heat burned into the city, likewise, the emperor's evil blazed into madness. He sought to prove himself capable of incredible feats. He dared to declare himself supernatural. A soothsayer named Thrasyllus had prophesied some years earlier that Gaius had as much chance becoming emperor as for someone to gallop on horseback across the Gulf of Baiae, and so it became the emperor's highest aim to ride his stallion over the sea.

He began construction of a monumental bridge, one that would span the bay from Baiae to Puteoli, a distance of more than three miles. During construction, one of the senators reminded him that King Ahasuerus of Persia had built a bridge upon the sea, and it had "rallied the king's army to victory!" Caligula, greedy for encouragement, found such comments more delectable than the roasted liver of a white goose fattened with ripe figs.

Soon a decree was announced at the crossroads of each neighborhood and posted with scarlet ribbon and imperial seal in the forum:

A minimum of two persons from each household
shall witness the triumphant ride of Gaius Caesar
Augustus Germanicus, our divine emperor, when he

crosses the Gulf of Baiae on horseback two weeks hence.

It mattered not whether the city's commoners could afford the trip, communal carts would bear them hence. In the depth of my own miserable sorrow, the emperor's decree was ludicrous. For Caligula, however, it was a serious matter. His decrees were to be obeyed. Soldiers would enforce them. All the world was expected to bear witness to his escapade and sear it in memory for generations to come.

One week prior to unveiling the emperor's bridge in Baiae, a letter arrived:

From Aquila to his dear Prisca and family. Greetings.

I hope you are well, as I am.

It is said that you suffer in the loss of your dear friend. I beg, however, that you take great care. You are dearest to me of all that is on the earth.

In accordance with the decree of Gaius Caesar, I am making plans to attend events in Baiae with my young sister. Please allow me to escort you along this journey. Mutual contact before marriage is not in accord with tradition, but I believe your recent loss would create an exception and an allowance for me to comfort your family. Please send word that your father will agree.

Father consented. Betna stayed behind with Miriam, and I walked at Father's side to Rome's southern gate, each of us bearing an amount of food and clothing in bags upon our shoulders. It was early morning, and Aquila had parked beside the Via Appia. He was perched atop a painted wooden cart pulled by a pair of roan horses, hands holding fast to leather reins. Tamar waved from within the cart's brown wooden shell, her petite hand extended from a square window hung with blue-colored drapes.

Aquila hurried to my side, his face drawn and pale. Saying he was grieved by my frailness, he folded my hands tight within his own. "Prisca," he said, "do you forget our plans?"

I couldn't answer. My mind was dull.

Aquila continued. "I am preparing our home, planning our future. Are you taking care of your promise as well? If you fade away ..."

"I am sorry," I said. But I was unsure why.

He brought his face close. "We are not meant to die of grief, my love."

Aquila drove the horses, and Father sat by him. Tamar and I bounced on a cushioned bench within the cart. She was kind but shy as the wheels started to rumble over our stone-paved road. Gloom had taken residence in me, and my voice was gone. Perhaps it had died with Hannah.

Many carts and horseback riders crowded the Via Appia as we began the journey; however, once possessed of distance from Rome, our route was unhindered, and the air smelled of growing things. Leaning from the window to fill my lungs, views of countryside held me there. Tamar soon joined me, pointing to golden hills and narrow bristled

255

trees. We took turns shouting colors of flowers that burst from grass-covered slopes. Purple! Yellow! Orange! Sunshine warmed my skin, wind whisked my hair, and the sound of hooves clapping against stone carried me, body and soul, from the heartache prevailing in Rome.

Our day was long. Tamar and I dozed through the warmest hours, and I later wakened to a smell of sea. Grand villas grew from fertile hilltops, their ornate columns seen from far off. Behind them were occasional peeks at silvery blue waves. We had ventured into a land of retreat and refreshment for Rome's wealthiest.

"Father!" I called. "Where are we?"

He leaned into our quarters. "So you wake up now."

I grinned.

He said, "We are at the southern border of Latium, soon to enter Campania. Tonight we lodge in the town of Sinuessa." His brows lifted. "On the Tyrrhenian Sea."

My heart beat faster. "On the sea. Tamar, did you hear? I've often longed to be in such a place," I said. "Betna's stories have tempted me. He said your feet sink into sand, and the water is so vast you cannot see land beyond."

We could not be pried from the window, though light weakened and breezes were chill. It was dusk when our carriage slowed beneath a rounded, rock-strewn mountain and flaming torches marked a low city wall. Sinuessa. It was situated near a shoreline. The town appeared to float in rosy light, its arms stretched long, receiving the sea unto itself.

My nose twitched. "What is that odd smell?" I asked.

"Hot springs," Aquila replied. "And they're close."

We were stopped in front of a low building on the northern reaches of town. A squat, pleasant fellow came bustling out to greet us, breathing as if having run a long way.

"Welcome!" he said. "I am Eli." He was some years older than Aquila and had a broad nose and plump face.

Father greeted him and presented letters; they had been expecting us.

"Malka—my empress," Eli winked, "will see your papers. She is inside."

"Do you have shelter for horses?" Aquila asked.

"There's a stable in the rear. I'll handle your rig for you," Eli said.

Malka was a female version of Eli, though shorter and younger. Her hair sprang from a neatly stitched scarf in a multitude of tight curls, and she wore a tunic that had been dyed a dark purple. (I would later learn that the purple dye came from a certain shellfish found in Sinuessa's bright blue waters.) Twin eight-year-old daughters with round faces and hair flowing in dark spirals were attached to Malka like a fresh and delightful fragrance, though they never uttered a word.

Malka received us like a mother soothing an ailing child. "Oh, you must be exhausted," she heaved. "Oh, let Eli take your things," she gushed. "Oh, let us help you to your rooms." She pointed to a basket filled with fresh fruit, urging us to, "Eat! Eat!"

Tamar and I lodged in a room that faced the sea. Standing on tiptoe, rolling waves were seen from a high window. Our walls were white and decorated with faded

257

frescoes of palm and fruit trees. Father and Aquila occupied a room across a narrow hall.

We all traipsed to the sea next morning. Shedding sandals and lifting the tunic from my ankles, I sank into hot, gritty sand. Nearby, a young woman walked at water's edge, chubby babe in her arms. The child's fingers curled around a strand of her hair, and she smiled, caressing the infant's face with her own. A lump grew in my throat, remembering Hannah with her newborn son.

"Menahem." My shoulders were weighted with guilt. Why hadn't I looked for him?

Aquila walked to water's edge and inhaled moist air. "The seaside can be a healing place," he said.

My thoughts were in the past, and I stared at white foam covering my toes.

"Prisca?"

Forcing myself to capture Aquila's words, my voice was cutting. "Yes. I must send a word of thanks to Gaius Caesar for our journey," I said.

Aquila chuckled. "He's not a man we should feel indebted to."

"Yet that is surely what he wants," I said.

"We owe him our allegiance as the governor of our lives." Aquila paused, his eyes searching distant blue waves. "But he cannot own our hearts."

"My heart." I swallowed. "Will it ever stop aching?"

Aquila came near. "In time."

"Even as we traveled through the countryside I began to feel better, but it seems such a betrayal to

Hannah," I said. "Why should I laugh again? Why should I have love, when she had only misery and suffering?"

"Because she's gone, we may think Hannah's life was unhappy," he replied, "but you know there was joy. She had your friendship. She was able to bring new life into the world. Many women never experience such things."

"Was I unable to see it, Aquila? Do you think she was happy?"

"You knew her probably better than anyone," he said. "What do you believe?"

My eyes traced puffs of white adorning sunny sky. "Miriam said her last words were for me: '*He has sent me to heal the brokenhearted,*' from the prophet Isaiah. I keep thinking her words were something God wanted me to know."

"Maybe it was what Hannah wanted you to know," he said.

Waves lapped the sand, and I stepped into them. Water hugged my ankles, sand massaged my feet, and sun soaked into my scalp. It felt good. Aquila came to stand by me.

"I once believed we each had purpose," I said. "But if that were so, why would Hannah be taken before accomplishing it? I've wished it was me that had gone from this world."

Aquila said nothing, but his chest heaved, and it gratified my heart somehow to know he still wanted me. Had I been doubtful? Oh, selfish thoughts! Did I truly wish to have died in place of Hannah? My stomach wrenched with the truth that I was glad to be alive, and I was ashamed. Miriam's story of a boy who risked himself for love still pursued me. Could I ever be of use in God's immense plan? It was clear there was no purpose for me; I was nothing.

"Why? Why did Hannah die?" I asked. "Is it wrong to ask why good people are taken when wicked men like Caligula live?"

Aquila watched a gull soar above us. "Even Job pondered such things." He picked up a stone and tossed it far into soft waves. "And God answered Job with a question: *'Have you commanded the morning since your days began and caused the dawn to know its place, so that it might take hold of the skirts of the earth and the wicked be shaken out of it?'*"

Wind-whipped locks of hair brushed the strong outline of his face. He turned toward me and took my hands into his. "If such decisions were left for you or me to decide," he said, "I wonder if we would choose rightly. We see only our narrow corner of the world, I think." Aquila squeezed my hands gently. "With every holy word left to us, Adonai promises love, care, and provision. I believe our Lord loved Hannah. Don't you?"

"I do believe that." Tears rimmed my eyes, and a sudden gust blew into my face. My eyes closed and then opened to see my betrothed studying me. "Maybe one day I'll understand," I said.

We walked down sandy coastline, no more words between us, and then I remembered what God said to our people after he rescued them out of Egypt. *"I am the Lord who heals you."*

႞ ႙

Caligula's "Festival in Baiae" was to take place on the next day, and so into our coach we climbed, purses filled with Malka's sweet cakes. It was painful to leave Sinuessa, and our ride began in silence. Before long, however, we crossed into a thriving land called Campania. How could Valeria and her husband part from such verdant fields? Variegated greens of olive groves and grape vines cascaded down gentle slopes in neat rows. Immense plains of rippling grains stood proud under searing sun, promising weighty loaves of bread to come. The Romans called this region *Campania Felix*—the "fortunate country"!

The first sign that we were near our destination appeared in the form of waving tent awnings. We were approaching a large encampment of Roman travelers, and from a distance, the hills appeared to be spotted with pale birds, wings ruffed and ready to fly. Father advised Aquila to roll on past, and our sturdy horses trotted away from crowds and closer to steep, triangular peaks, landing in a circle of natural rock walls. Gnarled trees lent drama to surrounding yellow-stone escarpments; it was our own private fortress. We had come to a place Lucullus had discovered and utilized for private picnicking grounds, a place my father had visited as a small boy. A westerly breeze infused with mineral-water odors greeted us, and a brief stroll from camp found a warm spring that bubbled over stony shelving into an oblong pond.

Two tents were erected, one against the other. It was my first opportunity to see Aquila's handiwork, and it was apparent why his business was thriving. Each structure was crafted with precision and care. The fabric, made from the hides of goats, was smooth. Our tents were assembled in swift order, an attribute that justified Aquila's craftsmanship in the eyes of Rome's military, and I admired the authoritative rise in his tone, the way his fingers hugged crisp seams and tapped the taut surface.

After camp was set, Tamar and I rejoiced in our luxurious secluded pool, bathing away travel's fatigue. Laying back into gurgling water, the current tugged my hair, and warm vapor seeped into thirsty skin. Grief had stolen my body's vitality, and I was dismayed to see a bony frame stretched out beneath an undulating curtain of steam and bubbles. Was this the body that would be given in marriage? I pondered God's plan for a husband and wife— for Aquila and me—and little bumps dotted the lengths of my arms. I was both thrilled and terrified.

Tamar interrupted my thoughts. "I never want to leave this place," she said. "Even the smell doesn't bother me!" She plunged beneath water's surface, bursting forth from it with a gleeful gasp.

"Makes me think of soured eggs," I replied. Stretching my limbs, I looked around and above at sharp rock ledges and the scrubby plants that softened them.

Tamar swam near. "May I ask you something?"

"Anything," I said.

"You've seen the senators. For me, that is a rare experience." She hesitated, shy about speaking her mind. "Tell me, what will it be like? Will they be close to us? How will they behave toward us?"

"I've seen them, but always distant. Most of what I know comes from hearing about them." Memories of how senators mistreated Hannah and Miriam surfaced, and my jaw tightened. "The senators are rich and proud. They have enormous ability to influence others." I groaned. "They have the power to make decisions for all of us, Tamar, but those decisions are not always for our good."

"But what about tomorrow, being around them?" Tamar asked. "I'm afraid to say or do the wrong thing."

"I've been afraid of them too, even though the senate has always been part of my life somehow. Try not to worry. We can ask Father about it."

Tamar said, "Ever since we came to Rome, I've been anxious. Aquila won't allow me to leave our home, and I sit at the loom for hours, but what do I weave? All I see are dismal walls." It became all too clear that Tamar deserved a better friend than I'd been to her.

"Dismal. That's a good word for Rome these days," I said.

Tamar spun about, peering overhead and around at the raw splendor enclosing us. "Here, there is endless color," she said. Her motions created subtle waves. I whirled as well, spotting dainty purple flowers that spilled from rock fissures and silver-green branches tickling a blue sky. Tamar's words were soft as the steam rising to bathe our pinked faces and produced a slight echo within the grotto. "Now I have ideas to fill my weaving," she said. "Don't you wish we could live in a place like this?"

I smiled and stretched my fingers, enjoying the press of water's flow. "Hmm, yes. To be in a place like this every day … it would be rejuvenating. You would have more ideas for your weavings than ever dreamed."

Tamar sighed, allowing herself to float and stare into sky.

Closing my eyes and laying low, wetting my face, knotted muscles started to unwind, and tears for Hannah began to release.

We soaked until our fingers were wrinkled and spongy, covered ourselves in air-freshened clothing, and then talked of the meal we would prepare over open fire.

"About tomorrow, one thing is certain," I said. "There will be lots of people, and it will smell much worse than this water!"

Giggling like little girls, we walked the small distance to camp.

ॐ ॐ

Father and Aquila carried in several fresh fish before dusk. With herbs and oil, Tamar and I cooked them over glowing coals and, as our ancestors long before us, our little band broke bread together in a rough and beautiful country.

Tamar beamed when Father complimented us on the meal. "Prisca found herbs growing wild near our footpath!"

She described our waterfall and pool, and her hands became animated, reminding me of the tall brother at her side. I felt growing affection for this sister of mine ... and compassion. Tamar had lost both mother and father, and she was far from the home she had known.

"We picked handfuls of rosemary," I said.

Father sniffed his plate of food. "*Rosmarinus*—dew of the sea."

"Dew of the sea." Tamar sighed. "I like it here."

Laying her plate aside, Tamar addressed my father. "Will we—will we see senators in Baiae tomorrow?"

"Yes," Father said. "They will be near the emperor, making certain that he sees them."

Aquila leaned against a large rock. "My sister has not mingled with Roman nobility. I think she suspects all senators are seven feet tall and dripping with gold."

Tamar shrank back, embarrassed.

"Gaius Caesar sees himself in that very way." Father's eyes were twinkling. "But, young Tamar, you must travel to Gaul to find men of such height. The Romans make themselves taller by building their sandals with thick nails."

Our laughter sounded against rugged walls and bounced back to us. Aquila leaned in to feed the fire, his features accentuated by light and shadow. I judged him the most handsome man, and a dizzy feeling rose in my middle.

I asked, "Can you tell us, Abba—I mean, are there respectable men among the nobility anymore?"

Father's face turned serious. "Of course we are wise to convey respect to every senator. Whether they deserve our respect is another matter."

Aquila said, "You'll see Caesar's guard at his side, the Praetorian Guard. They look respectable."

Father agreed. "Clemens is in command. I believe he is a man of honorable character, but his features can appear somber, difficult to make out."

"There is a military tribune named Chaerea among the guard," Aquila said. "I've heard differing opinions of him, Priscus. What is your view?"

Father rubbed his chin. "He's a man of about fifty and has been a victim of Caligula's relentless mockery, taunted with allegations of effeminacy in front of his fellow guards. Chaerea has a youthful bearing and wavy hair and, on occasion, has shown sensitivity toward others. These gentle traits the emperor has used as a weapon, subjecting him to ridicule by his own cohort."

"Is this Chaerea a respectable man?" I asked.

Aquila said, "My impression of him has been positive. Recently, I witnessed leniency on his part toward a delinquent taxpayer. But one never knows, in the current state of Rome, if such leniency is sincere or if driven by some sinister motive."

"You're right to question," Father said, "but my sense—and my experience—tells me that there is good in the man." He leaned forward and stirred the fire. "The guards are in a precarious role. Remember who it is they work for."

Tamar shifted on her cushioned stone seat. Her forehead creased with worry. "Forgive me," she said, "but what has become of this world, that we must question every man's goodness?"

"It is a sad state," Father said. "But be comforted by the fact that there are not so few worthy men, only that there are few men who risk revealing their own true character."

"What do you mean?" Tamar asked.

"The emperor is malicious," Father replied. "It is a dangerous thing to display one's opposition. Hence, many people walk around pretending to be like him."

Aquila sat up straight, lifting his chin. "One day," he said, "virtuous men will be free. We will know them well."

Father's eyes traveled upward to a wide sky blinking with stars. He sighed. "There was a day when tribunes represented the people's interests, in the days of the Republic, before emperors robbed them of their honorable—and to Rome, sacred—powers. Tribunes were then considered sacrosanct."

Tamar leaned closer. "What is 'sacrosanct'?"

Father explained. "Such term had more meaning when Rome was a Republic."

Tamar pinched her face. "Republic?"

He explained. "It was a form of government where the people were represented by selected officials and no one person made every decision. Even when the first emperor, Augustus Caesar, came into power, there were those who were still termed 'sacrosanct.' It is a word that means they have a sacred purpose; they are inviolable, not even to be touched, under any circumstances."

Father gazed again into night sky, feathered clouds now drifting like filmy curtains across the stars, and then he patted Tamar's hand. "For those of us who are foreigners and exiles," he said, "certain nobles would tell you that all Romans are sacrosanct."

His words brought needed clarity for me. I'd seen it in Roman faces throughout my life. Even a child's innocent and playful touch, if it came from other than a Roman child, would cause revulsion to flare in haughty eyes.

Aquila stood, pacing. He spoke like a centurion issuing orders. "And now we have military tribunes to lead

the soldiers, pecuniary tribunes to guard the treasury ..."
He shook his fist. "And we are expected to rely on Caligula
to represent morality to the people. Humph! Morality!" He
tossed a log into the fire and orange embers shot high on a
curling line of smoke.

Tamar looked like a hunted hare. "What if I touch
someone who is sacrosanct?" Her entire body quaked.

Father replied, "Because our people are not Roman
by blood, we must always use extreme caution." He
softened at her terrified expression, his voice reassuring.
"Don't fret, dear Tamar. Aquila and I will steer you in safe
directions. You will be well in our care."

Her brother smiled. "Yes. Stay close." He pointed
to me. "Both of you."

Father cleared his throat. "Forgive me, Daughter. I
didn't give a direct answer to your earlier question. There
are respectable men among the nobility. But my best
advice is to be discreet, as Aquila cautioned. Stay close. All
will be well."

ॐ ☙

It was a good night of sleep within our snug tent,
dreaming of a day when Aquila and I would share a tent of
our own. Though fresh scent of morning tickled my nose
and birds squawked and sang, it was tempting to close
dreamy eyes and return to sleep.

Tamar was watching a large, buzzing fly bump
against tent walls. At my movement, she turned and smiled.

"You're looking better," she said.

"Am I?"

Her brows rose. "You looked like a ghost when we picked you up."

"That bad," I replied.

She edged closer, her words soft. "I know how much my brother loves you."

ജ ൟ

Aquila secured our horses near the spring, and we left on foot for Baiae. It was a rocky trail, uphill and down, but it felt good to stretch and climb. We expected a hot day and had dressed to stay cool. My hair was tied into braids, Roman fashion. Tamar had tied hers high with ribbon, and it fell in a shining brown length like a fountain. Her tunic was dyed to match the sky; mine was the gentle white of myrtle flowers, its edges adorned with pink roses.

Father and Aquila wore tunics in darker shades of blue, Father's edged by a gold band. They had money purses secured to wide leather belts. I began to realize that this adventure was therapeutic for all of us. Father had relaxed—to the point of being humorous. Aquila's vigor was apparent in flushed, bronzed skin.

The vista of Baiae stopped us on the path. Jagged, tree-covered slopes curved around a shining bay shaped like a quarter-moon and opening to sparkling, turquoise Tyrrhenian Sea. To our right and left, villas stood proudly on hilltops; you could not gaze long at them for the reflection of light on polished marble. Grape vines tumbled over terraces, and private pools peeked from behind columned porticoes. Just below us, the coastline was teeming with crowds. Aquila clasped my hand, and our eyes met.

Father and Tamar had started down the slope, and we followed. While watching them, my emotions stirred. Hannah's absence was apparent. How I missed her. Just then, words came to me like a fresh blast of air, "*Lo, I am with you always.*" Words of Jesus. My feet seemed to lift from solid ground, and soft like a whisper I heard: "*Seek me.*" The sound was so clear in my mind I looked for a source but saw no one.

"We're lagging behind," Aquila said. I took his hand and gave my attention to the trail ahead.

Before ever reaching the valley, sumptuous fragrance greeted us, touting Baiae's many cook-shops. Passing into town, we saw fish searing over open coals and large pots of simmering lentils set into marble counters with low flames beneath. We walked near a bakery, and twists of bread were being pulled from a huge, dome-shaped brick oven. My stomach roared.

Aquila laughed. "Shall we get something to eat? If not, Prisca may distract attention from today's spectacle."

Father pointed. "If it's still there, I remember a place. Just a short walk."

Tamar and I shouted in unison. "Yes!"

We walked past two more streets and on the third turned north. A shop on our left was painted the yellow of lemons, and swirling blue letters reading "*Fructi Maris*"— fruits of the sea—garlanded its open doorway. The dining area was an open portico lined with smooth columns. Its floor was inlaid with black and white *tessellae* where, in the center, an artisan had designed a colorful tray of fish. On a long counter, pots of olives brimmed with scent, and a young girl stood on a stool nearby, pouring fresh water over a basket of lemons.

At the rear of the room, an older man worked with a knife, carving a piece of wood. His skin was brown and thick from sea and sun, his head thin of hair, and age spots peppered a reddish scalp. I supposed him a cheerful sort of man, for the lines that framed his mouth were deep.

Father took a few steps toward him, leaning to study his face. "Avram?"

"Would I know you?" The old man's voice was raspy.

Father replied, "You may remember me as the boy who once stole a fig and later offered a toy flute to repay you."

Avram looked up, squinting his eyes. His plump cheeks began to jiggle. "Ha, ha—the boy I knew still lives in your eyes. Eben Lucullus Priscus, you are a man now. I cannot count the summers that have passed."

My father held Avram's shoulders and kissed him on each cheek. "Days in your company were blessed days," he said. "And where is Shira? She must be in the kitchen."

Avram's smile faded, and he shook a bowed head. "It was not to be. She has been gone these many years." He looked up. "But, you see, she did not leave me without help. Eleven children, and always at least two at my elbow. '*Did you eat, Abba? Did you wash your face, Abba? Did you sleep, Abba?*'" He laughed and slapped his knee. "I am now an old man. Sleep will soon come."

Father gestured toward me. "I present my daughter to you, Avram. My Priscilla."

"Ah," Avram said, "she has the look of her mother."

271

"And you remember Nessa. Only once and she was quite young," Father said.

"No man can forget a charming woman whose eyes reflect the sea. She must have been near Priscilla's age when we first met." He took my hand and squeezed it. "Aha, I also see spirit—and mischief—like her father." Avram chuckled.

"Humph!" Father replied. I began to giggle.

Introductions were made all around, and we selected bowls of fish soup, thick with vegetables. There were also fist-size puffs of bread containing a honey-fig filling. Avram came while we dined and laid a gnarled hand upon Father's shoulder.

"We have many things to speak of. Will you be long in Baiae?" Avram asked.

"Just through tomorrow," Father replied.

"Come along again. It will bring joy to an old man."

"I cannot promise it, my good friend. But we will try," Father said.

ಬಿ ೞ

We departed Avram's company and set out for the bay. Near the waterfront, each person passed through a roped area and received a newly minted coin. Of course, we would not be allowed to spend it! The coins were to pay household taxes, proof that we attended the event and proof of payment when the publican collected. The engraving was of Caligula's laurelled head on one side, and then the reverse depicted the emperor's full-figure relief, right hand raised in honor of the Praetorian Guard. Is that what this festivity was about, to garner devotion from the powerful men closest to him? My brain mulled through it. If Caligula did not have the favor and protection of his Praetorian Guard …

Caligula's bridge was an astounding sight. Multiple ships had been commissioned as floats; all of these were part of a lengthy overpass upon which the emperor would travel. Some—dare I call them ships—had been expanded into elaborate lodgings and banqueting spaces set afloat. A long trough had been erected to carry fresh water from the mainland into each one. The bridge itself was mounded with a layer of soil. It was a perfect and, in the Romans' eyes, supernatural feat, forming dry land upon the sea.

Seating had been arranged for senators at the gateway to Caligula's bridge, and purple-bordered white *togae* filled every seat. These nobles appeared bored, chattering in small groups and waving hand-held fans.

Horns began to blare and onlookers were pressed back by the Praetorian Guard, creating sprawl the length of Baiae's wooden pier and even beyond, into shrubby rocks flanking the bay. Guards then diverged into two lines either side of the bridge entry; and children, dressed as sea nymphs, cast bright-colored flowers onto the ground. Gaius Caesar trotted over the floral path astride his prized racehorse, Incitatus.

I whispered to Tamar. "I've heard that Incitatus hosts his own dinner parties, complete with servants!"

"A horse?" Tamar looked incredulous.

Aquila said, "And he is fed a mixture of oats and pure gold flakes."

"In truth?" Tamar asked.

"Yes, Sister. In truth," Aquila replied.

There was no denying that Incitatus was a beautiful stallion. White as Grecian marble, neck encircled by a jeweled collar, Incitatus had drawn countless chariots to victory. With a quick pitch of his head and a swish of white combed tail, Caligula's horse exhibited the pride and admiration of its owner.

I spoke soft again to Tamar. "They say the emperor sleeps with his horse before every race."

Her eyes expanded to double their normal size.

Aquila groaned. "He treats that horse with more care than any other living thing."

Reclining in a shady pavilion was the emperor's wife, Lollia Paulina, wearing a tunic of purple silk. Her curled and braided hair was adorned with gold and pearls. It was well known that Caligula also kept a mistress named Milonia Caesonia, and perhaps she waited for him in one of the floating lodges upon the sea.

Caligula reared his horse. No matter that he had not run a race, he came forth like a hero! A wreath of oak leaves crowned his head, and as if he were riding into battle, a gilt sword hung from his waist. He carried a shield and wore a shining breastplate rumored to have belonged to Alexander the Great. A purple silk *chlamys* sat upon his shoulders.

Rome's emperor addressed the masses with pomp. "Do you see what I have done? I have bridged the sea!"

His audience roared while Caligula dismounted. He offered a sacrifice to Neptune, the Roman sea god, and then the *praefectus* of Baiae led the audience in a series of cheers, "Hail Gaius Caesar! The emperor shall cross the bay on horseback! A distance of twenty-six *stades*! Hail Gaius Caesar!"

Climbing again onto his gleaming steed, Caligula shouted at the multitudes filling the shoreline. "I am your emperor! Your god! You are my people! And you will remember this day. You will declare my fame to the ends of the earth, extolling my name for all time!" Like a fired catapult, he shot forward, and white doves were released into clear skies. Fast after him went nearly a century of Praetorian Guards, first cavalry and then foot soldiers. It was a magnificent scene.

In the crowd's fervor, Tamar was pushed, landing on the pier with a thud at the feet of a praetorian guard. Terror flooded her face; her paleness rivaled that of Incitatus. The guard looked grim, but one glance at her softened him.

"I'm sorry. So sorry," Tamar said. "I was pushed and—"

"Silence," the guard said. Tamar's mouth snapped shut. He looked to his right, noting a colleague's attention, and then reached down to lift Tamar from the ground. Aquila was beside her in an instant.

"Your wife?" the guard asked.

"My sister," Aquila replied.

The guard released Tamar and stepped back into position, but his eyes remained on her for some time.

Tamar stammered. "Is—is—is he sacro- ..."

"Sacrosanct?" Father finished her question. "No."

She relaxed.

Aquila shook a finger at her. "If, however, he believed you intentionally pushed him, he could have killed you instantly."

I glared at Aquila and then took Tamar's shoulders into my hands. "But he released you, even helped you! It's all right."

When the emperor passed from sight, the crowd withdrew like waves retreating into sea, and Baiae then became the attraction. Wine flowed liberally. Noise rose to deafening levels. Exotic women swayed among bustling streets. Something about the festivity reminded me of the first day I'd seen Gaius Caesar, another day on which he had ridden a powerfully built stallion. At that time, my heart had pulsed with eager hope for our future. That hope was now gone. I shook my head in disgust. Today's event was a ridiculous bit of theater.

"*Seek me.*" Again, the words were subtle but clear, suffusing my thoughts. I glanced each way; no source was apparent. Seek who? Where do I look? A bowl of bright lemons gained my notice, and I stopped. Avram's yellow shop.

"Father, may we go again to see Avram?" I asked.

"I long to see him as well, Prisca. But safety precludes—I would prefer to get beyond these crowds."

"Only for a few moments?"

He responded with a look that said he was going to give in, and my senses told me that was the right place to go. But why? What might be found at Avram's little seafood shop?

We strolled through the door of *Fructi Maris* just as a familiar party was leaving. It was Aedias, Hesperia, and five children, and we exchanged greetings in the portico's shade.

"Where are you camped?" Father asked.

Aedias replied, "Ah, my intellectual friend, we have been favored with accommodations at a nearby villa."

"At a villa," I replied. "It must be lovely."

"Ah, yes, quite nice. The freedman, Callistus, has afforded us lodgings," Aedias said.

Father whistled. "Well, then. You are experiencing luxury indeed."

Aedias chortled and stood taller. "There was a recent banquet for which Callistus secured my services. He was pleased with the abundant fare, and I must confess it as my proudest accomplishment." His chin lifted. "The feast was nothing less than stupendous! Shoulder of hare, broiled black birds—oh, and cold wild boar with pickled vegetables as an appetizer! My hunger stirs yet again with pungent memory."

Tamar and I looked at one another, trying not to show our horror. Aedias was boasting of food that none of us would have dared smell and would never eat.

"The Romans do love their palates," Aquila said.

The pompous chef narrowed his eyes. "True," he said. He tapped his lips with a swollen finger.

Hesperia was serene, dressed in a shimmering tunic that rivaled the Tyrrhenian Sea. Jewels hung at length from her ears.

Longing to speak of something other than Aedias' cooking, I approached Balbina. "How do you like Baiae?"

Her eyes met Hesperia's before answering. "It is a pretty place," Balbina said.

I smiled at Hortensia, her hand fastened tight to the older girl's. Cassius, Aulus and Livius were sorting seashells on a step below.

Hesperia leaned near Aquila. "The emperor's triumph was breathtaking; would you agree?"

"It was unlike anything I have seen before," Aquila replied.

"Come dear," Aedias said. "We must be getting back to our host."

Hesperia lowered painted eyelids, extending her long neck like a tall bird. She clicked her fingers, and the children gathered behind her. They left with correctness and style.

"She does have beautiful clothing," Tamar said.

"Maybe she would be willing to teach us. What if we arranged an afternoon of sewing and weaving?"

"I would like to learn from her skills," Tamar replied, "but do you think we could bring the food?"

"A banquet that we can eat! I agree. We could offer the meal as our thanks for her teaching."

Upon entering the vibrant environment of *Fructi Maris*, a fragrance of well-seasoned food summoned us. We found ourselves hungry again, and Father and Aquila began making selections.

"*Seek me*." Avram's careworn face was in sight, and I went to him.

"Please excuse me." I lowered my voice. "Have you heard of a man called Jesus?"

Avram beckoned me near with fingers tickling the air. His voice was pumped with excited bursts. "I have not just heard, Prisca. I know," he said.

"But what is it you know?" I asked.

"That he lives," Avram said, "here." He laid a hand across his heart.

"Someone else has spoken to me about Jesus. Please help me understand."

"It takes faith, child."

"Faith? Believing in something?" I asked.

Avram took my hands within his own. He said, "Faith is the certainty that something exists, though you cannot see it. It is something you've hoped for that you are sure of being true." He smiled. "What have you hoped for, child?"

"What have I hoped for? It's still not clear for me. But I'm trying."

"Do not worry that your faith is small," Avram said. He picked up an olive from the table and placed it in my hand. "Faith begins like a tiny seed and grows. With each step you take nearer the Savior, your faith will increase."

Ethan came to mind and his description of the encounter with Jesus. He said that the closer he got to Jesus the heavier his basket became. Even as I cupped the small green olive, my palm calculated its trifling weight. Is it like that? Is there faith starting in my basket?

Father approached us. "Hmm, is Avram telling you stories about my boyhood?"

"There is not time enough in a month of days to tell your stories!" Avram's smile digressed to a frown. "And now you have come to tell me good-bye."

"Once we've witnessed the emperor's return, we must go home," Father replied. He patted Avram's shoulder. "But let us not become strangers again, old

279

friend. Come to us in Rome. At least send word of your health."

Avram said, "My eldest daughter will write for me. Old bones do not travel well."

The enduring bond and fond history between this man and my father was heartening, and I yearned for more hours in Avram's company, listening to tales of times gone by. "I will pray to see you again," I said.

"And I will pray for even nobler things," Avram replied.

ಔ ಚ

On the following day, the emperor returned to Baiae, this time driving a chariot. We were led in cheers as he passed from bridge to mainland, but he was fatigued, perspiration streaming from beneath his wilting ring of oak leaves, and did not address his onlookers. The *praefectus* called for praises to the emperor's name, and many rang out freely. "Hail Gaius!" "Hail august one!" "Victory!" And then it was over.

With one final gaze across the bay, together, we started the journey home.

Again, Tamar and I beheld lush countryside with window curtains flapping at our sides. Inspired, Tamar talked of a design she wanted to try at her loom, and I contemplated Mother's best recipes that would be enhanced by fresh herbs we had collected and bundled to take home. We both spoke of homes that, one day, would be filled with flowers. I asked Tamar if she had heard of Jesus.

"Aquila told me of him," she said.

"What did he tell you?" I asked.

"Only that some call Jesus the Messiah. He did not know more."

"Do you think it is true," I asked, "that Jesus is the Anointed One?"

Tamar sighed. "I know so little, Prisca."

"Avram told me it takes faith. Faith in what we have hoped for." My eyes traced our cart's wood-ribbed ceiling. "Tamar, we've hoped for Messiah every moment of our lives. Our promised Savior."

The remainder of that day passed with few words. Instead of an overnight in Sinuessa, we camped in a thicket of trees. I closed my eyes to remember shore and sea but was not disappointed. It was pleasant to spend our last hours in privacy. Next day, when Rome's majestic walls loomed above the line of road, my muscles tensed, unwilling to return to many things—even less prepared to depart from Aquila. After arriving at the gates, he lifted me from the cart, pausing to search my face.

"When we were in Sinuessa," Aquila said, "you asked me about your heart. I think it is healing."

"Perhaps it is," I replied.

He said, "I could not part with you today if I thought otherwise."

"I don't want to part, for any reason. And I feel a little afraid."

"I am never far, my love."

Aquila enfolded my hand in his, and I wanted to stay at his side, but Father stood apart, baggage hanging from both shoulders, grinning. It was time to go.

Aquila smiled and nodded. "May our trip to Baiae comfort you in days to come."

It did.

                           ℰ ℭ

~ X ~

Though the fig tree may not blossom,
Nor fruit be on the vines;
Though the labor of the olive may fail,
And the fields yield no food;
Though the flock may be cut off from the fold,
And there be no herd in the stalls—
Yet I will rejoice in the Lord,
I will joy in the God of my salvation.
The Lord God is my strength;
He will make my feet like a deer's feet,
And He will make me walk on my high hills.

~Habakkuk 3:17-19

We returned from Baiae uplifted, though when Rome's towering structures tightened about us, my throat cinched in like manner. Father took my hand and spoke in a bright, cheerful tone. He was looking lean and tanned—almost youthful.

"When is a Roman happiest," he asked, "when dying a valiant death or when achieving vast wealth?"

"Oh, I can't guess. Perhaps heroic death in the midst of furious battle," I said.

"Hmm. A worthy try," he said. "But you must know the noblest Roman will only be happy with money. The Greek playwright, Aeschylus, said, '*Only when a man's life comes to its end in prosperity dare we pronounce him happy.*'" Father's earnest face had me searching for some life-important lesson there, but the glint in his eyes hinted at something else. He said, "A dead Roman with mounds of

283

gold ... now that is a happy man!" We laughed, but I presumed that, for many, it was a real life purpose. Eliam sprang to mind.

Rounding a final corner, our entry gleamed in welcome. Once inside, the men exchanged shoulder pats while I turned to my nurturer, teacher, and lifelong friend, awakened to the look of her: Smooth gray hairs—still thick—swathing a petite head, clothing of fine needlework and crisp dignity, narrow fingers on small hands dotted by signs of age, dark centers of her eyes that always saw me with clarity. I wanted to fold her image into innermost scrolls of memory.

"You have returned with health," Miriam said. I leaned into her, and she held me close, skin damp with tears. "It was my prayer," she said.

"I—I've neglected my promise," I said, "and will think of nothing above the pursuit of Menahem. It was my promise to Hannah, that I'd care for him."

"Child—"

"No." I squeezed her hands. "It is time to grow up, time to think of others. I've been selfish, consumed by my own sorrow."

"We have all felt this sorrow," Miriam replied.

I urged determination into my voice. "I will find Menahem."

‽ ⁐

My last communication from Lormah had been a cloth stitched with warning, so the search for Menahem proceeded in a different way. Betna took me to Rome's wharf where we sought a ship named *Piscator*—the Fisherman.

"It will not be large," Betna told me, "made for fishing in shallow waters." He described it with one square sail and a smaller, three-pointed sail in stripes of brown and blue. We had come before dawn, before most ships began their float into open sea, and it was difficult to see what was docked at a distance. Fewer ships crowded the Tiber since Caligula's ride across the bay, Rome's largest vessels having been requisitioned to build his bridge.

We first came to a broad, white boat with a sternpost shaped like a swan. Its curved hull lent an air of wings upon water. Beside it rocked a flat ferryboat ringed with thick ropes, and next there was an odd-looking cargo ship Betna called a "bucket." At the farthest point of the pier was the vessel we searched for, its crew setting out to sea.

Betna shouted. "Justus!"

The sailing master turned and waved. Betna and I scurried over wide, planked boards until at last we stood panting in front of a rugged sailor. Justus' arms were inflated with muscle. His tunic was tan and coarse, and on his block-like head he wore a woven hat that came to a point above his nose.

Betna said, "You remember, one night we had"—he lowered his voice—"we had little crates. We had many."

"I remember," Justus said.

There were stabs at my heart. I, too, recalled that tragic night.

The sailor shifted his attention from Betna to me, eyes red-rimmed with black pin-pointed centers.

"We are here to seek one package," Betna said.

Justus raised hands to belted hips. "That shipment is gone. It has been many weeks."

"But where?" I asked. "Can you tell us where to look?"

Betna laid a hand on my shoulder.

I added in a breath, "Please."

Justus inspected Tiber's pier. Stout arms crossed his chest. Activity was mounting around us, men and crates were shuffled from shore to ship. The *Piscator's* striped sail fought a rising wind behind him. Justus lowered his voice. "There is a man, a Greek named Hektor," he said. "He has a warehouse for grain."

"Hektor," Betna repeated.

"He may help you," Justus said.

I pressed hands together and lifted them to my mouth, tense with worry over Menahem. "Thank you," I said.

Justus cleared his throat. "I know nothing more." Untying his vessel and giving its bow a shove, he hustled aboard.

Betna nodded to his seafaring friend, who had already busied himself with a puffed sail, the boat picking up speed. "I will search for this Greek," Betna said to me.

"How long will that take?" I asked.

Betna patted my shoulder. "Hurry does not help."

And so I was patient—or at least tried to be. I waited while Betna searched, recognizing that a woman, particularly a young woman, would only meet with closed doors and silent glares or worse. Such thoughts lent understanding to Lormah's statement that, though a slave, she was given some freedom to move about; most could not. I yearned for that ability to come and go. Betna, of course, was diligent, but the very nature of the children's harbor was one of concealment. As each day passed and we saw nothing of Menahem, optimism began to fade.

ℬ ℭ

Within a week of returning to Rome, Alon came. Rain was falling. Drums of thunder were shaking our ground, and water streamed as from a bottomless amphora; splashing, humming, and funneling into rivulets. When the door opened to his rap, it seemed a black cloud had paused on our doorstep. Alon's beard had become long and unkempt and surrounded a gaunt face. I would not have known him among the masses.

He said, "It gladdens me to see you. You look well." His voice broke, and he hung his head, refusing my pleas to come inside and find dryness and warmth.

"Alon, you are a part of us," I said. "You can come here whenever you need—"

"No." His voice was gruff. "I'm going away."

I shook my head.

"I seek work in the East," he said, "and I am traveling now to Judea."

"The land of our people," I responded.

Alon looked down the road, as if sight of the Holy Mountain was already fixed.

He said, "I came here to tell you—I want you to know that—that I will remember your kindness to Hannah and to me. I only leave because she—she is ..." Alon raised his chin and forced a grin from quavering lips. "I've often dreamed of returning to our homeland. Now there is nothing to keep me."

"I would keep you, friend," I replied, "if I could."

He shook his head. "Rome is not where I belong."

"But your father. Surely he needs your help in his work."

He grunted. "He has hired someone with a desire for work, unlike his own son." Alon bowed his head. "Only one week ago I was not certain. Today, I realize everything here is useless. Hannah was the reason for all I did." Struggling to say more, he combed his beard with unsteady fingers. Then, drawing his hand into a fist, he turned to leave.

"Will you send us word?" I stepped out the door. "Send word of your journey?"

"I cannot promise," he said.

Alon's slumped figure dissolved into a shimmering curtain of rain, and I walked further into pelting raindrops, allowing them to hammer the roots of my hair.

ಬ ಚ

That night, I dreamt of a wide river and Menahem on its opposite shore, crying and kicking at a blanket. I went to him, stepping first ankle-deep in green water, then to my thighs, soon to my waist. Cupping chilled fingers and swimming into river's flow, my clothes grew heavier, sinking me, allowing waves to slap my face. A woman dressed in white appeared, gathering Menahem into a lengthy robe. She dashed into the trunks of leafless trees, and they were gone.

I woke, picturing Hannah there with me, laughing and talking as we once had done. She wasn't angry, but my stomach wrung with guilt. "I'm afraid he is lost, Hannah. I've failed you."

Remembering how, as little girls, Miriam taught us Daniel's prayer, I offered it as my own: "*Almighty Father, I do not make requests of you because I am righteous, but because of your great mercy. Please hear my prayer. Please forgive my offenses.*"

Ethan told us Jesus had come as an outpouring of the love and mercy of God—again, a reminder of Jesus. Is this man, born in Bethlehem, your answer, Adonai?

ಐ ಆ

Summer weather lingered, to the agony of all. Rome's inhabitants had been taxed to the bottom leather of their purses, compounding the weariness. Due to seizure of ships for Gaius Caesar's bridge across the bay, we also lacked viable transport for grain; so Rome next suffered a famine.

Never before had I considered how much bread was eaten in the city. It had always been plentiful and the staple of our diet. The Roman tradition of free bread to the needy was a better gift than ever imagined, and the scent of baking bread was noticeably absent midst crowded sewers and burning sacrifices.

Scarcity of seagoing vessels also affected delivery of fresh fish. Justus' little boat could not carry enough, and fish carted overland were also in short supply. Our family dined on garden vegetables. All homes despaired, but none more than commoners, deprived of free bread rations. It was dreadful to walk city streets in those days, hands reaching out at every corner, clutching at air; children with no heart for play, cowering under stairs and eating crumbs from filth at their feet.

As the calendar pointed to autumn and heat lumbered on, the emperor chose to divorce his wife. It was expected. We had often seen him on the arm of his mistress, and her figure betrayed the emperor's intent: Rome's heir was apparent. Everyone listened for announcement of his new marriage, but none came. I had expected that my own wedding would be held in September's golden days, but Father would only say, "Not yet, my daughter. Not yet," his face cautioning.

ଚ୍ଚ ଔ

When market week concluded, there began a celebration of Julia Drusilla's birthday. It was extraordinary that Father wanted to attend the ceremonies; we were not required to do so. He took several precautions, however. We sat among commoners in the highest rows of the Circus Maximus, a prudent distance from familiar senate faces. Our bodies were robed in shades of brown. According to Father, Aquila was near, and he could see me. I sighed to think he was close, ready to protect me at any sign of trouble.

Drusilla's divine name, "Panthea," was shouted in loud chorus, piercing the crowd's unruliness much like a towering Egyptian obelisk pierced the racetrack's elevated center. The circus's sandy floor had been painted red and green, and more than 200,000 writhing fans roused the stadium to life. An unexpected whirr of excitement rose from the lowest seats, and we looked to see two enormous animals pulling a golden cart into the arena. Within the cart was a statue of Drusilla.

Betna leaned forward. "Elephants!" he said. "These are in my country."

I was captivated. They squeezed into the arena, their leathery bristled hides brushing travertine revetments on both walls of the arched entrance. (Father would later speak of the "sheen from elephant rubbings.") Young children ran to the bottom rail, extending fingers to touch them and giggling as they passed. Such magnificence in a living creature! Raising a thick, snake-like nose into a curl overhead, one elephant released a blast louder than several horns together. His thick-legged companion echoed. Laughter filled the arena.

Men of darkened skin marched into the circus, wearing red-painted sandals that laced up to their knees. Little golden discs hung from white tunics, shining in sunlight and jingling. They danced moving only their legs, hands against their sides.

Music emanated from the throats of women following, who were dressed similar to the men, their lengths of hair wound with feathers and jewels. It was a simple chorus, half of the women singing in echo to the others:

"Dea, Dea, Panthea! Laudate! Laudate!"
Goddess, Goddess, Panthea! Praise! Praise!

Caligula's roofed platform intruded into layers of seats on the Palatine side of the circus. He stood and carried

291

himself to platform's edge with an air that professed he was as powerful as the massive creatures that had earlier fascinated us.

"Today we honor Panthea!" he shouted.

Hands were waving, people were cheering. Wooden carts tottered around the racetrack where bread loaves and fruit were tossed high into greedy hands, and it was undeniable that Rome's starved spectators were praising the free food and not their cold-hearted ruler. Caligula repeated Drusilla's name with less volume but with sentiment, and then food carts scuttled out of the arena. Turning first right and left, in one swift move, he cast a simple cloth into air. It was a signal for gates to open, a race to begin.

Proud charioteers pummeling across colored sand gained the audience, and I alternated joggling in my seat and biting my nails with each round. Caligula favored the Green team, which immediately wheeled ahead of all others. Horses nodded, necks stretched, manes flared. The Green driver tugged reins left, then right. It was amazing how his horses responded to slight pulls.

Several laps into the race, the Blue team dashed to Greens' right, vying for lead. At that precise time, a pale-painted chariot—the Whites—rushed to the inside before a turn. Caligula jumped to his feet as his Greens were pressed from both directions, wheels spinning into brief contact with the Whites' chariot, sand spraying into a plume. This action upset Blue team's horses in the outside lane; rearing, their chariot overturned. The Red team then came from behind, unable to stop or evade, and drove into the skirmish, tumbling over the blue team's horses, one of which was speared by a flying shard. The crowd squealed. Somehow, Reds managed to hold together and moved on.

White, Green, and Red teams proceeded around a turn, gaining speed into the straightway. They were just below us.

Within the track's raised oval center—called the *spina*—a golden dolphin was tipped to indicate an end to that round and start of the final lap. Chariots raced to the opposite turn and Reds took a slight lead, but their horses were lathered, spent; a bearded driver prodded them with strong lash and rod. Would the Blues be cleared from the track in time? My breath held as debris was carried away and, in a blurred instant, chariot wheels replaced it.

It was the last turn before rushing to finish past Caligula's balcony. His Greens made a decisive move, forcing their horses between White and Red teams, pushing the Whites into a wall edging the *spina*, Reds to the outside. Shouts and squeals crowded the air. White team lost control and rolled, its driver tumbling forward, leather reins encircling and dragging his body across sand and against stone. Fans around the ring waved colored banners; their bellowing never faltered. Reds gathered force and continued, but they were too weary to overcome the Green team who claimed the win.

Gaius Caesar stood, hands raised. It was clear he had invested into this race, and for him it would pay well. His apparent joy elicited growls from spectators. Cries of "No more Green!" rose from seats to our left, between us and the emperor, and guards rushed into crowded stands, carrying away any hecklers. Father shifted, shielding me from view, while men and women were dragged to racecourse below.

Angry voices fired further insults. "Bring back the Republic!" "Revolt!" "The gods condemn you!"

Caligula's face twisted. He returned their insults with a sneer. "If you had but one neck!" he cried. His fist came down hard on the railing. "If you had but one neck, I would silence you!"

The Circus Maximus then bore resemblance to a littered stage of Greek tragedy, its floor a rumpled mixture of grainy color and chariot debris, its stirring backdrop a terrified audience, heads rotating in search of escape. Guards were visible at every opening. Caligula acted as the compelling chorus leader, his angry words performed in vivid and exacting manner. Those men and women who had been dragged from their seats succumbed to fatal and final parts in the emperor's tragic play, knees sinking into sand, heads forced forward. Roman swords sliced the air. Then there was certain silence.

ಲ ೞ

Later, in the privacy of our kitchen, Father and Aquila discussed the day's events.

"I see now," Father said.

A rapid pulse throbbed at Aquila's throat. "He's angered the entire populace, not just senators!" he said.

A fist pressed tight to Father's lips.

"I believe—" Aquila set his jaw. "I think it will be soon."

"What will be soon?" I asked.

"Let us be the ones to worry," Father said. He patted my shoulder.

"Forgive me," Aquila said, "but maybe she should be told."

I crossed my arms, rising to full height, and a steady gaze passed between them. Father nodded.

"There are reports of a conspiracy," Aquila said. "The people of Rome are indignant, as you saw today in the circus. They oppose Caligula openly. I've heard it as well from the streets."

"A conspiracy," I said. "But who could be part of such a plan?"

Father held his chin for a moment. "Senators, tribunes, some of Caligula's own guards. I dare not speak their names," he replied.

I clenched my cup. "His own guards."

Aquila came closer, and I found myself thankful for a rising conspiracy, if only for a rare opportunity to be near my betrothed. "The conflict resides even within palace walls," he said.

"But who would have enough courage to stand against Caligula?" I asked.

"Courage?" Father asked. He shook his head and sighed. "No, it is not courage. People are needy. They are becoming desperate. Swift death is less painful than slow starvation."

"But because they starve they are also weak," I said. "How can people who are starving defeat someone like Caligula?"

Aquila said, "Even the clamor of lowly commoners can make a difference, when there are many."

"The commoners could bring down an emperor?" I asked.

"As Caligula well knows, Rome's enraged mobs have provoked rebellion in the past," Father replied.

"What does that mean for us?" I asked. "Are you saying we should join the conspirators?"

Father's response was abrupt. "No."

"What you must do," Aquila said, "is be quiet and remain unseen, go about normal chores, if that's possible. Any persons who even appear to be part of a scheme, they will be dealt with promptly."

"Dealt with," I repeated.

Father looked into my eyes. "They will face torture to force confession. And then execution."

"Unseen. You're talking about more than daily chores," I said.

"Your wedding date is being deferred," Father said. "No festivities in our neighborhood."

Aquila appeared troubled. "Or we could arrange for a secret—and quiet—wedding."

"Quiet. Secret." I bit my lip. "That will work for me." As the words parted my lips, a surge of guilt cramped my heart. Esther was not quiet or unseen, was she?

Father stood between us, a firm hand embracing each of our shoulders. "I've heard senators speak of a campaign. Gaius Caesar is planning an excursion to Gaul." He paused. "We could have the wedding then. I feel better about having it when he's gone."

I remembered how the emperor took a bride from another man's wedding, used her for a time and then cast her out. My body chilled. I said, "When he's gone."

Aquila took my hand. "As you wish."

ප ශ

We woke in the night to pounding on our door, and I heard Betna's voice and then sandals tapping on mosaic tiles.

Betna called out.

"I'm awake," I said.

Like birds set free from clasped hands, Hesperia's girls flew into my room.

I studied each of them. "Why are you here? And in the middle of the night," I said. "What has happened?"

Balbina stood tall. She had now surpassed my own height and would soon reach marrying age. "We ran away," she replied. Her voice sounded strong, though her eyes were wet.

Hortensia, tears tumbling down her cheeks, climbed onto my lap. She pulled her limbs tight and snuggled against me.

With broken speech and wringing of hands, the girls described their lives in the household of Hesperia and Aedias. It was one of hard work and steady punishment, and malnourished bodies added emphasis to their troubled tale.

"Stay here," I said. After nesting them into blankets, flickering lamp in hand, I went in search of Father.

"We cannot risk the anger of Aedias and Hesperia," Father said. "Already our standing in the community has been compromised."

"But it is compromised on a lie! Only because others accused Hannah of—" I didn't want to say anything more.

Father looked drowsy. "Still," he said, "we must not hurry into actions we'll regret. Are the girls injured?"

"Little Hortensia has a swollen foot and bruised legs from being hit with a broom handle. Balbina refuses to share any details, but her fingers are bruised and bleeding."

He continued to pace across the room. "No one knows they came here," I said. "Can't we hide them until the children's harbor is found?"

"Are you sure no one knows?" He shook his head. "Children usually leave a trail."

"It's only what the girls told me," I replied. "They took great care."

"Prisca, our laws do not allow for this."

"I know."

Before light, we walked the girls to Miriam's abandoned *insula*, encountering only a few ragged souls who dozed among rubbish. We were cautious about entering. Though Father had placed a solid bolt, those needing shelter might have found a way. Inside, it was cold and forlorn with no sign of habitation. We left food, bedding, and strict instructions to stay in hiding.

"What if someone comes to the door?" Balbina asked.

"Then you will conceal yourselves as I showed you," Father said. He laid a hand on her head. "Keep the door locked from inside. You'll know us by our knock. I don't expect it, but if someone enters, you're small enough to fit into that old clothing bin. No one will know. Just remember to be quiet."

I weakened at Hortensia's pale face. "Don't fear," I said. "We'll attend you every evening. And Alon's family is nearby. Remember Alon?" Balbina nodded. "We'll ask his family to keep watch over this place as well." I hugged each in turn and reminded them that these lodgings were temporary. "We'll find a better home for you—a safe one—soon."

Father was silent. I knew the arrangement was worrisome. We had to find the children's harbor.

ಹಿ ಐ

When next Betna and I walked to the fountain, I saw wavering beneath cool waters a small square of wool with three even stitches. Squeezing water away from its sodden fabric, I had reassuring thoughts of Lormah. But where did she intend to meet? It was odd to find her message at the fountain. Adding a trio of stitches, I then carried my reply to the fountain next day, letting it fall as if by accident into the basin, wishing to avoid inquiry from the many who had come with pots to be filled. It was hard to trust, hard to be confident that Lormah would find my message and then reveal a place of meeting.

As I bent into the font with my jar, Keziah was taking hers away. She was steady, familiar with repeated discipline, raising her water-filled vessel without a spill. Mara had died during our sojourn in Baiae, and I pitied her silent and cheerless daughter who had been segregated from others by meticulous mothering; Keziah was alone and friendless. Edging closer, my throat compressed, realizing grief at Hannah's passing was still near.

"It is long since I've seen you," I said. "Is your father well?"

"He has taken a new wife," Keziah said.

"At least—well, might that lift some of your burden?"

Keziah set her pot down and turned toward me with a hard look. "It helps me to know my mother died a righteous woman."

"And she was. It must console you."

Her fingers tapped a steady rhythm against the water pot in her hands. "A pity you do not have the same comfort," she said.

I stepped back, stunned.

"You act as if you don't know." Keziah's laugh was harsh. "Everyone knows. Your family is so proud. Your father, he looks quite prestigious in his Roman dress, but what are your lives before God? And have you not brought curse upon them all, associating with—with sin?"

Keziah began to walk away but turned to stand over me, crimson-faced and breathing loud. "Remember the Psalmist's warning: '*Here is the man who did not make God his strength, but trusted in the abundance of his riches and strengthened himself in his wickedness.*'" She grunted, embraced her jar, and left.

Coldness crept up my arms. Had we trusted in Father's position and pay and not in our God? The luxury of our travel to Baiae weighed against me, and I sat on fountain's brick ledge recalling sand and sun, the restful feel of hot mineral waters against my skin. Had I neglected to seek the Lord's direction? Most painful, could Hannah have lived if I had been more worthy? Might Menahem already have been found?

Noticing a leak from a slight fracture in my clay pot, it was certain that Adonai was pointing out flaws. I had been selfish, steeped in self-pity. Who was that proud young girl who dared believe she had a purpose not unlike Esther? What a fool. How could I have been so arrogant, to think Almighty God could use me? Keziah was right. And it was my doing. My head sank lower, empty as the vessel in my arms.

Just then a dark-skinned hand touched the sleeve of my garment. It was a woman dressed in plain, tan wool.

She looked on me through rounded eyes of eager youth, though her face was not young, and she gave my arm a tender hug. "I do not think her words are true," she said.

Ashamed that this stranger had heard Keziah's assertions, I looked down at the dusty road. "But my family has suffered. How else can I explain it? I've thought too much of myself."

"And can you explain the suffering of Job?" she asked.

"No. I—I cannot." Emotion was rising. "Though I must be cursed. Adonai has withdrawn his blessing."

"I believe that Almighty God calls you to deeper faith," she said.

"Deeper faith?"

"When the path is hard, who can you trust?" the woman asked.

"Well," I said, "I've been taught that God's law will bear me up. But sin, the law …"

"Our Lord gives us something beyond the Law of Moses. He gives himself. He is only asking that we come with our little faith. Do you believe God can be so good?"

My eyes pinched to understand. The woman had full, rounded lips and strong white teeth. Gentle lines of age told me she smiled often.

"Faith. Are you saying that faith overcomes the Law of Moses?" I asked.

"God himself fulfills the law by sending his own Son to save us. And with faith we can believe it."

In the fountain's depths, I saw Avram's reflection, his hand extended with a single olive. "I have heard something like you say. But, in recent troubles, those thoughts have become cluttered."

"I pray you will know the saving grace of God."

"Grace?"

"Yes," the woman said.

Her face was round, cheekbones high, and glowing with chestnut color. There was a depression in her right cheek when she smiled. She continued, "God's grace he gives freely to us. His love is so big, his own Son he gives," she sighed, "to die for us."

"His own Son." I whispered the words. "Do you mean Jesus?"

"You know him!" She clapped hands together.

"No. I've been told of him but never met—"

Several women approached the opposite side of the fountain, and I pulled my jar from the shallow pool. "I'm sorry. I must go."

"I pray we meet again," the woman said.

Rejoining Betna at a nearby carpenter's shop, we made our short walk home in silence. My thoughts were muddled, a bewildering blend of Keziah's words with those of the stranger. If God did give his own Son for us ... But Jesus was nailed to a cross! How could God let that happen? And if Jesus was dead, how could he save anyone now?

ᛒᎠ ᏣᏴ

My mind strayed often to the unknown woman at the fountain while waiting and watching for Lormah. Every dawn, I searched our street from my square of garden. When we walked home after attending Balbina and Hortensia, every balcony and shaded niche met my eyes. On the fifth day, slogging home with a full water pot, there she was, partly concealed by a hedge near an *insula's* stairway.

We were within sight of home, and I begged to go to her. "She can be trusted. Please."

Betna eventually consented because home was near, and he carried the container of water. Lormah motioned me into a murky gap between two buildings, and my body cooled in shade; the air was moist and still.

"My friend," I whispered. "I've missed you."

She touched my shoulder in answer, and I wrapped arms around her. It was difficult to hold back tears at seeing her again.

Lormah appeared startled but returned the embrace. "You did not forget me," she said.

"Never."

"Our meeting must be short, but you must know, I am soon to be sold."

"No, that cannot be. You must not leave me."

"But I am not sad. Our Lord gives me new work." Her eyes widened. "And maybe a master who will be kind."

"But something has happened to me. It's as though something has—you see, something happened to the girl I was. Maybe it began with Hannah's attack and then her—her death. It's hard to explain, but I grieve all the days."

"You think too much of death."

Leaning hard against the building's moss-covered wall, I sighed. "But those I have loved have died."

"Many that you love are living still." She paused. "Why are you not coming for Hannah's baby?"

"But we couldn't find you. We've been looking." Lormah frowned, and I heard myself rambling. "I couldn't think how to feed him or care for him, and the children were all moved, and—and then so much time passed. We could not—oh, maybe he is better without me anyway."

She closed the distance between us, her voice compelling. "The evil one is always working to keep God's people away from faith. Do not let him lie to you! If you pray, the Lord shows you these things. He makes a way."

"But you don't understand. There's something wrong with me. There's a sense of—I can't explain it. As if—as if my clothing—no, it's more. It's as if my entire body is soiled ... with sin. I am cursed."

She came close, studying my face. "You are not," Lormah said.

"You deserve someone better as a friend."

Lormah gasped, her mouth wide open. "Do you not know? When you come, I know God sends you. Even when you are sitting in the mud, I know it." Her eyes shone with amusement. "He sends you so Lormah will learn."

"But all my efforts—you see, nothing is going right. Miriam is getting frail. Father is burdened and sad. If only Mother had not died. If I had done something different, maybe she wouldn't have." Groaning, my words running at a fast pace. Lormah's forehead was creased, her brows arched as if she were hearing a foreign language. "And then Betna, he is so lonely. Dear Hannah is gone, and so is—"

Lormah grasped my arms. "And you are a god who makes everything right?"

"But—no."

"You command who suffers and who does not?"

"No."

"You are not God." Lormah's voice was firm.

Almighty God. Hannah once described him as a powerful commander, overseeing and disciplining his children. Could it be that God disciplines us with pain?

"Before you"—Lormah pointed at me—"before I know you, Prisca girl, I was one not loved. All I know is shame." Passion filled her words. "And so I trust babies. Babies do not hate." A hand went to her cheek. "My skin is ugly. But babies do not see these things."

"And I have failed you. I've failed Ethan too, putting the children's harbor at risk."

Lormah grunted. "We are in a world that has sin. There is always risk." She raised her brows. "Children's harbor?" It must have been her first hearing of the name I'd given it.

"But it's—"

Lormah stopped me with a raised hand. "Look for God's goodness," she said. "The evil one tries to hide it. Look. Have faith. You will find it."

The woman at the fountain said we were called to a deeper faith. Is that what Lormah had? The hardness of life was written all over her. She wore only rags. Yet, for one who had so little, she gave so much. How could she persevere in the midst of such circumstances?

"My name is a slap to me," Lormah said. "It tells me I am not loved. 'Lo-Ruhamah.' Even to say my own name, it is saying I am bad. And then God sends you to teach me, to show me there is no shame, that my name is a lie. Jesus gives me a new name, and I know 'Lormah' means '*loved*,' because he tells me." She lifted her eyes to mine, and they were brown and gold, rich and intense, moist with emotion.

I took her hands and held them. "It is a good name. And if I have helped ..."

I turned and began to pace, sensing a struggle within. "Could it be that I have a purpose after all? Maybe like Es- ..." I frowned. "But Hannah is dead. She is gone. Menahem is lost. And now you are to be sold and will go away. Grief trails me, and it's because I've been too proud, expecting God could use me."

She reached out a hand, but I pulled away. "Keziah made me believe I am cursed," I said.

Lormah raised her hands, speaking in eager tones. "The love of Jesus is about life! When do you go to him and live?"

"But he died too. It's all hopeless. Our God has forgotten us in this horrid place."

Lormah put hands to my shoulders, pressuring me to sit down, and then she positioned herself across from me. For a moment, there was silence, her eyes closed in prayer. And then she leaned near, speaking with boldness.

"Jesus dies for our sin." Lormah patted her chest.

"For our sin," I repeated. Father made payments for us, sent to the Temple in Jerusalem. His payments were to purchase sacrifices that would cleanse us from sin—spotless lambs, goats—and we were convinced it was the way, the promise, the plan given to our people for all generations. How could one sacrifice change everything? And without making any payment?

"Jesus is only someone I've heard stories about, Lormah. I've never met him and know little about his life, except how Ethan described it. What can Jesus mean to me?" I asked.

Lormah fell back as if I'd hit her. "He is everything to you! Jesus rose from the tomb. He is alive." She lowered her voice to a throaty whisper and pressed hands to her chest. "He lives in me."

Silent, I measured her words. "He lives in you?"

"Do you see? You can speak to Jesus. He hears you. He is the friend who never leaves."

"The friend who never leaves?" I asked.

Lormah smiled, rocking back on cool ground. She then leaned toward me and spoke each word with passion and distinction, urging the message. "He is with me all the day and night. His Holy Spirit whispers to my soul." She closed her eyes, and the calm of her presence arrested me. I craved that sweet solace that made her face shine.

"He is with you always?" I asked.

"When you tell God you believe, the spirit of Jesus comes to live—here." She reached across, tapping the area of my heart.

"You have spoken of the Holy Spirit." I searched Lormah's face for answers.

"When Jesus goes up to the Father," Lormah said, "he sends the Holy Spirit to us. His Spirit tells us right things, true things." Her voice softened. "You are never alone."

I was breathing, but each intake of air was labored. My eyes closed. "Adonai," I prayed, "show me. I really want to know. Please show me if it is right to believe in Jesus. Let me know if he is your Son."

Stillness surrounded me, exuding light and warmth. Lormah was standing, an arm reaching out for me. Seeing her extended hand, my breath held. The strange scar had disappeared. Every finger was perfect and in its proper place. I touched her hand, now smooth and healthy.

"The Lord hears you," Lormah said. "And I receive blessing!" She pulled me to my feet. "Do you see? Do you believe in Jesus?"

Odd, in that moment, I did see—myself. About my neck was a thick chain, each link inscribed with a tax against my soul: My need to please and fear of failing, my need to save others and claim importance, my selfish pride, weighty levies of guilt; worry after worry, fear upon fear. And Jesus stood there, his hand taking hold of the chain and lifting it from my shoulders.

"I do! I believe in Jesus."

"Do you believe Jesus is Messiah, our living Savior, sent from the God of Abraham, Isaac, and Jacob?"

"Yes."

A soft airiness floated around us. "This is what I've hoped for," I said. "Life. Freedom. I am no longer afraid."

Lormah's face had a fresh and thriving radiance that could only come from time with God. "Come," she said.

Our boldness was astonishing. We walked—or skipped—to the Tiber River, arm in arm. There was a place where the embankment closed around itself creating a small cove, and water splashed against rocks of gigantic size. A stone bridge loomed overhead. In that place, Lormah led me into soft, curling waves.

"Do you believe Jesus is God's son and he died to give you life?" Lormah asked.

"Yes."

"Do you accept God's gift of salvation and ask him to forgive you?"

"Yes."

"Like water washes you, Jesus washes sin away. He covers you with his righteousness."

Kneeling into tepid water, its current surged above my head, and then Lormah's hands drew me up. The Tiber had seen so much death. Now life.

A voice entered my mind: "*I will never leave you. I will never forsake you.*" Names of children came in and out of mind's sight—Menahem, Ira, Balbina, Hortensia—and a sudden awareness saturated my senses. They needed to be taught; I would be their teacher. The Lord's own hand would show me how. "I am the way," Jesus said.

"You are the way, and I will follow." Emotion stirred, sensing his loving presence and knowing he heard me ... and—precious miracle—I could also hear my Lord's gentle voice.

"You serve a risen Savior!" Lormah said. "You are alive in Jesus!"

Yes, alive. I wanted to cry out, "Jesus is the way!" and to share this gift with everyone dear to me and to share it with people I didn't know, to let it float from me like a swarm of multi-colored butterflies flitting about in daylight, imparting delight and hope. There was fullness, more joy than one could hold, yet it was not heavy at all, so unlike the weight of sin.

As Lormah and I parted, my feet were running. I had to tell Aquila. It was improper; it could be looked upon with scorn. Still, my feet carried me where they would. And soon, to my delight, there was Aquila running toward me! We almost collided on the street. He led me into a courtyard lined with trees and flowers.

I started: "There's something wonderful to tell—"

"Prisca, it's—"

"—and it just happened," I said.

"—the most amazing thing," he said.

We laughed.

"You first," Aquila said.

I waited a moment, fascinated by the timbre in his voice, the birds singing around us, the smell of roses floating on air.

"Aquila, I believe. What we have heard about Jesus is true."

His brown eyes opened wide. "Yes, it is."

"You—Aquila?" I drew a breath. "You believe in Jesus too?" My heart was thumping, filling my ears.

"I believe that Jesus died for me," Aquila said.

"And for me."

"Yes, my love. For us. For all," he said.

"How could this have happened?" I asked. "Both of us, today."

Aquila shook his head. "If I had not believed in the miracles of God before this! Here is yet another way God has increased my faith."

"How could we ever doubt?" I asked.

He replied, "Tychon told me today that '*Nothing is impossible with God.*' And I know it's true."

As he spoke, I remembered something more. Hannah's final words. Tears coursed down my face.

Aquila seized my hands, alarmed. "Beloved, what is it?"

"Hannah's words, '*Tell Prisca I believe.*' Aquila, I know where she is."

For us, on that day, time did not pass. We spoke of the mysteries of Almighty God and of excessive grace extended to us in his gift of Jesus, our Messiah. Our next question became, "And what would you have us do now, Oh Lord?"

When breezes swept into our enclosure and rattled crisp leaves on overhanging trees, my bridegroom stood to escort me home. We cared not what others might say; our love remained pure. And we knew that our God could see us, robed in the righteousness of Jesus. Soon we would be married. I knew it as sure as I knew the Lord had rescued my heart from despair.

Upon arriving home, we opened the door to a baby's cry and soothing voices. I stopped, curious at the sound, and then raced through the vestibule, Aquila close behind.

Betna stood in the center of the room, bouncing a baby in his arms. He arched wiry eyebrows in my direction. A young woman stood by.

"Menahem?" I asked.

Betna nodded. He looked almost giddy.

Filling my arms with the healthy baby, I realized he truly did have Hannah's eyes. I smoothed ringlets of dark hair, breathing in the scent of him.

"Oh, Menahem," I said. My hands went quick to chubby waving arms, embracing each little finger with my own.

Betna cleared his throat. "We have brought Ulrika. She is his nurse."

"We?" I asked.

Ethan stepped from behind Betna. "Hello, Prisca."

"Ethan." I studied his face, feeling my own pinch in pain. "I'm so sorry about …"

He shook his head. "The Lord has taken care of us—the Lord and your good friend." He motioned toward Betna.

That same "good friend" turned aside and mumbled. "I did nothing."

Ethan and I grinned at one another. We knew otherwise.

"I've been unable to come, to bring the boy." Ethan sighed. "Our situation has been tenuous. It remains so."

My voice shook, words halting. "Yes—well, I knew he would be safe, and ..." Pulling the baby close, resting my cheek against his, I sighed. Aquila laid a hand on Menahem's head.

"You call him 'Menahem,'" Ethan said. "We did not know." Ethan gestured to the young woman. "And he has brought comfort to Ulrika. Her own child—a girl—was lost."

"Ulrika," I said. I turned to the young woman, her hair streaked with gold. Tan-colored flecks crossed the bridge of a pale nose.

"I love him," she said. Ulrika's voice was delicate, matching her manner. "I have called him Gavriel, like the angel who spoke to Mary. To me, he is an angel."

"He is an angel." I enclosed his small hand in mine. "And will you continue to nurse him? Can you come here to nurse him?"

Ulrika looked down at her feet. "It is difficult," she said.

My brow creased with worry.

"I do want to nurse him," Ulrika said quickly. Her blue eyes were round and expressive. "But I cannot live in your home. And it is many roads to my dwelling."

Menahem twisted in my arms and reached for Ulrika. I tried to hold him tighter, to speak to him, but he began to cry.

"It will be all right," Ulrika said to the child. She took his small hand, and he wriggled away from me. I fought back tears, placing him in her arms and swallowing the regret in my throat.

Betna came closer, a hand on my shoulder. "I will take you. The child will soon know you."

"Will that be all right?" I asked. "We have clothes for him." I remembered blankets and baby things we had woven and sewn; Hannah would want her son to have them. Ulrika nodded, cuddling the baby in her arms. Her own clothing was clean and well-mended, and it was clear that Menahem was in good care.

Ethan stepped closer. "Do you still wish to help our children?"

"I do. In fact—well, I have a desire to teach them," I replied.

"Teach them? I will include that in my prayers," Ethan said. "Now that we have found each other ..."

"There are also two young girls in need of shelter," I said. "They have lived in harsh conditions. May I bring them to you?"

"As Jesus taught, we will turn no child away." Ethan studied me. "Though there are arrangements we must make. Betna and I have invented a way of corresponding, and I will get word to him."

I wanted Ethan to know that Jesus was now my "friend who never leaves," but Aquila spoke at my side. "Ethan, do you have need for a young couple to assist these children?"

"There is much to pray about, it seems." Ethan gazed at us with interest. Does our faith show?

I said, "There have been times I worried we would never see you again. Is the children's harbor safe?"

"We must persist in our caution," he said, "but God finds a way." He paused. "I like your name for it, a children's harbor. And you may be pleased to know that we are still housed near the Tiber's changeable waves, continually seeking to be a harbor of safety and hope for the helpless."

Ethan placed a hand on Aquila's shoulder. He looked tired. "You understand," Ethan said, "our caution is meant to include you, your family."

ೞ ೞ

Afternoons with Menahem became a tender blessing, his little hands pulling at my hair, a face of complete peace in sleep, and his small mouth mimicking mine and making soft sounds. One day he began to reach for me! Ulrika would chatter about each new discovery he would make, her happiness so apparent and innocent, and I remembered what Hannah had said to her newborn son: "For you brought me comfort even before your birth—and a will to live." Menahem had clearly brought those gifts. Yes, "comfort" was his name.

It gave me pause to think how God brings solace into dark times, by his grace. In my prayers, I asked about sharing my faith with Father, Miriam, and Betna, knowing there was much learning ahead. Time upon time, God would remind me of those first moments of meeting Ethan and his unwavering patience.

"Lord God," I prayed, "May I know that kind of patience that comes from trusting in you and your right time, your good plan." Hopes lifted and faith revived. My basket was filling.

ೞ ೞ

On one clear-sky day, messenger boys were dispatched throughout the city to announce the intended marriage of Gaius Julius Caesar Germanicus, our emperor. Floral wreaths graced monuments at crossroads once again. He would be taking Milonia Caesonia for his bride.

When the marriage occurred, it was so hot—even in late October—awnings had been placed about the forum to shade the bridal banquet. A little girl was born a few weeks later. She was named Julia Drusilla, in honor of the woman Gaius Caesar loved, his sister. The emperor proclaimed the birth miraculous, his child born only one month from the wedding, and we laughed that he would think Rome's inhabitants so blind and dim-witted!

Soon after Baby Drusilla was born, an interesting discussion took place in our household. Fresh from the senate house Father appeared, brimming with tidings. "Yesterday," he said, "Gaius Caesar laid his infant daughter upon the knees of Jupiter, declaring her already a goddess."

I asked, "And now are we being commanded to worship her? Is there some decree demanding we offer sacrifices to his child?"

Betna coughed and raised an eyebrow.

"There has been no decree," Father said, "though it will surely come."

I groaned. "There are always new requirements, new fees, new demands, and there is nothing left for people to give." I touched Father's arm. "Is this the news you promised?"

"My daughter, there is also good news. Our valiant emperor is heading north … at last. He's leaving for Gaul with the plan of pursuing a military campaign." He took my hand and held it.

"Our wedding," I said.

Father smiled. "We have reason to cheer," he said.

"At last," Miriam cried. She rose and came to us across the atrium, leaning on Hannah's old cane. "I shall have to sit at the loom once again."

ဆ ၵ

~ *XI* ~

Surely he has borne our griefs
And carried our sorrows;
Yet we esteemed him stricken,
Smitten by God, and afflicted.
But he was wounded for our transgressions,
He was bruised for our iniquities;
Upon him was the chastisement that made us whole,
And with his stripes we are healed.
All we like sheep have gone astray;
We have turned every one to his own way;
And the Lord has laid on him
The iniquity of us all.

~Isaiah 53:4-6

With the departure of Caligula, all of Rome released a profound sigh. It was that breath of relief one expresses after a devastating storm has passed and you see that you and your household have survived its fearsome blasts.

For his own amusement, the emperor had taken with him a collection of painted actors, exotic women, and gladiator showmen. Their absence was appeased by a surprising influx of visitors from the East, calling themselves "messengers of good news." One by one, they trickled into Rome promising new life in Jesus. First was a stout, longhaired man named Simeon, who stood in the marketplace and declared: "The Lord has commanded the blessing of life for ever more. And by what name is this called? It is Jesus!"

Next, there was mild-mannered Lucius, who came to assembly and told us with more passion than his slender body suggested, "Do not forget the promise that Israel would receive a Savior through David's line. The Savior has come!"

And then there was Salome, calling to passersby near a neighboring fountain. "Through Messiah's touch," she told us, "I was cleansed of a flesh-eating plague." Never had I seen a woman with skin more pure—pale and pink as a child's. Many came forward in faith and received healing by the power of God's Holy Spirit. Yet, for all these occurrences, I remained the only one in our *domus* who believed.

Our wedding day came. Standing in my room, I passed calm fingers over luxurious silk—Father spared no expense—expanding into the fabric with calming breaths. It was cool and quiet, and then there came a gentle whisper. "The time is now. Share your faith."

"Beautiful." Miriam held aloft the door's curtain, entering in her gentle way.

"It is the love of the Lord, you know, that brings beauty," I replied.

She paused, smiling at words she herself had taught. "And he has blessed you with a loveliness that increases," Miriam said.

I chewed my lip, offering silent prayers.

"Do not be afraid," Miriam said. She balanced on the edge of my bed. "Aquila loves you."

I said, "I'm not afraid, dear Miriam. The love of Jesus has cleansed me of fear."

Her eyes gazed into mine. "I still hear his name in my dreams," she said.

"You once said you would know when Messiah has come. What does your heart tell you now?" I asked.

"That he lives," she said. "Only my harried mind makes me question."

Warm memories stirred in me, Avram's sun-and-wind-beaten hands and a green olive dropping into my open palm. "It takes faith," I said. "Even if it's very small, it's a beginning."

"You believe," Miriam said. "You believe in Jesus."

"I do."

"Child, why have you not told me?"

"I wanted to, and the words would be on my tongue, but there was a compelling sense that I must wait, as if a warm hand rested on my shoulder to stay me. This morning, I knew the time was right."

Miriam sat very still. She said, "It is many months now since we talked of the box and its precious scroll." Her eyes were piercing, clear. "I have often repeated its verse, *'The sun of righteousness shall rise with healing in its wings.'* Each time, I sensed the Lord changing my heart and knew a day would come when I would have to choose."

"And Jesus says, *'You did not choose me, but I chose you.'*"

Miriam's eyes widened, but she did not speak.

"Ethan has told me about him," I said. "Oh, Miriam, the words of Jesus are like honey on my tongue!"

Her voice shook. "How did you come to believe?"

We sat close, snug, like those days when I was small and receiving lessons at her knee, but this time

Miriam was the student. I told her about Lormah, her hard life and solid faith; about Lormah's miraculous healing through prayer; about my chain of burdens being lifted; and then that breathtaking sense of peace ... God's words that came to me by the Holy Spirit.

"And if I believe," Miriam said, "what must I do?"

Her hands felt cold, and I pulled them to my face. "It is so refreshing and different from the many rules we've been taught," I said. "If you believe, you simply say so and open yourself to receive. Do you believe that Jesus is the Son of God?"

"I believe."

"Do you believe that Jesus died for your sin, one perfect sacrifice for all time?"

"Yes," Miriam said. "And I sense a word—a word that I am forgiven. He is—he is saying, '*I give you life everlasting.*'" She held her breath for a moment. "It is true, Priscilla. The Lord is speaking to me."

"The impossible becomes possible!"

"He chose even me." Miriam sighed. "And death is no longer my enemy."

"As Lormah has said, '*Jesus is about life!*'"

"Life," she said. "And I feel it in this old body. It is long since ..." She stopped, brightening. "And what of Aquila? Something tells me you have already shared your faith with him."

"Another miracle," I replied. "The very day I came to know Jesus, Aquila received God's life-giving grace. It seems miracles abound."

"Even in Rome," she said.

"Not even Rome can dim God's glory," I said.

"Oh, praise him," Miriam said. She began to rock with emotion, and I wrapped arms around her. We sat without speaking as precious Miriam surrendered to Jesus, allowing his grace to consume old sorrow and shame.

After a time, Miriam stood. "We should be preparing you to marry." She wiped away tears and smiled. "And, oh, blessed truth! Our Savior has come!"

Leading her to my basin, I bathed her head. "Beloved Miriam, you are redeemed," I said. "Your sins are washed away, and you have received the gift of eternal life."

Her hands rose to touch my face as if she were seeing it anew. "I believe the Lord will use you," she said.

"If only—you see, I still struggle with feeling worthy."

"I think I understand." Miriam pulled me close, pressing her face to mine. "None of us are worthy without Jesus. And, oh, my child, we have lived so long without him, in our old way. Such thoughts are difficult to change." She smoothed bedclothes and then stood, raising her head high. "Now I am encouraged. There is hope."

୫୨ ୯୫

Just as Abraham sent his loyal servant to retrieve a bride for Isaac many generations before, Aquila sent his trusted friend, Tychon.

I answered the door unaccompanied. Father, Betna, and Miriam stood by with tender faces.

Tychon was dressed in his finest, speaking the ancient words of Abraham's chosen man: "Pray, give me a little water to drink from your jar."

I held out a cup with water freshly drawn. "Drink, my lord," I said.

He emptied the cup and then produced two gold bracelets. I held my arm for him to place them.

"Tell me whose daughter you are," Tychon said.

"I am the daughter of Eben Lucullus Priscus of Rome, son of Eben and son of Judah."

My father stepped forward. "Behold, Priscilla, my daughter, is before you," he said. "Take her and go, and let her be the wife of your master, as the Lord has spoken."

Then Father turned to me, eyes bright, chin raised. "And will you go with this man?"

"I will go," I replied.

Father drew me into his arms and held me tight. Miriam appeared at his side, handing him an embroidered wedding veil, and he kissed both my cheeks before covering my head.

Tychon guided me to a waiting litter, made private with gauzy draping, and I climbed inside. Its interior was softened with colorful, stitched pillows. Aquila's men hoisted the litter on sturdy shoulders, and we started down the Vicus Albus with Tychon making strong, confident steps at the head of our procession. His tunic had been sewn with silver threads that flickered in occasional patches of light. Behind us, followed the collective footfalls of family.

We traversed the Tiber River, and as we drew near our destination, music was heard. Aquila stood apart, wearing a robe that was crisp, white, and trimmed with gold and blue threads.

He helped me from my carriage, and we walked through an exterior door that was shaded by flowering vines. A short passage brought us into a wide, tiled atrium. Natural light flowed into the room from an adjacent garden that spanned the home's northeastern edge. Four stout columns bridged the two spaces, and high garden walls made the entire space private and secure. At garden's far end, there was a round pool reflecting golden sun, and at the center, a canopy had been raised. Aquila led me toward it. This would be our beginning, our tent and our shelter, like ancestors of long ago.

Once everyone was present, my bridal walk could begin. Seven times I circled round Aquila, the number of days in which God Most High completed creation. My steps were even and slow-paced, eyes fixed upon my bridegroom, loving him more with every sacred step. The rabbi recited from the *Torah* during each rotation:

"And God said, '*Let there be light,*' and there was light … and God said, '*Let there be a firmament in the midst of the waters …*'"

As the rabbi spoke those powerful statements that had flown from the mouth of our all-knowing and wondrous God, I remembered that Ethan had explained Jesus was the Word; and, through him, all things were created. That magnificent vision had come to mean so much … Jesus issuing forth and instilling life into a meaningless void. Once more, the life of Jesus bloomed in the empty spaces inside me, and I trembled. Would it always be that way, a continued renewal that increased my faith? Thank you, Jesus.

The rabbi's voice pierced the air. "Then God said, *'Let us make man in our image, after our likeness.'*"

Having completed seven circles, I stood at my bridegroom's side.

"And God blessed them," the rabbi said, "and God said to them, *'Be fruitful and multiply, and fill the earth and subdue it.'*"

Aquila raised my veil, and his look recalled our first meeting, when he had studied me with eyes that missed nothing.

Our betrothal chalice was lifted high in the rabbi's hand. Seven blessings would be recited, and guests were chosen to impart each one.

Father began, his voice full and strong. "Blessed are you, Lord our God, Ruler of the World, who created all things for your glory."

And then Betna: "Blessed are you, Lord our God, Ruler of the World, Creator of man."

Miriam's voice was heard, quiet yet unwavering. "Blessed are you, Lord our God, Ruler of the World, who created man in the pattern of your own likeness, fashioning woman from man as his helpmate, that together they might perpetuate life. Blessed are you, Lord our God, Creator of man."

Alon's father, Ezra, shouted the next. "Blessed are you, Lord our God, Ruler of the World. May Zion rejoice as her children are restored to her in joy. Blessed are you, Oh Lord, who causes Zion to rejoice at her children's return."

And then Ethan: "Blessed are you, Lord our God, Ruler of the World. Grant perfect joy to this loving couple as you made your creation happy in the Garden of Eden so long ago. Blessed are you, Oh Lord, who grants the joy of bride and groom."

Once again, the rabbi spoke: "Blessed are you, Lord our God, Ruler of the World, who created joy and gladness, bridegroom and bride, mirth, song, delight and rejoicing, love and harmony, peace and friendship. Oh, Lord our God, may there ever be heard in the cities of Judea and in the streets of Jerusalem voices of joy and gladness, the voice of a bridegroom and the voice of a bride, jubilant voices of those joined in marriage under the bridal canopy, voices of young people feasting and singing. Blessed are you, Oh, Lord, who causes the groom to rejoice with his bride."

Tychon recited a final blessing, merriment apparent in his voice: "Blessed are you, Lord our God, Ruler of the World, Creator of the fruit of the vine."

We turned toward the rabbi, who placed the chalice in Aquila's hand. Aquila tipped it for me to drink and then drank from it as well. My stomach grumbled as wine entered, for we had fasted, and Aquila smiled. He placed our empty chalice on the ground and said, "Blessed are you, Lord our God, Ruler of the World. I shall have no other gods before you, and I place no earthly thing before my wife." He flattened the cup beneath his heel and cheers were shouted by all.

We were hastened then into a private room where a table had been set with food and a solitary lamp. Our first meal as husband and wife was to be shared separate and apart, though we could hear feasting and celebration outside our door.

Overcome with emotion, I could not sit down but, instead, swayed against Aquila's broad chest. "And now we are married, my husband."

Aquila embraced me and then took my hands, folding them within his own. "Yes, my love. And there is more. Prisca, I sense that it was no accident for us to know Jesus at the same moment and—I'm a little unsure how to say it—but there must be some higher purpose for our union, something special that God has for us, even beyond the love we share as husband and wife."

"Those thoughts have come to me as well," I said. "It's something you know but can't quite explain, isn't it?"

"It doesn't diminish the genuine love between us," Aquila said.

"No, dear husband. I believe that it enhances the love we share."

Aquila cleared his throat. "And—and so we agree."

I replied by hugging his warm hands with mine.

He said, "I want to say a prayer, one prayer between us, as we begin our life together."

My heart was filled with thankfulness for a worthy man who loved me. His sensitivity to our Lord's purpose was humbling, and I was attentive as he spoke in earnest to God.

Aquila said, "We now stand before you, Almighty God, having all faith in your Son, Jesus. May your Holy Spirit guide us in your way so that your grace will be seen in our lives and that we may be known as people who have faith."

"And I agree with my husband," I prayed. "May we live to please you in all things, dear Adonai."

Our eyes met and held, and then Aquila's arms came fast around me, his lips finding mine, gentle at first, and then the eagerness of his mouth met my own fervent longing. Warmth flooded me.

When Aquila lifted his face from mine, he removed my veil and pulled my hair loose, combing it with his fingers. "I've wanted to do that since our first meeting, when we walked through the market." He smiled.

"That monkey!"

Aquila chuckled. "He became my furry friend—but also my enemy. All those silky waves within my grasp, but I couldn't touch them!"

"Funny," I replied, "I felt the same about a yellow scarf, but dare not touch it for fear of Eliam." I laughed.

Aquila kissed my lips and then each rise of my face. Sitting down, he carried me with him.

"I don't know how to describe what I'm feeling," I said. "It reminds me of a time when I drank unmixed wine." My cheeks flushed. "Airy in my head."

Aquila raised his brows. "And they expect us to eat." He motioned to a table abundant with food.

I began to giggle, and though our guests might hear, I couldn't stop.

Aquila kissed my laughter away. "Until the celebration is over, my love."

I kissed him again. "I love you."

All too soon, bells were jangling outside the curtained door. We had eaten little. God had provided love to feast upon. We emerged, hands clasped, from our sanctuary—the bells had to be rung a second time—and joined the festivities. At unexpected moments during the dancing, singing and celebration, however, I felt my body become supple and yielding, remembering Aquila's earnest prayer, the sweet knowledge that we had been joined by God, and my husband's tender lips meeting mine. The experience would never be forgotten.

Tamar delighted us with a lilting voice and skillful playing on a harp. Miriam danced with Betna. Father had a perpetual smile that only dimmed when it was time for him to go.

"Abba, we have always been together. Are we now meant to live apart?"

He straightened, voice firm. "A woman must leave her home." My father then traced a finger down my face, over my nose, and I remembered a much younger Prisca, perched on a father's bouncing knee. "Adonai has placed you in good hands," Father said. "And so I go." His voice had begun to waver, and tears rose in my eyes.

"And I'm very relieved my husband isn't moving me away to Pontus!"

He smiled. "You will make a good home here," he said. "I have faith in you."

Looking up at him, I raised an eyebrow. "Next time we meet, I wish to talk more about faith."

Miriam had no words. Her hands wrapped my face, pulling me close. She then took Father's arm. Tamar embraced us both and turned to leave as well; she would be occupying my old room for a few days.

Betna lifted my hands, kissing each one. "And you are married." His eyes shone with amusement. "You remember the words?"

"Yes ... sir," I said. It was cheering to resume our playful banter, believing that some things didn't have to change. Solomon's song came easy to my lips, "*I am my lover's and my lover is mine.*"

"You do well." He kissed the crown of my head.

The contented little party faded to indistinct shadows, while I held tight to the tall man smelling of cloves at my side. We were alone. It had been a joyous celebration, and I was curious where we would rest our heads, realizing that the place Aquila had been preparing was yet unknown.

"Our wedding, it was—I'm thankful that you chose a garden," I said. "It was a beautiful gift, so perfect for us. But our home, Aquila, is it far from here?"

He looked confused at first. "Prisca." He chuckled, waving a hand. "This is our home."

Looking around, eyes wide, I couldn't speak.

Aquila's arms encircled me. "This is the place I have prepared for you, my bride. Will you be happy here?"

"It is more blessing than I can hold!"

We made a brief circuit around our garden, my husband pointing out places where he knew my spade and seeds were needed. We spoke blessings to God as day was coming to a close, and then Aquila escorted me into our private chamber. Passing into its stillness, my pounding heart was a distraction, but then he kissed me and lifted me into his arms where I belonged. Throughout that night we shared our words of love, our passionate youth, and our bodies ... God created us for such wonder.

৪০ ০৪

In the next months, affection for my husband ascended with every sunrise, and a pleasant pattern infused our days. Aquila's business in tent-making was growing, and he was able to provide work for other needy laborers. My life became a comfortable rhythm of cooking, sewing, gardening, and contentment within the delightful home he had provided.

Each evening, we strolled together. Sometimes we paused for a ready reunion with family or a visit with friends. Sometimes we talked about future plans. Sometimes silence lingered between us, and I mused about the many attributes of the one whom God had chosen for me: A man of physical strength and spiritual zeal with a sharp mind and grasp of important details, a man who was interested in how things were designed and built, a man who listened to and considered my interests and dreams, a man of faith.

A day came when we met together with Ethan and talked of our service in the work of God. Ethan was always patient, always inviting us to profound discoveries and fuller faith. I told him of my desire for purpose, and our earnest friend shared what he had learned while walking with Jesus.

"Knowing Jesus as your Savior means you stop trying so hard," Ethan said.

"But doesn't the Lord expect us to give with all our might?" I asked. "I mean, since we love him and appreciate what he's done for us, shouldn't we try even harder?"

"It is because of this love that you can trust him to establish his kingdom in his own way," Ethan responded.

"God will call you to work that you do not expect, but you should not expect particular work."

Impatience made me tense, and my jaw tightened. "Are you speaking again in riddles?" I asked.

Aquila was nodding. "What do you mean? We should '*not expect particular work*'?"

There was glee in Ethan's expression, not that he was mocking us, but his delight overflowed when teaching such lessons. He said, "Do you remember, my friends, when I spoke of that day on a hill, when I was a boy? It was the day I went to Jesus carrying fish and bread."

"And he blessed it," I said, "and fed thousands of people!"

"Yes. But it is the first miracle I wish to evoke, before Jesus blessed and shared my meek offering," Ethan said. "Though I had never met him, he knew me. In that moment, to realize my life was no mystery to him, that he knew my name and everything about me—it still captures my very breath."

"Something so impossible," Aquila said.

Ethan sighed. "And yet Jesus has told us what value we are to God. He said that even the hairs of your head are numbered. Can you believe that God created you and knows you so fully?"

It was hard to respond to Ethan's question. My mouth was quieted. What does the Lord Jesus think, knowing me so well? Nothing could be hidden.

Ethan said, "God is creator of all things, even of the works that he will bring you to. We are simply invited to walk in them."

"Tell us more," I said. "Help us understand."

"Can you see, if we would choose our own tasks, even well-intentioned, even wanting to do something good for our Lord, it would call attention to ourselves, making us proud that we did such things?" Ethan asked.

"I do see that," Aquila replied.

"And so it is when we abandon ourselves, when we think not in terms of what we can do but remembering who it is that we love," Ethan said, "that God can use us in miraculous ways."

My husband and I looked at one another and joined our hands.

"Love your God," Ethan said, "without any plan or scheme in mind. Let go and listen. And then he will fill you with his good purpose."

"When I first believed in Jesus," I said, "there were names of children that filled my head and an awareness that I would be teaching them. It was like you've told us. Nothing was planned or thought out, but there was a strange sense that it simply would be."

Ethan nodded. "I agree that you have been created for such a worthy task, and there is real need."

Soon thereafter, Aquila and I began to teach at the children's harbor. To work alongside Ethan and Lormah was a significant blessing. Twice a week, we varied our evening walk, taking a winding route through Rome's narrow streets and alleys and arriving at the children's harbor after sunset. By lamplight, I taught reading and writing in both Latin and Greek. My husband taught woodworking and leatherwork as well as mathematics using an *abacus*. Together, we prayed with them.

Balbina and Hortensia were now part of this growing family and gaining healthy weight. Menahem, nearing one year old, would curl onto my lap as I read or sang. When he called to me in his way, "Purka, Purka," it made me warm to the miracle that he was with us. Ira was toddling about, tall and gangly for his age. Surprising in one so young, his face was serious—still watchful—and filled with yearning for stories about Jesus. The little blonde girl I had met upon first visiting the children's harbor had begun to speak. Bel was the name she gave. She was intelligent and curious, an avid listener, and always seeking the seat closest to mine. Day after day, I marveled at innocent love pouring from each unique child, finding it unbearable to believe anyone would have hurt them or cast them away.

My husband and I were students as well. When children's studies completed, Ethan recited parables or told us about the life of Jesus on earth. Some experiences were firsthand; some he knew from talking with Jesus' disciples. They were rich discussions indeed. When it was time to go, we would emerge from a breathtaking realm where faith and hope were tangible, carrying what we had gleaned from our lessons for more contemplation at home.

Tamar, a happy member of our family, was included in our discussions, but she had not yet accepted the living gift of Jesus.

ဆ ⋈

When spring's sunshine warmed the land—oh, dread event!—Gaius Caesar came marching back into Rome. We heard his troops before seeing them. Clanking metal, stomping feet, and creaking wagons filled with raucous singers could be heard from far away, and they whisked a haze of dust that soared like a filthy banner announcing their unwelcome return. It soon became known that the military campaign staged against Britain was all pretense and show. In the "battle," the emperor killed some of his own soldiers described as rebellious, as well as a few wealthy patrons (after they had made last-minute bequests to him). With his triumphal return, Caligula's men carried dozens of tall baskets filled with nothing but seashells, which the emperor called his "spoils of war." I speculated how many Romans slipped behind bolted doors and fell onto their couches in hysterical laughter. And this man—Caligula—was the leader of the powerful Roman Empire?

A darker facet of Caligula's campaign was his discovery of a conspiracy. Implicated in the alleged scheme was Lentulus Gaetulicus, former consul, who had been commanding several military legions in the upper Rhine. Caligula had led his armies there straightaway, executing Gaetulicus with all swiftness.

Lepidus, Julia Drusilla's former husband, was also named in the coup as the very man who coveted the emperor's throne. He was ushered back to Rome in chains, tried at court, and executed. Caligula's two remaining sisters, Agrippina and Julia Livilla, were somehow involved as well, though we never quite knew how, and were sent into exile.

For us, the most frightening consequence of the plot was that the emperor began to suspect everyone of treason—its legal name *maiestas*—and spies littered the streets. In addition, the empire's resources had dwindled to such a degree that Caligula was again desperate for money. Suspicion and desperation; it was a deadly pairing. Mouths were stilled; valuables were hidden.

We existed in a sweltering metropolis, heat pressing annoying odors upon us in steady waves. Thankful for my walled garden, I required firm persuasion to leave it.

One day, a messenger came to us with a letter from Father:

To my dear Priscilla and Aquila, greetings:

I am writing to make you aware of a special delegation arriving from Alexandria. That great city has suffered a disturbance between Greeks and Judeans. A delegation of Judean leaders has begged an audience with our emperor to seek relief ...

I prayed for those brave Judeans, ambassadors of a worthy cause, that the emperor would not harm them and would listen to their pleas. Many trade goods came from the City of Alexandria. Betna had described well-built ships and rich merchants, and Alexandria seemed to be much like Rome. Perhaps dignitaries from that powerful province would have a favorable effect on Gaius Caesar, leading to improved circumstances for Judeans in both Alexandria and Rome ... and even beyond.

When the day arrived, Aquila and I escorted Tamar to my Father's home. Still rather shy, she had little interest in crowds and was eager to spend a day in Miriam's wise counsel, refining her latest floral design upon the loom. Father and Betna had already gone, hoping for private conversation with the delegates, wanting to lend support, so

Aquila and I proceeded toward Rome's center, eyes open, expecting to see them at every familiar turn.

The forum was bright with color and alive with activity. Extending overhead was Caligula's latest building project, a lofty bridge linking his residence with the "Temple of Jupiter Best and Greatest," which crowned the Capitoline Hill. Caligula's *domus* sat atop the Palatine Hill, and so the bridge soared high above, lacking only artistic details and embellishments.

Valeria had told me there were rumors of a riotous emperor clad in elaborate costume—or in nothing at all—running along the passage and shouting at Roman gods in moonlight. Her words reminded of those brutal days toward the end of old Tiberius' reign. Father had said then, "Great power has to affect a man. Only God is capable of unnatural power yet remains merciful." Unnatural power. We passed under the bridge, and visions of Caligula screaming and running its length made me shudder.

We walked near Basilica Aemilia, an extravagant building where carved scenes depicted the Romans' capture of Sabine women, and giant barbarian statues stood in alternating marbles of yellow and purple. At building's corner, men were performing gymnastic feats, standing one on top of another, three men high. Laughter rippled through the forum when someone on the basilica's tall balcony tossed the uppermost man an apple, then two, then three. He almost lost balance trying to catch them all.

Peacocks meandered among the crowds, trailing brilliant feathers, and children scurried after them trying to steal a colorful plume. The fearful birds ran shrieking.

"Should we have convinced Tamar to come?" I asked.

Aquila shook his head. "She is happiest baking bread and weaving garments."

I recalled Tamar's fright in Baiae, the soldiers who made her uneasy. She was now of the age …

My thoughts sprang to voice. "I wonder."

"Wonder what?" he asked.

"If we should be seeking a proper husband for her."

"What makes you think I haven't?" Aquila smiled, his head held high.

Of course Aquila had thought of those things. "I may have some ideas for you, my husband."

"And I have no doubt you will share them," he replied.

"In this you are correct." I hugged his hand.

There was a female vendor standing by her jewel cart singing an invitation to buyers. Her voice had a clear, high tone and made me think of coins tinkling into a dish:

> *Sparkling stones in red, blue, yellow, green,*
> *Bronze and gold, silver so fine.*
> *Come! See! Your dreams will be granted!*
> *The gods' own harvest of beauty divine.*

Leaning into the woman's cart was Quintilia, the stunning actress I'd seen on the day Miriam and Hannah were freed from the *carcer*. Quintilia raised sparkling yellow stones to her neck, and they glowed against pinked skin, accentuating cinnamon-colored streaks in her hair.

On the *rostrum*, a man was giving an oratory. I squeezed Aquila's hand. "Can we get closer? I'd like to hear his speech."

The actor was wearing a molded Greek mask, eyes and mouth outlined in dark colors and crowned with gold leaflets. I hugged Aquila's arm.

"Oh, he's not just an orator," I said. "This is Greek theater!"

Aquila appeared to be listening, but his brows were pinched. His eyes explored the crowding hordes that were fenced into the forum by tall rows of temples, basilicas, and monuments.

It was enthralling to see a play, even an excerpt of one. I nudged my husband. "It's a play by Aristophanes, I think." Aquila made no response.

Greek theater was known for employing a wise chorus leader who would reveal some life-changing moral to the audience. It appeared that our actor was portraying such a role, and we had arrived mid-scene:

> *"Our poet maintains that he has done much that is good for you; if you no longer allow yourselves to be too much hoodwinked by strangers or seduced by flattery, if in politics you are no longer the ninnies you once were, it is thanks to him. Formerly, when delegates from other cities wanted to deceive you, they had but to style you 'the people crowned with violets,' and at the word 'violets' you at once sat erect ..."*

Aquila took my arm. "Let's get out of the sun."

I exaggerated a frown. "But the play!"

Aquila's voice was quiet and controlled. "Not now."

He pushed through spectators, leading me into shade on nearby basilica steps and next to a wide granite column. My husband appeared grim, wary, and the statements of our Greek speaker began to grow, sending needles of fear. There was a row of short stairs that ran the length of the building and, having a higher perspective, we could see many faces from assembly having come to greet the delegation. My father and Betna were on the other side of the forum, and I gestured in their direction. Father had the same bleak expression as Aquila.

No Judean ambassadors were seen that day. No promising speeches were delivered. Instead, we were instructed that Gaius Caesar sought "an audience from the Jews" and were told to remain. Aquila hauled me even further under the basilica's tiled roof, and my stomach began to twist in remembered fear. Yes, Caligula had returned, and that meant our lives were never safe.

Rapid as fleeing peacocks, the scene transformed. Gone was the Greek actor and humorous acrobats. A murmur infused the crowd like a rustling fire, and Praetorian Guards circled the *rostrum*. Twelve *lictors* preceded Caligula carrying the *fasces*, a bundle of rods that were bound together around an axe. The *fasces* was Rome's emblem of ruling authority, and it was an intimidating display.

The emperor presented in glistening purple. Still a young man, he was now nearly bald. His face had become inscribed with a permanent snarl, featuring a bulbous, pinkish nose. An ivory baton was carried in his left hand, and he motioned for the crowds to quiet.

"Greetings, Jews of Rome," he said. "Many of you supposed today that there would be visitors from Alexandria. You, I venture, will be disappointed. The delegation's attendance took place in another venue." He spun about, swishing his glossy cloak, and smiled. "Let me be candid," he said. "Rome's primary irritation is that you Jews do not reverence the person you owe homage to, your lord and emperor."

Faces wet with anxiety, Caligula's listeners remained hushed in anticipation of his speech, one that we had begun to understand was a real threat. After inspecting the audience, his narrowed eyes ignited with malice. His hands appeared dramatic and accusatory:

"I will explain forthwith our differences, so you may understand. You call yourselves a nation: Israel. You have journeyed far from the roots of your own homeland, yet you appear satisfied to be flourishing in a land that others have fought over, a land that is not your own.

"The very soil cries out against you! This ground was made sacred by Roman blood. These seven hills bear witness to the excellence of those who were fated to possess them. Every fierce battle, every work of art, every triumph sings out to us—ah, yes, I hear them! They sing of Roman glory!

"You declare that the fiery hand of an invisible God emblazoned his laws upon stone tablets—merely pieces of stone—a reminder of his rule over your lives. Well, the true Roman has no need for such carvings! We live by following the examples of our ancestors, a noble and heroic line, whose actions speak through our poems, our plays, and in our military victories. We are guided and smiled upon by multifarious gods who reveal their wisdom in signs upon the skies and fragrant smoke from our sacrifices."

Caligula paced across the rostrum with clipped steps and returned to face the crowd once more, his face coloring in comparison with the dark-wine hue of his attire.

"It has been decreed that Rome should have command over you—yes, command—over your wretched little enslaved race. You are apparently the only persons by whom I am not esteemed a god, and the time has come for you foreigners to recognize your error." He paced the rostrum again, posture straightening. "The hand of Jupiter appoints me to that dutiful purpose! I alone govern this vast empire, and that includes the province of Judea."

Caligula lifted his baton to depart a silent forum. In hasty afterthought, he raised his voice. "I will tell you now, people from Judea, that my likeness shall soon reside within your very own Temple, on your hill in Jerusalem. It shall be of unspeakable size, a figure like no one has ever before seen." His voice grew in volume. "You will remember that I am your god."

As quickly as Gaius Caesar had appeared, he was gone. He did not wait for final applause; there was none. Senate business was scheduled to begin, and I saw Father walk toward the *curia*. How long, I feared, before Caligula took notice of him, a Judean freedman, inside senate walls? Panic knotted my stomach, and I pitied his shaky position. Aquila took my hand and held it tight for a moment. He understood me so well.

After exiting the forum, we saw Betna watching for us near the doorway of *Epulatus*. He grinned and waved. A roe deer with huge antlers hung inches from his head near a trio of brown speckled goats, and at his side a wild boar swayed, hanging by leather straps. Betna looked like the master hunter, lacking only a long spear, and my spirits lifted on seeing him. Hesperia was not visible, but I heard her voice from a balcony above. Did she know we aided in the escape of Balbina and Hortensia? A pang of guilt swept over me, and I was pleased to rush our steps.

ಶಿ ೮೩

The sun was high as we turned down Vicus Albus. Nearing my childhood home, I noticed Valeria standing back from her balcony's railing, figure darkened in shadow. Raising my hand in greeting, she did not respond and crept inside. Later, recalling her behavior, it occurred that she must have seen something of what took place that morning.

What had I expected to see as we entered? Miriam sitting at the loom? Tamar setting out food for midday meal? Those questions tormented my sleep later on. What we found was dreadful.

The door was open. From beyond it, Tamar's muffled sobs could be heard. We found her on the floor clutching a stone tablet with three names etched upon it: *Priscus, Miriam, Priscilla*. Miriam was nowhere to be seen.

Tamar described the morning's ordeal in broken sentences. Apparently, not long after we left her there, three soldiers had appeared.

"One is named Honoratus," Tamar said. "He is—it—it was the guard in Baiae. The one—you know, the one

343

when I fell and …" She began to sob again. The other two soldiers remained unnamed.

After some prodding, she continued. "They said they had—they had information regarding residents of this house, that there was—there was treasure withheld when making the year's assessments."

"This was about money?" I asked.

Betna laid a hand on Tamar's head. "Please, tell us."

Tamar choked back tears. "They said they had—had word of an older woman and—and you, Prisca. They named you both. How could—oh, how did they know your names?"

"They had word, you say?" I asked.

"Word of—of a—they said it was a box, a treasure of some kind."

My breath held. I had spoken of it as a treasure. The gift from Shema? Miriam had determined it should come to me. Warmth drained from my face.

"Tell us more," Aquila said.

"They came to take—take all of you. They—they took Miriam away." Tamar began to cry again, severe jarring sobs that prevented words to flow.

I sank to the floor, next to her. "They took Miriam?" My eyes swam with emotion.

"They wanted to ask—ask her questions. They said something about a—about a box."

A box. A box that had no value whatsoever to Rome. But who would believe it? And who would have told of it? Who even knew? I stared at tiled floor, searching my mind for anyone who might have heard about this "treasure" of Miriam's. Had she discussed it in the *carcer*? But the soldiers mentioned my name too—and Father's. Again, Miriam had been right to say we would never be free of pursuit. Those words haunted me now, along with the memory of burying the box as she begged.

Hands flew to my face. "Betna! What about Father?"

"I will see to Priscus," Betna replied.

Aquila pulled me to my feet. "Pack some food. We must go," he said.

"But wait. My father."

He stood firm. "Take only what you need."

I said, "But I can't go until I know—"

Aquila pulled me close, speaking with force. His hands held my arms. "They will return. We might have time to get you away while the streets are yet crowded." He extended a hand to Tamar. "Help Prisca. Gather food for two days, maybe three."

Aquila's command sobered us. Tamar and I fled the room.

My mind churned like a mounting storm. Would Miriam be okay? And what if they arrest Father? What should I take? Things that were Mother's? Father's treasury of books? The box itself, buried near the garden steps? Because of our haste, only Mother's baby blanket was selected, and it enfolded two loaves of bread. Tamar was securing vegetables into a basket even as we swept into busy street.

A short distance from our home, someone could be heard from behind, pushing through the masses who had exited the forum.

"Let me through. I must pass." It was a man's voice. Eliam. And next he was standing before us, soiled with perspiration and red from heat.

I stared at him, expressionless.

"You must allow me to speak to you," he said. "Please."

"What is wrong with you?" Aquila's look was fiery, and he was clearly working to keep a low voice. His wide-eyed glance swung between Eliam and the bustling faces shuffling around us. "You wish to speak here? Now? On the street?"

Eliam was wheezing. He pointed. "Just here. There's a portico between those walls. We can speak privately."

"And what would you say?" I asked.

"It concerns your friend." Eliam's eyes implored.

"Not now," Aquila said. He took my hand, and we walked several feet. Tamar had my other hand.

"But it is something you must know." Eliam sounded desperate.

Closing my eyes, breathing steadied. "Perhaps I should hear it," I said.

We entered the portico, and it was indeed a private setting. Large shrubs had been planted just outside its marble colonnade, effecting silence and cover. Tamar stood apart, her eyes just able to peer above leafy branches into busy street. Aquila placed protective arms around me. Eliam faced the wall for a moment and then turned to us, his shoulders low.

"I have done many wrongs," he said, "many things I am not proud of. When my home burned, my wife and son

346

with it, I wanted to take. I wanted to take from everyone."
He mumbled into a clamped hand. "Bitter—oh, I was
consumed with bitterness and anger. I wanted to ..." His
hand pounded the wall.

"We have little time," Aquila said. "What is it we
need to know?"

He walked a few steps away and then paced back,
his voice ragged and low. "I want you to know this is not
my doing. Those that I have been connected with, they
came to me. They asked me about some treasure box. I
know nothing and told them so. Though I like to joke with
these men, sometimes banter, it has never been my wish to
hurt your family."

I shook my head. "You say yourself that you have
done wrong. Why should I believe you would not wrong
me? Or Miriam?"

Eliam stared at his own feet. His voice sounded
small. "You see, young Priscilla, it—it was my pot. My pot
had fallen onto the road." Eliam's eyes became still pools,
focused on a scene somewhere beyond. "Has it been twelve
years? Yes, twelve years since I pulled my wagon aside and
started back to retrieve a pot that had fallen, one amphora,
filled with oil, that fell from the ropes and wedged next to a
stepping stone. But"—his voice shook—"my clumsy feet
were too slow."

Still dressed in finery, gold draping his neck, there
were shadows that outlined Eliam's inflamed eyes, and his
hands were trembling. What was he trying to say? It was all
vague, unclear.

His head bobbed, and then he continued on as if I
understood every straggling word. "I stopped," he said,

"stopped there on the road, pleased to look upon a beautiful woman and her daughter walking—ah, no, you were skipping—backs to the sun, wildflowers bouncing in a little girl's hands." He pinched his brows. "And my pot was lying there, something that a driver would not see, eyes blinded by setting sun, and jammed into place where it could wrench a wheel." He swallowed with effort, and his body was wobbling.

Mama. I remembered the cart, horses bolting, load overturning, but never noticed an amphora on the road. I felt queasy.

Eliam sniffed. "My heart has been burdened these many years." He groaned. "Even as my own family was burning—though unknown to me—I went to your house and found a dark foreigner there who sent for help." Eliam sighed and ran a hand over short bristles crowning his head. "Little Priscilla, I would exchange all of my days for that one day."

Emotion was affecting my speech. "I—I don't know what to—to tell you," I replied.

Aquila said, "You need say nothing. We must go."

"Yes, yes," Eliam said. He extended a hand, nearly touching me, his words coming fast. "But, little Priscilla, please know this: I will try to help. I will use my influence to clear Miriam." He was backing up as we walked, sandals tripping his steps.

"You have done enough," I said. If only something could blot his face from my eyes forever.

"Please. If you will trust me in this," Eliam said.

"Trust you?" I asked. "I believe you console me only to—to find what treasure they seek. And there is none. Your quest has failed."

"No! No! I have no desire for any—"

Aquila raised his hand in front of Eliam's face. "We are going now. If you wish to help, please do not approach this woman again."

My body was stiff. I could not look at Eliam, and we left without further words. He remained in my thoughts, however, in days to come.

೮ ೮ଷ

It was Aquila's idea to take us to Miriam's old dwelling outside the city. As far as anyone knew, it had been left to decay. Balbina and Hortensia had not met with any trouble while staying there, and that knowledge aided our confidence it would be safe. Could the authorities know of our marriage, our new home? Would they search there? Might they take our home and our possessions?

"We are simply being cautious," Aquila said. "We married while Caligula was gone and only select friends were aware—remember, they searched for you at your Father's. It could be that no one knows of our home."

Fear had tensed every muscle in my body, and I struggled to breathe. "But if they do, if someone told them, if they were somehow watching ..."

"Better we are not there to be taken ourselves," he replied.

It had been months since being at Miriam's and, even then, only to lodge two little girls for a brief stay. Its condition was shabby at best. The brilliant flowers of

Miriam's balcony were black, papery things. Every darkened corner hosted cobwebs, and there were signs that someone may have trespassed and slept there. But we had always known it as a place of sanctuary, so we cast out dirt and moved in.

Tamar, in bursts of memory, provided further details about Miriam's taking. She said first that the soldier—Honoratus—had been kind. The others had wanted to shackle Tamar as well and have her questioned, but Honoratus stepped in to prevent it.

Tamar described Miriam's last words as they took her away. "She said, 'Tell the child'—I knew she meant you, Prisca—'that the Son of righteousness has risen!' She said, 'Do not be afraid. I am in the Son's care.'"

I shared with Tamar the story of the box and recited for her those meaningful words from the scroll.

Tamar replied, "And if we gave that treasure to Caligula, he would not believe it, would he?"

"No doubt he would think we concealed the 'real' treasure," I said.

"The words of the scroll," Tamar said. "It says '*You shall see the difference between the righteous and the wicked*'? What I've seen is that the wicked do very well."

"I am ignorant about many things, my sister. Maybe what we are to learn is that the righteous are expected to behave different from the wicked; that, even in difficulty, our faith cannot be moved."

A knot closed my throat. And what of my own faith? Had I forgotten the power of Jesus already in the midst of our present trouble?

Tamar was staring into distance. "And '*the sun of righteousness has risen.*' Has the time come, Prisca, that our Lord is claiming his own? How will we know whether we are his 'special possession'?"

My shoulders dropped. "I had promised to be more prayerful, Tamar, and that neglected promise is grieving me during this sad time. Attentive to my own joys and new wifely duties"—I inhaled deeply—"I have forgotten that our Most High God has a purpose greater than me."

Tamar laid her hand across mine. "Some things are not your job, Prisca. You cannot know and do everything."

"My friend, Lormah, has said that very thing. 'You are not God.'" How I yearned for Lormah's humble insight. That old weakness of wanting to fix everything myself was getting in the way.

"She's right," Tamar said. "You have to let some things go."

"But I should be listening, seeking to know his will. It's time to turn thoughts to Jesus, not to myself."

"Jesus," Tamar said. "Aquila has spoken of him. You both believe. I see it." She lowered her eyes. "It is hard to accept. I want to trust your words but cannot forget what my mother taught. How can anyone be sure that Jesus is our Messiah?"

"Our words are not what you should trust, Tamar. Ask God to reveal the truth to you, dear sister. He surely will." I paused, amazed at the Holy Spirit filling me in response to the simple act of turning to Jesus, putting him at the center of my thoughts. "It requires faith," I said.

"Faith," Tamar repeated.

"Faith that God found a better way for us than the law. Jesus is that better way," I said.

"Jesus is the way?" Tamar moved closer.

"The one true way," I replied.

Tamar clasped her hands. "Prisca! I forgot. There was a woman with Miriam before the soldiers came. She said those very words, that 'Jesus is the way.'"

"A woman?"

"She came just after you left me there."

"Who was this woman?" I asked. "What was she like?"

Tamar chewed her lip. "Slender. Dark. She was a foreign woman, perhaps from Egypt. I'm sorry. I was at the loom when she talked with Miriam and was not listening."

"Do you think she told the soldiers where to come? Did she betray"—

"Oh, no. It was nothing like that." Tamar smiled. "She was so peaceful. I remember thinking Miriam was better—quiet, but glad—after the woman left."

Could it have been the woman from the fountain? She had such peace. And how had she come to visit Miriam? I prayed that the Holy Spirit would make these things clear.

We ate together in silence. Betna arrived after dark, and he came in the guise of a Roman man of mourning, dark hood covering his head. Aquila opened the door, and Betna slid through.

"Child," he said. It sounded like a timid wail.

I noted the shine of his dark skin, eyes puffed and fatigued, and took his hands into mine, holding them tight. "They've taken Father," I said.

"When Priscus came home, I begged him, 'Leave. Hide.' Your father, he sends me on a fool's errand. And I am the fool." Betna hung his head, face twisted in pain. "When I came back, soldiers are taking him away, and he waves me to hide." He slammed a fist into his palm over and over. "And I hid. To my shame." He turned away.

Aquila squeezed Betna's shoulder. He said, "There is no shame. Someone needed to come tell us; Priscus knew that. They would have taken you as well, and then we would be tackling worse peril."

Father taken. I didn't want to believe it. When I saw him earlier in the forum, he was looking his best, ready to meet with the Alexandria delegates, soft woolen cloth falling sharp from broad shoulders, his face immaculate, jaw firm, eyes clear. And here was Betna, broken in heart, tired in body, and ashamed. I laid my hand on his back.

"There was nothing more you could do," I said. "Now we must—where have they taken him?"

Betna pulled away. "He knows you will try to come," he said. "You will not."

"But you must take me to him," I said.

"And then we would have to free three people," Aquila said.

Tamar was crying.

"Only if I'm caught," I said. "Is he in the jails near the forum? There must be a way."

Betna shook his head, face to the floor. "It is worse."

"Worse? What do you mean?"

"I followed to see, to know where"—Betna's face pinched—"and Priscus, he is taken to Rome's quarries."

"The quarries." Dust, heat, whips ... certain death. I struggled to breathe.

Aquila helped me to a chair. "Beloved," he said, "it is time for us to remember Who lives in us."

I closed my eyes. Faith still lived in my heart, but I was afraid. "Aquila, how does our Lord help us in these cruel times?"

"According to Tychon, Jesus told his disciples, '*In the world you have tribulation; but be of good cheer, I have overcome the world.*'"

"But this is something I cannot see. If he has overcome the world, why do such things happen?" Squeezing my face tight, I recalled something Lormah had told me. "My husband, we are living in a world that has sin," I said.

He pulled me to him. "Prisca, do you trust me?" he asked.

At my lack of response, he repeated the question. "Do you trust me?"

I nodded.

"Your father is my own. I will do what I can." He lifted my chin and looked into my eyes. "Do you believe that?"

"Yes." Even as the word left my lips I doubted if it was true. I wanted to do something myself, to go running into the wilderness, to do anything—anything to keep me from thinking. Yet there was no mistaking it, the Lord's voice, "Trust in me. Trust your husband."

৩০ ০৪

In those days that became weeks, our cramped household adjusted. Tamar and I took turns preparing meals. Betna retrieved water for the household and went to market. Aquila continued his work. In every activity, we remained cautious of authorities, and I began to realize that residing in a city of Rome's size could be our best advantage. Aquila was doing whatever he could to locate the particular quarry where Father was taken, and that was an undertaking that required patience and anonymity.

Friends watched over our dwelling across the Tiber and advised that no one had searched for us there, but my husband insisted we wait. He was unyielding that we remain in our hiding place.

My childhood home we were unable to keep from relinquishment. It was sold, as were any possessions within. It had passed to someone of Caligula's choosing, benefiting the emperor monetarily, no doubt. When I was told of this fraud, it was like my own body had been assaulted. All I could do was separate my heart from it somehow and convince myself that our old *domus* belonged to a different time and place.

One afternoon, tormented by guilt, I defied my own husband's orders and went to see it. Dressed as a slave woman, I walked by, careful not to betray the emotion vibrating my limbs. It was quite altered, that structure that had sheltered us and listened to our many prayers. New residents had formed a receptacle inside the doorway for household gods, and our *mezuzah* had been stripped from the doorpost. It was as if they had desecrated our Holy of Holies. My garden—what had been my garden—was left to neglect and ruin. They had no need for it; their wealth was

355

sufficient to buy vegetables at market. Branches of myrtle, yet alive, peeked over the wall as if to invite me back, but I could not bear the anguish and turned away.

"Amicus!" a woman shouted. A small boy with clipped brown hair ran through the garden door in a dirt-smudged tunic. He had made trenches, little rivers with bridges, where spiked branches of rosemary had once thrived. Pebbles that had marked neat rows of vegetables had since become soldiers in battle.

Hovering beneath a veil of brown, I closed my eyes to shut out those ruinous images. How can one become so attached to a place? Is it not simply a shell made out of stone? Stones cannot see, cannot feel, and cannot hear the lives of those that dwell within. But there was that mark on the wall, the one Father made when I was nine years old and feeling tall; a view from the atrium into blue sky above, daylight falling into the room a specific way, the room in which I became betrothed; and the little cook stove where Mother baked sweet cakes and dipped my finger in warm honey. My eyes closed. I could taste the sweetness on my tongue. There was also the memory of Miriam's treasure—carved box and prophetic scroll—wrapped carefully and buried beneath fertile soil. Nausea came over me in a wave. It was now just a building and a sad reminder of what had been taken.

ဆ ☘

Betna came one morning with news from the marketplace concerning Eliam, idle gossip that flowed in the following fashion:

"Eliam was taken into custody! Bet he had that secret treasure after all!"

"Greedy old fool."

"Mm-hmm! Fool he is!"

"Withholding assets from the censor. Not smart."

"I heard he tried to defend that old Miriam woman. You know, the one they took away?"

"No! He'd never help a body in trouble."

"That's what I thought. Can't be true. Just thinks of himself."

"Ha! Well, they put him in jail too."

"Serves him right. He has plenty to pay for."

℘ ℘

On that last occasion of seeing Eliam, he appeared desperate, broken, and had insisted he would help clear Miriam. But I didn't believe him. Had he tried to help her? Was it true? There was a fleeting thought to pray for him, but it passed, and I became occupied with other tasks.

In the night, I woke more troubled than ever. In our work at the children's harbor, we were taught to care for others, to pray for our enemies. We were to be like Jesus who died for all of us, even though we were sinners.

For days, these meditations pursued me, until one morning, kneeling in prayer, I let go of my anger and asked God for the ability to forgive Eliam. What then came to mind were words that Ethan had shared with us, words that were spoken by Jesus: "*As you did it to one of the least of these, you did it to me.*" Eliam needed to hear about Jesus. He needed a friend to visit him in prison, and I was appointed to share the good news. Such revelation caused our first marital disagreement—in truth, it was a heated argument.

"You are not going," Aquila said. He planted a firm hand against the wall.

"How can you say that, when it's what the Lord is compelling me to do?"

He crossed his arms. "It's too dangerous. I forbid it."

"So you're saying God is not powerful enough to protect me?" I raised my chin.

"I'm saying you can't continue the work of the Lord if you are imprisoned ... or dead."

I moved closer. "Yet you know that God used Joseph, even as he landed in an Egyptian jail."

"And you think you are like Joseph," he said.

"More like Esther." I stood firm, hands on my hips. "And she faced death as well."

"Wife, you grieve me! Does it delight you to make me worry?" Aquila squeezed his brow with a firm hand.

Seeing the alarm in his eyes, I softened, stepping away into silent prayer, and then returned, leaning into his broad chest.

"I appreciate that you're concerned. But what if the Lord has called us to this very purpose? I once questioned how Esther could have so much courage and hungered for it; but now, through prayer, I know it is not our bravery that the Lord uses. He uses our weakness. True courage rests in the strength of God, and it rises on wings of sincere faith."

Aquila did not respond.

"Please. It's on my heart to go. Pray to the Lord. Seek an answer for both of us."

Aquila prayed, and we both surrendered, seeking the Lord's way, not our own. On that same afternoon, a letter was delivered to us by Alon's father. We opened the seal to read:

Greetings, Aquila and Prisca:

Grace, mercy, and peace from God the Father and Christ Jesus our Lord.

Thanks be to God for this journey. When we parted, I was emptied in spirit, defeated in heart and soul. Praise God that by his great power and unfailing mercy, I am new. By the gift of his own Son, he has ransomed me— and not only me. Jesus was sent for us all.

I have met a fisherman named Peter who walked with Jesus and learned to be a fisher of men! Peter teaches of power that comes to us by the Holy Spirit. As we heard from the prophet, Joel, God said, "I will pour out my Spirit; and they shall prophesy. And I will show wonders in the heaven above and signs on the earth beneath." These sayings have come true! Each day, I have beheld wonders that have no earthly explanation! God's miraculous power is freely given to all who call upon the name of Jesus.

It is my prayer to come again to you and share these blessings from my own mouth, but I know that the One who has called me also guides me according to his perfect will, and my path is in his hands. He has commissioned me to go forth and spread the good news! Even me, only a man.

I sense from the Holy Spirit that you have also received Jesus as your Savior. I pray your faith will increase and that you will comprehend the riches we have inherited by the grace of our Lord Jesus Christ. Peace be unto you, my friends.

Alon

After reading Alon's letter, Aquila and I lay on our faces before the Father and prayed in the precious name of Jesus Christ that we might be filled with his Spirit and that our feet would tread whatever path was laid for us. We then agreed that into the prison of Rome we would go, bearing the love of Christ to a lost soul. And I prayed, if it might be the Lord's will, that I would see Miriam ... even for a moment.

᠊᠊᠊ 🙰 ᠊᠊᠊

Before light dawned, we started on our journey. Humble cloaks hung upon our shoulders, and in my hand was a basket of small, round loaves. We would not pretend to sell these loaves, but in prayer we believed that God wished us to carry them to hungry prisoners.

It was a tranquil forum. Few persons were visible under twinkling stars and no moon. At the gateway to the *carcer*, one lone soldier paced. We approached, our sandals silent and slow. At the very moment we would address the guard, he was called away by a crashing sound in an anteroom nearby. No one stood to bar our entrance, so we advanced without making a sound.

The odor that rose from the passage was one of decay and death, and each step flooded my senses. Remembering the haggard forms of Hannah and Miriam in this brooding cellar, my stomach twisted. Miriam back again? I could not understand why the Lord would allow such suffering.

We passed several cells, too dark to see any occupants, whispering at every entrance:

"Miriam."

"Eliam."

Aquila passed bread loaves between the iron squares that made up prison doors. Eager hands accepted them.

"Miriam."

"Eli- …"

"Who are you?" It was a man's voice. Eliam.

My husband approached. "It is Aquila …"

I knew what my husband was thinking. Should he reveal my presence? Oh, Lord, give him the words.

"… and Prisca."

"You have come? Here?" Eliam's voice wavered.

"You must know. I—I discovered that it—it was Hesperia who told of the box. She wants to persuade"—

"That no longer matters," I said.

"But she may try something more," Eliam said.

My husband replied, "We will pray for God's protection."

Eliam's voice sounded raw. "But listen to me—"

"It is the Lord who prompted us to come to you," I said. The calm I felt amazed me. "Are you—Eliam, are you all right?"

He moved closer to the iron bars and cleared his throat. "Thank you for coming."

I know not how it happened on this moonless night, but then I saw him, illuminated within the moldy chamber. He was thinner, dark rings around his eyes giving him a skeletal look. His body had been beaten. Crusts of blood stained his clothing. One arm hung limp at his side. Pity swelled my throat, and I wanted to shut my eyes, but it was clear that God's desire was for me to see Eliam, to really see this broken man.

Aquila squeezed my hand. Did he see him too?

"We are here," Aquila said, "to tell you of good news. We bear witness that Messiah has come."

"And what good would that be to me?" Eliam asked. His head pressed against the bars.

I said, "You told me of your deeds."

"And I am condemned. Soon I will pay."

"But Jesus has already paid for your sin," I said. "I am here to tell you that Jesus, our Messiah, has sacrificed himself, taking the sin of all mankind upon him, sinless though he was."

Aquila spoke with whispered enthusiasm. "And Jesus rose again! He lives, that you might live."

Eliam choked back a sob. "I am a dead man."

I stepped closer. "Jesus offers forgiveness to you, Eliam. And so do I."

His voice quavered. "You—you would forgive me? That is not possible."

"Jesus has forgiven me," I said. "And by the power of his love, I am able to forgive."

Aquila's arm went around my shoulders. "We have learned," he said, "that nothing is impossible with God, if we only have faith in Jesus." He extended a hand to Eliam. "Do you believe?"

Eliam passed a hand across dry lips. "I have heard others speak of this Jesus. Even Miriam sings from her cell in praise of his name."

A quick breath filled my lungs. She was near.

"It is true," Aquila said. "We have both accepted the gift of salvation. Even now, the Lord speaks to me, my brother." Aquila moved close. "Eliam, he will never leave you."

"Jesus loves you," I said.

Eliam gripped his iron door. His voice seemed faint, as if coming from a gaping hole inside of him. "I could never have believed, except that he sent you. If Jesus could bring you to me"—he began to cry—"after—after what I've done, into a place such as this …"

Aquila placed a hand on Eliam's head. "I pray for you, Eliam, son of Omer, that you would believe in all faith that Jesus, God's only Son, died for your sin and rose again. I pray you will receive God's gift and have life."

I prayed in silence.

Eliam lifted his brow and inhaled. His mouth opened. He reached out and touched Aquila's hand. He could see us!

"My friends!" he said. His eyes blinked at the supernatural light. "I believe! Yes, I believe Jesus died for me. I am forgiven." He dropped to his knees, saying over and over, "Bless you, Jesus. Bless you, Jesus."

A couple of cells down, a familiar voice began to sing. It was a psalm:

> *The Lord is on my side,*
> *I do not fear.*
> *What can man do to me?*
> *The Lord is on my side to help me.*

Eliam said, "Blessed be the name of Jesus."

Tears slid down my face. "Yes," I said.

"It is time for us to go," Aquila said.

Eliam stood. "You are right." His voice was a whisper. "And may—may God grant you safe passage."

"God be with you." I cast these words upon Eliam even as I was moving in Miriam's direction. Unlike the experience at Eliam's cell, I could not see her, but her hand searched out mine.

My whimpering voice echoed within the black vault. "What can it mean for you to be locked away in this place?" I asked.

"It is to fulfill the Lord's purpose," Miriam said.

"I don't see it," I said. It was easier for me to understand Eliam's imprisonment as a means for awakening unto God's grace. But Miriam, why must she live in gloom and filth? What possible purpose could it serve?

She said, "God has placed me here to bring his kingdom into lonely places."

Another woman's gruff voice emerged from the blackness. "Because Miriam is here, I have learned to trust in Jesus. And there are others."

Miriam said, "Even the guards have softened hearts. One day they will receive."

The unknown woman said, "And now I am not afraid. Blessed be the name of Jesus!"

Footsteps were crossing our way, and Aquila spoke at my side. "Miriam, you know we love you, but I must carry my bride to safety."

"I rest well knowing you are with her," Miriam said.

"As long as I breathe," Aquila replied.

Her fingers began to slip from mine.

"But when will I see you again?" I cried. "I have prayed and prayed for your release."

"My release will come, child," Miriam said. Her words were delivered like a tender caress. "My heart tells me we will meet again in glory."

I could not speak.

"Do not fear," Miriam said. She sang, again, the psalm. From that day forward, "what can man do to me" filled me with instant courage.

Footsteps were nearing. A man spoke. "It is time for quiet, old woman."

Miriam was kind to him. "Ah, yes, only a bedtime song. Soon the sun will rise."

With healing in his wings, I thought.

Aquila and I were wedged into a corner. The guard's lamp created long shadows, and we hid in them. His beam shone briefly on Miriam, her gleaming visage peering at us behind rusted bars. In my foolishness, I had expected to bring her hope! Once again, it was made clear that it is God's purpose to live for and not my own.

My husband and I clasped hands and touched our heads together. We prayed. In the next moment, an extraordinary light appeared at prison's entry. It was not golden like a lamp, but appeared silvery blue and pulsating. We walked toward it. Nothing was distinct on either side, but a shimmering finger of the Holy Spirit of God pointed our way. When it dimmed, we found ourselves in humid, low-lying air on a street leading from the forum, safe and at peace.

Aquila looked at me, eyes wide. "If I ever doubt," he said, "remind me of this day."

ଚ୬ ଔ

~ *XII* ~

I hereby command you:
Be strong and courageous;
do not be frightened or dismayed,
for the Lord your God
is with you wherever you go.

~Joshua 1:9

Two days after visiting Eliam, my husband took me to a narrow street that had been decorated with dense plantings. Vines and flowers hung from every balcony, some in thick, leafy curtains that started from high above and nearly touched the paving. Trees and shrubs had been trained into hidden alcoves and luxuriant rooms. It was a captivating, thriving haven. We entered one lush nook containing a small bench, caught up in the splendor of such a paradise and grateful for its privacy.

"It's surprising such a place exists in Rome," I said.

"A friend told me of this place," Aquila replied. "It seemed right to bring you here for many reasons, but one is for us to have time apart from others."

"There is news? What have you discovered?"

"I know the quarry your father was sent to," Aquila said.

"Where is he?"

"North of here, in mountains beyond the River Arnus, a marble quarry east of Lucca."

"So far." I sighed. "What are your plans?"

"Tomorrow, after dark, I proceed north."

"In the morning, I'll pack a few things," I said. "It won't take much to—"

"You will stay here."

My heart beat faster. "But how will I know if you're all right? When do you think you'll come back? It is not—it's not safe to go unaided."

He smiled. "And who led me into the bowels of Rome on nothing but faith?" Aquila smoothed loose strands edging my face and kissed tremulous lips. "If I tell you the Lord is guiding me, can you trust that?"

"It's hard," I said. "I don't want you to go and, at the same time, it's the only way to help my enslaved father. I want to go with you, to be part of it, to be sure you make it back."

"And who would care for Tamar and comfort Betna?" Aquila pulled me close, his voice resonant and soothing. "The more I know Jesus, the more I believe he guides each of us in different ways. It's like Ethan said. There are special jobs for us, special tasks that we're made for—well, and more than that. His Spirit empowers us to do things we never thought possible."

I squeezed my lips and nodded. My husband was wise. And he was growing in faith. Emotions raged in me and thoughts tumbled about, but strong hands tilted my head gently upward, and there was no doubting the solid assurance residing in Aquila's face.

"I do not go alone. The Holy Spirit travels with me," he said. "And two of my workers will also be at my side. I leave Tychon here, to keep watch."

"To keep watch?"

"You may not always see him, but he will be nearby. There are few I would commend for such duty; only your father, Betna and Tychon."

"My father," I said. Snuggling closer to my husband, I laid my head against his heart. "Tell me one more time it will be all right," I said, "that you will come home to me."

"I'm counting on the effectiveness of your prayers," he said. "And there is confidence—not of my own—that urges me on. Do not fear."

ɞ ↺

Aquila's departure left me restless, weary, and—I had to admit—fearful of the unknown. Fear, I knew, was not from my God. As promised, I prayed for those I loved, each consigned to a bleak and hostile place. Father's location crept into my dreams, stark mountainsides swathed in veins of white marble, recalling the Roman legend about *snow the gods had made eternal.* I shivered. A scribe was not conditioned for harvesting marble slabs.

In prayer, there was peace, and my work at the children's harbor brought comfort and release. Betna first cried out to prevent my going, but in the end we were both convinced it was a task to be carried on. He remained my devoted escort, and we were always alert to the possibility of danger. Lormah had become adept at leatherworking and was real help during my husband's absence. Young students, eager with questions and sincere affection, kept our minds on worthy tasks.

Balbina, rescued from Hesperia's callousness, had gained an elegant beauty. Gone was her persistent anxiety.

A slender neck and fine features were enhanced with thick-lashed and thoughtful eyes; her oval-shaped head was crowned by reddish-brown hair that fell across slim shoulders in silken waves. Not only were her natural features remarkable; living in a sea of love had added grace and tenderness, and her generous heart made her even more charming.

She came to me one evening, in her careful and hesitant way. "Can we—can we talk in a quiet corner?" she asked.

It was then I realized that her changes were not only outward. She had become a young woman. We stepped into a corner and spoke in hushed tones. "How can I help?" I asked.

"Will you help me prepare for the days ahead?" she asked. "It seems that the more I have learned, there is more to be learned. My life feels like a filled round pot that rolls away and then rolls back empty." She laughed.

I took her hands in mine. "Already you know so much. You know the duties of keeping a clean home. You're an excellent cook and have improved at the loom." I softened my voice. "The intimate duties of a wife, we can find some time set apart to discuss those things."

She started chuckling and covered her mouth to stifle it.

"Tell me what I'm missing," I said.

"I'm sorry," she said, "but you don't understand. I want to carry God's message of grace into the world." She leaned close. "Each day, the desire increases. And the Holy Spirit fills my dreams with needy faces and places to go. But how does one follow such longing ... where to begin, when to go? And who would go with me?" She giggled at my astonished face. "You see, I have many questions."

My response was an embrace. "Your questions show how ignorant I am and a reminder never to assume—oh, Balbina." My head was shaking. "Well, first, we should pray, thanking God for planting such bold desire. I don't trust myself to give you answers; we must seek wisdom—as Betna says—'like it is treasure that is hiding.' We need the Holy Spirit to show the way."

ᛒᛟ ᛎᛄ

On another night, as studies completed and we prepared to leave, Lormah drew me aside.

"Strange rumors come to my ears," she said.

Had Aquila been captured? Had his plan been discovered? Had Miriam …

Lormah patted my shoulders, shaking her head. "It is not what you think, it is not what you think …"

I held my breath. "Tell me."

"The emperor, he makes his guards angry," she said.

"Caligula's guards? What are you saying?" I asked.

"Do you know a man, his name Pop—Poppa—Poppaedius?" She clamped a hand over her mouth, sniggering at her own stilted pronunciation.

"He's a senator," I said. "Some have called him an *Epicurean*."

"Hmm, a pleasure-seeker," Lormah replied. "That is easy to believe."

"What happened to him? What did he do?" I asked.

"This Pop—this senator, Caligula thinks he is spreading bad stories."

"Poppaedius is saying bad things? Bad things about Caligula?" I landed in a chair. "And somehow the emperor found out."

Lormah grunted. "The senator probably says only truth."

"I am sure you're right. But what did Caligula do to him? Has the senator been killed?" Already, images of the emperor's many abuses darted in and out of my mind. It was hard to douse those burning horrors.

"Not him." Lormah pulled a chair close, sitting across from me. "They take his woman."

"Quintilia? The first time I saw her, they were walking together in the forum."

Lormah explained. "Caligula makes his men cut her face. One man, his name is Chaerea, does the cutting."

I covered my mouth. The thought of it made me want to weep.

"Even then, she says nothing against her man. She is more brave than I think."

"Do you mean you—you know her?"

Lormah nodded. "One day, the Lord tells me, '*Go to her,*' and we talk."

Thinking of Quintilia's exquisite skin, now scarred, I leaned into my hands. "How can anyone be so cruel?"

"This is not all," she said. "Chaerea, he is sick, full of anger because Caligula makes him do this thing. He says, 'No more am I used by such a madman.'"

"How—how can you know his very words?"

Lormah grinned, her brows lifted. "You see, to be a slave means you are like the walls—you are there but not living—no one knows that you hear."

"But what does it all mean, Lormah? Do you know what's going to happen?"

"There are others who think that way, that the emperor needs to die," Lormah replied.

Caligula's death. It was something both craved and feared. And who or what would follow after him? Balbina wanted to step out into such a world, carrying a message of grace? I hugged my own face, feeling my skin, trying not to picture the emperor's atrocities.

She said, "I tell you, friend, I trust you. Pray to God, but do not speak of this."

஬ ௸

A knock on the door awakened us. It was Tychon, and we invited him into our confined quarters.

"A messenger came," he said, "with a note. Aquila frees your father today. We are to pray."

"I've been praying," I replied, "praying not to lose them and that they will be all right."

"I do not think you will lose a man like Aquila," Tychon said. He then laid a hand on Betna's shoulder. "There is more," he said.

"Is something wrong?" Tamar asked.

"I must take you from here," Tychon replied. "The authorities are coming. They know where you are."

I started fidgeting, chewing my nails. "But how? Could Hesperia have discovered us and ..."

"Nothing is certain. Only that the emperor thinks you hide a treasure," he said.

"But it is nothing to him," I said.

Tychon nodded. "Many battles have been fought over nothing but lies."

"Where do we go?" Betna asked.

"I know a place," Tychon said. "I'll take you."

We packed our few remaining possessions and left while it was yet dark. Betna was our rear guard, and Tamar held my hand to the point of aching. Thinking back to the day of Miriam's taking, I recalled the beautiful beginnings of Tamar's weaving ... all left behind when we had to flee. "Please, Lord, drive away her fright, give her hope that she can begin again."

We followed winding streets and alleys, some which smelled rank and passed near Rome's sewer. Our final stage in the journey found us descending one hill and climbing a high knoll in the northeastern corner of the city, ending in a one-room rectangle slightly larger than Miriam's and on the fourth floor. It was located near an intersection of four aqueducts, two of which were more than two hundred years old; the other two had been commissioned by Caligula and still under construction. Bustling streets crossed nearby, and so our newest lodging found us midst a perpetual burble of water, men working bricks and mortar, and a chatty clatter of travelers.

Betna left to explore and bring fresh water before sunrise. Tychon helped with repairs—loose windowsills and broken stair treads—while Tamar and I cleared out dust and endeavored to create a home. Busyness helped, but my eyes burned and my head throbbed.

Tychon laid aside his tools and approached. "You are anxious, my sister."

"And wouldn't you be?" I scratched at a speck on the table's surface that could not be removed, and then dropped my rag and pot of oil. "Once again, we move in darkness, pack and unpack, scrubbing till our fingers are nothing but nubs, only to end in a noisy, irritating place."

"Clamor can provide a mighty fortress to those who hide," Tychon said.

Was there nothing that perturbed this exasperating man? "I'm sick of hiding," I said, "sick of worrying about who might see me and what that could mean."

Tychon laid cushions on the floor and motioned for me to sit. I ignored him.

"And when will we know what is happening in Lucca?" I asked. "What if they kept Aquila, made him a slave too? What if he and Father are dead? How would we know?"

Tychon motioned again, his demeanor calm.

Arranging the cushion so that I could lean against the wall, I sat and held my head.

"My sister," he said, "when are you going to see beyond the cross?"

"What are you talking about? Beyond the cross?" It was too much for my overused mind to answer questions.

"We live in a world where death is entertainment and compassion is considered weakness," Tychon said. "In that kind of world, it can be easier to cling to Jesus' sacrifice and remember only his violent death. But when faith grows, you learn to look past that instrument of torture—though still remembering its shadow—to see

God's victory! Remember, our Savior rose again. He came to life."

Lack of sleep and worrisome tears had so wounded my eyes that they would barely open. "There are things I should have done and mistakes that—I was the one who spoke of Miriam's box as a treasure. Someone must have heard. These things might not have happened if—"

Tychon interrupted. "Who are you, Prisca?"

"What?"

"Tell me who you are," he said.

I chewed chapped lips, filling my lungs. "Aquila's wife, a daughter to a scribe, a teacher—well, learning to be a teacher, and ..."

Tychon stopped me. "Tell me who you are to Jesus."

My head ached. "I—I don't know. How can I see myself as he sees me?"

Tychon stood and laid his hand on my head. He said, "When you do, you will begin to live."

໖ ໕

After dwelling in our newest residence for little more than a week, we found ourselves adjusting. Because of the aqueducts, there was ample fresh water, and neighbors were accustomed to temporary laborers and road-worn travelers entering and exiting, so we remained inconspicuous. Added noise provided some privacy for conversations. Tychon was right; it was a good place for hiding.

Standing high above the city on our narrow strip of balcony, outlines of pointed and square-shaped buildings became blacker profiles against a contrasting pink sky. It had become a frequent venue for me, offering an ability to see far and wide, ever hopeful of our loved ones' safe return. Sometimes Tamar would join me, and we watched together.

When Tychon arrived, he came to stand at my side.

"Have you any news? Any sign?" I asked.

"Nothing," he said. "But he will find you. I left word with good people."

"Good people," I repeated. Continuing my gaze into vivid sunset, timeworn memories prompted a smile. "When I was a child, I met a woman named Elah, whose husband was in a construction accident and died. In her race to be with him, she fell, and so my mother went to tend the woman's injuries, taking me along. Even in pain, Elah was kind, thinking only of others, and though I was a little girl, I knew she was someone my father would call *bona fide* ... good, faithful. Elah's goodness has warmed me all these years. She was 'good people.'"

Tychon leaned on the railing, jaw twitching.

"There's something else," I said. "What are you unwilling to tell me?"

"Tonight, the *ludi romani* will begin." Our tinted sky was beginning to fade, and one star was flickering.

"Do the Romans think of nothing but games?" My hands clutched the wooden rail. "Don't worry. I have no desire for gladiator combats or wild beast hunts. Come inside. Have you eaten?"

A shadow paused on his face, and he stared hard across the city. "Caligula has come up with a new way to open the games. He intends a celebration at dark using human candles for light."

"Is there no end to his wickedness? Are you thinking to try and stop it or—Tychon, it's too much to do on your own."

He turned toward me with a look of one whose child was ill, a mix of worry and sorrow. "My sources say his store of human candles is the city prison. It may mean Miriam is—"

Before he could say more, I forced my way past him, running out the door and down the stairs. Tychon was fast behind. He pulled and begged but could not make me return to the *insula* and appeared reluctant to affront Aquila's bride.

"I am going," I said.

"But you don't know where to go."

"Any Roman citizen can tell me where the games are," I replied. "It's their prime amusement."

"Even if you get there"—his eyes narrowed with concern—"Prisca, it will be a fearsome sight."

"But I'm going to be there. Miriam will not die alone." I started walking.

Tychon caught up. He reached for my arm, his mouth forming a tight line.

"Wait. I understand," he said. "I'll take you, but we go my way."

After we passed Capitoline Hill, my neck dripped with sweat. People were everywhere, clogging every artery that traversed Rome. Tychon had taken us around some of the chaos to end up where Caligula's games were set to start, the Theater of Marcellus. When we arrived, soldiers were lining a passage that led to the theater where an official launch of *ludi romani* would be by actors on stage. Hundreds of crisp tunics, metal glinting in torchlight, stood erect and alert, ready at Caligula's command.

Tychon maneuvered us around the activity and into a temple's garden nearby, and we sat beneath an olive tree, its branches obscuring our presence.

One by one, prisoners were thrust from wagons, each one splashed with oil. Tied to rough wooden posts, their feet were supported by short blocks that lifted them high. A number of them were taken inside the theater. Some prisoners were calm; some fought their captors with every step. Many were Judeans and familiar to me.

When she appeared, Miriam was easily recognized. She did not struggle. Her head was lifted toward a starred sky. I moved, but Tychon held me.

He whispered. "You cannot save her. Neither of us can. There are too many soldiers. If you go near, they will only add you to the condemned."

"But I must do something. To just watch while Miriam is ..." Tears blurred my eyes.

"Aquila's last request of me was to keep you safe," Tychon replied.

"But he, himself, has gone into danger," I said.

Tychon held me, his eyes pleading. "When your husband climbed on his horse, he told me, 'I live only to see her again.' Prisca, will you keep your life for him?"

A rapid heartbeat filled my ears, remembering my husband's earnest face, his wedding promise: "No earthly thing before my wife." Even now, he was attempting to save my own father. I bit into my fist.

Holding my breath, fingers gripping tree bark, I stood, motionless. "I will not run."

Gaius Caligula led the parade, his maniacal face lit by handheld flames on either side. He shouted for all torches to be extinguished and, moment by moment, darkness overcame us. It was cold, eerie. A horn then sounded and, at once, prisoners were set on fire.

Tychon was right. It was terrifying. It was a spectacle that would forever invade my dreams. Flames soared like golden spikes, reaching into violet sky. Screams of pain fused with sounds of crackling fire, and an acrid odor of smoke permeated our chilly air.

And then, soft as summer clouds, Miriam's familiar voice sang to me. She knew I was there.

> *I am like an olive tree, an olive tree, an olive tree,*
> *Flourishing for all to see, an olive tree*
>   *in the house of God.*
> *I trust in God's unfailing love, for ever and ever.*

My choked voice sang with her the last line, and she was gone.

We remained, Tychon and I, hanging our heads as citizens were funneled through a blazing gateway of agony. There was no sound from spectators. And what might they be thinking? Would they, one day, beg God's forgiveness?

When Tychon stood and motioned our departure, I could not move. Without a word, he sank down at my side. Smoke surrounded us, like mist on a cooled sea. Olive leaves swayed. Dark crept in, flames faltering, and uniformed soldiers began to light theater lamps.

"She said we would meet again in glory," I said.

"It will be a blessed reunion," Tychon replied.

"Please pray I can survive this pain."

"I have not stopped praying for you, even before you first ran from the balcony."

Hugging the trunk of the tree, I cried. As if some essence of her life might still be there, I yearned to run to the beam where Miriam died. But that was foolishness. My spirit sensed her move away, carried off into the arms of God.

After a time, Tychon nudged me. "We must go."

In that moment, there came a sudden, odd sensation. Instead of her painful death, my mind became steeped in fond memories of her life and rich teachings she had planted.

"Tychon, can we walk by Miriam's old home?"

"But I brought only this small lamp," he said. He prepared to light it.

"Please. Just to be near. I know what it looks like."

Before long, we passed the pomegranate tree, and I envisioned a smattering of children in its shade, Ethan perched on a rock and telling them stories. Tears rolled down my face. Children.

"I am God's child," I said. "His beloved child."

"Yes," Tychon said.

Stopping there on the road, a new and profound understanding flooded my soul. "Jesus not only died for me," I said. "He came to life for me. *'I am like an olive tree in the house of God.'* He lives so that I can have life."

Tychon bowed over his small lamp. "Abundant life," he said.

"Thank you," I said.

Smoke had followed us. The air was a strange bluish gray, and lamplight that fell from a few homes cast feathery shadows. Shrugging pained shoulders, a stench rose from my clothing and nausea caused me to sway on legs that were at last letting go of relentless strain.

"We have to stop here," I said, "just a moment and then ..."

"Look!" Tychon shouted.

Someone was running towards us. It was a man. It was Aquila. Feeble legs pushed me toward him. Just as steady arms lifted me from the ground, I collapsed into them and sank my face into his warm, pulsing throat.

"Prisca. My love." His arms tightened around me. "Why are you—what has happened, Tychon?"

"It is Miriam," he replied. "She has been—she is with God."

There was a sound of uneven steps approaching and two shadowy figures, one taller and leaning on the other.

"My Abba," I whispered.

He came close and embraced my face with a calloused hand. "It is a strange turn of events, Daughter," he said. "I have become a slave. Your husband has purchased me from the quarry master."

I covered Father's hand with mine and offered him a weak laugh, and then relief at their safe return overtook me; tears of both grief and delight streamed.

Aquila bore me to our hideaway, Tychon leading the way. We were cautious and had no further conversation until a solid door closed behind, and then rejoicing filled the room for the return of those we loved. Our celebrating was, however, tempered by the loss of Miriam.

Aquila—patient and adoring—held me throughout that night. The heartbeat in his chest sang me to sleep. And, upon rising, my spirit was soothed by the Holy Spirit calling Scripture to mind: *"The steadfast love of the Lord never ceases, his mercies never come to an end; they are new every morning; great is thy faithfulness."*

৪০ ০৪

Father's right knee had been injured during his time in the quarry, which was one reason Aquila was able to purchase him from the quarry master. Included in the bargain was his slave companion, Straton, a man who had driven the bullocks, powerful animals who pulled sledges filled with marble. Straton was solid-built and strong but a man of short stature, and I asked him how he could drive such wild, dangerous animals.

He replied, "My head stood below the points of their sharp horns, you see! Many a man lost his life because he was too tall."

On the second evening after their return, Aquila recited a thrilling tale that he entitled *Liberation from the Pit*. Having no knowledge of quarry practices, the slave master's covetous nature, or how to arrange a purchase of slaves; for my husband, it was all a venture in faith. Taking on the pretense of a wealthy merchant in search of slaves to tend an olive harvest, Aquila rode on horseback to Lucca and then down a sheer, snaking trail into the quarry's wide cavity. Wearing an outlandish costume lent from an actor's wardrobe—scarlet robe festooned with gold leaves—he even shaved his beard to play the part. In addition, a friend had provided a saddle trimmed in gold-colored bells and red fringe; colorful feathers had been woven into the horse's mane.

Straton was enlivened by the memory. "Your man came prancing into the quarry," he said, "and Balbus, the slave master—old tub of oil and sweat—had never run so fast. He tripped over his square bloated feet in a big hurry to get shoddy slaves for Aquila and fat money into his own skinny purse!"

"And all the while I pretended not to know who Aquila was," Father said. "All I wanted to do was cackle and shout!"

Aquila said, "Well, it's a good thing the quarry master had eyes on the moneybag and not on you!"

Straton said, "Aquila tossed his bag of coins at Balbus—" The poor man then had trouble finishing his sentence, because horselaughs and knee slaps stilted his words. "It landed—ha—it landed—ha—ha—in a pile of horse dung! But the master—he—he didn't even care. He picked it up out of the stink and grinned. Ha! Never knew he had any teeth. First time I ever saw 'em. He had at least five, don't you think, Priscus?"

Father said, "Maybe as many as six, and every one as grimy as his moneybag!"

Our makeshift table of food nearly tipped over we laughed so hard.

"Because of our friends," Aquila said, "we had an amount of coins I never could have gathered on my own." He described how Alon's father, Ezra, had given all of his own savings for the rescue.

"And you should have seen Aquila ordering us to walk behind his horse," Father said, "hands and feet shackled. He played the part of a nobleman very well. Never saw him so stern. Straton and I scurried after him like a couple of short-legged ducks."

"Till we got up the trail and rounded the corner," Straton said, "and then we all jumped and slapped and bellowed. We could barely get the shackles off because we couldn't hold still!"

ဆာ ၄

While my father began his lengthy healing process, he assisted Aquila's tent-making business by creating a system of recordkeeping. It reminded of Betna's old tale about finding a ship that needed workers in Alexandria; here was my husband needing accounting help, and Father needed work!

Some weeks later, we learned that Eliam was among those set aflame near the Theater of Marcellus. It was sad to think that Eliam had been broken and grievous for so long. That God had sent us to bear news of eternal life to him was consoling, and it amazed us to remember and consider the miraculous workings of Almighty God. How he strengthens our faith, when all around we see only impossibilities!

We lived through winter's bleak months in the "house by rushing waters," and every day Miriam's absence was tangible. It was a different grief, though, from the time after Hannah's death, because from the moment Miriam left, I knew she was with our King, our Savior, our "friend who never leaves." Such thoughts made my breath catch. One day, we would be together again—Hannah too—and that heavenly appointment was too marvelous to lose hope.

℘ ℭ

In the cold month of *Ianuarius*, Gaius Caesar was assassinated. We heard it first from Lormah, who came at sunset wearing a new blue tunic, her hair braided and pinned, a basket of bread loaves on her arm. She giggled at the astonishment on my face. Never had she looked so healthy, so vibrant, so well-dressed.

"Oh, I am purchased," she said. She raised her chin. "As a maid for a good woman."

Aquila began to cough, then to chuckle, and Lormah joined him.

"What is so funny?" I asked.

Lormah placed both hands on my face and pulled me close. "I am free! Your husband says it is a gift to you, but it is a gift to me!"

Lormah's freedom was cause for a feast. And so, gathered close around our square table, we feasted and listened while a much-loved friend regaled us with news surrounding the emperor's demise. He had been hosting the Palatine Games when it happened.

"Some Romans say Caligula makes the gods angry," Lormah said. "They say he does a bad sacrifice."

"A bad sacrifice?" Father asked.

"Before the games. Blood from a flamingo gets on him," Lormah replied.

I wrinkled my nose.

Lormah continued. "Later, he was going to the bath with friends, and they attack him on the way."

"Who attacked him?" We all wanted to know, but Lormah didn't have the answer.

When Tychon joined the party, he supplied additional details. "It was colonel of the guards, Cassius Chaerea, who started it," he said.

"We've spoken about Chaerea before," Aquila said.

I said, "Chaerea was the one who cut Quintilia's face." At Father's questioning glance, I explained. "It happened while you were at Lucca. Caligula ordered his colonel to torture her, expecting she would implicate her beloved senator. But Quintilia never did."

Father replied, "It's perplexing, having worked among senators all these years, aware of their deeds, to lack knowledge about these things." He appeared reflective and then smiled. "Having been away, working at something quite different—in an odd way, it's freed me."

"If you want to know what is happening," I said, "Lormah can tell you. She educated me about what slaves can learn among the shadows—oh, but wait! She is no longer a slave."

Lormah grinned.

"It's interesting," I said, "that God has changed our circumstances. Sort of gives me an expectant feeling."

Lormah was impatient for more information. "And who are the others? I hear that many people attack the emperor."

Tychon said, "Another colonel, Cornelius Sabinus. And then several more helped him. They had been plotting for months."

Lormah said, "You see? I know this."

"Most of the assassins have been killed," Tychon said. "My friend, Demetrius, was near when it happened. He is a slave. He said Chaerea leaned into Caligula's face and, when his sword struck, shouted, 'It is always the heart that makes weapons work!'"

Father replied, "Caligula had tormented that man every day. It's clear what was in his heart."

"Chaerea was the first one to be hunted down and put to death," Tychon said. "But when the guards saw that people were happy Caligula was killed—most important, the senators were happy—they decided they were glad the tyrant was dead too. They ended the hunt."

"So much about death," I said. "But I'm not sad to see the emperor go."

Aquila nodded. "His death will certainly mean more people will live."

৪০ ৫৪

Warmer days came. Again, we packed our modest belongings for a trip, but it was a merry one, delivering us onto a familiar road. Inhaling a fresh drizzle of early spring, home was in sight. A day of jubilation had arrived. It was so exhilarating that I didn't know where to start, whether to dig in the garden or bake a cake! Aquila chose the cake.

Father and Betna had found a small *domus* close to ours, and Straton was rooming with them. Tamar remained with us, her nimble fingers and creative mind making colorful weavings upon the loom, and we grew closer each day … true sisters.

And so life resumed its comforting pattern of work, prayer, and song. When we found our way into the children's harbor for continued teaching, tears of joy met us there. The children had grown, and we remarked how their hunger for knowledge made us more zealous to teach.

In our family circle, Aquila and I were still the only ones who knew the saving grace of Jesus, but we lifted loving prayers and knew that the Lord would attract other hearts. As Jesus said, *"No one comes to me unless the Father draws him."*

ಬ ಛ

Appearing at our door one sunny day was the dark and lovely woman from the fountain, the one who had spoken of deeper faith when a grieving Keziah set sharp barbs into my soul. As soon as we were returned home, I had begun a dedicated search for her, longing to ask about the day of Miriam's arrest. On that tragic day, was it this woman who had brought cheer to my beloved mentor? If so, what did they talk about?

Since the unnamed woman knew Jesus, I had enlisted the help of friends who also believed, Lormah and Ethan. At last, she was steered to us.

Hurrying my guest into the atrium, I bubbled with exhilaration like the fountain where we first met. Would she be surprised to hear that I knew Jesus, really knew him? At the fountain, she had spoken of the grace of God, words that sang with glorious truth. There were many things to discuss.

We moved into warm light streaming in from the garden, and I began talking before my guest was even seated. "At last I see you again! How kind you were that day of our first meeting. You have no idea how your words—"

We were interrupted when Tamar and Betna walked into the room. Betna carried a satchel I had not seen for many months, a leather pouch that was buried on the night Hannah and Miriam were released from Rome's prison.

"Betna! You have it!" I ran to him.

He was silent, unmoving, and staring beyond me. My visitor was wearing the same enchanted expression.

Betna opened his mouth to speak, and it sounded as though he were in some faraway place. "Ketek," he said.

She leaned on the couch for support. "My man." Her eyes were filling with tears.

Betna's package landed in Tamar's arms, and he strode across the room. Taking Ketek's hands, he lifted and examined each finger, each lined palm, and then embraced them. "I look for you every day," he said.

Ketek said, "Always I know it in my heart."

"And you—you are married?" Betna asked.

She hesitated. "I am not married. But I have been a slave." She lowered her head, dark lashes making feathery shadows on high, rounded cheeks. "Men have used me," she said. "You may not want Ketek this way."

"I will always want Ketek," he said. "And will you be married to me?"

It was clear she wrestled with decades of held-back emotion. Her cheeks glazed with tears, and every word took effort. "Yes—oh, yes," she said.

Betna pulled her close, their foreheads touching, and it appeared that every muscle in his body began to relax. My mind could see them together those many years before, Ketek with yellow flowers in her hair, Betna youthful and strong, both with eager hope. And there, playing soft upon those lucid reflections, was the adoring tune Betna had taught: "*I am my lover's and my lover is mine.*"

৪৩ ৪৬

We waited until Betna had returned from escorting Ketek before uncovering our treasure. Pink light of evening had softened the atrium's walls, night crickets had started a chirping chorus in the garden, and our little family gathered in anticipation. Aquila sat at my side. Tamar sat by him and reminded me of the little girl I once was, eager to meet a litter of puppies. Father and Betna shared an opposite couch.

A familiar wooden box slipped from its leather sheath. "This," I said, "is the treasure Caligula was seeking. Betna, thank you for rescuing this special gift."

After Caligula's death, Rome greeted a new emperor named Claudius, and it was yet unknown how his reign would alter our lives. We experienced less unrest after Claudius attained the *curule* chair, but it was always unwise to dig in another person's yard by moonlight. Betna assured me it still looked like a little boy's battlefield.

It was difficult to hold back emotion. Resting on my lap was a gift from Miriam. Her fervent descriptions and excited utterances still sparkled in memory, reminding my heart of its weighty loss. Long, slow breaths helped.

Just as Miriam had done, my fingers traced carvings on the box while telling them about Shema, a little boy who tended the stables … and who also came to tend a priest named Matthias. Everyone was patient. We all knew about King Antiochus and his cruelty, but they had never heard about young Shema, who risked his life for love of another.

"Such love has the ability to transform someone," I said, "and Matthias was transformed, becoming a person known for compassion and selflessness."

Aquila said, "And we can be changed by the love and grace of God, who gave his only Son, Jesus, so that our sin would be forgiven. Jesus gave his life, so that we would have life forever."

I glanced around the room. All were listening. My hands shook as the scroll was pulled from the box.

"According to Miriam," I said, "this scroll was written by the very hand of Malachi." Unrolling it with care, ancient words sang from my lips.

"How beautiful," Tamar said.

"From Malachi himself," Father said.

Betna sat very still. "I want to know more," he said.

"Miriam said she believed Messiah would be more than a Savior, more even than a king," I said. "She believed he would be 'a holy bridge between us and the Almighty,' providing a better way for us to speak with God."

Aquila said, "We have experienced the fellowship of the Holy Spirit just how Miriam described. You see, when Jesus ascended to the Father, he sent the Holy Spirit to us."

I added, "To teach, to guide, and to whisper God's word."

"To fill us with God's holy power," Aquila said.

All of a sudden, Father and Betna said in unison, "I believe." That was the power of God!

Tamar was smiling and nodding. "I've heard his voice many days now, prompting and uplifting me. He tells me, '*I am the way, the truth, and the life.*'"

We prayed together, grateful for God's endless mercy. Hand in hand, we walked to the cove where Lormah had bathed me in the Tiber River. Washing in water was comfortable, having come to us from long tradition, but now the experience was emboldened by total surrender to Jesus, God's Son.

Kneeling into the swirling waters of the Tiber, my life soared with fresh faith. Overhead, two pinpoints of starlight peeked from a sky that had begun to darken, and I marveled that the One who could create such perfection by speaking it into being could also know me in a complete and exceptional way.

Breathing long and full, I offered myself to the God I loved. "I have found my purpose at last. It is to know You and trust You … for such a time as this and for always."

૪૦ ૦૪

80 CB

Acknowledgments

With the encouragement and prayer of others, this story grew from a gentle whisper into a written work. A debt of thanksgiving is owed to dear family and friends, their names too countless to list, although I wish to extend a special note of affection for my children, Matthew, Bradford and Amy, who have been constant in love and support. Also, to those who read through the manuscript and encouraged every feeble effort: Darryl and June, Kyla, Marcie and Ron, Miriam, Pam, Tamara and Tim; these dear friends continued to believe in me and in the calling on my heart, even as the years mounted and writing was yet to be complete. Thank you. I love you all.

I'm grateful for the wonderful women of Christian Life Church in North Park; women of grace, of faith, and of humble courage who prayed specifically for this project and for me throughout the journey, often while struggling with hardships of their own. Our Bible studies and prayer times were rich and honest, and though in time I had to move away, enduring ties of friendship and memories of our meetings continue to bring comfort every day.

Heartfelt thanks are also offered to dear Sue, who graciously housed me; and to Manda and Melva, loving and supportive colleagues during years of college.

Regarding historical studies, it would be terribly remiss not to mention the patient instruction of two key professors: Judy Gaughan, Ph.D. (CSU), and Elisabeth Fuhrmann-Schembri, M.A. (Rome). Experts in their fields but also passionate about the true life of antiquity, they helped me to embrace the realness of 2,000 years ago. My courses with these knowledgeable instructors became meaningful encounters with history that will never be forgotten. Thank you with all my heart.

And to Editor Jennifer Layte who was the first to fully edit the manuscript, my sincere thanks. Jennifer's straightforward observations helped to refine the text for publication.

Glossary and Historical Notes

(Some words have more than one meaning. The simple definitions listed below are those utilized within the context of this story.)

abacus – (Latin) instrument used for counting

Abba – (Hebrew) "Daddy"

amphora; amphorae (pl) – (Latin) two-handled jar or jars; depending on size, these would store oil, wine, perfume, etc.

arx – (Latin) fortress, castle; height, summit; bulwark, stronghold; in Ancient Rome, the Arx was a fortress on a hill overlooking the forum.

aulos – (Latin) a flute-like instrument borrowed from the Greeks

hasidim – (Hebrew) relating to piety; pious ones

atrium – (Latin) hall; open central room in a Roman house; forecourt of a temple

augur; auguri (pl) – (Latin) interpreter of mystical signs in Ancient Rome

bestiarius; bestiarii (pl) – (Latin) beast fighter in the Roman arena

Capitoline – in Latin, it is *capitolium*, the hill in Rome where the large Temple of Jupiter resided; the Anglicized version was used for easier reading

carcer – (Latin) prison

chlamys – (Greek) military cloak

cithara; citharae (pl) – (Latin) a stringed instrument in the lyre family, borrowed from the Greeks

curia – (Latin) senate house; senate

curule chair – (Latin) official chair; Emperor's chair

dea – (Latin) goddess

denarius; denarii (pl) – (Latin) silver coin first minted in the 3rd century BC

domus – (Latin) house

dupondius – (Latin) brass coin of small denomination used in both the Roman Republic and later in the Empire; it was valued at one-half of a sestertius and one-eighth of a denarius

ein sheva – (Hebrew) – literally "spring of seven"

El Gibbor – (Hebrew) "God of Strength"

El Ro'I – (Hebrew) "God of Seeing"

El Shaddai – (Hebrew) "God Almighty"

Elysium – (Latin) where Romans believed good souls would go in the afterlife

facile princeps – (Latin) literally means "easily first" or "easily the first one," a natural leader

fasces – (Latin) rods bound around an axe, symbol of Roman authority, adopted from the Etruscans in Rome's earliest days (8th century BC)

fresco – painting made by applying pigment to wet plaster, used extensively in Roman dwellings

garum – (Latin) sauce made from fermenting fish; used as a condiment in ancient Roman times

genius – (Latin) spirit; derives from the Latin *genui, genitus*, meaning "to bring into being, to beget"

gladius – (Latin) sword

harena – (Latin) sand; our word "arena" is derived from this Latin term

imagines – (Latin) wax masks of Roman ancestors, created at time of death and stored in a special place within the Roman home

Ianuarius – (Latin) "January"

imperium – (Latin) command; mastery; supreme authority

insula; insulae (pl) – (Latin) literally "block of houses," Roman apartment structure

karkadè – (Nubian) – hibiscus plant growing in East Africa

lar or **lares** – (Latin) Roman gods of the borders, household gods

lictor – (Latin) attendant who preceded a Roman leader carrying the fasces

Lucius Annaeus Seneca – (ca. 4 BC-65 AD) Roman philosopher, statesman and orator

ludi publici – (Latin) the public games

ludi romani – (Latin) the Roman games

maiestas – (Latin) treason; offense against the sovereignty of

mezuzah – (Hebrew) receptacle containing an inscribed parchment and attached to a Judean family's doorpost, signifying faith in God

mitzvah, mitzvot (pl) – (Hebrew) commandments observed by Judeans

mohar – (Hebrew) customary price paid for a bride

mons testaceus – (Latin) mountain of broken vessels [*mons*=mountain, *testa*=pot(sherds)]

nisu'in – (Hebrew) marriage ceremony

nuntius – (Latin) messenger; informative speaker

Palatine – in Latin, it is *palatium*, the hill in Rome where emperors resided; the Anglicized version was used for easier reading

palla; pallae (pl) – (Latin) woman's robe

piscator or **piscatoris** – (Latin) fisherman

pomarius – (Latin) fruiterer

pompa funebris – (Latin) funeral procession

pons – (Latin) bridge

praefectus – (Latin) overseer; governor

Purim – (Hebrew) a springtime festival to commemorate the defeat of Haman's plan to kill the Jews (ref: *Book of Esther*)

retiarius – (Latin) net-fighter

rostrum – (Latin) literally "beak," orators' platform in the forum

sacrosanct – (Latin) inviolable

secutor – (Latin) pursuer

sesterce or *sestertius; sestertii (pl)* – (Latin) small silver coin, during the Roman Republic valued at approximately one-fourth of a denarius; in the Empire, made of brass rather than silver

spina – (Latin) literally "spine"; raised center of Rome's racetrack in the Circus Maximus

stade, stades (pl) – (Greek) a term of measurement equaling 180 meters (approx. 600 feet), footrace length in ancient Olympic games

taberna; tabernae (pl) – (Latin) shop, inn

tablinum – (Latin) room in a Roman *domus* where family records were kept, generally across from the entry and opening into the atrium

taharah – (Hebrew) act of purifying for burial

tessella; tessellae (pl) – (Latin) a cube of mosaic stone

res publica – (Latin) literally, "the public thing"; public affairs; Roman Republic

toga; togae – (Latin) dress of a Roman citizen

toga virilis – (Latin) toga signifying manhood

tunic – generally a sleeveless, knee-length garment (in ancient Greece and Rome, worn by both men and women)

via – (Latin) way, passage, road

vicus – (Latin) street

Vergilius – (Latin) Publius Vergilius Maro (70 BC-19 BC), Roman poet; known commonly as "Virgil" or "Vergil"

Yeshua – (Hebrew) "Jesus"

Additional notes:

1) Readers may be curious about the absence of the Colosseum in this story. Between 37 and 41 AD, games and events would have taken place in the forum (utilizing temporary structures) or held within the Circus Maximus. Construction of the Colosseum did not begin until approximately 70 AD by the Emperor Vespasian, and it was completed in 80 AD.

2) Roman Senators Lucius Cornelius Sulla and Gaius Nonius Asprenas did exist during the time period of this story; however, any connection with an assault on our story's character, Hannah, is fictional.

3) Regarding Biblical accuracy, we do know that Priscilla (Prisca) and Aquila were Judeans living in Rome who became followers of Jesus and later met the Apostle Paul and began work alongside him. Paul described them as fellow workers in Christ Jesus (Romans 16:3); and, like Paul, Aquila was a tent-maker by trade. We know little more about them except that they were teachers as well, providing wise counsel to Apollo, another worker in the faith. This story was constructed using historical facts and interpreting, through prayer, how the lives of these notable believers may have been impacted by such history.

Historical Resources

Primary Sources:

Aristophanes: *Acharnians*. Jeffrey Henderson, Tran. *Focus Classical Library*. Focus Publishing: Newburyport, Massachusetts (1997). (Alternative translation: Daniel C. Stevenson. *The Internet Classics Archive*. Daniel C. Stevenson, Web Atomics (1994-2009). Permission for reproduction, classics@classics.mit.edu.

Cicero: *On Divination, Book 1, Translated with Introduction and Commentary*. D. Wardle, Tran. Oxford: Clarendon Press (2006).

Cicero: *The Nature of the Gods, Translated with Introduction and Explanatory Notes*. P. G. Walsh, Tran., Oxford: Clarendon Press (1997).

Dio Cassius: *History of Rome*, c. 220 CE, Book LIV. Book LIX. *The Loeb Classical Library* edition (1924).

Herodotus, *The Histories*, c. 430 BCE, Book III.

Hesiod, *Theogony*. [Reference article in *Perseus Encyclopedia*].

Hippocrates, *On Ancient Medicine*, Part 20; *On Ulcers*, Parts 1, 2, 4, 5, 7, 11 and 12.

The Holy Bible, New Revised Standard Version. Oxford University Press: Oxford, New York (2001).

Flavius Josephus: *Antiquitates Judaicae XIX 1-273.*

Flavius Josephus: *Death of an Emperor*. T. P. Wiseman, Tran. (Exeter Studies in History, 30): University of Exeter Press (1991).

Inscription of Ezana, King of Axum, c. 325 CE.

Philo: *In Flaccum* and *De Virtutibus Prima Pars, Quod Est De Legatione Ad Gaium*. C. D. Yonge, Tran.

Pliny the Elder, *The Natural History*, Book XXIII, Chapter 20. (Eds. John Bostock, M.D., F.R.S., H.T. Riley, Esq., B.A.).

Polybius: *The Histories*. Evelyn S. Shuckburgh, Tran. London, New York. Macmillan (1889). Reprint Bloomington (1962).

Procopius of Caesarea: *History of the Wars*, c. 550 CE, Book I.xix.1, 17-22, 27-37, xx.1-13.

The Selection of Aspalta as King of Kush, c. 600 BCE.

Strabo: *Geography*, c. 22 CE, XVI.IV.4-17; xvii.I.53-54, ii.1-3, iii.1-11.

Suetonius, *The Twelve Caesars*. Robert Graves, Tran. Penguin Group: London, England (1957). Revised, Michael Grant (1979) (2003).

Tacitus, *The Annals*. Alfred John Church and William Jackson Brodribb, Tran. Random House, Inc.: New York and Canada (1942).

Virgil: *The Eclogues (Eclogue IV)*, 37 BC, a Public Domain book.

Vitruvius, *De Architectura*, Book II, Chapter 6. "On pozzolana."

Secondary Sources:

Boatwright, Mary T., Daniel J. Cargola and Richard J. A. Talbert. *The Romans, From Village to Empire*. New York and Oxford: Oxford University Press (2004).

Card, Michael. *The Parable of Joy, Reflections on the Wisdom of the Book of John*. Nashville, Tennessee: Thomas Nelson Publishers (1995).

Casson, Lionel. *Travel in the Ancient World*. Baltimore and London: The Johns Hopkins University Press (1994).

Claridge, Amanda. *Rome, An Oxford Archaeological Guide*. Oxford, New York: Oxford University Press (1998).

Clarke, John R. *The Houses of Roman Italy, 100 B.C.-A.D. 250, Ritual, Space, and Decoration*. Berkeley, Los Angeles and Oxford: University of California Press (1991).

Clarkson, Rosetta E. *Herbs, Their Culture and Uses*. New York: The MacMillan Company (1967).

Hamilton, Edith. *The Roman Way*. New York, London: W. W. Norton & Company (1932, 1964, 1984, 1993).

Jackson, Robert B. *At Empire's Edge, Exploring Rome's Egyptian Frontier*. New Haven & London: Yale University Press (2002).

Jeffers, James S. *The Greco-Roman World of the New Testament Era, Exploring the Background of Early Christianity.* Downers Grove, Illinois: InterVarsity Press (1999).

Kidd, D. A. and Mary Wade. *Latin Concise Dictionary.* Glasgow, Great Britain: Harper Collins Publishers (1997, 2005).

Osiek, Carolyn and David L. Balch. *Families in the New Testament World, Households and House Churches.* Louisville, Kentucky: Westminster John Knox Press (1997).

Simmons, Adelma Grenier. *Herb Gardens of Delight, With Plants for Every Mood and Purpose.* New York: Hawthorn Books, Inc. (1974).

Stambaugh, John E. *The Ancient Roman City.* Baltimore and London: The Johns Hopkins University Press (1988).

Stephens, William H. *The New Testament World in Pictures.* Savage, Paula A., Designer. Nashville, Tennessee: Broadman Press (1987).

Tyler, Varro E., Ph.D. *The Honest Herbal, A Sensible Guide to the Use of Herbs and Related Remedies, Third Edition.* New York, London and Norwood (Australia): Pharmaceutical Products Press (1982, 1987, 1993).

Made in the USA
Charleston, SC
12 June 2016